What in hell were horses doing out here in the middle of the night?

Shadows approached through the red from the truck's taillights. Sweat glistened off the flanks of huge, muscle-corded horses. The riders bent forward slightly, cleaving the wind. Something caught the light, gleaming. Something metallic.

The truck coughed, back-fired, began to pick up speed. He had no thought now but to get back to Bethany's Sin. He could hear the wild, hoarse breathing of the horses bearing down behind him. Coming closer.

A movement beside him made his nerves cry out in alarm. One of the riders had pulled up beside his window. The figure's raven-black hair streamed like the mane of the huge, red-eyed horse. The lips were contorted in a terrible scream of hate.

And in the blink of a second the rider's arm whipped out, carrying with it an object of metal . . . an axe shimmering with moonlight.

There is no escape from the secret of

BETHANY'S SIN

"Not for the weak-hearted"
Publishers Weekly

A NOVEL BY
ROBERT R. McCAMMON

BETHANY'S SIN

AVON
PUBLISHERS OF BARD, CAMELOT AND DISCUS BOOKS

BETHANY'S SIN is an original publication of Avon Books.
This work has never before appeared in book form.

AVON BOOKS
A division of
The Hearst Corporation
959 Eighth Avenue
New York, New York 10019

First Avon Printing, January, 1980

AVON TRADEMARK REG. U.S. PAT. OFF. AND IN
OTHER COUNTRIES, MARCA REGISTRADA, HECHO EN
U.S.A.

Printed in the U.S.A.

For my grandparents and for Penny.
Thank you for bringing me this far.

I

HARBINGERS

ONE

NEAR THE BLACK SEA, 1965

The woman's shadow, falling across the diagrams spread out on a folding metal table, made the men look up.

In the air were the thick smells of heat and dust, sweat, sweet Turkish tobacco; the sun baked the droppings of the stray, slat-ribbed dogs that occasionally yapped around the timber-enforced excavation, and dark circles of flies danced above the men's heads, nipping at unprotected ears and cheeks. Had it not been for the large timber-stilt-supported roof of corrugated tin over the excavation, the sun would have driven the men insane weeks before. From the main excavation, a rectangle that sloped from six feet to over twenty, trenches snaked out in all directions, angling around huge boulders and mounds of broken stone. There were the noises of digging: picks striking rock, shovels pushing aside coarse, stubborn earth. Occasionally the wind brought the sharp salt tang of the Black Sea rolling across the pit like a breath from another world. It was hot July, and the sun was the blazing eye of a cyclops in a face of azure.

"Good morning," Dr. Vodantis greeted the woman, nodding his head slightly. Sweat had collected in the pockets beneath his dark-rimmed eyes. He had been at the site since six-thirty, and while the Hotel Imperiale in the four-mile-distant village of Caraminya was hot, it was nothing like the heavy heat out here in the hill country. He felt scorched and covered with dust, though his khaki suit was relatively clean compared to those worn by the others.

The woman returned the nod. She was tall and large-boned, with a deeply tanned face framed by a well-groomed mane of loosely curled hair the color of midnight

3

shadows. She wore old, faded denims and brown work-boots, a cotton blouse, and a simple gold chain around her throat. An olive-green backpack was strapped around her shoulders.

"Here. This is what I wanted you to see. Excuse, please." Dr. Vodantis leaned across his young field assistant and turned one of the diagrams toward the woman. There were distinct lines to indicate the trenches and the central pit, and broken lines in circular and rectangular and oblong shapes. He traced a finger along one of the trenches. "Here," he said. The finger angled to the left and tapped at a broken-lined square with a question mark at the center of it. "It's perhaps . . . oh . . . a hundred yards from this amphitheater. One of the Turkish workers found it yesterday morning."

The other men watched her. Her eyes—stunning, deep sapphire against the darkness of her flesh—narrowed very slightly. In the distance there was the rumble of a bulldozer. "I see," the woman said finally. "An opening? Into what?"

"How far back into the mountain it goes we don't know yet," Dr. Vodantis said. "Dr. Markos's assistant crawled into it for a distance yesterday." He glanced across at Dr. Markos, a gaunt man with a shock of white hair and a bristle of beard.

"For only four meters," Dr. Markos said, addressing the woman. "I called him back because I feel the tunnel is too dangerous to explore fully yet. The ceiling is unstable; we'll need hydraulic supports before we can send anyone in."

"What did he find?"

"That it has a gradual downward slope. It began to constrict before he turned back." He tried to keep his gaze steady, but it was difficult because in this woman's eyes there was a piercing kind of . . . yes, power. He knew her reputation well; he had worked on a Crete dig with her three years before, and though he did not like her techniques, he respected her intelligence. He'd seen firelight reflected in her eyes once, on a night when the stars were strung like a vast tapestry across the sky and the voices of ghosts whispered in the corridors of a ruined temple; some dark and awesome determination

4

had crept across her face, shadowing her features, and he had thought in that instant that the spiderish hand of the oracle had been laid upon her shoulder. "Before I send any of my team in," he told her, "I want to make certain of their safety. A shift of stones could bring the mountain down into that tunnel. After all"—he smiled slightly while the woman's face remained expressionless—"whatever lies inside has been there since 1200 B.C. I think it will wait." He glanced over at the others for support.

"An approximate date," the woman said quietly, her eyes expressionless. "And it would seem to me as an archaeologist you would be more . . . willing . . . to take necessary risks."

"Necessary. Ah. There's the key word." Dr. Markos took a chipped briar pipe from a breast pocket, struck a match, and touched it to the already charred tobacco. "Has it occurred to you that it might be a natural cave with no connection to these ruins at all? If that's the case, there could be a drop-off, a wall of solid rock, a winding labyrinth of passages from which no man could ever find his way out again. I find nothing about that particular site so remarkable that it merits a hasty and dangerous exploration." He tapped another square on the diagram. "Now, here where the weapons were found . . ."

"I disagree," the woman said, still calm. "I say that the city was built in a semicircle around the mountain's base for two reasons: strategy, in case of attack, and . . ."

Dr. Markos raised his eyebrows; a tendril of tobacco smoke wound itself above his head.

". . . as protection," she said, "perhaps for what lies within that tunnel."

"Pure speculation," Dr. Markos said, smiling slightly.

"I'm sorry, but I'll have to agree," Dr. Vodantis said.

"You have a right to disagree with me," she told them. "I have a right to believe in what I feel is true. Dr. Vodantis, I'd like to see that opening now." Without waiting for him, she turned her back on the group of men and began walking down into the pit toward the trenches. Each step took her backward in time. Teams of Turkish and Greek workers huddled around the gradual, painstaking uncovering of rough, time-etched brick-works; there were tables of chalk-numbered stones and fragments of stones, each part of the multilayered puzzle of this ancient place. At the far side of the pit a long stone stairway was beginning to emerge from the earth. Dr. Vodantis stepped in front of her.

"This way, please," he said, entering a trench that sloped downward at a thirty-degree angle.

The earth has moved in its wary sleep, the woman thought as she followed Dr. Vodantis down; the earth has shrugged its shoulders, drawn a deep breath, shifted beneath the harsh touch of nature and the harsher touch of men. On each side of the trench the brickworks were slowly asserting themselves again through the walls of yellow dirt. There were windows and doorways, clogged with rock and ancient debris; on one of the walls there was a great black scorch mark, the signature of flame. The woman paused and touched it, her eyes glittering. And then she followed the man into the maw of time.

Her blood was racing. High above her there was an open space in the makeshift ceiling, and she could see the blinding blue sky and the ominous, purple black outline of the mountain towering overhead. Something dark sailed across her field of vision toward the rim of the nearest cliff. An eagle, flying to its aerie overlooking the emerald plain of the sea. "Watch your step, please," Dr. Vodantis said. "A wall's just taking shape here." They stepped over black-crusted rubble and continued down.

Who has walked here before me? she asked herself. Whose flesh and blood moved through the narrow corridors of this sprawling fortress? For that's what it was; she'd known as soon as she'd read the excavation progress reports and seen the diagrams and photographs at her hotel. A huge walled fortress with its back to the mountains and its stern face to the Black Sea. Built by whose hand? This city would have remained lost had it not been for the earthquake in December, a tremor that had jarred most of Caraminya into rubble and killed more than thirty people. Now the streets of Caraminya looked haunted and silent, just like this centuries-older place. A split in the earth had uncovered a single wall of ancient bricks, blackened by flame but with a soul-jarring story to tell.

For the woman already knew.

Not just hoped, no, because hope had an element of fear in it as well. And she was not a person to feel fear. She knew.

She had the sudden feeling that the mountain was looming before her like a huge house of solid rock. A house waiting to welcome her home. A cloud of flies hovered greedily above her head, as if their collective genetic memory recalled a heap of rotting, sunbaked, sword-hacked corpses lying in these pathways. A stagnant breeze, filled with the breath of the dead, blew across her and then was gone. In its wake she thought she heard the clash of weapons and the harsh, high laughter of warrior hordes, but it was only the noise of shovels scraping stone and two of the university volunteers laughing over a private joke.

"Here," Dr. Vodantis said.

Where the trench ended lay a jumble of large broken-edged boulders. A pile of irregularly shaped stones had been marked with chalk and covered with a sheet of clear plastic, and two young workers in denims and T-shirts were busy brushing the loose earth away from an emerging wall; they glanced up and nodded at Dr. Vodantis. He motioned toward the jigsaw of boulders. "You can see where the opening's been cleared," he told the woman.

She moved closer to it. There was a dark, triangular hole between two of the largest stones; she knelt before it and reached in with one arm, feeling the jagged rocks wedged together at the ceiling. She shrugged off her backpack, unstrapped a compartment, and withdrew a plastic flashlight. Switching on the light, she peered into the tunnel. It continued far beyond the light's range, like an empty eye socket leading into the black recesses of a time-ravaged skull; jagged teeth of stone glittered, and she saw that the tunnel was perhaps two feet high and barely the width of her shoulders. "I'm going inside," she said after another moment.

"Please," the man said, stepping toward her. "I can't

7

allow that. At least wait until the safety equipment arrives, perhaps three days at most. . . ."

But she hadn't heard because she was already moving forward. Before Dr. Vodantis could stop her, she had slipped into the opening, working her shoulders in and then pushing with her legs. In another moment the ribbed soles of her workboots had vanished into darkness.

"God in Heaven," Dr. Vodantis muttered, shaking his head from side to side. He felt the eyes of the student volunteers on him, and he turned toward them and threw up his hands in frustration.

Within the cramped tunnel the woman crawled behind the thin beam of light. Dr. Vodantis was a fool, she thought; worse, he was as much a coward as Markos. Archaeologists all, and on the verge of a discovery that might very well rock the world. It was foolish not to take necessary risks to uncover the truth, if it *was* the truth these men were seeking. She worked her way deeper. The walls and ceiling were ragged rims of rock; something caught at her sleeve, and with her next movement she heard the cloth rip. Farther ahead the tunnel turned to the right, and she was aware of descending, a degree every few feet. Poised above her like a waiting juggernaut was the mountain, all the many thousand tons of it, and she could smell the cold, iron-dry smell of the rock itself. The tunnel began to constrict gradually; rock scraped her shoulders with every movement until her raw flesh screamed. In the distance she heard a voice, and she stopped, letting the echoes wash over her like ocean waves. It was Dr. Vodantis, calling her name from the tunnel's entrance. She hunched her shoulders together and continued on. For ahead of her, buried in tons of stone, buried by the deceptions and lies and crooked paths of time, lay the past. And today she would uncover the truth.

She stopped after a few meters because her shoulder had scraped something strange. She shone the light on the wall to her left, ran a hand across it. Smooth stone, cold to the touch. A wall fashioned by human hands. Before thousands of years of rockslides and earthquakes, this had been a passageway into the heart of the mountain. The hand of mystery was on this place, and as she crawled forward she thought she could hear the powerful voice of a Jason shouting orders to his Argonauts, the thundering gait of a Heracles striding a battlefield, the rumble and clash of a storm of armored warriors fighting face-to-face in a sea of carnage. Her blood was singing ancient songs. A cold chill grasped her spine and slowly worked its way through her.

For ahead, outlined in the cold touch of the light, was another hole.

The breath hissed through her teeth. Shoulders scraped and bleeding, she pushed herself toward the tunnel's end. There was another jam of rocks, and the hole was so small she couldn't look into it and probe with the light at the same time. A musty, dry reek of age hung within that hole, beckoning her with a skeletal finger. She realized she was having trouble breathing because of the denseness of the air, and she was going to have to work fast. She placed the palm of her hand against one of the smaller stones bordering the hole and pushed against it; it wouldn't budge. She tried another. There had to be a keystone here, a rock that would slide off balance and loosen the others so she could move through into . . . what? Her heart hammered. She put her shoulder against stone and pushed, the effort raising beads of sweat across her face. Harder. Harder. It was solid; there was no way. Her shoulder and spine ached, and she planted her feet against the tunnel walls for more strength. Something shifted. She gasped, held her breath, pushed again. There was the noise of rock grinding over rock.

And when it gave way—abruptly, as if something on the other side had suddenly ripped the stones away in an effortless grip—she fell forward, unable to keep her balance within the tunnel. Rocks, both large and small, crashed down around her in a thunderous cacophony, and curtains of crushed-rock dust descended on her in yellowish folds. She dropped the light, opened her mouth to cry out; a rock struck her elbow, numbing her arm; her chin hit stone, clicking her teeth together and opening a small gash in her upper lip. She had fallen onto a smooth surface, and for a long while she lay and let the echoes of the rockfall thunder around her like marching armies; dust whitened her hair and flesh, and to her it smelled like sweat and blood.

Before her the flashlight's beam was splayed across an unbroken stone floor. When she was ready to move again, she crawled to the flashlight, gripped it in a white-knuckled hand, and rose to her feet.

Slowly, she shone the light in all directions; her eyes glittered above it.

A long, smooth-walled chamber. Swirls of dust around shadowy forms.

She had left the outside world—that place of automobiles and towering skyscrapers and huge ocean liners—and stepped into the world of the ancients, so different and stunning it made the blood icy in her veins. And so silent. So very, very silent. She moved into the chamber, and before her the waves of dust undulated.

There were figures on either side of her. Life-size statues, frozen in poses of combat, bearing spears and swords. Impassive, blank-eyed faces stared back at the light. "Beautiful," she heard herself say, and the voice echoed *beautiful-beautiful-beautiful* a hundred times over, each time fainter than the last. These statues had been carved of glowing marble, and as she neared one of them, playing the light along its surfaces of battle dress, she saw that they were—

Her blood trilled.

Yes. Yes. They are. They . . . are. . . .

The flashlight trembled in her hand, making the shadows dance darkly.

With another few steps she saw the remnants of battlefield murals on the walls, cracked by age but still retaining some of the original, bold reds and greens and blues: warriors raising swords over the fallen; huge war-horses trampling down rows of armored enemies; archers firing arrows toward the sun; scenes of slaughter—broken limbs and decapitated heads with ragged necks, slaves bound by chains and dragged behind golden horses. Her heart pounded in her head; the air smelled of ancient, secret, terrible things, but she could not bring herself to leave this chamber, with its exquisite beauty and horror.

She thought she heard Dr. Vodantis calling her name again, over and over, but in another instant the sound had faded into the walls and she was alone. She stepped forward, into darkness, the noise of her footsteps echoing as if someone followed close behind. Someone or something, avoiding the light.

And at the far end of the chamber the light fell upon something that gleamed blackly. A large, dark, rough-edged slab of stone, waist-high. The woman moved forward, her shoes stirring more of the thick dust, and then stopped. She aimed the light down at the floor. Scattered about were dozens of crudely forged metal objects, rust-flaked and falling to pieces, recognizable only to a trained eye. The hilt of a sword; what might have been the point of a spear; a few ravaged helmets, one of them completely flattened; scarred and rusted fragments of armor, bleeding in the mounds of white dust. She searched with the light, moving it back and forth: more weapons, lying as if suddenly discarded, among them the ragged remnants of ax blades, dully reflecting the light into her eyes. She blinked; the beam of light tripped and fell over something on the floor. She found it again in another moment.

A bone.

And now, as she moved toward it, she began to see other bones lying among the weapons and dust. A scattering of bones, lying intertwined in the long and terrible darkness. Here a broken skull grinned at her. She moved the flashlight up above the bones, saw that the walls and ceiling were thick with black char. And then she staggered back a step, drawing in her breath with an audible gasp.

For there was a pedestal jutting out from the far wall, above that black stone, and another figure stood, arms seemingly outstretched to her. Frozen, to watch forever over the dead. The eyes of the idol were upon her, and the statue was so lifelike and intricate, the woman thought for an instant that those sightless orbs moved. Shadows fled the light. And she was certain she heard her name called now; Dr. Vodantis calling for her from a strange time and place. No. Not Dr. Vodantis . . .

But another.

A rustle of shadows, gathering shape, gathering strength.

She drew a lungful of air, found it bittersweet and . . . strange. Whirling, she played the light on the honor guard of statues. Had they moved? Had they drawn themselves toward her? Had those heads turned slightly on their marble necks? One of them, a figure armed with a bow, seemed to be watching her. The blank white gaze burned through to her soul and marked it with fire.

A whisper. Her name, spoken from vast distances.

Poised above the black stone—an altar?—the protective idol seemed to be waiting, and around it the dust spun and swirled like something alive. A voice, clearer now, borne to her by a cold wind that stirred dust into patterns that merged and broke and remerged kaleidoscopically, scrawling strange shadows before the path of the flashlight. The language was unfamiliar—no, it was some kind of garbled Greek. A crude, ancient Greek, a dialect filled with a rising urgency and raw, brute strength. She dare not let the light fall to the floor, but it seemed a tremendous effort to hold on to it. She could understand only fragments of the message, above the pounding noise in her head that sounded like the beat of an army's war drums. Backing away from the black stone, from the idol poised overhead, she swung the light from side to side; the voice was stronger now, imploring, becoming many voices, powerful and inescapable, echoing from all sides. She cast the light upon those haunted faces, and when the voice came to her again, it carried a power that made her stumble, fall onto her knees in supplication to the idol; in that instant she thought she saw the idol's head turn slightly, very slightly, and she thought she saw blue flames flicker across those marble sockets, there and then gone in the briefest of seconds.

And something moved within the thick, smoky folds of dust, like someone slowly walking out of a fire. The figure, a thing of shadow and light, dust and stone, approached the woman with vaporish strides and undulated before her; where the face would have been there was a dark outline. Orbs of glittering blue, like burning diamonds, flashed with a power that rocked the woman's head back; she felt that same terrible, awesome power wrench at her heart, exposing blood and bones and muscle. Ages passed between them, and when she opened her mouth to cry out, she failed to recognize her own voice. The figure wavered before her, and the shadowy outline of what might have been an arm brushed past her face, leaving the odors of dust and dry, brittle age. And then the dust welled up again, an ocean of it, obscuring whatever it was that the woman had thought she'd seen; she found the strength to rise to her feet and began backing away, her senses raw and screaming. The voice—no, many voices merged into one—fading now, gradually, back beyond the wall it had slipped through. And finally gone.

Reaching the opening to the tunnel, she pulled herself up through it and sucked at the fresher air until her lungs were filled. Her body felt strange; her nerves vibrated, and her muscles twitched as though she had lost control over them. She wanted to look back into the cavern, to see for one more moment the commanding murals and the black stone and the protective idol, but there was no room to turn her head in the tunnel; she began to crawl back toward where Dr. Vodantis waited for her, toward a world of madness and pollution, crime and brutality.

The voices were gone, but in the depths of her soul she could hear the echo, again and again and again. . . .

Flames of electric blue danced briefly through the woman's eyes, and she followed the tunnel back to where the men waited.

TWO

VIETNAM, 1970

He had been bound to the coarse-clothed cot by harsh wires around his wrists and ankles, and now, naked and spread-eagled, he waited.

Sweat had beaded and trickled and beaded again over his body, and beneath him the cot was as wet as the rain-filled hole he'd huddled in while the mortars had ripped the jungle into black shreds all around him. But this was worse, because it was quiet and there was no way to know when the next shell would fall or where it would hit. One by one, they had taken them all from the bamboo cages: Endicott, Lyttle, the nameless corporal who had dysentery and cried all the time, Vinzant, Dickerson, and now him. He hadn't wanted to be last. He'd wanted to get it over with, because he'd heard their screams and seen their faces when they'd been dumped back into the cages, left to whimper and moan or contort their bodies, fetuslike, to escape the unendurable reality of torture.

He'd prayed to God that he wouldn't be last. But hearing his prayers, God must have laughed and turned away.

Because now it was his time to be alone. To wait.

He tried to gather memories; he tried to relive them to take his mind off this dark hut that had been built of black-painted boards and then camouflaged with green netting so that it blended in with the jungle. *Faces: his mother and father in the front room of their small house in Ohio, snow falling steadily outside the windows, a Christmas tree freshly cut and glittering with ornaments in the corner. His brother . . . no, Eric was dead that year, but bring him into the memory anyway, make everything right, as it should have been.* How do they torture you? Beatings? *Bring Eric into the room; let him sit down in front of the fire the way he liked to; let the flakes of snow clinging to his hair and jacket slowly melt away. Let the fire touch his face, and Mother's and Father's faces, too.* No, not beatings. The others hadn't been beaten, had they? At least not where the wounds and bruises showed. The recollection of the Christmas pine stirred younger, fresher memories. *His mother knitting that forest green sweater she'd given him that year. Even though he'd known what his present was, she'd wrapped it in a box with golden cornets on the paper. Now count all the cornets. One. Two. Three.* But if they didn't beat you, then how was it done? He hadn't seen the others' fingers; had they driven the bamboo spikes under the nails, or was that only done in black-and-white war movies? *Four. Five. Six. Seven. Eight cornets. Firelight licking the walls. He*—hadn't Eric gone, too?—*had helped his father cut wood out in the deep forest for the fire that morning, and his father had knelt down in the snow and showed him the path a deer had taken as it made its way toward the protection of the hills. "Progress makin' 'em run,"* Father had said. *"They know the towns are eatin' up the forest land, and it's not right."* How do they do it, then? Why had they taken off his clothes like this? Why did they make him wait?

And in the light of the fire Eric—dead Eric—turns his head very slowly. His eyes are white and filled with fluid, like the liquid eyes of a doe Father had shot once by mistake in the fiery days of autumn. His eyes are unseeing, yet they pierce through souls like shrapnel and they uncover the secrets lying there.

"You did this," Eric says in a whisper. *The fire snaps behind him, like the closing of a steel trap or the sound a tripwire makes when you trigger it and you know Holy Christ my number's up.* "You killed me because you knew. You killed me, and I'm never going to let you forget it." *That dead, familiar yet horrible face grins. The teeth are flecked with grave dirt.*

"Now, Eric," Mother says quietly, absorbed in her knitting. *"Stop that kind of talk. Let's have a nice Christmas."*

The man on the cot trembled, squeezing his eyes tightly shut because his efforts to avoid torture had turned into a deeper, more terrifying ordeal than they could ever dream up. He shook his head from side to side, letting the images fade into blue and then vanish, like pictures drawn in disappearing ink.

"Lieutenant Reid?"

A man's voice, and Evan knew immediately who it was: the tall, lean Vietcong officer who always wore a clean uniform, the one who detested even going near the filth-covered prisoners. The one with a cat's smile, and eyes that could bore through steel; the Smiling Gentleman, Dickerson called him.

And now the man stepped into Evan's line of vision. In the light of the single overhead bulb the man's bald head glittered with pinpoints of perspiration; he mopped his head with a white handkerchief and then smiled into Evan's eyes, very slightly, the cheekbones jutting out from the rest of his skull and dark hollows beneath. "Lieutenant Reid," he said, nodding. "Finally we meet without cages between us."

Evan said nothing. He closed his eyes to escape that light-haloed face. Was that why his clothes had been taken away—because they were filthy with mud and excrement, and the Gentleman might have been offended?

"Why do Americans find a strength in silence?" the Gentleman asked softly. "In unfriendliness? Surely you know that for you the war is ended. Why insist . . . ? Ah, well. I expect you'll be like all the others were at first. Except for the young corporal, and unfortunately he's too . . . ill . . . to be coherent."

Evan ground his teeth.

"I'd like to ask some things of you," the man said, trying hard to enunciate correctly. "I'd like to get to know you better. Would that be agreeable?"

Don't speak, Evan warned himself. Don't let him in, don't. . . .

"I'd like to know where you're from, where you were born," the Gentleman said. "Surely you can answer me that? Ah, well. Wherever it was, I'm sure you miss it very much, don't you? I have a wife and two girls. A fine family. Do you have a family as well? Lieutenant Reid, I don't care for monologues."

Evan opened his eyes and looked deeply into the face of the man who stood over him. Deeper. His gaze probed

16

through the facial muscles, back through bone. The Gentleman was smiling like a long-lost friend or brother. And as Evan concentrated, he watched that face suddenly change, begin to melt like the face of a waxwork figure. The teeth lengthened, became fanglike; the eyes were centers of a seething red hate that seemed to grip at Evan's heart. Yes. This was the true man behind the facade of smiles.

"You see?" the Gentleman said. "I'm your friend. I wish you no harm."

"Go to hell," Evan said, immediately wishing he'd remained silent.

The Gentleman laughed. "Ah. A response. Not a good one, but a response. How did you join your military, Lieutenant? Were you—what is it called?—inducted? Or did you join by choice, out of a misguided patriotism? That doesn't mean very much now, does it? I'm sure it doesn't mean very much to the young corporal. I fear he may die."

"Then why don't you get a doctor for him?" Evan asked.

"You'll all have doctors for your injuries," the man said in an even tone of voice. "You'll all have good food and drink and real beds. If you show your worth. We won't waste our time and effort on those who would be . . . unappreciative. I was hoping you would show your worth, Lieutenant, because I like you and I—"

"Liar," Evan said. I can see through you. I know what you are. He could see himself, bleary-eyed and shaken, standing before a whirring camera to denounce the evil military imperialism of the United States. Or would they parade him through the streets of Hanoi with a rope around his neck and let the little children throw filth at him?

The Gentleman stepped nearer. "There's no point in this. I can make things good for you, or I can make them bad. We have some things we would like you to do for us. It's your choice, really. I can see you're afraid because you do not know what is ahead for you. Neither do I, because soon the matter will be out of my hands. There is another here who wishes to harm you." His eyes glittered tigerishly. "Someone skilled in the arts of fear. Now, Lieutenant Reid, why don't we talk as civilized men?"

A drop of sweat rolled into Evan's eye and burned as if it were a torch. He remained silent.

"Do you hate yourself so much?" the Gentleman asked softly. "Ah, then. I'm very much sorry for you." He stood over the cot a moment longer, and then he disappeared into the shadows like a wraith.

And for a long time—an hour? two hours?—nothing moved.

When the next shadow came, it came quietly, standing in the circle of light over Evan's cot before he'd even known it was there.

"Lieutenant Reid," the figure said, a voice of silk that made a chill work its way up his spine. "Let us consider for a moment the female of the species."

Evan blinked. The wires were red-hot at his wrists and ankles, and he couldn't feel his hands or feet anymore.

A woman stood over him; she was Vietcong, dressed in a neat uniform with a black scarf around her throat. Her hair was gathered into a sleek black bun, and the eyes in that face were almond slits of cold contempt. She ran her gaze across his body. "Most dangerous is the female," she said softly, "because she strikes without warning. She appears soft, and weak, and directionless, but that is the basis of her power. When the time is right"—she drew a fingernail across his stomach, and a red welt rose slowly —"the female has no hesitation."

She paused for long moments, her eyes motionless; one hand left her side, moved beyond the circle of light. "The female's capacity for revenge and retaliation is legendary, Lieutenant; why else does the male try to control and placate her? Because he is afraid." The hand came back; something dangled from the fingers. "The bite of the female can be excruciating. And deadly as well. For instance, this"—the woman held a small bamboo cage in her hand, dangling it over Evan's stomach—"female here. You see?" In her other hand there was a jagged bamboo shoot. She jabbed it several times into the cage and began to smile. Something scuttled within the cage. "Now she has received an injury that will make her senses scream for revenge." Once again she jabbed the shoot into the cage; Evan thought he heard a sharp squeal, and a strand of dark liquid oozed from the bottom of the cage onto the floor. Not blood, no, but—

Venom.

"If you do not wish to talk," the woman said, "perhaps you wish to scream. . . ." She unsnapped a latch and, holding the cage at arm's length, shook it over Evan's cringing, sweat-filmed body.

And what fell out onto his thigh drove a whine of pure terror from his throat.

A jungle spider perhaps half the size of his hand, flecked with sleek, greenish brown hairs. Black eyes the size of pencil points searched for the source of its agony. It scrabbled forward, through the risen blisters of sweat, along his thigh; he lifted his head, eyes distorted and wild, and saw the red cup of the spider's mouth centered between black mandibles. He wanted to scream and thrash, but with his last threads of willpower he kept himself still. The woman stepped back, the light splayed across her shoulders, and he could hear the noise of her ragged, excited breathing.

The spider moved onto his testicles and poised there, eyes twitching. "Get off me, you bastard," Evan breathed at the thing, feeling his nerves beginning to give way. "Get off get off get off. . . ." The spider crawled forward, across the testicles onto his stomach, through the forest of light-brown hair.

"Do you still wish to be silent?" the woman asked.

The black eyes twitching in all directions, the spider began crawling for Evan's chest; it paused on his breastbone for a moment, tasting his sweat. Evan felt his pulse pounding, and inwardly he screamed a scream that left him hollow and on the edge of black madness. The spider crawled upward. For the vein that throbbed in his throat.

"Silence will kill you," the woman whispered, cloaked in darkness, only her mouth moving—and it as red-cupped as the spider's.

The spider moved to the base of his throat and stopped there. A drop of fluid oozed onto the man's flesh. He smelled the sickly-sweet aroma of the poison, and his body began to tremble, out of control.

The spider waited.

And in the next instant the woman stepped forward. Her shadow fell across the man on the cot, blighting him. She raised her hand, the one with the bamboo shoot in it, and jabbed it down onto the spider. There was a quick squeal and a thick, sour odor; the spider fixed itself onto Evan's throat. He felt a razor touch of icy pain and then a sticky warmth, as the venom flooded from the sacs; the spider shook, emptying its fluid into the white beast below it. The man cried out in animal fear and wrenched violently at the wires; the spider scuttled across his throat, leaving a thin, brownish trail, dropped to the floor, and scurried for the darkness. But the woman crunched her shoe down onto it and ground it into a bloody mass.

The man was still screaming and writhing; blood smeared his wrists and ankles. The Gentleman stepped into the light, eyes narrowed and eager, two armed soldiers accompanying him. One of them grinned.

The woman was fascinated by Evan's reaction to pain. Her tongue came out, licked along the lower lip. In another moment Evan lifted his head, the cords in his neck straining and a small red puncture marking the spider's bite. When his head slumped back, his breathing was harsh and irregular, and beneath the half-closed lids his eyes rolled back and forth like bone-white marbles. The Gentleman motioned for the wires to be loosened.

"The one called En-di-cott has possibilities," the woman told him. "Also the one called Vin-zant. They will cooperate. The others are useless." She nodded curtly at the Gentleman and watched the other two unbind the American, then turned and vanished into the shadows.

After she was gone the Vietcong officer looked distastefully down at the mangled spider and shuddered. Using the spiders had been her idea. He saw with a rise of disgust that a strand of venom lay across his shoe, and he hurried away to his quarters to clean it before the French leather was ruined.

II

JUNE

THREE

IN THE DARKNESS, 1980

In the darkness he listened to the distant, hollow sound of a dog barking, and, his brain still misted with the need for sleep, he wondered why that noise made his flesh crawl.

Is it because, he thought, that dog has to be barking at someone? Or something? A presence that prowls the midnight streets of Bethany's Sin like an avenging juggernaut? He turned his head slightly to look at the digital clock on his night table. Twenty minutes after three. The longest hours of the night yet to come, the quietest, the hours when nightmares tremble on the edge of reality. He waited, not willing to return himself to that dark place of sleep, because fear gnawed at him now and there seemed to be a growth of thick tension in his stomach, like a knot of twisted muscle and intestine.

Because he knew when they came for him, they would come in the night.

Abruptly, as if the earth had swallowed it up, the dog stopped barking. The man lay still beneath pale blue sheets, stripes of moonlight like bands of softly glowing neon splayed across the bed through the open curtains. Clear skies for the next few days, the weather report had said; good weather for the first weekend of June, but showers probable by Tuesday. He saw the silhouette of a tree in the moonlight, a thing with many heads, a Hydra swaying and hissing and waiting just outside his window. With the next breath of breeze he could almost hear the thing whisper: Come outside, Paul, where the stars and the moon are bright, where the night is thick, where no one will see while I rip you to pieces.

Dear God, he thought suddenly. They're coming for me.

No. No, stop it! There's nothing out there but darkness and trees and barking dogs and the familiar streets of the village. Why didn't I leave today? he asked himself. Why didn't I get in my car and drive to Johnstown, get a room at the Holiday Inn, read, watch television, feel safe? Because, he heard the stricter voice of reason within him say, you cannot be certain. Your home is here. Your work is here. Your responsibilities. When he'd gone to Dr. Mabry last week for his physical—he'd put it off as long as he could, but since Elaine's death three years ago he'd been lethargic and had experienced stomach pains—he had felt compelled to open up, to spill some of these things that had taken root inside him and now grew wild and tangled. The doctor had listened quietly, nodding in all the right places, eyes attentive and concerned.

I've heard clicks on my telephone, he'd told Dr. Mabry. As if someone is monitoring my conversations. I've heard them several times, but only very faintly. And then there are the prowlers. . . .

Prowlers? Dr. Mabry had raised an eyebrow.

Not every night, but I know when they're there. I have insomnia sometimes, so I've been awake to hear the noises.

Have you ever seen anyone lurking around your house at night?

No. But I've seen shadows, things that move in the corner of my eye when I stand at the window looking out. And there's a dog that barks down at the end of McClain Terrace; I know it sounds funny to you that a dog should bother me, but it's like . . . an early warning. That the dog has seen or sensed something . . . terrible.

Well, the doctor had said, why don't I prescribe some pills for you that will help you sleep? Maybe you're overworking at the bank, and not getting enough exercise; that could be causing your insomnia. You already know what the problem is with your ulcers. Have you thought about taking up golf again?

Too many things had built up within him, too many noises and skeletal shadows in the darkness. The raindrops of suspicion and unease had become pools, streams, rivers, oceans surging behind a weakening dam. The pressure was about to blow him wide open. Of course he'd gone to Wysinger, but the man was little or no help. Sure,

Wysinger had told him, I'll bring the patrol car down McClain Terrace a couple of times a day if you think that'll help. My number's in the phone book, too, and you can reach me at night if anything happens. How about that?

Please, he'd told the man. Whatever you can do.

But he knew Wysinger wouldn't find them. No, no. They were too smart, too cunning to be caught.

And now a word burned in his brain: paranoid, paranoid, paranoid, like a child's strange rhyme, a jump rope singsong. You let little things bother you too much, Paul, Elaine had always told him, even when they were living in Philadelphia. Learn to relax. Learn to take things as they come.

Yes. And now they're coming for me.

Suddenly he craved light. Snapping on the night-table lamp, he squinted until he could see. My eyes are going fast, he thought, feeling a new pincer of panic. They were myopic and weak from years of reading fine print on loan applications. He took his thick-lensed glasses from the night table, put them on, threw aside the sheets, and stood on the floor. He crossed the room and looked out the window to where the rectangle of yellow light from his own bedroom lay on the green lawn. Craning his neck, he looked right and left along McClain Terrace. Dark, empty, silent as the grave. Darkest before the dawn, he thought, glancing back to the digital clock. Returning his gaze to the window, he thought he saw the glimmer of a light in a house far up the street, but instead of being comforted by that light, he felt a new seed of fear burst into raw bloom. But it wasn't a light after all, he realized in another moment; it was the shimmering white reflection of the moon on window glass. Everyone was sleeping.

Except him. And whatever had disturbed the dog at the end of the street.

Stop it! he told himself. You're wrong! Am I losing my mind, going crazy in middle age? Paranoid, paranoid, paranoid: that was a word used for nuts, wasn't it? He went out into the hallway, turning on the overhead light, walking barefoot to the staircase and descending. Then through the downstairs den, pausing to snap on the color television. Of course there was nothing on the screen but a blizzard of multicolored snowflakes, but somehow the noise of it reassured him just as when he'd been a child left alone in his parents' house, watched over by the flickering black-and-white guardian. He walked into the kitchen.

Bathed in the stark white light of the refrigerator, he rummaged through leftovers. That was the only part of living alone that still gave him trouble: cooking, making use of what was at hand. The refrigerator was full of little Tupperware bowls holding leftovers, cans of beer, a pitcher of two-day-old iced tea, a blue platter with slices of roast beef wrapped in aluminum foil. He smeared mustard on two pieces of bread for a roast beef sandwich.

He'd taken one bite of the sandwich when the lights flickered.

Fading to brown, as if the darkness outside were finally and inevitably slithering in through door and window chinks. He was staring at the lightbulb in the open refrigerator when the house went black and the refrigerator's motor wound down like a long human moan. And then he stood in darkness, surrounded by a silence like the aftermath of a gunshot, or the spaces between ticks of the clock.

Christ! he thought, stunned for a second, his heart giving a violent kick in his chest. He heard something plop onto the kitchen floor, and the noise startled him until he realized that he'd dropped the sandwich. What now? he wondered, waiting without moving, hoping the lights would flicker on again. The damn fuses had been overloaded. Or maybe it was a power blackout; he thought he'd read an article in the paper that said Pennsylvania Power was going to be doing some work on the lines this week and next. He turned, groped in a drawer, and found a flashlight, but the batteries were weak and cast only a dim brownish beam. Strange, he thought, how familiar objects look foreign in the half-light; in the den the furniture seemed to crawl, to twist into hideous shapes awaiting his passage. If there was a bad fuse, or the fuses had blown, he'd have to take care of it before the food in the refrigerator went bad; when he reached the door under the staircase that led down into the basement, he paused. Shouldn't he call the power company to check first? He put a hand on the doorknob and felt its coldness travel through his veins all the way to the heart. Call the power company. No, they'll think you're stupid! They'll think you're paranoid, and if you keep this up, sooner or later the people at the bank are going to be talking about you in whispers.

He turned the knob, pierced musty-smelling darkness with the flashlight, and began to descend the series of wooden steps. It was cooler down here, and quiet as a tomb. The stone floor of the basement was cold against his bare feet. He came down here infrequently, using the basement as a storeroom for things from his past: old trunks filled with ill-fitting clothes, a chair with a broken arm, a cracked ceramic-base lamp, a few pasteboard boxes that held some of Elaine's old clothes, musty books and *Life* and *National Geographic* magazines. He'd paneled two walls in pine; the other two were bare brick, and there were circular concrete columns as supports for a ceiling crisscrossed by pipes and copper tubing. On the far side was a door with four glass panes, and on either side of it, windows looked out onto a small backyard. The dark mass of the furnace stood silent; metal reflected the light into his eyes. He swung the flashlight beam around toward the fusebox, mounted on a wall just beyond the staircase; the light brushed past the doorway of a utility room filled with paint cans and dirty tarpaulins. He glimpsed a naked lightbulb, dangling from its cord like a severed head.

The fusebox was stubborn; rusted hinges squealed. On both sides of the flashlight beam, the darkness had begun to creep in, like slow waves of a black ocean. He wrenched at the box, shaking off a cold hand that seemed to be poised over the back of his neck.

The fusebox came open. He fumbled with the light, shone it inside.

And it was then that he saw the fuses had been ripped away.

He sensed rather than heard the movement behind him, and as he whirled around to see his arm coming up defensively with the flashlight, he heard something shrieking at him from the darkness, from the doorway of the utility room. He had a split-second glimpse of something glowing a hard electric blue, turning over and over as it cleaved the air, but he had no time to step back, nor to breathe, nor to scream.

For in the next instant a shimmering, neon blue, double-bladed ax struck him directly between the eyes. Shattered from the inhuman force of the blow, his eyeglasses parted over the bridge of the nose and fell away on each side of the head, while the ax blade tore through flesh and bone and brain. His body was slammed against the wall, the head snapping back so fast there was a sharp *crack!* as the neck broke. Blood streaming through the nostrils and the widened, horror-struck eye sockets, the corpse sagged down onto the floor like a mass of gore-splattered rags. It twitched spasmodically, the death dance of the muscles and nerves, and through the severed tongue, teeth clicked like bones thrown by ancient oracles.

And then the corpse lay still, in pooling red, the flashlight still gripped in a slowly whitening hand. But before dawn the batteries would be drained as well.

And through the basement, making glass rattle in the windows, echoing through the house and off along McClain Terrace, rose the savage shriek of a blood-hungry, victorious eagle.

When the last echoes had faded minutes later, a dog began to bark somewhere, frenziedly, like Cerberus at the gates of Hades.

FOUR

THE VILLAGE

BETHANY'S SIN, the roadside sign read, in white letters against a background of green. And below that; POP. 811. The sign looked immaculately clean, gleaming with the morning sun; Evan Reid remembered the contrasting sign that had marked the LaGrange town limits: pocked with bullet holes, bleeding rust, bent crazily out of shape by an errant car fender.

Good damned riddance to that place, he thought bitterly, as the dark blue station wagon swept along a blacktopped highway overhung by the spreading green arms of elm trees, toward the life that lay ahead, toward the village of Bethany's Sin.

"We're here!" Laurie said from the backseat, pulling herself up between the man and woman in front to see. Her face was filled with the honest excitement of a six-year-old who has seen the sun streaming out from behind swollen-bellied storm clouds; it was finally summer, after a long and terrible time of freezing weather, and her expectant eyes were as blue and soft as the Pennsylvania sky. She had been absorbed for most of the morning in a coloring book, but when they'd reached the green and rolling hills, the forests shadow-dappled and surely filled with the white-bearded elves of bedtime stories, Laurie had laid aside her Crayolas and let her mind drift. Beside her on the seat, her rag doll, Miss Prissy, nodded silently with the movement of the car.

What was especially good, she thought, watching a crow turning lazy circles in the sky, was that Mommy and Daddy hadn't been mad at each other for a long time.

"Not there quite yet," Kay Reid said, turning her head to glance back and smile at her little girl. She had the

29

same blue eyes as Laurie, set in an attractive oval face framed by auburn hair that fell softly onto her shoulders. "You'd better be putting away those crayons, though; it won't be long."

"Okay." Laurie began lining them up in the green-and-yellow box, her golden hair blowing in the air that circulated through the open windows.

Kay looked across at her husband; she knew he was weary from the driving, and concerned about threads showing in a couple of places on the left front tire. "Almost home," she said, and he smiled a little bit. Home: the word sounded strange because she'd said it before, in different times and places; now it was like one of those words that lose meaning after you repeat them over and over again. There had been no permanence in those other places she'd called home, neither the cramped upstairs apartment with its clattering radiator pipes nor the shingle-roofed house that had always seemed thick with the reek of the steel mills. Those had both been places of suffocation, gritty no matter how often Kay cleaned and vacuumed, bad places for a little girl to grow up in, hopeless places in which to try to heal strained scars. No. Don't think about that. Her mind sheered away from the black drop-offs of memory. She watched him, saw his eyes follow the white line in the center of the road. What is it I see there? she wondered. Hope? Or fear? She thought suddenly how much older than his thirty-two years he looked; how the lines had spread around his deep-set gray eyes and around the mouth, how minute traces of gray had prematurely speckled the temples of his unruly sandy-brown hair. It was the creep of stress and pain, of anxious times when the world with its dark, outstretched claws seemed to be closing in on them, confining them, trapping them.

He felt her gaze on him. "What is it?" he asked.

"Just nervous," she said, and smiled.

"No need to be. Everything's going to be fine."

Rising up from the forests on either side now were white picket fences, mailboxes, and driveways leading to unseen houses. Around the next curve was a white-painted brick wall, a black wrought-iron gate with a scrolled *D* at its center, the roofs looming over the woods behind. As they drove past that house, Kay could see black and white and dappled horses grazing in a distant pasture; some of them lifted their heads to watch the station wagon sweep by.

They came to an intersection with a blinking yellow caution light; there was a Gulf station with a banner proclaiming TIRE-SALE—Have to remember that, Evan thought as he stopped at the intersection—and across the street from it a large sign with an array of medallions and lettering: THE LION'S CLUB** THE CIVITANS** THE ROTARIANS** WELCOME YOU TO BETHANY'S SIN. And then they were driving along a street lined with elms and oaks; there were spacious, well-kept green lawns and dignified-looking brick and stone houses. More picket fences and gates and driveways, quiet streets, the hint of a breeze ruffling leaves overhead. A mailman in shorts, carrying a shoulder bag, making his rounds; a young blond woman in denims pushing a baby stroller; a summer-tanned teenage boy mowing a lawn, sweat glistening on his bare shoulders. A yellow Volkswagen, newly waxed, passed them going in the opposite direction. On the block ahead, a dark brown Buick was turning into a driveway. Evan suddenly felt ashamed of his station wagon; he wished it looked better. It was riddled with dents and nicks from five years of hard use and seemed like a vehicle from another world in this neat, everything-in-its-proper-place residential neighborhood; if there were a roadside sign in that other world, it would read JUST SCRAPING BY—POP. 3.

They passed a McDonald's on the right, and then the street they were on, Fredonia, carried them directly into the main part of the village. Quaint little stores were ringed around a street called, appropriately, the Circle; it was a beautifully planned community, Kay thought, glancing around at the shops: Eve's Florists, Bryson's Gifts and Crafts, the Lamplighter Restaurant, the Talmadge Rexall drugstore, the Perky Pot coffee shop. But what was loveliest of all to her, and filled the air with the sweet scent of summer flowers, was the small park in the Circle's center; peonies and marigolds and daisies, three different varieties of roses, violets of deep, sun-splashed color, were all planted in orderly rows at the village's

31

heart. There was a stunning range of hues, from pale white to flaming red to dark purple, the colors reflected in the window glass of the shops. Streets led out from the Circle in all directions, like spokes from the center of a huge wheel.

"It's soooooo pretty," Laurie said, pulling Miss Prissy up into the window to see. "And it smells so nice, too. Are we near our new house yet?"

"Almost," Evan said, following the curve of the Circle past the blue-and-green-striped canopy of the Village Thrifty Delicatessen, past a swapshop bookstore called Chapter One. He turned onto Paragon Street and drove away from the center of the village, passing the sheriff's office, a red-brick building with white-trimmed windows and door, and the modernistic glass-and-marble Wallace Perkins Public Library. Evan and Kay had visited Bethany's Sin three times: the first in April, when she'd gotten the job at George Ross Junior College, the second in May to hunt for an affordable house, the third during the first week of June to make final arrangements. Though it was smaller by far than the surrounding villages on Highway 219—Spangler, Barnesboro, Saint Benedict, and Carrolltown—Bethany's Sin had a refreshing character that both Evan and Kay found appealing. The lawns were as green as emeralds, the streets free of litter, the houses cozy and inviting. Fringes of woodland were allowed to grow wild within the village limits, so that there would be a block of homes right on the edge of the forest, or a vale of pine and wild honeysuckle separating one street from the next. And lining the streets, like summer's sentinels, were the trees, looming high over the Bethany's Sin rooftops to throw kaleidoscopic patterns of shade.

As he drove, Evan checked a map Marcia Giles had made for him on their last visit. Bethany's Sin stretched barely two miles from north to south, but there were many turn-offs and narrow, meandering streets that Evan hadn't yet learned to navigate; they passed the old flagstone Douglas Elementary School on Knollwood Street, turned right on Blair Lane. He looked down at the map again: Blair connected with Cowlington Street, then a left on Deer Cross Lane and up a small hill onto Mc-

Clain Terrace. It would gradually become familiar to him, but now it was a maze of houses and greenery. Off beyond Deer Cross Lane, Kay saw a couple of shaded tennis courts and a covered-over barbecue pit; there was a concrete jogging track, on which a solitary figure in red running shorts was loping around the far turn.

They reached McClain Terrace, as immaculate and fresh-looking as all the rest of the village. Perhaps the houses were a little newer and smaller, but Kay didn't mind; they were going to live in one of them, and that made all the difference. She mentally checked off the names on the mailboxes: Haversham, Kincaid, Rice, Demargeon. And then there was one with no name on it yet.

Evan swung into the driveway. "Here we are, troops," he said.

The house was two-storied, white with dark green trim and a dark green front door. Elms grew in the front yard, and there was a walkway to the door, lined with monkey grass. Though the backyard wasn't visible from the street, Evan knew it sloped gently downward to where a chain-link fence ended the property; beyond the fence there was a concrete drainage ditch and then the wild green tangle of the forest, unbroken until almost Marsteller, the nearest town, over two miles west. As Evan stopped the car, he was thinking about what Mrs. Giles had told him: *It's a very quiet neighborhood, Mr. Reid, and in your line of work I know how highly you must value peace and quiet. In this day and age it's a vanishing commodity.* He cut the engine, took the keys out of the ignition; the key chain had been made heavier by two after he'd come to terms with Mrs. Giles, over in her real-estate office on Kinderdine Street.

"Are there deers around here?" Laurie asked him as he lugged two heavy suitcases out of the back of the station wagon.

"Mrs. Giles says they've been seen a couple of times," Kay told her. "Here. Why don't you put Miss Prissy in this box and carry it in for me, okay? Be careful now, there's glass in it."

She took the cardboard box. "How about wolves? Any of them?"

"I doubt it," Evan said. "We're not far enough north."

Kay took the keys from Evan and carried a box filled with kitchen utensils up the three steps to the front door; a brass knocker reflected golden sunlight. She waited for Laurie and her husband and then slipped the key into the lock, turned it to the left. There was a quiet *click!* and she smiled, then opened the door and held it for them.

Even stood in the doorway, a suitcase gripped in each hand; there was an entrance foyer with a parquet floor, and off to the left a large, high-ceilinged living room carpeted in beige. It still looked bare, even with the new sofa and the coffee table and chairs they'd brought over from LaGrange in a U-Haul. Pictures were needed on the walls, knickknacks on the table; but that would all be done in time, he told himself. Right now it looked as good as anything in the home-decorating magazines Kay had begun buying as she feverishly counted off the days until they were to move in. God, he realized suddenly, this entrance foyer and the living room combined are probably about the same size as that entire house in La-Grange, under the towering smokestacks, where the siding was the color of rust and the rain on the roof sounded like gunshots.

"Well," Evan said, his voice giving life to the room as it floated up the white-banistered staircase and echoed back down again, "I think we're home." He turned, gave Kay and Laurie a half-smile because smiles still did not come easy, and then carried the suitcases across the threshold. He set them down in the living room and stood for a moment looking out the picture window onto Mc-Clain Terrace while Kay and Laurie went back to the kitchen; he knew the layout of the house by heart now, after negotiating those stairs with lamps and mattresses and pasteboard boxes that held the accumulated odds and ends of a ten-year marriage: paneled den, a small dining area and kitchen in the back, a porch with stairs leading down to the backyard; upstairs, two bedrooms, a bathroom and a half. Plenty of closet space. Even a full basement. The doorway beneath the staircase led down into it. Evan looked at the houses across the street and wondered who lived over there; he heard Kay talking in the kitchen, and Laurie giggling at something she said. There would be time later to meet the neighbors. Right now there were two more suitcases in the car. He went outside, hearing the distant breeze making its way lazily through the overhang of branches. Shade-dappled sun fell upon him, warming his shoulders as he reached into the back of the station wagon and pulled out the battered cases. Here were their lives, he thought; packed away into suitcases and pasteboard boxes, folded over, tucked into place, pushed down deep and covered over with newspaper so they wouldn't rattle. It had been a long, hard road from LaGrange; the memory of that terrible place was like the jab of an ice pick in his soul. Let it go, he told himself; let it go because that part of our lives is finally over. It's going to be good now, here in Bethany's Sin, everything as it should be. I'll make it be good. He glanced across the lawn at his house and felt proud for the first time in a very long while. Evan saw curtains being pulled aside in a window at the back, where the kitchen was, and Kay peered out and waved to him. He gave a little broken-back pantomime and shuffled toward the door with the suitcases, and he saw her smile before she let the curtains drop back again. He heard a lawn mower start up perhaps two streets over, the drone of insects rising in harmony with it.

And then the flesh at the back of his neck crawled, as it did whenever he sensed things without form or name, and he turned his head to gaze across the street. The houses there were sun-splashed hulks of wood and stone. Each one a little different, trimmed in dark brown, blue, painted white and forest green and burnt umber; but each one similar to the others in its silence. He narrowed his eyes slightly. Had a curtain been pulled aside at a window in the brown-and-white house two doors up the street? No, he decided after another moment; nothing had moved over there. And when he started for the house again, he caught the figure out of the corner of an eye.

Someone sitting in the shadows of a front porch next door. Staring at him, hands clasped in the lap, chin slightly upraised. Across the roof of the porch the shadows of tree limbs were intertwined like the bodies of pythons. Evan knew it had been the gaze of that figure, fixed on the back of his neck, that had given him a brief, needlelike chill.

Evan took a step forward. "Hello!" he called out.

The figure, wearing shadow robes, did not move. Evan couldn't tell if it was a man or a woman; his eyes slid toward the street, to the name on the mailbox: DE-MARGEON. "We're just moving in," Evan said; the figure remained motionless, and Evan imagined himself trying to carry on a conversation with a department-store dummy. He started to put the suitcases down and step toward the Demargeon house, but suddenly the figure moved, turning noiselessly in its chair; as Evan watched, the entire chair swiveled and began to glide smoothly forward. Then the figure vanished within the house and there was the noise of a door closing quietly. He stood for a moment, still gripping the suitcases, staring at that front porch; it hadn't been an ordinary piece of porch furniture that figure had been sitting in. It had been a wheelchair.

"Jesus H. Christ!" Evan said under his breath. He shook his head and turned back for his own doorway. But before he reached it there was the quick honking of a horn and a black, shining Buick swerved to the curb. The woman inside waved and cut the engine, sliding out from underneath the steering wheel.

"Good morning," Mrs. Giles said, coming up the walkway toward him. She was very tall, almost as tall as he, and looked skeletal, as if she'd gone a little too far with her faddish liquid-protein diet. The last time he'd seen her she'd been wearing a blouse and skirt, but now she wore a short-sleeved navy blue jumpsuit; bracelets dangled noisily from her wrists. "How long have you been here?"

"Not very long. We're still unloading the station wagon."

"I see." She had darting dark eyes that reminded Evan of some kind of insect, a high forehead crowned with light brown hair that held ribbons of gray. She was smiling, her face full of even white teeth. "How was your drive?"

"Fine. Please, come inside. Kay and Laurie are in there exploring." He followed her through the doorway and set the suitcases down near the stairs. "Kay!" he called. "Mrs. Giles is here!"

"Okay; be right down!" Kay's voice floated from the master bedroom.

Evan ushered the woman into the living room, and she sat down on the sofa. "I can only stay for a minute," she said as he took a seat in a chair across from her. "I wanted to come by and officially welcome you to the village, also to ask if there's anything I can do to help you get settled."

"Thank you," Evan said, "but we're almost in. There's still some furniture on our shopping list—"

"You might try Broome's Furniture over at the Westbury Mall; it's not far from here."

"We'll probably take our time about it. There's no hurry."

"Indeed," Mrs. Giles said, "there isn't. I think you'll find that you've made an excellent investment; there's no point anymore in renting apartments when you can put your money into solid property. At least not around Bethany's Sin. There's a rumor circulating that International Chemco may be buying land near Nanty Glo for a new research facility; if that's true, Bethany's Sin's going to be sharing in the area's growth, and all property owners are going to benefit—Listen to me go on! Isn't that how I talked you out of renting that apartment in Johnstown?"

Evan smiled and nodded. "I believe it is."

"Well," she said, and shrugged, "progress would be nice, but just between you and me, I hope the village won't ever become much larger than it is right now. There's a character and a mood here that I would hate to see altered by the crush of huge industrial complexes; I expect you had enough of that in LaGrange. For myself, I couldn't have stood that nasty air and the noises—ah, here's that pretty little girl with the golden hair. . . ." She had glanced over as Kay came into the living room, holding Laurie's hand. "How do you like having your own room, dear?" she asked the little girl.

"It's very nice," Laurie said.

"But she thinks the bed's too big for her," Kay said. "I've explained that when people get their own bedrooms

37

they can expect to sleep on full-sized beds. Anyway"—
she smoothed Laurie's hair—"now there's room for Miss
Prissy, isn't there?"

"Yes," Laurie said, "but she always sleeps on the
same pillow as me."

Mrs. Giles smiled. "I think that can probably be arranged. Well"—she glanced up at Kay—"I expect you'll
have quite a lot to do before the beginning of the summer
session."

"So much I don't know where to start. I'm driving over
to George Ross in the morning to check with Dr. Wexler.
Do you know him?"

"I don't believe I do."

"Then, on Wednesday morning, there's a conference
for the new instructors and some kind of luncheon. Work-
shops after that. I'm glad I won't be thrown into it cold."

"Even if you were," Mrs. Giles said, "I'm certain you
could handle the situation. You're a very intelligent
woman, and this seems like a perfect opportunity for
you."

"It is," Kay said. "Of course, I'm nervous because I've
never taught at a school anywhere as large as George
Ross. But at the very least it'll be a good experience."
She glanced quickly over at Evan. "For both of us."

"I'm certain." Mrs. Giles stood up from the sofa. "I'd
better be running along now; there are some calls I have
to make at the office. You have my number; if there's
anything I can do for you, please call me. All right?"

"Yes," Kay said, "we will. Thank you."

Mrs. Giles moved out into the entrance foyer, with
Evan behind her; she stopped and turned toward the little
girl. "Such beautiful golden hair," she said softly. "It
glows in the sunlight, doesn't it? You're going to break
some hearts when you get a little older, I'll tell you that."
She smiled into Laurie's eyes and then stepped through
the open door.

"Thanks for stopping by," Evan said as he walked her
out to the car. He looked over toward that front porch; a
shaft of sunlight now lay like a fork of lightning upon the
porch's flagstone floor. "By the way," Evan said as they
reached her Buick, "I saw one of my neighbors this
morning, just before you drove up. There was someone

sitting on that porch over there. In a wheelchair, I think. Do you know who that was?"

Mrs. Giles looked over at the Demargeon house, one hand on the door handle. "Harris Demargeon," she said, her voice taking on a darker tone. The tone, Evan thought, of calamities and accidents. A hospital-and-graveyard tone. "Poor man. Several years ago he was involved in a . . . rather nasty accident over on the King's Bridge Road, to the north of Bethany's Sin. There's a roadhouse up there called The Cock's Crow, and they're not above selling a few beers to minors on a slow Saturday night. A drunken young boy in one of those painted vans hit his car, almost head-on. The poor man's paralyzed from the waist down."

"Oh," Evan said. "I see." An image flashed through his mind like a multicolored comet: a red semi with ALLEN LINES on the cab door, crashing over a freeway median. Kay screaming. "I tried to speak to him," he told the woman, "but evidently he felt like being alone."

"He stays to himself." She opened the car door. Pent-up heat rolled out. "I'm sure you'll be meeting Mrs. Demargeon; she's a good friend of mine." She slid beneath the wheel, turned the key in the ignition. "In fact, they bought their house through me." The engine roared to life. "Good luck to you and your wife, Mr. Reid," she said. "We're so happy to have you in Bethany's Sin."

"Thanks again," Evan said, and when he stepped back from the car, she pulled away and disappeared at the far end of McClain, turning left toward the village. Something caught his eye as he turned back toward the house, and he looked again in order to locate it. Through the jigsaw of elm branches cutting the sky, there were the gables of a slate-colored roof; Evan judged it to be just this side of the Circle. A large building or house of some kind, though he hadn't noticed it before. Now, for some reason, he felt transfixed by it. Felt his heartbeat increase. Felt the blood burn like bile in his veins. Heard, as if in a mist-shrouded dream, his own voice screaming inside his head: *Stop it! Stop it! Stop it! Stop . . .*

The elm branches, moved by the breeze, intertwined themselves into leafy new patterns; shade fell across his eyes, and for an instant that gabled roof was out of sight.

"Evan!" Someone was calling. Someone close. Someone. Kay. "Evan, I'm putting coffee on! Do you want any? Evan, what's wrong?"

He tried to turn his head toward her, but his neck was stiff. His shoulder was throbbing.

"Evan?" There was a familiar panic in her voice now.

Answer her, he told himself. Turn toward her and answer her.

"Evan!" Kay called from the doorway. She could see his back, could see his head tilted slightly upward and to the side, in that strange way he had of staring at things, of sinking his soul into things, of becoming one with them. She started down the steps and across the lawn.

But before she reached him he had turned and smiled, his eyes clear of any disturbance, his brow calm. "It's okay," he told her. "I was just . . . letting my mind drift, I guess."

Kay felt her lungs heave. Thank Christ, she told herself. Thank Whoever listens to my prayers about . . . that thing. "Come inside." She held out her hand to him, and he nodded and took it. "You're hot," she said.

"Is that an invitation to something?"

"No," she said, leading him toward the open door, "I mean it. Your body feels hot. Are you okay?"

"Sure," he said. "Why wouldn't I be?" She didn't answer.

When they reached the house he realized how badly he was sweating; perspiration covered his face and neck in tiny blisterlike beads. Funny, he thought. Damned funny. But not funny enough to make him laugh, for his face burned and felt swollen.

As if seared by a huge, all-consuming fire.

FIVE

THE GIFT AND THE CURSE

Sleep waited for Evan, and he was afraid.

The remainder of the day had been spent settling into the new house: unpacking the suitcases and pasteboard boxes, hanging up clothes in the closets, sorting silverware and putting pots and pans away in kitchen cabinets, sweeping and mopping floors, stocking the refrigerator and pantry with what they'd brought with them from LaGrange. During the afternoon Evan had taken the car down past the Circle again, to that Gulf station with the tire sale, and had passed the better part of thirty minutes trying to talk the manager, a slim man with a shock of unruly red hair and the name Jess sewn onto his shirt, into coming down on his price. He finally agreed to, by five dollars, since Evan was new in town and he wanted the man's business in the future. Jess pulled the station wagon into the garage, and while a teenage boy with close-cropped red hair—the same shade as his father's—put the new tire on, Jess and Evan sat down in the office and had a quiet talk.

Good to have you here, Jess had told him. Bethany's Sin's a real nice place. Kind of quiet around here for me —me and my family live over in Spangler. Been there for the last four years. What do you do for a living?

I'm a writer, Evan had told him. Or trying to be.

Books, huh?

Not yet. Short stories, magazine articles. Whatever.

Good work if you can get it. Me, I guess I've done just about everything. Drove trucks for a few years. Construction work. Went into the house-building business with my brother-in-law, but that kind of fizzled. Tried my hand on the rodeo circuit back when I was a kid, growing up in South Dakota. Yeah, that was a rough way to make a

41

buck. You take those big horses, they're mean. The bigger, the meaner; and they don't have any love for humans. It was all I could do just to grit my teeth and hang on. Well, there you go. Looks like Billy's got that new whitewall on for you. Come back anytime, we'll just sit around and shoot the breeze, 'cause I don't get much of a chance to talk with the Bethany's Sin folk.

Driving back home, Evan made a wrong turn and found himself on Ashaway Road, a street that circled back into Highway 219 and northward. At the northern limit of the village stood a grassy knoll studded with elm and oak trees. Also gravestones. It was the Shady Grove Hill Cemetery, bordered along Ashaway Road by a low rock wall. Evan turned the car around in a driveway before he reached the junction of 219 and wound his way, still uncertainly, toward McClain. At the corner of Blair and Stevenson he happened to turn his head slightly to the right to look for oncoming traffic—of which there always seemed to be miraculously little—and that was when he saw it framed by the backdrop of a white glowing cloud: the gabled roof he'd seen that morning, now only a single street over. What street? he wondered. Cowlington? He could see windows just beneath the roof, glazed with reflections of other roofs and windows, of streets and houses and perhaps even the Circle itself. Like eyes that saw everything, set in a face of dark, weathered stone.

Behind him, the driver of a white Ford honked; Evan blinked, snapping his gaze away from that house, and turned toward home.

And now he lay in the bed beside Kay, she with her eyes closed and her warm body pressed against him, he feeling a heavy weariness but unwilling yet to let go. Distrustful of that time of rest because for him it was often not rest, but like sitting in the front row of a movie theater in the dark, waiting for the show to begin and dreading it. He remembered as a child, in New Concord, Ohio, going to the Lyric Theater on Hanover Street on Saturday afternoons. Eric with him, hand digging into a red-and-white-striped bag of popcorn; around him the chatter of children cut loose from the real world for a couple of hours, free to lose themselves in the shadows that would soon crawl or creep or slither across the time-worn screen. And when the monster appeared, slobbering vile fluids or gnashing vampiric teeth, the hail of popcorn would continue until the red-jacketed usher paced up and down the aisles with his flashlight, threatening expulsion from the school of silver dreams. Some of those monsters were fake and funny, men in rubber suits zapping fleeing earthlings with bizarre rayguns, Japanese centipedes crawling through underground tunnels, hunchbacks with popping eyes that looked oddly like sunnyside-up eggs. You could laugh at those, and trust that all would be okay when you got up out of your seat and turned your back on them in favor of some Red Hots or Chocolate Soldiers.

But there was one Evan still remembered. Still feared.

It had been one of those old, flickering, black-and-white serials, the chapters ending terrifyingly at a moment of excruciating danger. It had drawn him back to that theater again and again to see each episode because no sane person would have dared to turn away from the thing that crawled across that screen. Each Saturday you had to reassure yourself that it would still be there, that it wasn't gone, hadn't broken free from that movie to slither like the cold fall of night through New Concord. The Hand of Evil. Something never quite seen, and always felt too late. Something that could have been man or woman, or not even human, but the frozen, coagulated breath of a demon. Something that struck without warning, and what it was, no man knew or dared to guess. But some ventured that in its passing it . . . scuttled.

Like a spider.

And you never never never turned your back on it, or let it get behind you. Because when you did, it would either consume you or, if unable yet to sink its fangs into your throat, would devour whoever was at hand and bide its time. At the end of the serial the Hand of Evil escaped, oozing through a box the hero—Jon Hall? Richard Arlen?—had captured it in and thrown into the river. Such was the stuff of nightmares, of things that would resurface later in life and grip at throats and spines. Because even as a child in that theater Evan Reid had known there really was such a thing as the Hand of Evil;

43

not called that, no, because that was just a story, but darkness and evil and terror in some black, hideous, lunatic form that stalked its victims in absolute silence.

Beside him, Kay moved slightly on her pillow. He was only dimly aware that he was drifting into a place of thick darkness, where things waited.

The place he found himself in might have been some dream counterpart of the Lyric, but it was very cold; so cold he could see the floating breath in front of his face. There was absolute, ear-cracking silence, and his first thought was: Where are the other children? It's Saturday afternoon, isn't it? The show's about to start. Where are they? At first he thought he was alone, but very slowly something was taking shape just beside him. A form of many shadows and colors, merging into the illusion of solidity. Cold. Very, very cold. In the briefest of instants Eric's features slid across the face of the form, then were gone. Other eyes, noses, jaws, cheekbones, emerged from that face and then slipped away; some Evan recognized, some he did not. It was like watching photographs of the dead being flipped by at high speed. Some of those eyes and mouths gaped in ragged terror.

Perhaps shadowy ushers had torn tickets for this theater; perhaps it was wholly within Evan Reid's mind, or perhaps it actually stood somewhere along the line of demarcation between reality and dreams, between facts and premonitions. Wherever it existed, he now waited for the beginning.

Because he knew there was something they wanted him to see.

It began within him, a tremble of red across his mind that began to grow, to stretch out feelers that touched nerves here, and here, and here. It grew into a spiderish form that gnawed at his brain with a red-cupped mouth, and he was unable to scream or draw away. The thing crawled over him, inflicting pinpricks of pain with its furred claws. In a whirl of color the pictures loomed out at him, blinding him momentarily with a burst of white light: a barren, weed-choked woodland field and the sudden, terrifying noise of cracking wood. A flight of crows taking to the blue sky like a black pentagram. A sharp scream, abruptly ending. Then rising again, a de-

monic shriek that made him want to cry out in pure terror; earth exploding, spewing geysers of dirt and jungle
vines and tree branches. Mortar shells. Faces shadowed
by the bars of bamboo cages, watching him struggle with
two black-garbed guards. An American face over him,
peering down, saying take it easy, you're okay, you're
okay, you're okay now. A brief glimpse of Kay and
Laurie, both younger, Laurie as a baby in her mother's
arms. Steam-pipe rattles. Angry voices and someone crying. Crumpled wads of paper being thrown into a wastebasket, and a searing pool of yellow light.

And then, finally and most disturbingly, a roadside sign
that read BETHANY'S SIN.

Followed by utter darkness.

He shook his head, wanting to escape, to scream himself out of this place; but he realized after another moment that they weren't finished with him. No, not quite
yet. Because, after all, he had been brought to see the
next episode.

The darkness whitened, very gradually. Until it was the
color of sunlight, and there were the streets and houses of
the village, laid out in an orderly and pleasing pattern.
He could see the colors of the flowers in the Circle, and
all the shops ringing it, but it seemed that the streets were
deserted and the houses empty, because nothing moved.
He walked alone, following his beckoning shadow, surrounded by silence.

And he stood before that large, dark-stoned, gabled
house.

Moving through a wrought-iron fence topped with
spear points, walking along a concrete pathway toward an
imposing door of solid oak. He could taste a dry fear in
his throat, but there was no turning back, no running. Not
here, in this place. His hand slowly reached out, gripped
the brass knob and pushed. The door opened noiselessly,
and he stood on the threshold.

Darkness within; cold, the smell of ages past and bones
dissolved into ashes. The sun burned on his back; the
shadows ahead froze his face. And as he watched, unable
to move, dust boiled in a long corridor that seemed to
stretch into eternity before him. It finally came together like a curtain, and it was through this curtain

that Evan saw a shadowy figure moving, slowly and steadily. Formless, ancient, terrible. Striding closer. Closer. And closer. One arm coming up, fingers piercing that maelstrom of dust, clawing it away as if it were the sheerest fabric or the thick webs of a huge and lurking spider. The fingers stretched out toward him, and Evan threw up his arms before his face, but he could not step away, could not find the strength to move, could not slam that massive door upon whatever evil thing it was that neared him in that corridor. The hand began to come through the dust for him.

And the faceless shape of a head, cloaked in darkness.

He thrust his arms out against it to hold it back, his mouth coming open in a cry of terror. He gripped something, pushed at it. Hands on his wrists; someone shaking him. The lights coming on, stinging his eyes. Someone saying . . .

"Evan!" Kay. Shaking him. His fingers clamped around her wrists, and her hands on his shoulders. "Evan! Come on, wake up! Wake up! What's wrong with you?" Her eyes were sleep-puffed and wild, and she shook him harder to make him see her.

He wiped away the webs of sleep and sat up on the pillow. Beads of sweat clung to his cheeks and forehead, drying now. He blinked, trying to remember where he was. That house. No. Our house. Kay beside me. Outside, the sleeping village. All is well in the world. That other place, where they showed him the things, had faded and was gone. He waited a moment, trying to regain his equilibrium; his breathing was ragged. "I'm . . . okay," Evan said finally. "I'm okay." He looked into Kay's eyes, and she nodded.

"Was it a bad one?" she asked him.

From the bedroom across the hall, Laurie's frightened voice: "Mommy? Daddy?"

"It's nothing," Evan called to her. "Just a bad dream. Go back to sleep."

Silence.

"Do you want a glass of water or something?" Kay asked him.

He shook his head. "It's over now. Jesus, some first night in our new house!"

"Please . . ." Kay touched his lips with a finger. "Don't talk about it. Everything's all right now. Can you go back to sleep?"

"I don't—no, I don't think so. Not yet, at least." He waited a long while, aware that she was watching him, and then he turned his head toward her. "I don't want to ruin things," he said.

"You won't. You never have. Don't even think anything like that."

"Hey," he said, looking into her eyes. "I'm your husband, remember? You don't have to kid yourself, and you certainly don't have to kid me. We both know."

"You blame yourself for too much. There's no need for it." She felt uneasy saying that, as if she were fully aware it was a lie. She could see that his eyes looked distant and haunted, as if he'd seen something terrible that he'd failed to fully recognize.

"I want things to be good," Evan said, "I want them to work out."

"They will," she said. "Please . . ."

"But they haven't before, have they?" he asked her, and her silence stung him. "Always these dreams. I can't get away from them. I can't make them stop! Jesus, when are they going to stop? Now they've caught up with me, and I'm having nightmares about Bethany's Sin."

"Bethany's Sin?" Kay's eyes iced and narrowed. "What about it?"

"I can't make any sense out of it. I never can. But this seemed . . .worse than any I've ever had before."

Kay stared at him without speaking, because she didn't know what to say, because there was nothing to say. His eyes said everything. Torment. Pain. Guilt. She had the sudden sure feeling that in the other bedroom Laurie wasn't asleep at all, but was listening, perhaps fearfully. Laurie had heard her father cry out in the night too many times not to be afraid.

Evan was making an effort to control his breathing. The details of the nightmare were fading rapidly; just the cold terror remained lodged like a thorn down around his stomach. "I can't deal with this," he said finally. "I've never been able to. All my life I've cried out in my sleep; I've gone through insomnia and sleeping pills and stay-

awake pills. But I just can't shake the damned dreams!"
He threw aside the sheets and sat up on the edge of the
bed. Kay found herself staring at a small semicircular
scar on the muscular curve of his lower back where his
pajama top had bunched up. Shrapnel from a world
away. That was what had brought him home from the
war. Purple Heart and all. She touched it very slightly,
as if afraid it might burst open again and spill bright red
blood across the blue sheets. It seemed foreign to her, as
many things still did, even after all this time. "I don't
even know what the hell they mean," he said. "When I
try to examine them as bits and pieces, my brain turns
to slush. The fragments escape me just as I try to grab at
them. And this time . . . this time they were about Bethany's Sin. God knows why. But they were."

"They're only dreams," Kay said, trying to keep her
voice calm. How many times had she said that exact same
thing to him in the middle of the night? Only dreams. Not
real. They can't hurt. "There's nothing to them; I can't
understand why you let them . . . worry you so much."
Careful, careful, she thought; this is tricky, have to choose
the right words, like picking flowers in a bed of nettles.
She stared at the back of his head, the unruly hair standing out from the top and sides. He ran one hand through
it, and she saw his shoulders sag forward a fraction.
"They don't mean anything, Evan," she said quietly and
calmly. "Just maybe that you put too much mustard and
a pickle too many on your meatloaf sandwich. Come on,
lie back down. What time is it, anyway?" She turned her
head to look at the night-table clock. "My God," she
said. "Almost five." She yawned, still squinting from the
lamp's whitish glare.

"They mean something," he said in a dull, empty
voice. "The one about the truck meant something, didn't
it? And the ones before that . . ."

"Evan," Kay said. "Please . . ." She heard herself:
weary, irritated. Perhaps more than a little frightened as
well. Yes. Admit it, she told herself. Through the cold
layers of skepticism she had slowly troweled down over
the years as a protection against things she failed to
comprehend, that twinge of unease, of unreasoning fear,
had often penetrated. But only for a moment, because

then she'd been able to gain control again, to say no, no, it's only coincidence, there's no such thing as—

"I'm sorry if I frightened you," Evan said. "Jesus, I'm going to have to start sleeping with a strip of tape over my mouth so you and Laurie can get some decent rest for a change."

—what did they call it—

"I thought I'd left them behind," he told her, without looking at her. "I thought they were still in LaGrange. Maybe lurking under the bed, or something like that. The last one was about Harlin, and a month after it I'd lost my job at the journal."

—second sight?

"I remember," Kay said, without bitterness now because, after all, things had worked out well, hadn't they? Coincidence; all of it was coincidence. "I want to turn out the light," she said. "Okay?"

"Okay," he told her. "Sure."

She reached over, switched it off. Darkness reclaimed the room except for a single shaft of clear moonlight that filtered through the curtains. She lay on her back, her eyelids weighted by weariness, but did not immediately return to sleep. Instead, she listened to his breathing. It reminded her, oddly, of a frightened animal she had watched in a cage at the zoo when she was a little girl. She lifted her hand and touched his shoulder. "Aren't you going to try to sleep?"

"In a few minutes," Evan replied. He wasn't ready yet. The old fears had resurfaced, laced like scars across white flesh. The whole thing was unreal, like Poe's dream within the dream. *Why won't they leave me alone?* he asked himself. *This is a new start. I want everything to be right. I don't want the dreams anymore!* From the distance of time Jernigan's voice came to him: *Old Reid can see! Bastard can fuckin see! Said he saw that tripwire stretched across the trail in a dream, saw it glowing blue like it was on fire or somethin'. And Bookman on point found that goddamned thing, stretched tight, smeared with mud, just waitin' for us, because old Reid told him to watch for it! So Bookman traces it up into the trees and there's this fuckin' Claymore, and after everybody's got his ass hid we yank that wire and there*

49

she goes like a Roman candle, boom! *When the Cong came in to loot deadmen, they caught some lead between their teeth.*

Sure. Evan stared at the blank wall, feeling the darkness and silence of the house like an alien marrow in his bones. This dream he'd had tonight was . . . very different from any he'd ever had. Shifting shapes, formless things lurking in a dark maelstrom: what were they? What did it mean? Or did it mean anything at all? Like everyone else, he had dreams that were only insensible fragments, sometimes comedic, sometimes chilling. Dreams that were, as Kay had pointed out, brought on by too much mustard or spicy chili or things remembered from midnight television flicks. But through experience Evan had learned to tell the difference. If they—the formless escort-things that brought him to the movie in his mind—wanted him to see, then there was a purpose to it. A deadly serious purpose. And he had learned not to dismiss lightly the images they allowed him to see; that sight had saved their lives before, more than once. Of course he knew that Kay turned her back on it; she dismissed those happenings as coincidence because she couldn't understand, and she feared it as well. He hadn't told her about it before they were married, because in those days he was still trying to come to grips with it himself, to understand why he was burdened with a strange half-enlightenment, half-affliction. His mother's voice: a gift. His father's harder voice: a curse. Yes. Both of those.

He decided he did want a glass of cold water, so he rose up from the bed, switched on the light in the blue-tiled bathroom, and drew tap water into a plastic cup. In the bathroom mirror his face looked haunted by the things that lived behind it: dark circles beneath the grayish green eyes, lines deepening on his forehead and around his mouth, premature flecks of gray glinting at his temples. On his left cheek, just above the line of the cheekbone, was a small, crooked scar; there was another over his left eyebrow. He had ignored a dream once, in the fatigue of jungle fighting, in the day-to-day hell of survival; in that dream they had shown him a red sky filled with flaming wasps. When the mortar shells had come that morning, he was out in the open, and the shrapnel had pierced his left side, one piece imbedding itself dangerously close to his heart. Remembering that was difficult; it was a jumble of noise and faces and blood smells and hospital smells. How the medic, a young man named Dawes, had kept him from bleeding to death he never knew. He remembered, dimly, whirling copter blades and men shouting. Then there was blackness until a glaring white light shone over his face at a field hospital; he heard someone moaning and, weeks later, realized that it must have been himself. Now, standing before the mirror, he knew that the fine lines of the scars across his chest and ribs would look somewhat like a road map underneath his pajama top. Before the war he had slept with Kay in the nude. Now he didn't, though Kay said she didn't mind, and he thought she meant it, but that field of crisscrossed flesh made the images well up in his mind like burning drops of blood.

Four years before, when he was still inside the barbed-wire cocoon of cold terror the war had closed around him, he had tried to grow a beard. He wanted to hide: he didn't particularly like Evan Reid anymore; he didn't know the man, wouldn't have known him if he'd met Evan Reid on the streets of LaGrange. In the war he had killed human beings at first with sick horror and revulsion, later with an empty feeling, as if he were the M-16 itself, hot and smoking. And at the end, after what had been done to him in a Cong prisoner-of-war holding camp, he even found himself hunting them, every impulse and nerve vibrating with the killer instinct. The hardened men, the ones whose eyes looked funny, slitted, and who never liked people to stand behind them, said that after you got the killer instinct you never lost it. He had prayed to God that he would; and perhaps that was why he chose to ignore the dream and freeze in his tracks when he heard the mortar shells screaming in. Because it was time to stop. Or be stopped.

The beard was gone a week after it was begun, because the hair grew ragged around the scar on his jaw, branding him with memories. Another reminder of what he had been and what he had done.

He drank down the water, drew another half-glass and drank that as well. In the mirror his eyes stared back at him over the rim of the glass. Then he turned off the light and walked into the bedroom, where Kay's sleeping form lay motionless in the sheets. As he crossed the room the beam of moonlight fell upon him.

Abruptly, in the distance, a dog began to bark. Perhaps, Evan thought, from a backyard at the far end of McClain Terrace.

He paused, stepped toward the window, and drew aside the curtains with one hand.

Evan peered through the glass. Leafy elm branches cut the moon's pearly luminescence into jagged shards of ice. The dog began to bay. Something moved past the window, the flash of a phantom wraith there and then gone along the street. Evan, craning his neck but unable to see because of the trees, had the split-second impression of something black. And huge. For an instant his flesh had crawled and the hair at the back of his neck had risen. Now he could hear his heart hammering in his chest, and he strained to see through the night, his senses questing for the slightest movement.

But there was nothing.

If there had been anything at all.

Shadows? He glanced quickly up at the sky. A cloud passing briefly over the face of the moon? Possibly, but . . . if not that, then what? All along McClain the houses were dark; nothing moved, no lights shone, nothing nothing nothing . . . He felt bitterly cold, and he shivered suddenly. And drew away from the window, letting the curtains fall back. He slipped beneath the sheets, and Kay murmured, moving closer to him. For a long time he could feel his heartbeat as it seemed to strum his body like an off-key guitar. What had that been? he asked himself on the borderline of sleep. What was out there on the night-lit Bethany's Sin streets?

And why was he certain he would not have gone outside to see it for any price on earth?

Falling into the black crater of sleep, he heard that dog bark again.

Again.

And again.

SIX

LITTLE FEARS

Bird song filled the morning air along McClain Terrace, and fingers of sunlight moved in the forest beyond Kay's kitchen windows as she started breakfast. Laurie wasn't yet awake, but that was okay because starting next week she'd have to be getting up around seven-thirty to go to the day-care center while Kay drove on to George Ross Junior College, a few miles north of Ebensburg. Evan was showering upstairs, and as Kay put the water on to boil for coffee, she heard the noise of the shower cease.

When she was getting the cups—white with a dark blue band around the rim—out of the cupboard, her hands suddenly trembled and she dropped one of them onto the linoleum-tiled floor. It cracked, teethlike chips flying out in all directions, and she called herself a stupid ass and put the broken cup into the trash can.

But the truth was that a spring had begun winding itself tight within her.

She envisioned the inside of a pocket watch her grandfather Emory had once shown her, all the tiny gears clicking and turning, the mainspring coiling itself tighter and tighter as he wound it with his age-spotted hand. Won't it break, Pa-Pa? she'd asked him. And then it won't be good anymore? But he'd only smiled and wound it as tight as it would wind, and then he'd let her hold it and watch the gears go around, clicking in what seemed to her a mechanical frenzy. Perhaps now, she thought, the mainspring that controlled her nerves and heartbeat and even the workings of her mind was being wound by an invisible hand. An invisible Pa-Pa. Wound and wound and wound until she could feel the first threatening throb of pain erupt at her temples. She opened a drawer, searched through it for the bottle of Bufferin she'd placed there the day before; she took two with a glass of water. That helped a little bit. But they were tension headaches, stubborn and painful, and very often so bad the Bufferin did nothing against them. She shrugged her shoulders to ease the tight band across her back. The water began to boil on the stove. To her the kettle's whistle sounded like a shriek. She reached for the pot, feeling the heat on her hand, and lifted it off the glowing eye. At the same time she concentrated on dismissing the nagging fears that seemed to have crept up around her, vaporish things that might have stepped through the woodwork. Things that had followed them from LaGrange and now sat watching her, grinning and chuckling, from perches atop the counter or the cupboards. In the war of nerves they always won.

In another few minutes she heard Evan coming down the stairs. He came into the kitchen wearing a pale blue short-sleeved shirt and gray slacks, and kissed her on the cheek as she fried bacon. He smelled of soap, and his hair was still damp. "Good morning," he said.

"'Morning." She swept a mental hand across the kitchen, and those little fears scuttled away into nooks and crevices to wait. She smiled and returned his kiss. "Breakfast is almost ready."

"Great," he said, and looked out the windows across the sun-and-shadow-dappled woodland. "It's going to be a pretty day. Isn't Laurie awake yet?"

"No," Kay said. "There's no reason for her not to sleep late."

Evan nodded. He glanced toward the sky, half-expecting to see looming factory chimneys and a reddish tinge of industrial smoke, but there were only the distant clouds against a soft blue. How many mornings, he wondered, had he stood at the single kitchen window in that LaGrange house and seen that smudge of blood in the sky? Those cramped, low-ceilinged rooms had been like a cage, except the bars were of wood instead of bamboo. And in that dark brick building far beyond the company parking lot the Gentleman waited, except this time the Gentleman had a name and his name was Harlin. Evan's mind sheered away from all that, and he let the sunlight reflected off the trees warm his face; but in backing away from those thoughts he remembered the nightmare, with its Bethany's Sin road sign and its shadowy thing emerging from a cloud of dust. Something tightened suddenly at the base of his spine. What could that dream-form have been? he wondered; what evil, twisted thing reaching for him? Only the Shadow knows, he told himself. And even the Shadow can be wrong.

"Here we are," Kay said, putting the breakfast dishes on the small circular table in the kitchen.

Evan sat down, and Kay joined him. They ate in silence for a few minutes; in an elm tree in the backyard a blue jay screeched and then wheeled for the sky. After a while Evan cleared his throat and looked up at her from his plate; he caught her gaze and held it. "I'd like to tell you what my dream was last night. . . ."

She shook her head. "Please. I don't want to hear it. . . ."

"Kay," he said quietly, "I want to talk about it. I've got to get it out in the open where I can see it clearly and try to understand it." He put his fork down and sat silently for a moment. "I know my . . . dreams frighten you. I know they make you uncomfortable. But they frighten me much, much more, because I have to live with them. I wish to God I didn't; I wish I could turn my back on them or run away from them or . . . something, but I can't. All I'm asking is that you help me understand."

"I don't want to hear it," Kay said firmly. "There's no sense in talking about your dreams with me, because I refuse to see them as you do. For Christ's sake, Evan, you torture yourself with them!" She leaned slightly over the table toward him, ignoring that haunted, pleading look in his eyes that she had seen so often. "And you insist on trying to torture Laurie and me with them as well! Everyone has dreams, but not everyone believes that their dreams are going to influence their lives somehow! When you start doing that, you"—she searched carefully for the correct words—"make them come true yourself!"

Evan sipped at his coffee and put the cup back in its saucer; there was a tiny chip on the rim. "I don't dream like a normal person does," he said. "You must realize that by now. I'll sleep without dreaming for months at a time, and when they finally come they're . . . very strange. And real. Terrible and threatening; different from ordinary dreams. And always they try to tell me something. . . ."

"Evan!" Kay said sharply, more sharply than she'd intended. Slashed, Evan looked at her and blinked, and she dropped her fork down onto the table. "I don't care what you say or think," she told him, trying hard to keep herself under control. Her temples throbbed. Oh, no! she told herself. Damn it damn it here come those headaches! "They are not premonitions. There are no such things as premonitions." She held his gaze, wouldn't let him look away. "You make those things come true by your own actions, don't you see that? Can't you realize that it's you?" Bitterness rose in her throat, tasting like an amalgam of salt water, bile and blood. "Or are you too blind to see it?"

He kept staring at her, his face frozen into the mask he wore when she struck out at him. In the backyard a robin warbled on and on.

Kay rose and took her plate over to the sink. There was no use in talking to him about this thing; of all the tiny day-to-day thorns that pricked their marriage, this was the largest and the sharpest. This had drawn blood and tears. And what was most terrible, Kay thought, was that it was a hopeless situation: Evan was never going to stop seeing his dreams as a window onto some other world, and she was never going to agree with his often utterly ridiculous "premonitions." Those things that had come true in the past had come about due only to him, not to anything supernatural. Not to Destiny, nor to Evil, but only to Evan Reid. And the simple truth of the matter was for her the most painful: he had allowed those dreams to shape his own life and, worse, their life together. Middle-class gypsies, she told herself, almost humorously. Carrying our crystal ball with us. Living in fear when the dreams told Evan there was going to be a fire in the apartment building—he'd left the electric heater on one morning, a frayed wire had shot sparks, a lot of smoke but not much damage. His fault again. Living in fear under Eddie Harlin—don't think about that! —and so many other times.

And now it's begun again, she told herself. Only one day here, where there are so many opportunities for all of us, and it's already started. And why? Yes. Because he's afraid. Isn't that what the Veterans Administration psychologist, Dr. Gellert, had said years ago? Evan has a problem trusting people, the doctor had told her in one of those terrible sessions. There's a great deal of stress within Evan, Mrs. Reid; it's a result of the war, his feelings about himself, his idea that he's personally responsible for many of the things that happened. It seems to be a complex problem; it goes back to his relationship with his parents and, especially, his older brother, Eric. . . .

Evan finished his coffee and brought the plates over to the sink. "Okay," he said. "I know they disturb you; I know they frighten you. So we won't talk about them anymore." He waited for her response, and finally she turned toward him.

"They do scare me," Kay said. "And you scare me when you believe in them so much. I'm sorry I get upset, Evan; I'm sorry I don't understand, but . . . we've both got to put those bad things behind us." She paused for a moment, watching his eyes. "All right?"

"Yes," Evan said, nodding. "All right."

Kay reached out and took his hand, drawing him toward the windows. "Look at that," she said. "A whole forest for us to wake up to in the mornings. And that clear, blue sky. Did you ever make cloud-pictures when you were a child? What does that large one over there look like to you?"

Evan looked at it. "I don't know," he said. "What do you think?"

"A face," Kay said. "Someone smiling. See the eyes and the mouth?"

To Evan it looked like an archer, but he didn't say anything.

"I wonder what the rain looks like through these windows? Or the snow?"

Evan smiled and put his arm around her. "I doubt if we'll see very much snow this summer."

"It must be entirely white," Kay said. "And the branches thick with icicles. And in the spring and the fall it'll be different again." She turned toward him and looked into his eyes; he'd pushed away the haunted darkness, for a little while at least, and for this she was grateful. She put her arms around him. "It's going to be good," she said. "Just like we've always wanted everything to be. I've got my teaching position, you'll be writing, Laurie's going to be meeting new friends and having a real home; that's very important to her right now."

"Yes, I know it is." He held onto her and looked out across the forest. It would be beautiful under a cover of snow. And then in the spring, as the first green buds appeared on the thousands of bare brown limbs, there would be nothing in sight but fresh green and the slow and sure growth of new thicket; and in the autumn, as the weather cooled day by day, the trees would take on the appearance of fire, the leaves scorched with gold and red and yellow, slowly turning brown and curling, dropping to the earth. Beyond those windows Nature would be constantly changing her colors, like a beautiful woman with many dresses. It pleased Evan that there was so much beauty to look forward to, for in the past few years there had been achingly little.

There was a sudden *bing-bong!* from the entrance foyer. The doorbell, Evan realized.

"I'll see who it is," Kay said; she squeezed her husband's hand briefly and then turned away from the kitchen windows, going out through the den and a connecting corridor to the entrance foyer. Through the panes of frosted glass set into the door she saw the head of the person on the other side; she unlocked and opened the door.

It was a woman, perhaps in her late thirties, wearing a canary yellow tennis outfit; a locket initialed with the letters *J* and *D* hung around her neck. Her flesh suntanned but amazingly unlined, she looked as if she practically lived outdoors, and in her rather square-jawed but attractive face her gaze was steady and calm. She held a basket of tomatoes. "Mrs. Reid?" she said.

"Yes, that's right."

"It's so good to meet you. I'm Janet Demargeon." The woman motioned with a tilt of her head. "Your next-door neighbor."

"Oh, yes," Kay said, "of course. Please come in, won't

you?" She stepped back and the woman came into the entrance foyer. The aroma of freshly mown grass wafted in through the open door, reminding Kay of wide, luxuriously green pastures.

"I see you're all moved in," Mrs. Demargeon said, swinging her gaze in toward the living room. "How pretty."

"Not quite," Kay told her. "There's still some furniture to buy."

"Well, it's coming along nicely." The woman smiled again and offered her the basket. "From my garden. I thought you might like some fresh tomatoes this morning."

"Oh, they're beautiful," Kay said as she took them. They were, too; large and red and unblemished. Mrs. Demargeon walked past her into the living room and looked around. "Just a hobby," she said. "Everyone should have a hobby, and gardening's mine."

Kay motioned for her to sit down, and she did, in a chair near the picture window. "It's so nice and cool in here," Mrs. Demargeon said, fanning her face with a red-nailed hand. "My air conditioning has been breaking down since the first of June; it's a real problem getting the Scars serviceman over from the Mall."

"Can I get you something? A cup of coffee?"

"I'd love some iced tea. With plenty of ice."

Evan, hearing the voices, came through the foyer into the living room. Kay introduced them and showed him the tomatoes; Evan took the woman's outstretched hand and shook it, finding it as hard and dry as a man's. Her eyes were very attractive though, green veined with hazel, and her dark brown hair was swept back from her face. Glints of blond showed in it. Kay took the tomatoes back to the kitchen and left them alone.

"Where are you and your wife from, Mr. Reid?" Mrs. Demargeon asked him when he'd settled himself on the sofa.

"We've been living in LaGrange; it's a small mill town near Bethlehem."

Mrs. Demargeon nodded. "I've heard of it. Were you with the mill?"

"In a way. I was a writer and copy editor for *Iron*

Man, the mill's public-relations journal. Mostly I wrote headlines."

"A writer?" She raised her eyebrows. "Well! I don't think we've ever had a writer in the village before. Have you ever had anything published?"

"A few things. I had a short story in *Fiction* magazine in April, and before that an article on truck drivers in a CBer's publication. There've been some other articles and short stories, all in minor markets. Things like that."

"Interesting. At least you've seen some money from your efforts; I'm sure that's a lot more than most can say. Do you have a job here in the village, or in Johnstown?"

Evan shook his head. "I'm looking. We left LaGrange because of some . . . well, complications. And Kay's going to be teaching during the summer session at George Ross."

"Oh? Teaching what?"

"Basic algebra," Kay said, bringing Mrs. Demargeon's glass of tea across the room to her. The woman sipped at it gratefully. "Strictly a summer-session course, but I'm hoping for a math concepts course in the fall." She sat down beside Evan.

"That sounds way over my head," Mrs. Demargeon said. "Anyone who can handle that has my immediate respect. I saw you drive in yesterday; wasn't there a little girl with you?"

"Our daughter, Laurie," Kay said. "I think she's still sleeping."

"Too bad. I'd like to meet her sometime. She looked like such a pretty, sweet little child. How old is she?"

"Just turned six in May," Kay told her.

"Six." The woman smiled, looked from Kay to Evan. "A beautiful age. Then she'll be attending first grade at Douglas in September? That's a fine school."

"Mrs. Demargeon . . ." Evan began, leaning forward slightly.

"Please. Janet."

"Okay; Janet. I noticed the street was very dark last night. Are all the houses on McClain Terrace occupied?"

"Yes, they are. But most of the people on the Terrace are early-to-bed, early-to-rise types. A bit sedate, if you get my meaning. Also, I believe the Rices are on vacation this month; they drive up into the Allegheny forest to do some camping every summer."

"What about the house directly across the street from us?" Evan asked her. "I didn't see any lights at all over there last night."

"Oh? Well, I suppose Mr. Keating may be on vacation, too. As a matter of fact, I haven't seen his car there for a few days. He's a widower, but I believe he has relatives living in New York; he may be visiting them. He's a very nice man; I'm sure you'll like him." She smiled and sipped at her tea. "Oh, how cooling that is! Of course, June isn't really our hot month in Bethany's Sin. It's August you have to watch out for. That's the killer month; everything wilts. And dry. My God, is it dry!" She swung her gaze over toward Kay. "So. Have you met many of the villagers yet?"

"You're the first neighbor we've met," Kay said. "Of course, we know Mrs. Giles, but that's about it."

"It takes time, I'm sure. I wouldn't worry. They're friendly people." She shifted her eyes to Evan. "Most of them are, at least; some of them, the ones who live in those large houses down near the Circle, stay to themselves. Their families have lived in the village for a few generations, and, Jesus Christ, they're more family-conscious than the DAR!"

Kay smiled; she felt relaxed with this woman, and glad that she'd come over to make them feel welcome. It was, after all, an indication that they were being accepted into the village, if only by one neighbor. And acceptance was always a good feeling.

"The Circle's very beautiful," Evan was saying. "Someone's gone to a lot of trouble and expense to keep those flowers looking nice."

"The Beautification Committee does it. Let's see. Mr. and Mrs. Holland, Mrs. Omarian, Mr. and Mrs. Brecker, Mr. Quarles. A few others. They take turns planting and watering and weeding and such as that. They wanted me on the committee last year, but I had to turn it down. That garden of mine keeps me close enough to the earth."

"I'm sure it does," Evan said. "I was wondering: what's that large house over on Cowlington? I can see its roof from my front yard."

Mrs. Demargeon paused for a moment. "Large house? Let's see. Oh, right! That's the museum."

"Museum?"

She nodded. "Built by the historical society."

"What kinds of things are in there?" Kay asked her. Mrs. Demargeon smiled wryly. "Junk, dear. Just junk. Those society ladies think junk and dust make history. Don't even waste your time going over there, because usually the place is locked up tighter than a drum! Do you play tennis, Mrs. Reid?"

"Please call me Kay. Oh, I used to play a little bit, but I haven't in quite some time."

"Great! This place could use another tennis player! At least we do. I'm in a tennis club—the Dynamos—and we play every Tuesday morning at ten over on the courts just down the hill. There're five of us: Linda Paulson, Anne Grantham, Leigh Hunt, Jean Quarles, and me. Maybe you'd like to play some Tuesday?"

"Maybe," Kay said. "It depends on my classes."

"Of course." The woman finished her tea and put the empty glass on a table beside her. The ice cubes clicked together. She rose, and Evan and Kay did the same. "I'd better be getting on," Mrs. Demargeon said, moving toward the front door. Stopping to look back, she asked, "Are you two bridge players?"

"Afraid not," Evan said.

"How about canasta? Poker? It doesn't matter. I want both of you over at my house on Friday night. Can you do that?"

Kay glanced at Evan; he nodded. "Yes," she said. "Of course."

"Perfect." She looked down at her wristwatch and made an irritated face. "Oops! I'm running late! Leigh's waiting for me over at Westbury. Kay, I'll call you later on in the week and we'll set up things for Friday, all right?" She opened the front door, moved out onto the steps. "Well, have a good day. And I hope you enjoy the tomatoes." She waved a hand, gave them one last smile, and then walked off along the pathway to the sidewalk. Kay watched her for a moment and then closed the door.

She put her arm around Evan. "She's very nice. I'll

take something over there on Friday. How about potato salad?"

He nodded. "Okay."

There was a noise on the stairs, and Laurie came down, still in her pea green pajamas, rubbing sleep from her eyes.

"Hi, honey," Kay said. "Do you want some breakfast?"

She yawned. "Cheerios."

"Cheerios it is. How about some banana slices on top?" Kay took the little girl's hand and moved toward the den.

"Mrs. Demargeon didn't say anything about her husband," Evan said, and Kay looked back at him quizzically.

"Her husband? What about him?"

He shrugged. "Nothing, really. I saw him on their front porch yesterday, and Mrs. Giles told me he'd been in an accident several years ago. He's paralyzed and in a wheelchair."

"Mrs. Demargeon is probably sensitive about his condition," Kay said. "What kind of accident was it?"

"Car crash."

"God," Kay said softly. "That's awful." Brief flickering images of ripped metal, blank staring headlights, gashed flesh and nerves, swept over her. That could have happened to us once, she heard a voice inside her say. Stop that! "I'm sure we'll meet him on Friday." She tugged at Laurie's hand. "Come on, honey, let's get your breakfast." They disappeared into the den, and for a moment Evan stood where he was in the corridor, surrounded by shadow and shards of sunlight. After a while he realized he was working his knuckles, and he remembered doing that a long time ago, while he'd waited inside a bamboo cage. While he'd waited for them to come for him and make him scream. He shrugged his shoulders, almost unconsciously, as if shrugging off an uncomfortable coat or an old, age-wrinkled skin. He moved into the living room, stood where he could draw aside a curtain and look out the window at the Demargeon house next door.

"Evan?" Kay was calling him from the kitchen. "Where are you?"

He didn't answer, thinking numbly that she was trying to keep track of him as she would Laurie. The Demargeons' driveway was on the other side of the house, and in another moment he saw their car—a white Honda Civic—back out and then turn away in the direction of the Circle. Only one person was in it.

And as he watched, Evan thought he saw a shadow move across one of the windows facing his house. Moving slowly and with effort. Moving in a wheelchair.

"Evan?" Kay called, the hint of disturbance in her voice barely hidden.

He looked up. "In the living room," he said. And she was quiet. He heard Laurie ask something about how many children would be at the day-care center. Kay said she didn't know, but she was sure they'd all be nice.

The shadow was gone from the window. Evan turned away.

Out in the cradling branches of an elm in the front yard, a bird began to sing. The notes rang out across McClain Terrace and echoed away into silence.

SEVEN

THE LAW IN BETHANY'S SIN

At noon Oren Wysinger turned his white-and-blue Olds-mobile patrol car off Fredonia Street and into the McDonald's parking lot. Watching from under the brim of his hat, he saw a few people stop eating to stare at him; only when they were certain the blue light wasn't flashing round and round the rooftop glass bubble did they return to their lunches. That feeling of power made Oren Wysinger happy, as if he'd just been reminded that he was an important man. Maybe even the most important man in the village. He circled the restaurant slowly, looking at the cars parked in their yellow-outlined slots. Mostly locals. There was a red sports car he didn't recognize; somebody out for a drive, maybe some young guy from Spangler or Barnesboro trying to pick up girls. He parked his own car and watched that red job for a few minutes. After a while a teenage boy and girl, both wearing blue jeans, she in a halter top and he in a short-sleeved white shirt, came out of the restaurant and got into the car. The boy noticed Wysinger and nodded, and Wysinger tipped a finger to the brim of his hat. The sports car pulled out of the parking lot slowly, but Wysinger had the distinct feeling that boy would get out on Highway 219 and drive like a devil with a pitchfork up his ass.

Oren Wysinger was forty-six years old. He had the face of a man toughened by the weather: squint lines around eyes so deeply brown they were almost black, creases and cracks and gullies in the flesh that looked like dried-up riverbeds. Gray sideburns, close-cropped, came down from underneath the hat, and below it the hair looked like so much salt and pepper sprinkled across pale skin. His hooked nose was made even more hooked by a large bump of bone on the bridge, where he'd been caught by a beer bottle during a fight three years ago at the Cock's Crow. He looked wary and cautious and dangerous, distrustful of strangers and fiercely protective of Bethany's Sin. Because that was his job as sheriff. On both seamed hands the fingernails were bitten to the quick.

Wysinger stretched, his six-foot-three bulk completely filling the driver's side of the front seat, and his ornate belt buckle scraping up against the steering wheel. He was hungry as all hell; he'd had scrambled eggs and ham at five-thirty this morning in his small brick house on Deer Cross Lane, and during his morning rounds he'd chewed on Fig Newtons and Cracker Jacks and drunk a couple of pints of milk. The wrappers and containers lay on the rear floorboard. He got out of the car, walked across the lot into the restaurant. He knew the counter girls because he was a man of strict habits. They were cute little high-schoolers, two from Barnesboro and the other, the prettiest one, whose name was Kim, from Elmora. Kim had his lunch waiting for him: three hamburgers, French fries, and a large Coke. She smiled and asked him how he was doing, and he lied and told her he'd run down a speeder over on Cowlington just an hour before. He took his food, nodded or spoke to a few of the people at the tables, and then went back outside to his car. He switched on his radio and listened to the troopers while he ate. One of them was asking about a registration on a pickup truck. Codes were talked back and forth. Static, different voices, during one transmission the unmistakable scream of a siren. He found himself idly fingering the roll of fat at his midsection; it was no more than a bicycle tire, but it bothered him nonetheless. He could press all the way down through the fat to where the muscle was still firm; at one time the muscles and sinews had stood out like piano wires all along his body, and when he moved he could swear they vibrated. But now he wasn't getting enough exercise; he used to be able to walk his rounds, but in the past few years the village had been expanding outward and he found it more practical to take the patrol car. He thought of the troopers out on the highway, hard-muscled men in their streamlined metal-and-glass machines. They would be wearing green- or gray-tinted sunglasses to ward off the reflection of sun from asphalt, and those Smoky Bear hats that gave them impressive profiles. He'd wanted to be a trooper, and many years ago enrolled in the program, but things hadn't worked out. It was his attitude, he's been told; his reflexes were too slow as well. That was a fine thing for a pencil-pusher to tell a man who'd been All-State halfback at Slattery High in Conemaugh, his hometown, about seven miles northeast of Johnstown. Slow reflexes. Shit. And that bullshit about attitude, too. What did attitude ever count for, anyway? They had it in for his ass because he was from a small town and hadn't lived in Johnstown like the rest of them; they didn't like him because his picture and a story about the ex-football star joining the state trooper program had been in the *Conemaugh Crier*. They'd laughed at him for that. The sons of bitches. Whole goodamn program wasn't worth shit anyway. And he had nothing in Conemaugh, all of his friends having died or moved away, all the landmarks of his boyhood fallen to progress and concrete.

He wolfed down his last hamburger and, after finishing the Coke, crumpled the cup in one large hand. So what? Those bastards could have the open road, and they could run their asses ragged on it for all he cared. In another few minutes he heard the troopers talking about a red Jaguar convertible out on 219, clocked at sixty-eight. That would be the sports car he'd just seen; he nodded and smiled to himself. At least his instincts were still sharp. He turned the key in the ignition, and the engine growled. As he pulled out of the McDonald's lot, he was thinking of the fine light down on Kim's bare arms. What was her last name? Granger. Pretty girl. Probably had a lot of boyfriends, too. All of them football players.

As he drove, his eyes flicked from side to side; he drove along the Circle, nodding as a couple of people waved from the sidewalk, and he turned toward his office. Tree-branch shadows, cool and dark, moved over his car, engulfing him. He could still hear the troopers on the radio. They sounded very near, but he knew they were actually many miles distant, absorbed in their own lives. How simple it would be to break into one of those trans-missions, to scream into that radio, to startle them from their daily rounds, to shout out wildly, *This is Oren Wy-*

singer in Bethany's Sin: we need some cars up here and some help because . . .

No. No, couldn't do that.

There was no microphone on his radio.

As he listened, the voices seemed to be fading away until there was only an occasional muffled sentence or two. Voices from another world, fading in and out through thick clouds of static. On Cowlington Street a huge shadow loomed over the patrol car, and Wysinger felt a brief chill in its presence. He pressed his foot down a fraction on the accelerator. When he turned right at the next intersection, he glanced quickly into the rearview mirror and caught a glimpse of the three-storied stone house before it was covered over again by the maze of leafy branches. He didn't like to pass by there, though that was part of his job, too. It reminded him of the Fletcher house on the outskirts of Conemaugh; that house had been smaller, but it still stayed in his memory after ten long years, like someone lurking in the dark basement of his soul.

He'd been driving a patrol car in Conemaugh then, working with two other local men as part-time deputies. And it had been a cold morning in February when he'd gone to that house on the hill, summoned there by Mrs. Kahane, a teacher at Slattery, who'd told him something was wrong. Tim and Ray, Cyrus Fletcher's boys, had been absent for three days, and no one answered the telephone or the door. He tried the front door and found it locked; all the windows were closed and curtained, and he couldn't see in. But the back door swung open at his touch. And when he stepped in, he smelled something high and sweetish, not unlike the odor dead dogs gave off when he pulled their car-flattened, brain-crushed carcasses off the highway. It was cold in the house, though, and it wasn't a rotten-meat smell or a blood smell, but the scarlet smell of Death. He found everything in order in the kitchen. Tepid coffee in two white cups on the kitchen table. Plates set in their proper places; four of them: for the boys, Fletcher's wife, Dora, and Cyrus himself. Bacon and green-veined eggs on the plates. He called out for Cyrus and Dora, but no one answered, and after a long time he climbed the oak-banistered staircase to the second floor, where the bedrooms were. Somewhere a clock ticked in that house; he remembered that very distinctly, even now long afterward. Somebody must be here, he'd thought; somebody had to wind that clock.

He found the boys in their beds, with quilts and a blanket still over them. They had no faces anymore; their features had been hacked away. One of them—Tim?—had his mouth open, and Wysinger could see the glittering teeth were streaked with thick, dried blood. Their throats had been slashed, too.

In the other, larger bedroom, it was worse. Dora, in the robe she wore every morning as she made breakfast for the family in the predawn hours, lay on the floor on a mat of blood. Her head had been almost severed from the body, and one leg had been cut off and lay in a corner now, like a discarded walking stick. It was then that he became sick, and he struggled to get to the bathroom without puking his guts out on the rug.

But in the bathroom lay Cyrus. Parts of him were scattered on the floor, and Cyrus Fletcher had been a large, strong man who cut firewood and hauled it into town for his customers. Now it seemed that there was very little left of him except strings of flesh and muscle, jagged white shards of bone. The remnants of a staring, screaming face, and even that had been crushed by the blow of a heavy object. Long afterward, when Wysinger had stopped shaking and throwing up, he noticed the marks in the bathroom walls. Slashes. Like the blows of an ax. Those same slashes in the room where Dora lay. And as he ran to his car to call for help he realized the ticking of the clock, not wound for three days, had suddenly stopped.

From that moment on, unknown to him then, the true horror had begun. Like the spinning of huge, time-spanning webs. But he knew it now, and he disliked passing that stone house on Cowlington because it was filled with dead things, too, dead relics and things he didn't understand. Things from a strange, ancient past. His car was covered by shadows, and he felt cold, though the sun was burning brightly beyond the overhang of trees, and birds sang, and the wind breathed through the leaves like ancient whispers that no man could understand.

Nearing the small red brick building that was the sheriff's office, Wysinger instinctively put his foot to the brake. Parked in front of his office was a battered old Ford pickup, a crazy quilt of rust-eaten paint. The tailgate was down, and a young man was sitting in the truck's bed, his legs dangling. Wysinger narrowed his eyes slightly as he pulled into the parking space with the sign that said RESERVED FOR SHERIFF. He didn't know the man—at least he didn't think he'd ever seen him before—and he was suddenly both curious and suspicious. But he took his time getting out of the car, pretending to check the radio and the contents of the glove compartment before he swung his legs out and stood up; he closed the door and locked it, then glanced over toward the young man with a careful eye.

"Good afternoon," the man said. A flat accent unfamiliar to Wysinger. Beneath aviator-style eyeglasses his eyes were light brown and friendly-looking, as if he expected Wysinger to stride across the few feet of pavement that separated them and give him a hardy, good-to-meet-you handshake.

Wysinger nodded; he looked at the license plate. Nebraska. Filed it away in his mind. The man looked to be about twenty-eight or twenty-nine, certainly no older than that. He had curly brown hair and a brown mustache; his hair was unruly but clean, and the mustache looked newly trimmed. But the Nebraska tag and the young man's denims and blue workshirt immediately told Wysinger what he was: a drifter. Somebody looking for handouts; one of the legions of people who roamed the country, often living out of their cars or trucks, looking for odd jobs, anything to get them by. People who had left home early, lured by the call of the open road, searching for something only they seemed able to understand.

"I'm the sheriff," Wysinger said unnecessarily, but he wanted this young man to know exactly who he was dealing with, right here and now.

"Yes sir," the man said, with a cheerful air that immediately irritated him. "That's just who I want to see." He got down out of the truck and neared Wysinger; in the bed Wysinger could see an assortment of tools, odds and ends of wood and brick, a folded tarpaulin.

"What can I do for you?" Wysinger asked.

"I'm Neely Ames," the man said, offering a hand. Wysinger took it slowly, and they shook.

"Do I know you or something?" Wysinger eyed him.

"No," the man said. "Unless you were in Greenwood yesterday, 'cause that's where I was. No, really I'm just sort of passing through, on my way up north."

"Uh-huh," Wysinger said.

"I do odd jobs," the man said, nodding toward his truck. "Hall off stumps, cut grass along the roadside, take garbage to the dump——whatever needs doing. I was passing through and I noticed you had a pretty little town here, and I was wondering if any of the folks needed some work done. But before I asked around I figured I'd check with the sheriff so there wouldn't be any misunderstandings, you know?"

"Right," Wysinger said.

Neely could read the distrust in the sheriff's eyes. That was nothing new to him; he'd seen it before, plenty of times, in towns like Hollyfork and Whiting and Beaumont and a hundred others. It was a little drama he'd gotten used to playing out, and it required him to stand with a serious yet imploring expression on his face. Not too imploring, though, because then they thought you were making fun of them. He had to look honest, too, not the kind of person who would break into the bank in the middle of the night and run away with the town's life savings. Neely disliked posturing for people like this, but a man had to eat and rest from the road sometimes, and that meant having folding money in your wallet. And often that was hard to come by. But in four years of traveling he'd never stolen; once, in Banner, Texas, he'd found one of those small plastic wallets that come open in the middle and there had been a little over a hundred dollars in it but no identification. He'd kept the money but never thought of it as stealing. Just getting lucky. But he'd been unlucky, too, like the time he'd been thrown into a putrid-smelling jail cell in Hamilton, Louisiana, on suspicion of robbing a Majik Market of seventy-five dollars. The teenage girl who'd been working the counter said she thought he was the one but she couldn't be sure. After a day he was released for lack of evidence and told by a square-jawed policeman to hit the road and doan you eveh come back this way, you heah? He was grateful to get out, and though he hadn't been anywhere near that Majik Market, he had a sudden mean impulse to swing by it and rob the place of every damned penny in the register. But he hadn't, because the road, stretching out ahead until it vanished from sight, beckoned him on like the line of his destiny.

But in those four years he'd learned two things: all towns are basically alike; and all officers of the law are basically alike. Two lessons of the road that had been drilled by repetition into his head.

"So you want work, do you?" Wysinger asked him. The sheriff's expression had never changed.

"I thought I might find some here, yes," Neely replied. He sensed he was about to get the old we-don't-like-drifters-around-here speech; he'd heard that before, too.

Wysinger motioned toward the pickup. "Where are you on your way to? You got a home up north?"

"No. I'm just traveling. Seeing the country."

"What for?"

Neely shrugged. "Seems like a good way to pass some time. And it's something ,I've always wanted to do."

"Seems more like a waste of time to me." He narrowed his eyes like a wolf. "What'd you do, run out on a wife and three or four kids?"

"No," Neely said easily. "I'm not married. No kids, either."

"In trouble with the law somewhere? What'd you say your name was again?"

"Ames. Like the brothers." He could tell this was a lost cause. He made a move toward his truck. "Well, Sheriff, I've got some miles to travel yet, to borrow loosely from the poem."

"Poem? What poem?"

"Frost," Neely said, opening the door on the driver's side and starting to climb in. He could move on north to Spangler, Barnesboro, Emeigh, Stifflertown, dozens of tiny dots on the red ribbon of 219. There'd be work ahead. The hell with this guy.

"Talk about the law scare you a little bit?" Wysinger said, coming around to the side of the pickup. "Make you run?"

Neely put the key in the ignition and started the engine.

"I thought you wanted some work," Wysinger said. "Where you goin'? Why don't you get out and we'll talk about it, and maybe I'll make a few telephone calls and find out what you've been up to?"

"Sorry," Neely said. "I've changed my mind."

"Well, maybe you'd just better—" Wysinger stopped in mid-sentence.

Neely looked at him. The sheriff was gazing off to the right, his mouth half-open, his eyes glazed. Neely glanced into the rearview mirror. There was a black Cadillac parked across the street, and he could see the outline of a figure sitting behind the wheel. Motionless. Watching. Wysinger, without speaking to Neely again, walked across the street to that car, went around to the driver's side, bent to the window. Neely could see his mouth moving. The figure nodded its head. Then Wysinger seemed to be listening. Neely shook his head, put the pickup in reverse, and started to back out.

"Hey! Hold on a minute!" It was Wysinger, calling out from beside that car. The sheriff's head bent back down; he was listening again. In another minute the black Cadillac pulled smoothly away from the curb and vanished down the street, and the sheriff unhurriedly walked back across the street to where Neely waited. Wysinger ran a hand across his mouth, and his eyes were dark and uneasy.

"What's going on?" Neely asked him.

Wysinger chewed at a thumbnail. "Seems you've got yourself a friend in this village, Ames. Somebody wants you to go to work."

"Who?"

"The mayor," Wysinger said. "If you want to work, you'll be put on the village payroll. It won't be much, though, I can tell you that from experience. And you'll be working long hours, too."

"Just what is it I'm supposed to be doing?"

"Anything and everything. Hauling trash, cutting down weeds, keeping grass mowed, picking up litter on two-nineteen, such like as that. The pay's a hundred a week. You'll be on call from me whenever there's something needs doing." He glanced up in the direction the Cadillac had gone. "What do you think?"

Neely shrugged. The money sounded pretty good, and he was in no hurry to get anywhere. Bethany's Sin was a pretty little village, inviting and clean. No sense in not trying to make a couple of hundred dollars before he headed up into the New England states. "Why not?" he said. "Sounds okay to me."

Wysinger nodded. His eyes were like black mirrors, and Neely thought he could see himself reflected in those orbs. "There's a boardinghouse on the corner of Kittridge and Grant, one street behind the Circle. Lady by the name of Bartlett runs it. It's clean and not too expensive. Why don't you drive on over there and tell her I sent you. Tell her you're working for the village now, and she'll give you a nice room." His eyes were strange and motionless. Dead, Neely thought suddenly; his eyes look dead.

It was then, looking into the sheriff's black and fathomless eyes, that Neely almost said no, don't think I'll take it. Think I'll drive on north and try my luck there. But he didn't because he needed the money. He said, "Okay. Sure. I'll go on over there right now."

Wysinger held his gaze for a moment, and then the sheriff said, "Go on. And then come on back here as quick as you can. There's a dead tree needs cutting down a couple of streets from here; I've been scared it's going to fall across the road some morning." He stepped away from the truck and glanced both ways. "It's clear," he said. "You can back up now."

Neely raised a hand and pulled the truck out into the street, then drove back toward the center of the village. Then it had been the mayor in the black Cadillac, he told himself. He hadn't been able to see the man's face. He grunted. Never had a mayor give him a job before. He felt uneasy, though, around that sheriff. He'd have to watch that guy, because he sensed a cruel streak in Wysinger, and when you give a cruel man a badge you only sanction his cruelty. But what else had he sensed in the man, just moments before? Something dark and intangible, something like . . . fear? Yes, it probably was true that Wysinger was afraid of the mayor. Obviously the mayor of Bethany's Sin holds a lot of clout. Good to have him on my side, Ames told himself.

Wysinger watched the truck disappear from sight around a corner. His teeth tore at the nail of his left index finger. Within him his heart beat like the noise of a fist whacking an empty container. He didn't like very many people, and he didn't care much for that Neely Ames, either, because he didn't like those who had no responsibilities, who took life pretty much as it came. He didn't like people who didn't live in cages. So the feeling inside him now was more akin to pity than to anything else.

"May God save your soul," Wysinger said, and then he turned away and vanished into his office.

EIGHT

KAY, GETTING IT TOGETHER

Kay had spent most of the day at George Ross Junior College, and now, on the drive back to Bethany's Sin, she reflected on what had gone before.

She'd had lunch in the college cafeteria with Dr. Kenneth Wexler, the gray-haired, fiftyish head of the mathematics department, and discussed her algebra courses that would begin next Monday. She was going to be helping during registration on Friday and Saturday, and Dr. Wexler told her there would probably be between twenty and twenty-five students in each of her three classes. It's going to be a snap, Dr. Wexler had said, and good experience as well.

Dr. Wexler had shown her to her office; actually, it was a cubicle in the new brick-and-glass Arts and Sciences Building, with a desk and a chair and a window. On the other side of a partition was a Mr. Pierce, a gaunt-looking man in a dark suit who, Dr. Wexler told her, taught a class in calculus. Mr. Pierce came over to say hello and then returned to the papers he was filing away. Kay had gazed at the beige-colored walls of her office, at the cork bulletin board above her desk. Pictures were needed, she decided. Something to brighten it up. A few potted plants on the windowsill. On the bulletin board were about a dozen of those little red and blue and green and yellow pegs with needle-sharp tips. Some of them impaled small pieces of paper, and Kay wondered what had hung there before. Looking through the desk drawers, she'd found paper clips and pens and a memo pad marked FROM THE DESK OF GERALD MEACHAM. Her predecessor. When she'd asked Dr. Wexler about the man, he'd been evasive, and it puzzled her.

In Room 119, the classroom she was going to be using,

Kay had stood at the lectern beneath the overhead fluorescent lighting and looked across the empty desks. She even practiced writing her name on the blackboard, in yellow chalk: MRS. REID. It still stunned her that what she'd dreamed about for so long was within reach. The chance for a full-time teaching job if her summer work was acceptable. Jesus, she thought. It's not real. It can't be. While Evan had worked on the mill journal in La-Grange, she'd been teaching a couple of classes at Clarke Community College and taking advanced courses herself in the afternoon. Her doctorate was still a long way off, but she'd decided she had plenty of time. She could settle in here, teach her algebra classes and maybe tutor some students in the afternoons, and work gradually toward her degree. No rush. After a long time she'd switched off the lights in Room 119 and walked along the linoleum-floored corridor to the soft-drink machine in the teachers' lounge.

As she drank her Coke at a table in the corner, she kept her eye on the door, and watched other teachers who came in for a cigarette or just a conversation break. There was an elderly woman who wore her white hair in a tight bun; she bought a grape drink and introduced herself as Mrs. Edith Marsh. She taught poetry and smiled sweetly at almost everything Kay said. Mr. Pierce came in and lit a cigarette, but he spoke with Kay for only a moment before sitting in a chair across the room and gazing out the window onto the nearly empty parking lot. A man in his thirties, wearing blue jeans and a dark blue sport coat, came in and lost a quarter to the soft-drink machine. Kay gave him change for a dollar, and the man puffed on a battered pipe and told her he was a professor in the classics department when she told him it would be her first semester. He wished her good luck and lost another quarter in the machine, and after that, threw up his hands in mock rage and stalked out of the room, leaving a trail of smoke.

She'd returned to her office one last time, to try to figure out what sort of pictures to bring—still lifes? abstract posters? pastoral scenes?—and then had left the building. And now, reaching the limits of Bethany's Sin and winding her way toward the Sunshine School nursery and kindergarten where she'd left Laurie for a few hours, she wondered who Gerald Meacham had been. A mathematics instructor, of course. A very fine, intelligent man, Dr. Wexler had said; Mr. Meacham had lived in Spangler. He'd either been fired or had left of his own accord, but there had been a strange look in Dr. Wexler's eyes when she'd asked which. He seemed not to want to talk about the man. But why not? A scandal or something? Had Mr. Meacham been grading his tests with an eye glued to his female students' skirts? Anyway, Kay thought, thank God for what had happened to Gerald Meacham; if she hadn't gotten this teaching job, the family would be on the rocks by now.

The Sunshine School was a yellow-and-white house on Blair Street; there was a fenced-in backyard, and as Kay got out of the car and walked up the pathway to the front door, she saw a few children swinging on jungle bars. She could hear their laughter, like the noise of brook water running across flat stones in cool forests. There had been a brook near her house when she was growing up, and she had called it her secret brook and gone there every day one summer to watch that water run. She had thrown rocks into it and made wishes. One for a happy life. Two for a handsome prince. Three for a beautiful castle to live in. The next winter the construction men came and began clearing for a new highway, and they swept away the pine and oak trees with machines that got hungry at six o'clock every morning. When she had gone back with the first touch of spring to make more wishes, concrete had been poured over her secret brook, and staring at the smooth concrete, she had the distinct and lasting thought that at that precise moment someone she didn't know and would never know had laughed. Because that someone had stolen something that had belonged, at least for the fleeting days of a seven-year-old's summer, to her.

And perhaps, even then, she had become a little bitter. And a little afraid.

She rang the doorbell; through the panes of clear glass in the door she could see some of the rooms within: walls covered with children's drawings of horses, scarecrows, stick-people, buildings, and cars; a small table ringed by six small chairs; a bookcase filled with Golden

Books and Dr. Seuss *Cat in the Hat* stories; an aquarium with guppies. Two little girls, one dark-haired and the other with long, beautiful red hair, sat reading at the table, and now they were looking up at Kay. Through the hallway came a slender woman wearing a white, uniformlike pantsuit. She smiled at Kay and opened the door.

Kay had met Mrs. Omarian, who operated the Sunshine School, on their last trip to Bethany's Sin, before they'd left LaGrange for good. Mrs. Omarian, whose first name was Monica, looked to Kay to be about thirty; the woman had a friendly, attractive face framed by a full mane of dark hair, and she carried herself calmly, as if running a day-care center was indeed child's play.

When the door came open, Kay felt the cool touch of the air conditioning. It was very quiet inside the Sunshine School, as if all the children were napping somewhere.

"Hi there," Mrs. Omarian said. "How was your morning at school?"

"Fine. Better than I expected."

"Were you nervous?"

Kay smiled. "Very much so, I'm afraid."

"I guess that's to be expected," Mrs. Omarian said. She opened the door wider, and Kay stepped into the house. The two children at the table went back to their reading. "I taught for a few semesters at George Ross myself," she told Kay.

"Oh? In what department?"

"Psychology, under Dr. Anderson. It was just an introductory course in child psychology, nothing very challenging. But fun, anyway." She gave a quick shrug. "That was about four years ago, and I miss the academic life sometimes. The teachers' conferences, luncheons, and all that." She gazed at Kay without speaking for a few seconds. "I really envy you."

"I don't see why. I'd say you have your hands full right here," Kay said. "And you seem to be doing a good business."

"I am. There are more working mothers in Bethany's Sin than you'd think. Just a minute and I'll get Laurie; she's in the back, playing." Mrs. Omarian turned away from Kay and moved through a corridor to the back door. After another moment Kay felt a tingling sensation at the back of her neck, and she looked behind her.

The little girl with red hair was staring at her. The other child was reading *Black Beauty*. The red-haired girl said, "Are you Laurie Reid's mother?"

"Yes, I am."

"I'm Amy Grantham."

"It's good to meet you, Amy," Kay said.

The child was silent for a few seconds, but her eyes never left Kay's. "Is Laurie new here?" she asked.

"That's right. We just moved to the village yesterday."

"It's nice here," Amy said. Her eyes were blue, like deep tunnels to the soul. They were unblinking. "My mommy says it's the best place in the world."

Kay smiled. She heard footsteps in the corridor. Mrs. Omarian was holding Laurie's hand.

"Hi, honey," Kay said, smoothing her little girl's hair and giving her a kiss on the forehead. "Did you have a good time today?"

Laurie nodded. "We had fun. We played on the swings, and we played with some dolls and saw cartoons."

"Cartoons?" Kay said.

"There's a projector in the back," Mrs. Omarian explained. "What did we see today, Laurie?"

"Roadrunner. And chipmunks. And . . . Daffy Duck."

Mrs. Omarian smiled and winked at Kay over Laurie's head. "That's right."

"Well"—Kay took Laurie's hand—"we've got to be going. Tell Mrs. Omarian we'll see her again on Friday morning, all right?" They moved toward the front door.

" 'Bye, Laurie," Amy Grantham said. The other little girl looked up and said good-bye, too.

" 'Bye," Laurie said. "See you Friday."

At the front door Mrs. Omarian said, "That's a beautifully behaved little girl you have there. If the others were as good as she is, I could watch shows like 'Ryan's Hope' and 'One Life to Live' all day."

They said good-bye to Mrs. Omarian, and in another few minutes Kay was driving again toward McClain Terrace while Laurie talked about the other children she'd met. She seemed to have had a good time, and that pleased Kay because Laurie would be spending most of the summer there. Kay wished Laurie could have stayed at home with Evan, but she knew Evan was going to be putting together an office down in the basement and he'd want as much time as possible to work. So it was best that Laurie stayed at the Sunshine School.

On the way home they passed a modernistic-looking brick building with a glass front, on a corner lot where the overhanging trees cast black shadow-shapes. A simple white-on-black sign outside read MABRY CLINIC. Kay knew it was what served as the hospital in Bethany's Sin, but she'd never been inside and had never met any of the doctors. She'd been concerned about the quality of health care in the village when they'd first been thinking of moving, but Mrs. Giles has assured both her and Evan that the clinic was fully staffed and well equipped, and that Dr. Mabry, the director of the clinic, was the type of physician who insisted on house calls in emergency cases.

Coming through the front door of their house, Kay heard the muffled machine-gun chatter of Evan's battered black typewriter from the basement. Laurie went up to her room to play, and Kay opened the basement door and descended the staircase. Evan sat at the rolltop desk they'd bought at a garage sale several years before; it was nicked and scarred in places, and Evan had replaced three of the four legs, but he'd hand-sanded some of the worst spots and refinished it until it was a beautiful dark oak color that glowed beneath a couple of coats of varnish. He'd positioned the desk on the far side of the basement, near a screened window that he could pull up so he could both look out across the backyard and enjoy the fresh air. Boxes of books were piled up alongside him, awaiting the shelves he'd planned to build since the first day he'd stepped down into the basement and seen its possibilities. He'd brought down two framed posters—one a replica of a Graf Zeppelin travel poster from the thirties, and the other an authentic Harry Blackstone magic show ad, also a garage sale find—and hung them on either side of the window. A metallic desk lamp cast a pool of light over his right shoulder onto the paper in the typewriter, and beside him there was a pad of clean paper and several sheets of what he'd written that day. On the floor beside the desk was a wicker trash basket, and near that, a couple of pieces of crumpled paper. Kay stood behind him for a moment, watching him work. He would type a few lines and then stop, staring at the paper without moving. Then type a few more. Then, with a burst of speed, a dozen or more lines. Followed by silence.

After a few minutes Evan suddenly straightened up in his chair. He seemed to be listening for something. And then he looked around at her, his eyes wide, and his sudden movement frightened her.

"What is it?" Kay asked, taking a step backward.

Evan's eyes cleared at once. "Sorry. I didn't mean to scare you. But the truth is, you scared the hell out of me. How long have you been standing there?"

"Only a little while. I wanted to watch."

"I felt something down here with me, but I couldn't figure out what it was. Did you have a good day? Meet everyone you're supposed to meet?"

She nodded and came over to him, putting her hands on his shoulders and kissing the top of his head, right on one of his funny cowlicks. She knew those cowlicks drove him nuts when he was trying to comb his hair, and usually he just gave up and let it go wild, which to her looked sexy. "I checked in with Dr. Wexler," she said. "And I've even got my own office, too."

"Great," he said, and motioned toward his desk. "Is it as plush as mine?"

"What yours lacks in comfort it makes up for in charm," she said, and kissed him again. "I had a very good day, Evan. I felt like I really belonged there."

"And you do," he told her. "I'm very glad for you, and I'm proud of you."

She glanced over his shoulder at the paper in the typewriter. "What are you doing?"

"Nothing, really. Just some writer's doodling. I've been getting down on paper my first impressions of the village. You know, colors, sounds, smells,—that sort of thing."

"Interesting." She looked over the paper, saw it was an impression of the ring of flowers in the Circle. "That's very nice. What are you doing it for?"

"I'm playing with an idea," Evan said. "There's a

small magazine in Philadelphia called *Pennsylvania Progress,* and from time to time it runs stories about the smaller towns in the state. History, type of people, businesses, outlook for the future. I was wondering if they'd consider something on Bethany's Sin."

Kay grunted. "I think they probably would," she said. "But you're a newcomer here; how are you going to get your story together?"

"Old-fashioned research," Evan said. "And legwork. I'm sure there's historical information at the library, and certainly a lot of the older people living here know something of the village's beginnings." He shrugged. "I don't know; maybe it won't go anywhere, maybe *Progress* won't buy it, but I think it's worth working on."

"Then do it," Kay said.

He paused for a moment, looking at the paper in the typewriter. "Besides," he said, looking back at her, "wouldn't you be interested in finding out what the sin was?"

"The sin? What sin?"

"Whatever Bethany's sin was. You'll have to admit it's an unusual and intriguing name for a village. I'd like to find the meaning behind it."

She smiled. "Maybe it has no meaning. Why should it?"

"Why shouldn't it? Most towns and cities are named after something specific. An event, a person, a season. Whatever. Take the name Bethany. A person's name? First name or last name? I'd like to find out."

"Do you think the library would have that information?"

"I don't know. But I suppose that's where I'll start looking."

Kay fingered her husband's hair. "What would you like for dinner? I've got pork chops in the refrigerator."

"Sounds like pork chops would be fine."

"Okay. That's the menu for tonight, then. And I'd better get started on it, too. I like your idea about the story. Really I do." She moved toward the staircase.

"Good. I'm glad." He turned back to his typewriter and sat in silence.

She watched him for another moment, and when he

began typing again, she went upstairs and through the den to the kitchen.

After dinner they drove over to Broome's Furniture in Westbury Mall, but most of that store's goods were a little too expensive for them. They walked through the Mall for an hour or so, browsing in the shops, and Evan bought Kay and Laurie ice-cream cones at the Baskin-Robbins. Then there was a stop at the supermarket to buy groceries for the rest of the week, and they were on their way back to Bethany's Sin on Highway 219, the head-lights of the station wagon cutting yellow holes in the black curtain of night. Laurie said she could see stars, and Kay helped her count them. They passed a few cars and a large truck heading north, but as they neared the turn-off onto Ashaway and Bethany's Sin, Evan noticed that the traffic was sparse. It was very dark without the headlights of other cars to help light the way, and the trees and tangle of wild vegetation along the highway reminded Evan of impenetrable walls. The moon was white and full, like a luminous silver disk floating spirit-like above them. Laurie said it looked like the face of a princess who lived high among the stars and watched everything on earth. Kay smiled and stroked her hair, and Evan watched the road because something within him was drawing back. He tried to shrug it off, as one would shrug off the tightening of a muscle across the shoulder blades. The wind shrilled through the open windows; the headlights picked out the crushed carcass of a large dog on the side of the road. Its teeth glittered briefly, and the eyes were rotting black sockets. Evan instinctively turned the wheel, and it was then that Kay asked him if he were all right.

"Yes," he said, smiling. "I'm fine." But in another few seconds the smile had faded and was gone. He narrowed his eyes slightly, feeling rather than seeing the twisted trees that bordered the road. Ahead, finally, was a blinking yellow light that marked the turn-off onto Ashaway. Evan slowed the station wagon and swung off to the left, and then they were moving past the cemetery with its tiers of tombstones. On the streets of Bethany's Sin, lights burned in most of the houses; in a living room here, a bathroom, a bedroom, a kitchen. Porch lights glowed

white or pale yellow. Evan felt comforted by the knowledge that the residents of Bethany's Sin were settling
down for the night: reading the newspaper, watching television, talking over what had happened during the day,
preparing themselves for the next. He thought for an
instant that he could see through those walls and observe
the many families of Bethany's Sin, all secure and comfortable in their attractive brick and wood homes, all
going about the daily business of their lives. But something deeper within him nagged, and he couldn't figure
out what it was.

After another moment, when they were a couple of
streets away from McClain, Kay sighed and said, "It's
really quiet out tonight, isn't it?"

And then he knew.

He slowed the car gradually. Kay looked at him, first
amused, then irritated, then concerned. He pulled the
car to the curb in front of a white, two-story house with
a chimney. A light burned behind white curtains in a
large picture window. The upstairs of the house was dark.
Evan cut the engine and listened.

"Daddy?" Laurie said from the backseat. "Why did
you stop here?"

"Shhhhhhh," Evan whispered. Kay started to speak,
but he shook his head. She watched his eyes, feeling a
pincer of fear grab her guts.

When she could no longer stand the silence she said,
"What are you doing?"

"Listening," he said.

"To what?"

"What do you hear?" Evan asked her.

"Nothing. There's nothing to listen to out here."

"Right," he said, nodding. When he looked at her, he
saw she didn't understand. "No noise," he told her. "No
sound of cars. No radio or television noise. No conversation leaking through open windows and around us. No
one humming or talking or arguing or—"

"Evan," Kay said, in that voice she used when she
thought he was acting childish. "What are you talking
about?"

"Listen!" he said, trying to keep his voice low. "Just be
quiet and listen."

She did. From the woodland came the quiet drone of crickets. A night bird chirped sharply from perhaps a street over. But that was all. That's odd, she told herself. Really odd. No. I'm getting like Evan. It's not odd at all. It's simply a quiet village, with quiet people, at a quiet time of the night. She waited for a few more minutes without speaking, and then she thought of the frozen steaks they'd bought, now slowly thawing in the back of the car. "Let's go, Evan," she said.

"Can we go home now, Daddy?" Laurie asked.

Evan looked into his wife's eyes. She was waiting for him to turn the key in the ignition. Beyond her shoulder something moved. Evan's eyes focused on it. A shadow had moved slowly across that picture window, silhouetted against murky light, and paused for just an instant to draw the curtain back a fraction. Then it was gone. Evan blinked, not knowing what he'd seen.

"Hey!" Kay was tugging on his sleeve. "Remember me? Your long-suffering wife? We've got frozen meat and ice cream and milk in three bags back there, and we'd better be getting our tails home."

He paused another moment. The shadow did not return. He said, "Okay. We're going." He turned the key in the ignition and the engine started; they pulled away from the curb, and Evan threaded his way toward McClain.

Evan's right, Kay thought as they got within sight of their house, dark in a row of lights. It is very silent tonight. Strangely silent. But . . . better silent than noisy as all hell. Isn't that one of the reasons we moved to Bethany's Sin?

As they pulled into their driveway, Evan was trying to conjure that shadow in his mind. Something funny about it. Something unsettling. Something . . . something not right.

"Here we are," Kay said, getting out of the car. "Who's going to be good and help with the groceries?"

"I will!" Laurie volunteered.

"Okay, there's one Good Samaritan," Kay said. "Evan, aren't you going to get out?"

He sat motionless for another second. And then his head turned toward her. "Yes," he said. He went around to the back of the car to get a bag, and suddenly shivered because he realized what had disturbed him about that shadow.

When it had turned toward the window, with the light streaming from behind, Evan had seen that the figure was missing its left arm.

He didn't know why, but that made his nerves tingle as if an ice cube had been dropped down his back.

Kay, carrying a bag, walked on to the door. Laurie, with a smaller bag, followed. Kay turned her head toward him. "Come on, slowpoke!" she called out.

And at that instant, if Evan had been listening to the faint sounds carried on the breezes of night, he would have heard a noise from three streets over, where Blair and Cowlington met.

The sound of hoofbeats.

NINE

VISITING

". . . and every Labor Day there's a village festival in the Circle," Mrs. Demargeon was saying. "The merchants close up their shops and all but a few streets are blocked off; there are picinic tables and a bandstand and prizes for the best cake and cookies and relishes. Two years ago my tomatoes won first prize in their category, but last Labor Day, Darcy McCullough got the blue ribbon. Oh well, we've all got to have some competition, I suppose. Keeps us alert. But autumn is a fine time of year in Bethany's Sin; by mid-September the winds are cooling, and the frosts come toward the first of October. All the trees are yellow and gold and deep red. It's truly beautiful. You'll see." She took a sip from her coffee cup with its monogram of *J* and *D* and then glanced at Evan to make certain he was paying attention. He was. "And then there's winter. The sky grays almost overnight, and the snows come around Christmas. But it's a powdery, sugar-white snow, not that wet, heavy mess they get up in New England. Bethany's Sin goes all out for Christmas. The clubs compete with each other in raising funds for the children's homes in Johnstown, and there's a contest with a fifty-dollar prize for best lawn and house decoration. We won that"—she gave a quick glance at the man sitting on her left—"oh, four years ago. Yes, that's right. Four years. We strung little blinking white lights through the trees, and it was really very pretty."

"It sounds beautiful," Kay said.

"Oh, yes." Mrs. Demargeon nodded. "Christmas is always a nice time of year. But winter lasts a long time here, and there's usually snow on the ground through the first of March. By early spring you'll be ready for those flower buds to come popping out again. Evan, can I get you something else to drink?"

He'd been fingering the handle of his empty cup. "No, thank you," he said. "I've had enough."

"It's the decaffeinated kind, so you don't have to worry about staying up all hours of the night," Mrs. Demargeon explained. She gave Kay a quick smile. "I know how it is not to be able to sleep after you've had too much coffee." She turned her head to look at her husband. "Would you like something else, Harris?"

The man in the wheelchair pushed himself past her. "Only some fruit," he said. He reached a small table where a green bowl of apples and grapes had been set, and, picking up an apple, he bit into it and then rolled back to join the others.

"One thing I've been wondering about," Evan said, and Mrs. Demargeon looked at him and smiled in anticipation. "What churches do most of the people here attend? I've noticed a Presbyterian church to the south, just beyond Bethany's Sin limits, and another off Highway Two-nineteen about a quarter-mile north. I didn't notice what denomination that one was. . . ."

"Methodist," she said. "The Methodist church. That's where Harris and I go. I suppose it's split pretty much down the middle between Methodists and Presbyterians here. What church do you attend?"

"Actually," Evan said, "we don't—"

"Episcopal," Kay said.

"Oh. Well, let's see. There's a nice Episcopal church in Spangler, I think. Just a few minutes' drive."

"I was wondering," Evan said, "because I hadn't seen any churches within the village itself, and I thought that was a little odd."

"Odd?" Mrs. Demargeon gave a brief laugh. "No, no. The churches are nearby. Most people here are deeply religious."

"Oh, I see."

"Ten years ago, this village was nothing," Mrs. Demargeon said, turning her head toward Kay. "Just a spot on the map, with only four or five families and a store or two. Now look at it. And it's doubling every year. Think of what it's going to be in another five years, or even in three. Of course I'd hate to see the basic character of the village change. It seems to me if we keep a rein on so-called progress and we're not in such a hurry to invite any-old-body here, we'll come out better in the long run. What do you think?"

And while they talked, Evan found himself watching Harris Demargeon.

The man was sitting across the cheerfully decorated living room, to the left of the floral-print-covered chair his wife occupied, and it seemed that his attention kept drifting during their conversation. He would be polite and interested for a few moments, then Evan could see his pale gray eyes slide over toward the picture window; the man's gaze would darken perceptibly, as if he'd seen something beyond the closed curtains that no one else could discern. Mr. Demargeon had been a large man once, because he was big-boned, but now it looked to Evan as if he'd wasted away over a number of years. His cheekbones jutted, and around the rather deep-set eyes were webs of wrinkles and cracks. His hair was still dark, but it was thinning rapidly, and there was a circular bald spot at the crown of his head. He was dressed well, in dark slacks, white short-sleeved shirt, and striped tie. The knot of the tie was awry, and a button on the shirt unfastened, leaving Evan with the impression that perhaps the man had allowed himself to be dressed like some sort of department store mannequin; a picture of Mrs. Demargeon dressing her husband flashed through Evan's mind like the streak of a meteor. Struggling with the pants on his paralyzed legs, pulling them up and belting them around his paralyzed waist. God, how terrible that would be, Evan thought. For a brief instant he imagined Kay dressing him, and he in the place of Harris Demargeon. Unable to walk or run, unable to do a multitude of things that Evan took for granted. Unable to make love. Half a man.

Mr. Demargeon glanced at him, as if he could see through Evan's skull to his brain. His eyes lingered only a second and then moved away.

Evan hadn't known what to say to the man. Mr. Demargeon was very quiet, anyway, seemingly withdrawn in comparison to his wife's personality. He was friendly in a reserved way though, and he'd answered Evan's questions about the other people on the *street readily, but Evan sensed something in the man that he couldn't put his finger on. Hesitation? Aloofness? The man rarely smiled, but when he did, there were the clear indentations of laugh-lines around his mouth, the traces of earlier, happier years. For some reason, that disturbed Evan more than anything else.

They'd eaten dinner with the Demargeons, and Kay had provided a bowl of potato salad and a pretty cherry gelatin dessert with chunks of apples and orange sections suspended in it. Mrs. Demargeon was a charming hostess and a good conversationalist, and she'd been openly admiring of both Kay's position at George Ross and the fact that Evan had sold several stories. With Laurie she'd been adoring, and Laurie had basked in the attention for a while before going back to the Demargeons' den to watch television; Kay had looked in on her a few minutes earlier and found the child sleeping peacefully on the sofa, so she'd let her be. Kay had noticed that Mrs. Demargeon was a fastidious housekeeper: everything looked clean and fresh; the silverware, glasses, and dishes sparkled, and the expensive looking furniture in her house was tasteful and well maintained. The house made her feel very comfortable indeed, and it made her want to get her own home into shape even more.

Mrs. Demargeon had given a brief history of her life with her husband: they'd met and married in Philadelphia, where she was a legal secretary and he was a consultant with a financial firm called Merrill-O'Day. Her first marriage, his second. He'd branched off on his own a few years after they were married and had made quite a bit of money, but handling a large business was bothersome to him and he wanted to step back and play the market. They'd decided to leave the city and had seen the listing for their present house in a real-estate guide. After two visits to Bethany's Sin they'd decided to buy in; Harris had thought it would be a good investment, and Mrs. Demargeon thought it would simply be a wonderful place to live. "Now," she asked, "how did you two meet?"

"At Ohio Central University," Kay explained. "Evan

was there on a creative writing scholarship, and I was studying for my master's in math. Ours was kind of a storybook romance, I guess. We had to share a table in a crowded cafeteria, and as we talked we found out we shared an elective course in early civilizations. And we were both from the New Concord area. So we started dating. I don't really see what he saw in me then; I was pretty much of a bookworm, and I was very shy. But anyway, one thing led to another. After Evan's graduation" —here her face darkened slightly, but only Evan saw it— "he . . . had to go overseas for a couple of years. To fight. We were married when he got back. And Laurie was born about four years afterward." She touched Evan's hand and squeezed it. "I guess you could say we've been through a lot together."

Mrs. Demargeon smiled. "Who hasn't? In this day and time it's a miracle that young couples like you stay together at all. So many, many pressures. Money and all that."

"Lack of money," Evan put in good-naturedly. Everyone laughed.

Then, watching Mr. Demargeon, that strange, cold, uneasy feeling began to creep over Evan again. Something lurking behind the man's face. Behind those eyes. In that brain.

Something was said. Mrs. Demargeon and Kay were looking at him.

Evan said, "I'm sorry. What did you say?"

"What are your plans?" Mrs. Demargeon asked. "Now that you're in Bethany's Sin?"

"I'm going to be putting together an office in our basement," he told her. "And writing. Also I'm going to be looking for some sort of an outside job. Maybe with the newspaper in Johnstown. I don't know; I haven't looked into that yet."

"There's a community paper in Spangler," she offered. "And in Barnesboro, too."

He smiled. "Maybe I should start one here."

"Quite an ambition," Mrs. Demargeon said, glancing over at Kay and then back to him. "It's never been done before."

"Something I've been thinking about. Really." He

leaned toward her slightly, feeling her husband's gaze on him. "I'd like to know more about Bethany's Sin itself, and about the people here."

"Oh? And why is that?"

Evan explained to her his idea of doing an article on the history of the village for *Pennsylvania Progress*. She listened as if intrigued, nodding her head at all the right places. "Interesting," she said when he'd finished. "Have you begun your research yet?"

"No. I thought I'd talk the idea around a little first."

"I don't know that the village really has that much of a history," she said. "It's been incorporated for only—oh, about ten years. I don't think we have any famous residents or landmarks or particularly historic buildings. If it's history you're looking for, you might drive up to Saint Lawrence, to the Seldom Seen Valley Mine. Now that's something to—"

"Bethany's Sin," Evan said, trying to bring her back on track. "Where did that name come from?"

She screwed up her eyes, glanced at her husband. "I don't really know. Harris, do you?"

He thought for a moment. "No, I've never heard," he said finally.

"Weren't you ever curious about it?" Evan asked the man.

"Oh, sure," he replied. "I was when we first moved here. But no one seemed to know." He gave a shrug. "I guess it's one of those names that don't mean anything; it just sticks and that's that."

Evan grunted, feeling a twinge of disappointment. He'd envisioned a tantalizing story behind the village's name, something rooted in a mysterious past, but now, he thought, maybe there was nothing to it after all. His imagination had run away with him. Isn't that what Kay always said? That he lived on the rim of his imagination and someday he'd fall totally into it and nothing would be real anymore? Yes. Yes, she was probably right.

"If you'd like," Mrs. Demargeon offered, "I'll ask around for you. You know, try to find out something you could use in your article. But on the whole, all I know is that Bethany's Sin is a quiet, peaceful little village. Maybe there's nothing more than that about it." She smiled at Kay. "Actually, I prefer it that way. I don't want history or notoriety or anything else. And I'm probably echoing the feelings of most of the villagers."

"Do you think, then, that the others might be opposed to my doing anything on the village?"

"No, not opposed. Just . . . perhaps a bit reluctant. They value their privacy a great deal, and you've got to remember that most of them moved here, like Harris and I did, seeking a place to get away from the cities. A restful place, you see, certainly not one thrust into the public eye."

Evan paused for a moment, thinking over what the woman had said. Mrs. Demargeon finished her coffee and put aside the empty cup. He shrugged. "I don't think any article I would write could ever disrupt the village as much as all that. I even thought that maybe the people here would enjoy seeing something on Bethany's Sin in print."

"Well," the woman said, "I'm not so sure about that. But I'm not saying it isn't a fine idea. On the contrary. I'm just telling you that you might run into some resistance."

"I guess I'd better think it over some more, then," Evan said.

"Please don't listen to me," Mrs. Demargeon told him. "Do what you feel is best."

Evan looked at his wristwatch and saw it was after eleven. "Kay," he said, "I think we'd better get Laurie and head back home. It's getting late."

"Nonsense!" Mrs. Demargeon said. "It's early yet!"

"No, I'm afraid Evan's right," Kay said, rising from the sofa. "I'm a little tired from this morning; I never saw so many students in one building before in my life!"

They awakened Laurie, who sleepily followed them to the door as they said their good-byes to the Demargeons. Kay took Laurie's hand and went out onto the porch; Mrs. Demargeon followed, telling Kay she could come over anytime for conversation or fresh vegetables from her garden.

And Evan was about to step across the threshold of the front door when he felt Harris Demargeon wheel up very close behind him, almost on his heels. Evan turned and looked down at the man. Harris was staring at him, his eyes pale pools that hid strange, freezing depths. Evan felt himself drawn into that stare, and inwardly he shivered. The man's mouth twitched, started to come open.

"Harris?" Mrs. Demargeon, smiling, peered into the doorway. "We'd better not keep them if they're tired."

"I . . . I'm very glad you came," he told Evan. "I enjoyed our conversation very much."

"Thank you. So did I," Evan said. "We'll have to continue it sometime."

Mrs. Demargeon took Evan's hand; her flesh was cool, and there were calluses on her fingers. From gardening, Evan thought. He allowed her to pull him out onto the porch, and it was then, with an instant of pressure she applied to her grasp, that he realized how very strong she was. He felt as if he'd briefly put his hand into a vise, but there was no pain because it was over so fast.

"Come back and see us again," Mrs. Demargeon said from her porch steps. Behind her, Harris was framed in the light streaming through the doorway. "Come see us real soon."

"We will," Kay told her. "We really enjoyed it. Good night."

"Good night," the woman said, and then disappeared into the doorway. The door closed, but the white light on the porch stayed on.

They walked over to their house. Evan realized he was unconsciously massaging his hand.

"It was a nice night," Kay said when they reached their door.

"Yes," he said. "It was." He brought his keys out of his pocket and unlocked the door, and they stepped through into darkness. Kay turned on the entrance-foyer and living-room lights. Laurie could hardly keep her eyes open, so Evan picked her up in his arms and carried her up the stairs to her bedroom. Kay changed her into her nightclothes and tucked her in while Evan went back downstairs to snap off the lights.

He checked the front door to make sure it was locked, turned off the foyer light and then the light in the living room. And then, standing in the grip of darkness, he drew aside the curtains and gazed out at McClain Terrace. The Demargeons had turned out their porch light, and now the street was returned to silence and the night, except for the golden squares cast on the lawn from his and Kay's bedroom. He stood there for a long time, seeing nothing, until he gazed across at that dark shape on the other side of the street. Who had Mrs. Demargeon said lived there? Yes. A widower named Keating. On vacation, she'd said. Where do widowers go on vacation? Evan wondered. Visiting places where better memories lay in wait like gentle traps? Places where he'd taken his wife? Evan was curious about the man and interested in meeting him. He wondered when he'd be back from his vacation.

There was the glow of a white light from a window a few houses down. No, not a light, but that silver sphere of the moon, gazing down with benevolent eyes onto the sleeping village, reflected off glass. He ran one hand over the knuckles of the other, unconsciously.

Bethany's Sin: the two words came to him without warning from the back of his brain as he stared into the cold eye of the moon.

It had to have meaning. His curiosity insisted on it. But what was it? Something from ten years ago, when the village was incorporated? Or something further back, buried in the smoky folds of time?

He decided he would have to find out.

And as he went up to where Kay waited for him in the bedroom, he realized, suddenly and numbingly, that he was afraid to sleep.

Because he feared what his dreams might show him.

TEN

NO WAY TO DIE
IS ANY GOOD

For Muscadine John, the night was a friend. Maybe the night was his only friend, now that Old Mack Tucker and Salty Reese were dead. At least he thought Mack Tucker was dead. Tucker had missed their meeting at the campground under the railroad trestle three miles south of Latrobe, and asking around about the man, Muscadine John had learned from a sallow-looking 'bo named Wintzell that Mack had fallen from a northbound freight only a week earlier, outside Charleston, West Virgina.

"Yeah," Wintzell had said as he rolled a cigarette between browned fingers, "I seen it happen. Frail old man, he was. Couldn't've stood the road much longer, anyways." Light from the cooking fire touched his face. It looked like the leather pouch he carried his tobacco in. "He was up jumpin' and dancin' around, don't you see? Happy, like. Said he was headin' up toward where he was born and he was goin' to see some old friends. Anyways, he slipped. Fell right out through the door, and us burnin' the tracks at fifty, fifty-five miles an hour. Sharp gravel bed, too. We jumped up and looked out, tried to see him, but by then we was on around a curve, and it was too dark, anyways."

For a long time Muscadine John said nothing; he stroked his long silver beard and sat staring into the fire, his legs crossed in front of him. Across the foliage-surrounded campground the other 'boes played cards or talked quietly, catching up on stories or mapping out railroad routes. "You sure his name was Tucker?" Muscadine John asked finally.

"Tucker?" Wintzell narrowed his eyes in thought. He scratched the bridge of a nose that had once been badly broken and never properly set. "Now wait a minute.

97

Wait just a minute. Tucker, you say? Well, I think this here fellow's name was Tuckey. Or maybe it was Tucker, now I'm thinking of it."

There was no use in trying to match a description because Mack Tucker had looked different every time his and Muscadine John's paths had crossed. Once the older man had sported thick white hair and a walrus mustache; the next time John had seen him, Mack had shaved his head bald and had grown a stringy goatee. So there was no way to know the real fate—death on the tracks? small-town jail? vagrants' work farm?—of Old Mack Tucker. All Muscadine John knew was that the man had failed to show at that particular connection point for the first time in seven years.

Which saddened him, because he knew that friends were few and hard to come by, and there would probably be no more real ones in his life.

He talked of the road with the other 'boes gathered around the fire; he was heading up into New England, he told them, and then probably over toward the Lakes.

"You goin' northeast from here?" a lean, taut-jawed man named Dan asked.

"That's right. Up through Pennsylvania."

"Uh-huh." Dan chewed on a weed and seemed to be examining him; he seemed intrigued by the battered olive-green Army surplus knapsack John carried with him, and John made a mental note to sleep on the opposite side of the camp from this man. "You best watch yourself," Dan said quietly.

"What's that supposed to mean?"

"No offense. Just thinkin' about something I heard once. You movin' up into the state kinda reminds me of it." He glanced around the ring of hollow-eyed men. "Any of you know Mike Hooker? Tommy Jessup?"

"Heard of Jessup," one of them said. "Four Fingers, they called him."

"That's him," Dan said, nodding. "Crossed their paths right here, two, three years ago. They were takin' the route up to Maine. Had big plans. Hooker was goin' into the lumberin' business with his brother-in-law. I sat right here and talked to them and wished them good luck, and then they were gone. And by God that's the last anybody ever heard of 'em."

"Law?" Muscadine John asked.

Dan shrugged. "Nobody knows. I mean, hell, it was funny. Sooner or later you hear tales on the road of just about everybody you know. You listen and you pass 'em on. But in all that time nobody knows what's happened to Hooker and Jessup. They're just . . . gone."

"Same with Perkins Casey," said a younger man with longish brown hair as he rolled a cigarette, tucked it, and licked it. "Good old fellow, too. He was moving cross-country through Pennsylvania last time I saw him, maybe eight months ago. I've asked around about him, but . . . well . . ." He shrugged and was silent.

Firelight played across the faces of the listening men. Someone coughed, and someone else tipped up a bottle that glinted orange.

"Yeah," Dan said. "I'll tell you men what I hear. And I hear it from more men than one or two, men who ain't scared of the law, either. Tough, smart men. There's a place up northeast of here swallows 'boes whole. That's what they say, and you can laugh if you like, but I know what I hear. Little town by the name of . . . I don't know, Brittany or somethin' like that. Swallows 'boes up. You go through there, you don't come out again."

"Ain't Brittany," another man said from where he sat on a stump. "It's a funny name. Bostany. Bostany's . . . Sin."

"Sin?" John raised furry eyebrows. "Seems like I've heard of that place somewhere before."

"Well, listen to what you hear," Dan told him. "If I were you, goin' up that way, I'd stay plenty far from there. Got some bad-assed troopers hang their hats around those parts, too."

"Hey," one of the others said, "we got some hot cards over here getting cold. You men going to spin tall tales or you want in on a matchstick pot?"

All this Muscadine John remembered at the same time he remembered that the night was his friend. It protected and shielded him, and he preferred traveling when it was cooler, when the night birds were singing hobo lullabies. The midnight breezes nestled against him, and the weight of the knapsack—filled with an odd assortment of rags, shirts, socks, an extra pair of shoes, a red golfing cap he'd found on the side of the road, a couple of empty muscadine wine bottles—was familiar and reassuring rather than cumbersome. He wore his road uniform: black, threadbare trousers, sneakers with dirty laces, a Coors Beer T-shirt, won in a beer-drinking contest in a California bar and one of his proudest possessions. His silver hair was still luxuriant on the sides of his head but had almost disappeared from the top; he took pains to keep his long beard looking good. He combed it and washed it whenever necessary, and it never failed to get comments most everywhere he traveled, which had been many times across the face of the United States and twice into Mexico.

Walking northeast along a narrow Somerset County road, Muscadine John stared into the face of darkness and wondered where he was. He'd seen only a few cars going south in the past three hours, and he'd seen no road signs at all. There was a map somewhere in that knapsack, but he didn't want to take the time to find it. The road unfolded at its own speed; he knew that from experience. Overhead, the sky was a canopy of stars, some bright, some distant, like memories. The moon lay over his right shoulder, as if protecting him, and he could see the faint outline of his moon-shadow walking ahead of him on the concrete. On all sides lay a thick black blanket of forest, and from it Muscadine John could hear a dozen different kinds of noises: shrill bird cries, crickets sawing, small nocturnal animals skulking through thicket. His own footfalls were all but silent, and as he walked he felt himself truly part of the night world, a passing shadow, perhaps, the rustle of the breeze through leafy branches, the chirruping of insects bedded down in high roadside weeds. In another hour or so he would find a spot off in the forest to sleep, and then, in the morning, maybe he could scout out some good neighbor who would part with fifty cents or directions to the nearest soup kitchen.

He had taken three more steps when he froze. His

heart leaped, beating furiously, and his eyes widened involuntarily.

Perhaps twenty yards ahead, a figure stood at the side of the road, framed against the outreaching arms of the trees. Muscadine John stood motionless, eyes narrowing slightly to see better in the darkness. The figure did not move.

He took a tentative step forward. Then another.

"Jesus God," he muttered after another moment. "Damned eyes are shot to hell." He rubbed them and looked again at the roadside sign. It had appeared briefly as a tall, gaunt human being, and the sight of it had sent a cold chill up John's back. Now he muttered under his breath at his stupidity and neared the sign. He dug in a pocket for a book of matches and lit one; it blew out, and he lit another to read the white lettering: COLVER —2. ELMORA—7. BETHANY'S SIN—9. Never been through Colver, he told himself; might be a friendly little town. Have to see. His eyes dropped to the last name. Bethany's Sin. Heard of that one somewhere, haven't I? Yeah, somewhere. And then it came to him like the rush of blood to his face after a three-day drunk. Around the hobo campfire. What Dan had said. *Place swallows 'boes up. Stay away from there. Bad place.* He ran the back of his hand across his mouth, still staring at the name. The match went out. He flicked it to the side and continued walking, a little faster now, not knowing why but remembering what Dan had said and the way that man's eyes had looked dark and strange when he'd said it. Maybe it was time to bed down for the night, get an early start with the birds.

He'd walked perhaps another mile when he decided to make camp, and he pushed his way off into a maze of trees and sharp thornbeds in search of a hidden clearing. No use letting the troopers see his coffee fire. As he walked he thought of Mack Tucker. He hoped the man wasn't dead; he hoped they'd meet again somewhere, but if he was dead, John wished him well in that next and better world. But that would be a bad way to go: head cracked open on stones and the brains oozing out as a freight howled lamentations above the corpse. His mind sheered away from that thought. No way to die was any good.

Muscadine John glanced back. The road was gone, hidden by dense foliage. He smelled the sweet green smell of the woods, of the rough tree bark, of the charcoal black sky with glittering diamonds strewn across it. He continued deeper into the forest, thorns catching at his shirt and trousers.

And then he stopped; he cocked his head to one side, listening. His eyes glittered.

He'd heard something strange. Something distant. The echo of a noise. But from what direction it had come he couldn't be certain.

The high, shrill cry of . . . sure, he knew that sound. An eagle. Hunting.

And that was funny, Muscadine John thought, because there weren't a lot of eagles in this part of the country. And they didn't hunt in darkness.

He listened, his ears burning, but the sound did not repeat itself. He moved on, only dimly aware that the palms of his hands were wet.

In a few more minutes he thought he heard it again, but he couldn't be sure if it was his imagination. Yet it sounded nearer, over to his right. He turned toward the left, pushing aside thicket. A thorn scraped across his forearm, drawing a thread of blood. "Shit!" he said.

Another eagle cry. Or was it? Damn it to hell, John thought; I can't tell. I hear it, but I can't tell where it's comin' from. He was facing into the moon now, and that white orb burned down on him as if he were struggling in the heat of a searchlight. He glanced up at it, realizing that tonight the man in the moon looked more like a woman. Too bad about Old Mack; too damned bad. Woods are plenty thick. Maybe I'd better get my ass back to the road. What do you say, old-timer? A cry catching in the night breezes, closer now, much closer; moving over his head and gone. His flesh crawled, and he abruptly stopped pushing through the brush. Yeah. Get back to the road, troopers or no. Go on, right now. He turned, fighting his shirt free of thorns, and struggled back the way he'd come; he thought he could feel the touch of the moon, soft and hot, on the back of his neck. He shrugged it off.

Damn these friggin' woods, he thought. I'll take my chances on the road. That fella Dan was probably crazy. Bethany's Sin. What kind of a name for a place was that? What the hell did that fella Dan know, anyway? He craned his neck, looking for the familiar ribbon of concrete. A clump of high foliage stood before him, dark and shapeless.

He stepped forward.

And realized too late.

It was not foliage, no. Not foliage, but—

In the next instant something roared a challenge that almost shattered his eardrums and made him stagger backward, his heart beating in cold, absolute terror. The thing leaped forward, rising, rising on muscle-corded rear legs, its front legs pawing the sky; moonlight glittered off pistonlike hooves and from red, distended eyes on either side of a massive, triangular head.

Muscadine John's nerves screamed. A horse. A god-awful huge, solid-black horse.

And something more terrible astride it.

A human figure, one hand in the short-cropped mane. The eyes staring at him fixedly from a shadowy face: eyes of burning electric blue that uncapped the terror boiling within John's throat and drove out the scream that ripped at his vocal cords. He spun around, his flesh tingling. Another dark shape. Another. Another. And more, ringing him in. All of them with eyes like furnaces, burning now beyond blue to a hideous, terrible white-hot hatred. Gossamer robes flowed about the bodies, colored silver by the moonlight, and in that instant John knew he had stepped into a place where time stood still, and if he could somehow break free of that ring and run for the road, it might not be there, nor would Colver or Elmora. There were human-seeming forms astride those huge black horses, but they were not human. No, not human anymore. But things of nightmarish evil and hideous intent.

John's foot caught in a tree root; he staggered and fell, pulled down finally by the weight of the knapsack. Empty bottles clinked together. He held out his arms for mercy, crouched on his knees, sweat rising in beads on his face, and all of them reflecting the moon as they rolled down and glistened in his beard. His heart hammered. Around him the riders were silent, but the horses rumbled like the thunder of storms worlds away. The eyes, unblinking, scorched his soul.

He searched for his voice, found it in a deep cavern within himself. "Who . . . are you?" he whispered. "Who are you?"

They said nothing. He could hear them breathing.

"Please," he said, his voice cracking now. "I'm just an old man. I don't . . . want to hurt nobody." His outstretched arms were trembling. "I don't want no trouble," he said.

And it was then that the figure behind Muscadine John leaned slightly forward; one arm flashed out, leaving a trail of bright and brittle blue, the color of raw, unchained power.

John felt the hot sear of pain, and a tremor rocked his body. He gritted his teeth, and tears trickled from his eyes. He heard water running. Peed myself, he thought; fuckin' peed myself. But no. It wasn't that. It was the blood running from the stump where his right hand had been. The full impact of the pain hadn't reached his brain yet.

Another figure raised its ax; moonlight burned on the killing edge. The blade fell with a hissing, metallic sound.

Muscadine John's right arm fell off at the elbow. He found himself staring at the threads of flesh and the ghostly white, wet glimmer of bone. His hand clutched air a few feet away. And it was then, as the sick heat set fire to his veins and nerves and the marrow of his bones, as his mouth opened and his eyes bulged from their sockets, that his scream filled the night like the sound of a wounded and dying animal.

An ax fell.

The stump of his right shoulder gushed thick, glimmering red blood. Red rain spattered the trees. Muscadine John's body trembled as if touched by an electric wire; he saw their eyes on him and he knew he must get to his feet and run, run, run for the highway. Screaming in horror and pain, he staggered up

and forward, off balance, then fell against the side of one
of the horses and down into a clump of spined thorns.
The things turned toward him, their axes rising. He ran
for his life, tripping, screaming, staggering from tree to
tree; but they were only footfalls behind him, slowed by
the dense foliage but not slowed enough. Bleeding.
Bleeding too much. Oh God oh sweet Jesus God bleeding too much put hand in that socket hold the veins
oh God bleeding too much JESUS HELP ME BLEEDING
BLEEDING TOO MUCH . . . !

They guided their horses expertly around the trees
and the thicker growth; their faces were split by moonlight and shadow, and their fingers were clamped like
vises around the hafts of their glowing axes.

He tripped again, almost fell, but caught himself. His
legs were weakening; there was a buzzing in his brain
and a numbness that had claimed more of him with each
step. One side of the knapsack dragged because there
was no arm to secure the strap. And then he turned his
head, sweat burning on his face, to see them.

And it was then that the thing just behind him bent
down and, with an almost effortless blow, cleaved the
head from the fleeing, bloodied body of the man. It
sailed out into the night, turning over and over, the
silver beard catching moonlight, the eyes staring and seeing nothing. The body staggered on, jerking crazily, and
in another second crumpled down in a gore-splattered
mass of rags.

With eaglelike screeches of hatred and vengeance,
the things urged their horses forward. Hooves pounded
the body into a bone-crushed jelly. One of them found the
head, and it shattered like a porcelain bowl that had
held a wine-soaked sponge. For almost ten minutes the
things screamed and their mounts danced the dance of
the death-giver, and when they were finished, nothing
was recognizable except a battered, split-seamed Army
surplus knapsack. With one final, chilling cry they turned
their horses northward and slipped into the forest like
wraiths. For a long time after they had gone, no animal
in the forest dared move, and even the insects sensed
the quick, consuming presence of ax-wielding Evil.

In the sky the moon hung as mute witness. Very slowly

it began to sink toward the horizon as gray light crept over the rim of the world. A few trucks passed on the road, heading for distant cities to the north that might have been eons away from the forest surrounding Bethany's Sin.

And in the forest the flies gathered for a feast.

ELEVEN

THE OUTSIDER,
LOOKING IN

Because the neighborhood had been so deathly quiet all morning, Evan distinctly heard the noise of a lawn mower. He was working on a short story in his basement office, now complete with mounted bookshelves packed with aged paperbacks, a few valuable first-edition Hemingways and Faulkners, and assorted odds and ends; he'd left the windows open to catch the morning breezes.

The high whine of the lawn mower came from across the street, he realized after a moment of listening.

Keating's house.

Today, the last day of June, marked two weeks they'd lived in the house on McClain Terrace. Working on a regular schedule, he'd completed one short story and mailed it the day before to *Harper's,* but he'd had two rejection slips from them and was prepared for a third. No matter; he was certain his material was good, and it was just a matter of time. Kay seemed happy indeed now that the term at George Ross had begun; when Evan sensed in her an insecurity about her abilities as a teacher, he helped her talk those feelings away, and eventually her mood would lighten. He was glad to see that Laurie had adjusted very easily to their new home; she actually seemed to look forward to going to the Sunshine School every weekday, and in the evenings she bubbled over about the games she and the other children played. It pleased him to see both his wife and his daughter so happy, because they had come down a long, grinding road and thank God all those bad times were in the past. They had bought some new furniture, drawing the money from the savings account Evan had built up while working in LaGrange, and Kay was making plans to repaint the living room in soft peach.

It was only when he was alone and allowed his thoughts to drift that Evan felt the old, clinging spider-touches of doubt. They hadn't met that many of the families in Bethany's Sin, and though they'd seen the Demargeons a total of three times, Evan was beginning to sense, and fear, a lack of acceptance. He'd tried to talk his feelings out to Kay, but she'd laughed and said getting to know new people in any town takes time. There's no need to push it or to worry about it, she'd said; it'll happen in time. He'd finally agreed she was probably right.

The outsider, Evan thought; always the outsider, looking in. Imagination, he'd tried to tell himself. Only the imagination and nothing more. But he was different from other people because there were things he sometimes saw that others could not, and perhaps they sensed that about him and that was why he had trouble making friends or trusting people. Because of the feelings he'd sensed, Evan had postponed his research on Bethany's Sin; Mrs. Demargeon was so halfhearted in her encouragement that Evan was afraid to risk the disapproval of the other villagers. Afraid: that was the key word, the key emotion. Afraid of many things, some glittering in the light, some hidden in the dark. Afraid of failure and hate and violence and . . . yes, even afraid of the sight that lay behind his eyes.

He'd had no more dreams since that first night in Bethany's Sin, but the lingering intensity of that one still nagged at him. In the eye of his mind he saw the letters across a road sign: BETHANY'S SIN. And something approaching from a maelstrom of choking dust. He had no idea what it was, but the raw memory of it plucked painfully at his nerves. He'd tried to forget about it, telling himself it was caused by anxiety or weariness or whatever, but instead of forgetting he had only dug a grave for the nightmare—without warning, it often came back, bringing with it the small of death and dark glittering terrors.

But there were other things that disturbed him as well, not all of them confined to the sleeper's world. One day he'd left the house and walked the streets of the village for the sake of curiosity, admiring the flowers in the Circle, watching the tennis players on the courts off Deer Cross Lane, listening to the soft voice of the breezes through the treetops. Winding his way deeper into the village, he'd found himself standing near the corner of Cowlington Street, frozen to the spot. Ahead of him a shadow stretched across the earth, a thing of sharp angles and massed blackness; beyond a spear-topped wrought-iron fence stood that dark-stoned house, the roof of which he'd seen from McClain Terrace. The windows blazed with reflected sunlight, like white-hot eyes with orange pupils. From the street to the doorway was a concrete walk, lined on either side by neatly trimmed hedges, but along the windows on the ground level the shrubs had been allowed to grow thick and wild. The grounds were green and slightly rolling with large oak trees placed at intervals, casting mosaics of shade. Nothing moved around that house, and Evan could see nothing beyond the windows. After a few minutes Evan had felt a sudden, spine-rippling chill, even though he was standing in the full sun. His pulse throbbed, and when he raised his hand to his forehead, he found a light sheen of perspiration ready to break. He turned away quickly and retraced his steps until he'd left that place behind.

But why he'd felt a sudden surge of fear he didn't know.

And there were other things as well: the shadow of a one-armed figure, a shape that had moved rapidly past his bedroom window and on down the street, the barking of a dog in the still hours of the night. The haunted eyes of Harris Demargeon.

Imagination?

Nothing is real but what you perceive, Evan told himself as he listened to the drone of that lawn mower. But is what I perceive real? Nagging doubts bred of old insecurities and fears? Or something very different? Kay wouldn't listen; there was no need to burden her with the things that churned inside him anyway, but whether those demons were imaginary or real, they were beginning to scream within his soul.

And now they had taken on the voice of a lawn mower.

Evan stood up, climbed the stairs out of the basement, and stood in the front doorway, looking across the street at the Keating house.

Keating looked to be a younger man than Evan had envisioned; he was dressed in faded jeans and a sweat-soaked T-shirt, and as Evan watched, Keating paused momentarily behind his red mower to mop at his face with a white handkerchief. In the driveway there was a battered-looking, paint-smeared pickup truck with its tailgate down. Not exactly the kind of vehicle he would've associated with the man. Evan closed his door and walked across the street; he stood on the sidewalk watching him work. Keating wore eyeglasses patched together with adhesive tape. The man glanced up, saw Evan, and nodded a greeting.

"Hot day to have to do that," Evan called over the mower's noise.

The man looked at him, squinted, and shook his head because he hadn't heard. He reached down and cut the engine, and as it died, the silence came slithering back. "What'd you say?" he asked.

"I said it's a hot day to have to cut grass."

Keating wiped his face with a forearm. "Hotter than hell," he said. "In the shade it's not so bad, though."

Evan stepped forward. "I'm Evan Reid," he said. "I live across the street there. Are you Mr. Keating?"

"Keating?" The man paused a few seconds, glanced over at the mailbox: KEA, it read, the rest of the letters gone. "Oh. No, I'm not Keating. I'm Neely Ames."

"Oh, I see," Evan said, but he didn't, really. He looked toward the attractive split-level house, saw it was quiet and seemingly deserted. "I guess he's not back from his vacation yet, then."

"Guess not," Neely said. He drew a package of cigarettes from a back pocket and lit one with a battered Zippo lighter.

"Are you a relative or something, taking care of his house while he's gone?"

"No. I work for the village. I do whatever they tell me to do, and so here I am."

Evan smiled. "I noticed the grass over here was getting a little high, but I didn't think the village would send somebody out to cut it."

"You'd be surprised," Neely said around his cigarette. "In the last couple of weeks I've done just about everything. They're trying to break my ass around here."

Evan was moving toward the house. He stepped up to the front door as the other man watched him, and peered through a window. It was a typical living room, with chairs, a brown sofa, lamps, a coffee table. Magazines lay on the table: *Sports Afield, Time, Newsweek.* Evan saw two flies spinning around near the ceiling; they dropped down onto the coffee table and crawled across the cover of the *Sports Afield.*

"Nobody's home," Neely said.

"Yes, I see. Too bad." He turned back toward the man, then froze. In the distant sky, close to the horizon, was a grayish layer of smoke. "Something's on fire out there!" Evan said, pointing.

Neely looked, shook his head after a few seconds. "That's the landfill, a couple of miles on the other side of the woods. Most of the villages around here use it as a garbage dump. Somebody's just burning trash."

"Won't the fire spread?"

"I doubt it. The landfill's as barren as the moon. But if it did spread I can tell you who'd be fighting it. Me, either with a garden hose or my bare hands, because I'd have to be the whole damned fire department around here."

Evan looked at him and smiled. "That bad, huh?" The other man nodded vigorously. "I've been looking forward to meeting the man who lives here," Evan said.

"I kind of got the impression that whoever lived here has moved away."

111

"Why?"

"I went around to the back for a drink from the outside faucet. The basement door's open. And wide open, too. Like I say, nobody's home."

"Shouldn't the sheriff know about that?"

"I went inside," Neely continued, "on up to the hallway. There was a phone, and I called the sheriff because I thought somebody had broken in, maybe stolen something. Anyway, he told me not to worry about it, said he'd have it taken care of. But he raised hell at me for going inside."

Evan narrowed his eyes slightly, looked over his shoulder at the Keating house. "That's strange," he said quietly.

"There's furniture inside," Neely told him, "but not much more. The closets are all open and empty. And another thing: there are no fuses in the fusebox."

Evan looked at him. "No . . . fuses?" he said, almost to himself.

Neely shrugged. "I don't know. Maybe . . . what's his name? Keating . . . maybe Keating decided to move and just took off. A lot of people do that, you know."

"But why would he?" Evan asked, turning and gazing along the street at the other houses. The smudge in the sky seemed nearer. But the unasked question burned at him: Why would anyone want to leave the perfect village of Bethany's Sin?

"No telling," Neely said, watching the man. He drew on his cigarette again and then said, "Well, if you'll excuse me now, I'd better finish this lawn." He pulled a couple of times on the starter cord, and the mower kicked to life; guiding the mower toward an uncut section on the far side of the lawn, he concentrated on how good a beer was going to taste after this job was done.

Evan stood where he was for a moment more; from the corner of his eye he caught a brief glimpse of that high roof before the tree limbs covered it over again in the wake of a breeze. The museum.

He turned away, crossing the street again and disappearing into his own house.

And after he was gone, Neely Ames stared in the direction he'd gone. What was the man's name? Reid? He seemed okay, worlds better than most of the people he'd met so far. At least the man hadn't looked at him with something akin to disdain, as the others did. Neely swung the lawn mower around, cutting a swath through knee-high weeds. He hadn't told Evan Reid everything he'd found inside; he hadn't told him of that wide, dark stain on the basement floor, just below the empty fusebox. That he'd decided to keep to himself. He wiped sweat out of his eyes and put his back into the mower.

Day cooled into evening. The noise of the lawn mower stopped, and slowly the subtle blues of nightfall shaded the far forest, creeping toward Bethany's Sin. Evan watched them coming as he stood at a window in the den. He watched them as Kay made dinner in the kitchen, as Laurie laughed at a Soupy Sales rerun on television. It seemed to him that out there a tidal wave of darkness was gathering, gathering, taking awesome form and hideous strength, rolling across the woods, driving down the earth beneath blackness, rolling nearer and nearer and nearer. He tore himself away from the window and helped Kay make iced tea in the kitchen.

". . . some really smart kids," Kay was saying. "They're asking me questions that I find tough to answer sometimes. But God, that feels good. Being challenged like that is . . . well, it's one of the most fulfilling things in the world."

"I'm glad," he said, popping ice from their trays. "It sounds terrific."

"It is. You know, it'd be great if you could come over and have lunch with me someday. I'd like to show you around and introduce you to the other teachers."

He nodded. "I'd like that. Maybe some day next week."

"Thursday would be good," Kay said. She stirred the rice, listening to his silence. He'd been very quiet since she and Laurie had gotten home, and at first Kay had thought Evan had gotten a rejection slip in the mail, but all that had come was an electric bill and a Penney's mail-order catalogue. He was often quiet when his work wasn't going well, when he felt at odds with a character or a situation in a story. But this was somehow different. This was like . . . yes, like the morning after one of those . . . dreams he had. Oh God, no.

"Aren't you feeling well?" she asked him finally, not looking at him but rather into the rice.

And he heard the trepidation in her voice. The fear of what was to come. He said, "A little tired, I guess."

"Trouble with your story?"

"Yes."

"Anything I can help you with?"

"No," he said. "I don't think so."

But of course she knew that wasn't it.

"I went across the street today," he said. "To Keating's house. You know, the widower Mrs. Demargeon told us about? There was a guy over there cutting the grass. He said the back door was open, the lock broken. He said he didn't think anyone lived there anymore."

"Who was he?"

"Someone the village hired. A handyman, I suppose." He gazed out the kitchen window, saw black. Blackness creeping, spider-forms in the clouds. "I looked in through a window myself, and I—" Say it. You've got to say it and get it out by God or your soul will scream. "I didn't like what I felt."

"What did you see?"

He shrugged. "Furniture, magazines. Flies."

"Flies?" She looked at him questioningly.

"Two of them," Evan said, "circling the living room. I don't know why, but that bothers me."

"Oh, come on," Kay said, trying to keep it light and easy. "Why should that upset you so much?"

Evan knew why, but wouldn't tell her. Because he'd seen many, many corpses in the war. And most of them had been specked with greedily eating flies. Around the lips of rictus-grinning death masks, around the bullet holes and ripped arteries. Since then, he'd always equated flies with death, just as he equated spiders with rank, crawling evil.

They sat down to dinner. Evan thought he could hear the darkness breathing beyond the windowpanes.

"We watched cartoons today, Daddy," Laurie said.

"We had a fun time. And Mrs. Omartian told us some stories."

"Omarian," Kay corrected.

"What kinds of stories?" Evan asked her between fork-fuls of beef stew.

She gave a little-girl shrug. "Funny stories. About old things.

"Old things, huh? Like what?"

She paused a moment, gathering her thoughts. Mrs. Omartian was such a nice lady; she never talked loud and never got angry, no matter what any of them did, no matter if they swung too hard or laughed too loud or threw rocks. The only time she'd ever seen Mrs. Omartian get upset was when Patty Foster had fallen down and cut her knee real bad. "About an old place," Laurie told her father. "Funnier even than Oz."

"I'll have to meet this Mrs. Omarian sometime," Evan said, glancing over at Kay. "I'd like to hear these stories." He smiled at Laurie and continued eating.

When they'd finished dinner, Kay and Evan did the dishes, and then she settled down in the den with a stack of mathematics texts she'd brought home from the George Ross library. Evan played a game of Crazy Eights with Laurie at the kitchen table, but his mind kept drifting from the cards he held. He kept thinking of the darkness outside the walls, and how the moon would be shining now on the windows in that looming house on Cowlington Street.

And when Laurie was sleeping and the lights were out, Evan and Kay made unhurried love in their bedroom, entwining and falling apart and entwining again. Kay breathed steadily beneath him, and clutched at his firm back and shoulders, but even in the ebbing warmth of their afterglow, when on the rim of sleep they both held to each other, Evan's mind turned and twisted into the corridors of the past.

Eric. The cracking of a high, decayed branch. A fall-ing body, thudding to earth in a golden field. Crows taking to the sky, fleeing death. And Evan, young Evan, who had seen his brother clutching at empty space in a dream but hadn't recognized it as a premonition, standing over him, seeing the blood trickle from both sides of his mouth, seeing the small chest heave for air.

Eric had made a move to grasp his arm, but Evan had spoken. "I'll go and get Dad I'll go and I'll hurry and get him I'll hurry!" And then he'd run, stumbling all the way back to the small house on the hill, screaming for his mother and father to help because Eric had been hurt badly, he'd fallen while branch-walking and now he was broken on the ground like some sort of carnival puppet. He'd shown them the way, afraid afraid afraid that he was taking them along the wrong path, afraid he couldn't find that place again, afraid. . . .

And when they'd gotten there, Eric's eyes had been glazed and steady, staring at the hot orb of the sun, and the flies were already tasting the blood around the young boy's mouth, like water from red fountains.

Evan's mind, tumbling through a labyrinth.

Faces peering through bamboo bars. Evan, dazed and weak, fighting off two black-garbed guards with all the strength left in his body. Gripping a knife and slashing, one of them swinging at his head with a rifle stock, the other falling back with liquid gushing from a torn jugular. The noise of screams and shouts, more guards coming from the jungle-camouflaged compound, the shadows converging toward the bamboo cages. Evan grabbing at the rifle stock, knocking it aside, driving the knife deep through the rib cage up into the lungs. Throwing the Cong aside, turning toward the cages where the crazed men babbled and frothed. Machine gun fire, bullets streaking across the ground between Evan and the cages. Searing flame across his left shoulder as a bullet whined past. And then he'd turned away from the cages and run for the jungle with the guards behind him, firing at his shadow; he'd dived into dense foliage and hidden there for what seemed like hours until the shouting had died away, and then he'd made his way back to where he knew his own camp lay, miles to the south.

He'd reported the capture of his recon patrol, and a rescue mission had been organized. He'd led the men back through the jungle, relying on his memory and his instincts, and the next day they'd found the Cong camp.

But only the dead remained. The others had been executed in their cages, their bodies riddled with bullets, and the stench of death hung there like a dark mist. And already the flies had come in swarms, ancient armies always victorious.

And it was then that Evan had known.

Yes, there was something like the Hand of Evil that crawled over the world, spiderish and dripping with venom. Seeking bodies and souls. Twice Evan had been in its presence and escaped, and twice that hideous thing had taken the lives of others instead of his. But whatever it was waited, and watched, and breathed the breath of night.

Because someday it would come for him again.

He opened his eyes, pulled Kay to him, and kissed her forehead. She smiled sleepily, and then he let his mind topple over the brink.

Into a terrible, familiar place where the show was about to start, and he could not be late.

For they had something to show him.

A roadsign, with light blazing behind it: BETHANY'S SIN. Images of the village: neat houses in rows, spreading elm trees, the Circle. And that house: the museum on Cowlington Street. The opening door; fear thundering in his soul. A sudden whirlwind of dust, a darkening of the light, a coldness that made his bones ache.

And that movement in the dust, a figure draped in shadows coming slowly nearer and nearer, walking soundlessly and with coiled, terrible strength. He wanted to cry out but could not; he wanted to run but could not. And now the figure parting the curtain of dust, reaching through it for him, coming closer, closer, fingers grasping for his throat.

And now Evan could see only the eyes in a dark, hovering face.

Electric blue, crackling with power that threatened to rip him to pieces. Unblinking. Below them, lips parted in the snarl of hate, showing glittering teeth.

Evan screamed, felt the scream tear at his throat like a claw; he fought his way out of it, Kay beside him now saying dear God dear God not again please no no not again no Evannnnnnnn. . . .

"Okay . . ." he breathed finally, trying to steady his nerves. He felt wet and clammy, cold and alone. "Don't worry. I'm okay. Really. I am."

"Dear God in Heaven!" she said, and it was then he realized she had moved away from him and wasn't touching him anymore.

He looked into her eyes, saw them widened and afraid. He ran a hand over his face and shook his head. "Go back to sleep."

She stared at him in silence, as if she were staring at someone with a terminal disease: sadness mixed with fear.

"I said go back to sleep," Evan said, his gaze drilling a hole through to her brain.

She shuddered inwardly from the expression in his eyes. She'd seen something like it before, when he'd awekened and told her there was going to be an accident and they might get hurt, there was going to be a red tractor-trailer truck marked ALLEN LINES that would lose its brakes and veer across a median toward them. But no, this was worse, and it frightened her to the very core of her being. His eyes were hollow and haunted, lit by an internal fire to banish the terrible cold that had crept through his bones.

"Go to sleep," Evan whispered.

She started to speak, thought better of it, and laid her head back down on the pillow. Through the window she could see the moon, and it seemed to her in that instant that the moon was . . . grinning.

"My God," Evan said softly. "Oh, my God." He settled back, his heart pounding in his chest like a sledgehammer. There was no waiting for sleep; it had passed him by this night, discarding him like a cracked, useless container. He threw aside the sheets and let the air cool the sweat on his body; beside him, Kay stirred, but she neither touched him nor dared to speak.

Those eyes burned in his brain; when he closed his own, he saw them still, orbs of fire somewhere within his forehead.

And now, with this second dream, he knew. And feared the hideous knowledge.

Something in the peaceful village of Bethany's Sin was stalking him.

Drawing closer.

And as they lay like fearful strangers, June slipped into July.

III

JULY

TWELVE

NIGHT ON THE KING'S BRIDGE ROAD

"We're closing up, hon," the woman with the bun of bleached-blond hair said.

Neely Ames glanced up at her from behind his glasses and nodded, and she turned away, moving from his table back toward the bar. Light glinted off the amber glass of four empty beer bottles precariously stacked two-on-two before him; another beer bottle, half-drained, lay on the floor beside his chair. He watched the woman—what'd she say her name was? Ginger?—go back behind the bar and start counting money out of the cash register. He strummed a few more chords on the time-worn twelve-string Gibson guitar in his lap, and Ginger looked up, gave him a quick and tentative smile, then continued counting where she'd left off. Vic, the bartender, a burly man with a reddish beard and a gut that preceded him by a foot or so, cleaned beer mugs with a cloth and listened to the younger man play.

They were old songs, but of course neither Ginger nor Vic had ever heard them before because Neely had written them himself. Some of them had lyrics, some didn't; some were complete, some were fragments; but each one in its own way was special; and each one sprang from a particular event or feeling in his life, something that had burned through his gut and finally made its way out, with much pain and often confusion, through his fingertips, to be voiced by that guitar. He was good at it, and he'd left home in Nebraska years ago to join a group of musicians called the Midnight Ramblers, but nothing had ever really broken for them and eventually they'd gone their separate ways. For some time after that, he'd made a fair amount of money playing in clubs and roadhouses

123

like this one, but he didn't really know a lot of the new, popular songs, and people seemed to want to drink rather than listen to music, anyway. Most times, he'd play a couple of his tunes for club managers and they'd shrug and say sorry, that kind of guitar music doesn't sell too good anymore. And of course that was true, but he'd decided a long time ago that he'd play his own music or nothing, and he'd paid for that rather brash vow by a succession of menial jobs like the ones he'd been doing in Bethany's Sin. It was money in the pocket though, and there was no use complaining.

From time to time, when he sat in a darkened bar with an ashtray full of stubs before him and empty bottles lined up like friends who've come and gone, something came to Neely: the memory of a voice, a sight, a taste, an aroma that made his mind slip back. Back through the years, back through lifetimes. He remembered his father, a strapping man with a crew cut and a preference for red cowboy shirts, playing guitar with a band called the Tru-Tones on the country carnival circuit; through him Neely had learned about music and pain. Neely's father had been an alcoholic, a man who drank at night and screamed at the moon like a wounded dog; his mother, a graceful and intelligent woman who had been a minister's daughter, became in time both a borderline drinker and a tent revivalist who passed out pamphlets on the saving mercy of Christ. Neely remembered her praying beside her man as he hung his head down in a pool of vomit that smelled of moonshine. But his mother had slipped, too, giving up the almost impossible task of trying to get him on the wagon in favor of crawling through the ruts at his side. Theirs had been true love.

And now Neely sometimes found that drinking helped the creative juices flow: he wasn't an alcoholic, he wasn't bound to it, but by God it eased some of those bad memories, and took him through lonely nights, and mostly just helped him forget the day his aunt and uncle had come for him and had his mother and father taken away to one of those white-walled hospitals where everyone's eyes looked like holes that had been drilled through to the brain. He'd grown up fast, taut and smart with lessons no school could ever teach him. Sometimes when he drank raw whiskey, which wasn't often, he thought he could see the same vision his father must have seen: that real life started tomorrow, down the road, around the next bend. Real life was waiting ahead.

After a few minutes more, Neely clutched his guitar by the neck and stood up. The beer bottles wavered, making the light dance a jig. Ginger smiled at him again, and Neely wondered what would happen if he asked her to go home with him. She was probably ten years older than he, but what the hell? No, no. Shouldn't do that. Maybe she was the bartender's wife; he'd seen Vic put his arm around her waist a couple of times that night. He watched her for a moment more and then moved toward the door.

"Hey," Vic said, "you okay?"

He nodded. "Yeah."

"You got a long way to drive?"

"Bethany's Sin," Neely said. "I work over there." His tongue felt a little swollen, but other than that, he felt fine.

"Well," Vic said, "you take it easy on the way home."

"Thanks. I will."

"Good night," Ginger said. "I like the way you play that guitar."

Neely smiled at her and then was through the door, walking in the glow of the red neon sign that said COCK'S CROW; above it was a rooster, outlined in neon, crowing toward the sky. Only his truck and a Chevrolet station wagon remained in the red-neon-licked gravel parking lot. He slipped into the truck, eased his guitar onto the seat next to him, started the engine, and turned toward Bethany's Sin. As he drove, he glanced at his wristwatch, saw it was only a few minutes before two. Breathing the night air as it swept in through the truck's open windows, he was feeling pleasantly light-headed; he didn't want to think about six o'clock when Wysinger would probably be calling him with some work to do. The King's Bridge Road stretched out before his headlights, a smooth asphalt ribbon that was one of the better-kept roads in the area surrounding the village; it led him past the darkened Westbury Mall and intersected with 219 for the last few miles into Bethany's Sin. At this time of the morning there were no other cars, and the night ran before the truck's lights.

He found himself thinking about that yard he'd cut today. Whoever lived there was gone; there was no doubt about it. All the clothes gone from the closets, nothing left but the furniture. That bothered him: why cut the lawn of an abandoned house? In the last couple of weeks he'd seen two other houses like that one, both dark and silent, one over on Blair Street and the other on Ashaway. Of course it was summer, vacation time for those who could afford it. After all, there'd still been names on the mailboxes. The locals were fanatics for keeping their village looking immaculate, and of course there was nothing wrong with that, but Neely wondered if a great deal of it wasn't just to impress those who happened to drive through the village. Or maybe to entice more families into Bethany's Sin. Whatever. It wasn't his concern anyway.

His ears were filled with the insect songs of the forest. There was a bend in the road coming up ahead, and Neely decreased his speed—no need to run off into a gully and get in trouble with the troopers. They'd sure as hell smell the beer on him because he could smell it himself. Hell, I'm okay, he told himself. I'm doing damned fine.

And as if to emphasize that point, he hit the accelerator a fraction as he rounded the wooded bend.

Too late he realized that something was in the road.

The glare of headlights off something dark and moving. Several figures. Black things. Animals. He heard a low-pitched rumble and realized only then that they were horses; they scattered before the truck, hooves flashing, and then he was through them and around another bend. He glanced quickly into the rearview mirror, tapping the brakes. Horses? What the hell were horses doing out here in the middle of the night? He hadn't been able to take a good look at the riders because he'd gone through them so fast, but he'd had the split-second impression of torsos and head turning swiftly toward him. The headlights had gleamed sharply off eyes that had been widened and unblinking and . . . yes, by God, as blue as raw electricity passing through power cables. He shivered suddenly, staring into the mirror, the truck slowing, slowing, slowing. . . .

Stopping.

Night birds cried off to the left. Crickets shrilled with their buzz-saw voices and then died away. Beyond the range of his headlights the road was so dark as to be nonexistent. He watched the rearview mirror, saw the splay of red from the truck's taillights.

And that was when he saw them coming.

Shadows, approaching through the red. Sweat glistening off the flanks of those huge, muscle-corded horses. The riders bent forward slightly, cleaving the wind. Something catching moonlight, gleaming. Something metallic.

His hands tightened involuntarily around the wheel. He plunged his foot down on the accelerator.

The truck coughed, backfired, began to pick up speed. Now he couldn't see them following but he knew they were there, and though he didn't know how many or what they were, he had no thought now but to get back to Bethany's Sin. The truck's aged engine rattled and groaned like an old, rheumatic man; the wind roared in through the windows, tangling his hair. In another moment he thought he could hear the wild, hoarse breathing of those horses bearing down behind him. He glanced in the rearview mirror, saw nothing; looked over his shoulder, saw nothing. But they were there; he knew it. Coming closer. And closer. The engine racketed, and he gritted his teeth and mentally urged it on. With one hand on the wheel he leaned over, rolled up the far window. Then the window beside him. He could smell his own sweat. Something screamed just behind him: a wild, high cry that made his heart thunder with fear, and in that second he knew that something out on this shadowed road was alive and dripping with a terrible, vibrating hate. He could feel the tendrils of it reaching for him like so many black fingers gripping at his throat. On both sides of the road the tangled silhouette of the forest swept past, dark against dark. The speedometer needle quivered between forty-five and fifty. And again Neely heard that cry, apparently from just behind his head; he flinched from the eerie, piercing whine of it. The noise seemed to be driven through him like icy steel. A hand clutched at his stomach and he hovered on the brink of nausea. He felt like screaming and laughing at the same time, laughing wildly and hysterically until his voice cracked, because he knew this had to be the DTs or beer jitters or something like that; it couldn't be real, no, it couldn't actually be happening. He'd scared a group of deer crossing the road, that was it, and then his imagination had taken over. Glance in the mirror. Nothing back there. Everything dark. Nothing. Deer. Long gone by now, all scared as shitless as he'd been. You're drunk, by God.

Another curve in the road, a wicked one. He put his foot to the brakes, heard the tires begin a squeal. The speedometer needle dropped to thirty-five.

A movement beside him that made his nerves cry out in alarm. He twisted his head to the side. And stared, his mouth coming open to release a horrified, guttural croak.

One of the riders had pulled up beside his window. The figure's raven-black hair streamed like the mane of the huge, frothing horse it rode. The figure was hunched over, one hand at the base of the massive, muscular neck, urging the horse faster and faster. There was no saddle, no harness. And then the rider's face came around and stared in at Neely. The lips were contorted in a terrible scream of hate, teeth glittering with moonlight. And those eyes: orbs of fierce, glowing blue, a power deep in those sockets that almost literally jerked Neely's head back to snap his neck. Cold terror flooded his body, and he fought to maintain control over the steering wheel. And in the blink of a second the rider's other arm whipped out, carrying with it an object of metal, something that brought another cry from him and made him throw one arm up across his face.

Which saved his eyes. Because in the next instant the ax blade smashed through the window glass, filling the truck's cab with stinging wasps. The arm rose and fell again with blinding, terrible strength; he heard the blade bite metal on the doorjamb and then scrape off. Neely twisted the wheel, his foot going for the accelerator but hitting the brake instead; the truck began to swerve, then fishtailed off the road, crashing through brush and wild vegetation, glancing off a thin poplar, shaking Neely as if he were the dice in a cup held by an ancient, laughing god. He hit the accelerator again, felt a bone-jarring crash as the truck smashed down a scraggly mass of thorns; he heard glass break, and one of the headlights went out, leaving him in murky semidarkness. Neely could hear the breathing of the horses now, and could see the figures all around him. How many? Ten? Twelve? Twenty? He braced his arms and twisted; the truck screamed, battering its way through the brush like a fear-maddened cyclops, and regained the road. Another ax blade struck his door, glanced off. He sank his foot to the floor; his glasses had fallen off and lay somewhere on the floorboard, and his guitar had slipped down as well, making moaning noises as the tires slammed against asphalt. The speedometer needle reached fifty and vibrated crazily.

And there, perhaps half a mile ahead, was the blinking caution light that was the turn-off onto Ashaway. He took it at fifty, the tires shrieking so loud he was certain the noise echoed across Bethany's Sin like a banshee's wail. He whipped the truck through the village's darkened streets, past silent houses, through the Circle, and toward the two-story wooden boardinghouse where a middle-aged woman named Grace Bartlett rented him a room for twenty-five dollars a week. When he pulled up before the boardinghouse, the noise of his tires made windows vibrate.

Fearfully he looked over his shoulder, his breathing harsh and forced, his heartbeat out of control.

Nothing had followed.

Shaking, he ran a hand over his face. Nausea rushed him, almost overtaking him before he could open his door and lean out. Glass tinkled off the seat and out of the doorjamb. Jesus, he told himself, trying to steady his nerves; Jesus Christ, what did I see out there? The sour stench of beer rose into his face, and he turned his head away.

Noises seemed to be gathering over him like dust stirring in heavy folds. The sounds of insects in trees; the lone calling of a bird over toward the Circle; the gentle stirring of branches in a hint of warm breeze; a dog barking repeatedly in the distance. Neely found his glasses, put them on and stared into the night for a moment, then took his guitar and slid out of the truck, his head still spinning and his limbs leaden. With a nerveless hand he traced the scrapes along the driver's door; bare metal showed through the layers of paint, and he could see the dents where the powerful blows had been struck. If it were not for those ax-blow signatures and the broken glass, Neely would have talked himself into believing he'd had some kind of nightmare on the road, that he'd drifted into a beer-induced sleep where something terrible and evil had struck.

But no.

The window was shattered, and tiny bits of glass speckled the underside of the arm he'd thrown up in self-protection. He looked again into the darkness, felt his spine crawl, then heard a voice within him shout out, *Get inside quickly quickly quickly!* Neely turned away from the truck and almost ran into the house. Climbing the hallway stairs, he fumbled for his key and then twisted it in the lock of his door. He switched on the overhead light, illuminating the bedroom papered in a dark brown bamboo design. After setting the guitar in a corner, he crossed the room and slid open a window overlooking the street. And there he stood for perhaps fifteen minutes, watching and listening—for what, he didn't know.

But nothing moved down there.

He ran a hand over his face; there was glass in the palm. Wysinger should know about this, he decided finally. Something tried to kill me, and I saw its face; I saw those eyes, and I know what it was.

Something hideous and breathing hatred. Something in the form of a woman. But . . . no, not human. Not really human at all.

After a while he shut the window, picked the glass from his arm and hand with a pair of tweezers, and finally tried to sleep. It came to him shrieking and bearing a moon-glittering battle-ax.

Just before dawn a shadow climbed the stairs, paused at Neely's door. Quietly tried the doorknob. Then vanished the way it had come.

THIRTEEN

WHAT NEELY SAW

Sheriff Wysinger leaned forward slightly, his feral eyes narrowed above the cigarette stub in his mouth. Behind his desk there was an oiled walnut rifle cabinet and a shelf with gleaming football trophies. The goldflake paint had begun to crack on several of them, exposing ugly and valueless metal. He took the cigarette from his mouth and laid it on the rim of a red plastic ashtray. "Ames," he said quietly, "it's a little early in the mornin' for these kind of stories, don't you think?"

"What kind of stories?" Neely asked him from where he stood on the other side of the desk, his hands resting on his hips.

"Yarns. Fairy tales." Wysinger drew on the cigarette again, exhaled smoke through his nostrils in a dragonish stream, and then crushed it out in the ashtray. Tiny red embers flared, glittered, died. "Now just what sort of shit are you trying to hand me?"

"Hey!" Neely said, lifting his arm so the other man could see the cuts. "And look at these!" He pointed out two small gashes he'd found in his chin that morning. "You want to come out and have a look at my damned truck?" He stood waiting for the man to move; he could see the overhead lights glittering on the pink flesh of Wysinger's scalp.

Wysinger sat still for a moment. Finally he shrugged with disdain and hefted his bulk out of the swivelchair. Outside the sheriff's office the light of morning was pearlish, and a thin haze of wet ground-fog still haunted the curbs. Neely walked around to the other side of his pickup truck, and Wysinger followed at his own pace.

"There," Neely said, motioning toward the scrapes and

the broken window; in the morning light, the ax-blade gashes were clearly visible.

Wysinger moved past him, ran a hand across one of the cuts. "What'd you say you were doing last night?" he asked.

"I was at the Cock's Crow until they closed," Neely explained again. "On the way back to the village I drove through a group of horses and riders, crossing the road, I guess; I slowed to see who they were, and then they came after me. You can see for yourself what they did."

"Yeah, I see. What time did you say this happened?"

"Around two."

"Two?" Wysinger grunted. "Awful late for people to be ridin' their horses on a country road. How many were there?"

"I don't know. Jesus, I was just trying to get my ass out of there!"

"Uh-huh." He stepped over to the window, examined the jagged edge. "What'd you say they were using? Hammers?"

"No. Axes. One of them was, at least."

"Axes?" Wysinger turned from the window and looked into Neely's face. "You know that sounds wilder'n hell, don't you?"

Neely stepped toward him, his jaw grim. "Now listen to me," he said, not caring about Wysinger's position in the village anymore, not caring about the damned job he held, not caring about anything but making this ox of a man believe. "I know what I saw last night. Riders, chasing me down. And by God one of them smashed my window with an ax! Tried to fucking run me off the road!"

"Watch your language," Wysinger said quietly as a car drove past.

"They were trying to kill me!" Neely said, louder than he'd wanted to; he could hear his voice echo off the side of the truck. "I don't see that you understand that yet!"

"I understand it. I just don't understand who they were, or why they should try to hurt you. You hit one of their horses? That why your headlight's broken and the grille's all smashed to hell and back?"

"No," Neely said, shaking his head. "I didn't hit any of them. That happened when I went off the road."

Wysinger smiled slightly, sensing that he had Neely where he wanted him. "Well, now," he said, watching the other man. "Maybe all of it happened when you went off the road? Huh? Maybe you had a bit too much to drink last night and you slammed your heap into a gully, broke that window, and beat up the driver's door? So to keep me from findin' out you were drunk-drivin' and had a wreck, this morning you made up a cock-and-bull story in your sleep and ran over here to—"

"No," Neely said, his voice firm and cold as steel, his gaze matching the flint of Wysinger's. "That's not how it happened at all."

"You're sticking to this shit about horses in the middle of the road? Jesus!" Wysinger snorted. He turned away from Neely and moved toward the door. His lungs ached for the second cigarette of the morning.

"Wait a minute! Wait!" Neely stepped forward, put his hand on Wysinger's shoulder, and twisted the man around. Wysinger's eyes blazed briefly, and Neely dropped his hand away. "I haven't told you everything yet. I saw one of the riders. I looked into her face—"

"Her? What the hell do you mean, 'her'?"

"It was a woman. But I've . . . I've never seen a woman who looked like that before. It was like . . . like looking into a blast furnace. Or a volcano. I could feel the heat from those eyes, like they were burning holes through me. I've never seen anything like that in my life, and Jesus Christ, I hope I never see it again."

Wysinger waited for a moment, his gaze probing. When he spoke, his voice was hard and emotionless. "Okay," he said. "You want me to take a drive up Two-nineteen to have a look, I will. But I'll tell you one thing. I don't like you. I don't like fuckin' drifters on the make with their hands out for money. And worst of all, I don't like drifters who drink in the middle of the night and then lie like rugs to stay out of trouble. I don't believe a word of this shit you've been spreading, and nobody else will, either. If I could prove you were haulin' ass down Two-nineteen last night with a bellyful of beer, I'd either throw you in jail or kick your ass out of this place!"

Fleshy lids shawled his eyes. "Now get on over to the tool shed and get the mower. Cemetery's weeded up." Without waiting for Neely to speak again, Wysinger turned his back, strode toward the door, and disappeared into his office.

"Son of a bitch!" Neely growled under his breath. But he'd known even before he'd left Mrs. Bartlett's that his story was strange and unbelievable, and that Wysinger would probably laugh in his face. At breakfast, in Mrs. Barlett's yellow-walled kitchen, the ample, rather motherly woman had eyed him with concern and asked him what time he'd gotten to bed the night before. It's not right staying out all hours, she'd told him, moving about the kitchen in her peach-colored robe; when my Willy was alive, she'd said, he was early to bed and early to rise. He was a hardworking man, too, and a good man. I can see in your eyes that you didn't get a good night's sleep, and that's what a body needs most. You're feeling all right, aren't you?

He'd told her he was feeling fine, but he hardly touched his breakfast. He'd told her nothing of what had happened on the road.

Now Neely shook his head in disgust and went around to the other side of the sheriff's office, where a chain-link fence surrounded a metal shed. Neely used one key to unlock the fence's gate and another to unlock the door of the shed; inside were various hand tools, cans of gasoline, shovels and hoes, the red lawn mower Neely had grown so familiar with. He found a swingblade and wheeled the mower out, locking everything behind him because he was responsible for all the tools and there'd be hell to pay if anything happened to them. His biceps and forearms already sore, he loaded the mower into the truck bed, then threw the swingblade into the front and drove off in the direction of Shady Grove Hill. He felt a gray, desolate mood coming over him; alone, that was what he felt. Utterly alone. So perhaps it was fitting, in his desolation, that he spend the hottest part of the day in the cemetery.

As Neely drove away, Oren Wysinger let the blinds fall back across the window. He turned the lock on the door, crossed behind his desk, and took a key from the middle drawer. Then he walked to the file cabinet on the other side of the office and knelt down to unlock the lowest drawer. At the back of it, buried beneath blank sheets of typewriter paper, was a dark-brown book about the size of a photo album. Wysinger took the book out, laid it on his desk, and snapped on the gooseneck desk lamp. Sitting down, he drew on his cigarette and let the smoke dribble liquidlike from one side of his mouth. Then he opened the book.

Taped across the first page was a yellowed newspaper clipping with the headline CONEMAUGH FAMILY SLAIN. There was a picture of the Fletcher house. He turned the page. Another newspaper clipping: SPANGLER RESIDENT KILLED. A mug shot of a smiling middle-aged man wearing a tie, the name Ronald Biggs beneath it. On the next page two smaller items: WIDOWER SLAIN and BARNESBORO MAN KILLED. The book was filled with grim reminders of murder: photographs of houses where bodies had been found, of cars that had been discovered on the sides of country roads, of blankets covering what could only be horribly mutilated corpses. Like those of the Fletchers. They covered a span of ten years; the last one was a few paragraphs on how a Barnesboro woman had discovered the mutilated body of a George Ross mathematics teacher named Gerald Meacham. That had been a little over three months ago.

Wysinger smoked in silence for a few minutes, looking at the next blank page. When he felt the sudden heat on his fingers, he crushed the cigarette out. There was a dull, heavy feeling within him, as if his bodily fluids had pooled into a lake that became more stagnant every day, thickly slimed with some kind of evil filth. He knew the thread that ran through these killings. Most of them men living alone. All killed by tremendous blows of a sharp, heavy object. All killed in the night, between midnight and dawn. Three years after the mayor of Bethany's Sin had given him the job of sheriff, Wysinger had sat down with a bottle of Jim Beam and a map of the county. For a long time before that, he'd been clipping the articles about the slayings from the small local community papers, probably because nothing in his life had shocked and sickened him so much as seeing the Fletchers ripped to pieces like they'd been. Possibly it was curiosity about the other murders, or a strange and sure feeling that they were all somehow connected, or a feeling of terrible destiny, but he'd clipped and saved and studied for years, while the police in other villages blamed maniacs or drifters or hoboes armed with bludgeons. And that night, his spine stiffened by Beam, Sheriff Wysinger had drawn circles around the towns on the map where they'd found bodies or, in some cases, just empty cars on the roadside or off in the woods. Then connected those circles with lines.

And it was then he saw that Bethany's Sin lay in the center, like a spider hanging in the midst of a web.

Now he touched that next, empty page in the brown book. His fingers felt contaminated, blighted, diseased. Often he awakened in the night, alone in his house, listening to the dark speak. The disease had crept into the marrow of his bones and festered there; sometimes the sores boiled over, and he wanted to scream. But he never did, because he was too afraid.

There would have been a new entry had Neely Ames's truck crashed into the roadside thicket. The troopers would have found the man's corpse battered beyond recognition. If they'd found it at all. Christ! he thought. Too close to Bethany's Sin. Too damned close. Investigations, troopers probing around, people asking questions. Too damned close. He closed the book and turned off the light but did not move from his desk. He dreaded what was to come because now he'd have to talk to the mayor. And even though he knew from the calculations he rigidly kept that the moon was beginning to wane, he was deathly and numbingly afraid.

Kay thought: At three o'clock, silence is the instructor in the classrooms, teaching lessons on how time can slip away. She was sitting in her small office with test papers from her morning class before her, waiting to be graded. Most of the classes at George Ross were held in the morning and early afternoon, and by this time of the day almost all of the students and teachers were gone. About fifteen minutes before, she'd walked down the corridor to the teachers' lounge and that unpredictable soft-drink machine that always had indignant notes taped to it. The halls had been silent and empty, doors closed, fluorescent lights switched off. She'd brought her Coke back to her office and continued working because to her there was something strange and slightly . . . yes, forbidding about a large building when all the noise had seeped out of it, when all the people had gone away. Silly, she told herself. That's silly. I can work better when it's quiet; I can get these papers finished and then pick up Laurie at the Sunshine School and go home to Evan. She was glad Pierce had gone home early. That man made her nervous.

Kay turned to the next paper. Roy Sanderson's. Nice, bright young man. He did well on the pop tests Kay sometimes threw at them. She checked through the first few problems, found an error in the fourth one, and circled it with her red pen; she reached across the desk to her right for the half-drained Coke can.

At first Kay saw it from the corner of her eye and wasn't certain what it was. When she turned her head to look, she shivered and gasped in amazement.

There was a human figure standing on the other side of the pebbled-glass door to her office. It stood motionless, and how long it had been there Kay had no way of knowing. She expected the doorknob to turn and the door to come open, but for frozen seconds she was certain a pair of eyes watched her own form there at the desk.

"Who's there?" Kay asked, realizing her voice sounded strained.

In the blink of an eye the figure had slipped away.

Kay put aside her pen, opened the door, and looked out. The corridor was empty. Off to the right, where another hallway angled out, she thought she could hear footsteps drawing away. "Who's there?" she called out again. The footsteps stopped. When Kay, her own footsteps echoing, moved forward to see around the corner, she heard whoever it was ahead begin walking again. Kay turned the corner into a corridor that would have been completely dark but for sunlight streaming through the slats of a drawn window blind. Ahead she saw a door just swinging shut. Kay stopped, the heat of the bands of sunlight on her like fiery fingers, and stared at that door. Who had it been? she wondered, her eyes narrowing slightly. One of the other teachers? A student, perhaps? She started to step forward and then paused. A sudden chill had passed through her. Go back to your office, she told herself. You've got a lot of work to do yet. Go back. Go back. Go back. You're being damned ridiculous, she heard another voice within her say. Are you getting scared of shadows now, like . . . Evan? No. I'm not. She moved forward and quietly pushed the door open.

Into another corridor.

The dim glow of fluorescents. Closed doors with numbers. Silence. No, not silence, Kay realized after another moment. She could faintly hear the noise of metal clattering, then a rhythmic slapping sound. A wet sound. Kay let the door swing closed behind her, and then, trying to walk as swiftly as possible, she followed those noises. Windows with drawn blinds. A series of frosted glass doors, like hers, with names on them: DR. CLIFFORD, DR. HEARN, DR. PERRY, others. Kay thought for a moment. History professors, weren't they? Yes, this was the history wing of the Arts and Sciences Building. She moved on, listening, feeling that chill working within her again, wanting to turn back yet curious about who it had been standing like a statue before her office door. Those noises of metal just ahead, the rhythmic sound echoing from wall to wall. Kay realized they were coming from the end of the corridor, just around the next corner, where a pocket of afternoon shadows had gathered in wait.

Go back, she told herself.

Then, in the next instant: No, I'm not like Evan. I'm not afraid of shadows.

And then she had gone around the corner, and too late she realized there was someone there, hunched over. A face looked up, eyes widened, mouth coming open.

"Jesus!" the woman cried out shrilly, stepping back and dropping her mop at the same time. The mop handle whacked dully against the floor. She almost lost her balance across the metal bucket that lay at her feet, filled with sudsy water. "Jesus!" the cleaning woman said again, trying to recover herself. "Oh, you scared the very life out of me, creeping up on me like that out of nowhere! Oh, my heart's just pounding!"

"I . . . I'm sorry," Kay said, her face flushing. "I didn't

mean to frighten you. I'm terribly sorry. Are you okay?"

"Oh, God, I've got to get my breath." She put her shoulder against the wall and took a few deep lungfuls of air. She was a stocky woman with white hair and a heavily lined face. "Usually there's nobody around here this time of the afternoon," she said. "I don't expect anybody to come creepin' up on me like one of those haunts on the late show!"

"Please," Kay said, feeling foolish and embarrassed. "I didn't mean to scare you or anything like that. I was just . . . looking around."

"Been a long time working here," the cleaning woman said, "and nobody's ever scared the life out of me like that! What were you walking so soft for?"

"I didn't know I was."

"You sure were! Oh, Lord have mercy!" She suddenly looked full into Kay's face with dark eyes. "Are you a student here? All the teachers are gone home for the day."

"No, I'm not a student. I'm Kay Reid, and I'm a math teacher."

The woman nodded. "Oh. Well, Myrna Jacobsen cleans up the math wing. I didn't remember ever seeing you before. No need for me to have." She paused a moment more, shook her head, and bent to pick up her mop. "My back's not like it used to be. Guess my nerves are shot, too. But it's so quiet here in the afternoons, you see, I just naturally thought that nobody was around."

"I see," Kay said. "Really, I'm sorry."

"It's okay, it's okay," the woman said, taking another deep breath and then going back to her mopping.

Kay started to turn away and then stopped herself. "You weren't over in the math wing by any chance, were you?"

"Me? No, not me." She looked at Kay with caution in her eyes. "Myrna works over there, like I said. Nothing's missing, is it?"

Kay shook her head.

Relief flooded back. "That's good to hear. Myrna's a pretty nice lady, and a good worker, too." She threw herself back into the circular swirling of the mop; the wet strands slapped against the tiles.

"Someone was over there a few minutes ago," Kay persisted. "I was just curious."

"You must mean Dr. Drago," the woman said.

"Dr.—who?"

"Drago." The woman motioned with her head. "She came through here a minute ago. Only she was walking loud, so I could hear. Her classroom's just down there, number one-oh-two."

"Who is she?"

"I don't know what she does. Just teaches, I guess. History." More mopping, the mop slap-slapping on the floor.

Kay didn't know the name, but then she didn't know any of the history staff. She could see the door with 102 on it just ahead. "Is this Dr. Drago in her classroom right now?"

The woman shrugged, more interested in her work now. "Don't know. I saw her go in, though."

Kay moved past her. "Watch the wet floor!" the woman called after her. Kay stepped over wet smears and pushed open the door of 102. What she saw stunned her for a moment. It was a large amphitheater-type class, with seats in a semicircle around a lectern. Long windows were now curtained, and glass spheres suspended from the ceiling glowed with pale white light. Kay stood at the top of the amphitheater for a few seconds, looking around, and then slowly walked down the carpet-covered steps toward the lectern. This classroom made her own look minuscule, and the temptation to stand at that lectern, gazing out across the seats, was too strong. She stepped up onto the speaker's platform and ran her hand along the face of the wooden lectern. Then she stood as a teacher would, hands gripping the lectern's sides, looking out upon the empty amphitheater. How many students would sit in this classroom? Over a hundred, certainly. She gazed across the room. There was no one here at all; if Dr. Drago had come into the room, she'd left before Kay had entered. On the far side of the dais where the lectern stood there was another door, and above it a green-glowing exit sign, probably leading out into the parking lot.

And Kay was about to step down from the platform when a cool, unhurried voice said, "No. Stay there. You look very natural."

Kay's head came up sharply, but she couldn't see who'd spoken. Nevertheless, she didn't move from where she stood. "I . . . I can't see where you are," Kay said.

There was silence for a few seconds. Then, "I'm here."

Kay looked to the right. There was a woman walking down from the top of the amphitheater; Kay knew she hadn't seen the woman because one of those glass spheres had been in the way, and it unnerved her now that she'd been observed without realizing it.

The woman approached Kay. "You seem very comfortable there. As if you're at home behind that lectern." Her voice was well-modulated and compelling, with a hint of a foreign accent that Kay found difficult to identify.

"I was just . . . curious," Kay said, watching her as she came nearer. "I wanted to know what it felt like."

"Yes. I began like that as well. Quite interesting, isn't it? Now imagine one hundred and twenty students watching and listening. Does that stir something within you? I think it probably does." Still coming nearer, light beginning to rest on her features.

Kay nodded, tried to smile and found it difficult. "I didn't mean to . . . to wander in here. I was looking for someone."

"Oh? Who?"

"Dr. Drago," Kay said.

The woman stood just below her, at the foot of the dais. "Then I believe you've found me," she said quietly. And Kay found herself looking into the woman's eyes. Dr. Drago was, Kay guessed, in her early forties; she was a tall, large-boned woman, but she moved with the fluid grace of an athlete, smoothly and powerfully. A mane of ebony hair was swept back from a rather square-jawed face, and veins of gray swirled from the temples toward the back of the head. Her face was tawny-colored and smooth, with only a few lines around the eyes and the mouth; she looked to Kay as if she spent a great deal of time outside in the sun, but without the premature aging that prolonged exposure to the sun brought on. In this woman's face there was a purpose and a strength of will that Kay could almost feel physically. But it was Dr. Drago's eyes that, oddly, both disturbed and compelled her; they were deep-set and clear, an aquamarine color like the depths of distant oceans. Kay's own gaze seemed locked with this woman's, and she felt her heartbeat suddenly increase. Though Dr. Drago was dressed simply, in pressed denims and a powder blue blouse, she wore the ornaments of the wealthy: glittering gold bracelets on both arms, a couple of gold chains about her throat, a dazzling sapphire ring on her right hand. No wedding ring.

"Kathryn Drago," the woman said. She smiled and offered her hand. Bracelets clinked together. "And please call me Kathryn."

Kay took the woman's hand, found it rough-fleshed and cold. "I'm—"

"Kay Reid," the woman said. "You live in Bethany's Sin, don't you?"

"Yes, that's right. On McClain Terrace. How did you know?"

"I live there too. And I'm always interested in the newcomers to our village. You're married, aren't you? And your husband's name is . . . ?" She waited for the answer.

"Evan." Kay picked up the cue, trying to look away from Dr. Drago's gaze and finding it all but impossible.

"Evan," she repeated, letting the name rest on her tongue as if it were food to savor. "A nice name. Do you have children?"

"A little girl," Kay told her. "Laurie." She thought Dr. Drago's eyes widened, very slightly, but she couldn't be certain. "We've only been in the village for about a month." Those eyes riveted her; she couldn't blink, and she felt her own eyes going dry.

"Oh? And how do you find life in the village?"

"Quiet. Restful. Very nice."

Dr. Drago nodded. "Good. That's good to hear. Many families come to Bethany's Sin and yearn for the cities again. That I've never been able to understand."

"No," Kay said. "I wouldn't understand that, either. Bethany's Sin seems . . . perfect." What was it about this woman that made her heart beat so hard, hammering in her chest? What was it that made her blood thick and sluggish? She started to step down.

"Please," the woman said. "Stay there, won't you? Imagine yourself here with all those seats filled. Imagine them waiting for you to speak. Imagine them wanting a part of your knowledge for themselves."

Kay blinked. Dr. Drago was smiling slightly, a friendly smile, but those eyes above her mouth were . . . strange and cold. Burning through her now. Strange. Very strange. I'm not like Evan. No, I'm not. Not afraid of shadows. Who is this woman? Why does she . . . look at me like that?

"This is my classroom," Dr. Drago said matter-of-factly. "I'm the head of the history department here."

Kay nodded, impressed. "That must be a big responsibility." Eyes burning. What was it?

"Yes, it is. But a great deal of reward as well. I find a great pleasure in exploring the mysteries of the past. And passing those mysteries along to my students."

Kay's heart was beating fast, and her face felt hot. "Isn't it air-conditioned in here?" she asked, or thought she asked, because Dr. Drago didn't answer, only continued smiling at her.

"What's your field?" she asked Kay after another moment.

"Math," Kay said, or thought she said. She put a hand to her cheek. Her flesh wasn't hot, as she expected, but cool. "I'm teaching an algebra class."

"I see. You shouldn't have much difficulty with that. The summer semester's very quiet."

. . . very quiet very quiet very quiet. The words seemed to be ringing within Kay's head. Damn it! she thought suddenly. I'm coming down with something. A cold? Dr. Drago's eyes gleamed like beacons. "I live outside the village," the woman said. "One of the first houses you pass on the way in."

"Which house?"

"You can see it from the road. There's a pasture with—"

"Horses," Kay said. "Yes, I see it every day. It's beautiful; I don't think I've ever seen a house quite like that one before."

"Thank you." The woman paused for a few seconds,

examining Kay. She touched Kay's hand again with her own. "Aren't you feeling well?"

"I'm fine," Kay lied. She felt chilled and hot at the same time, and unable still to look away from the woman who stood before her. Her heart beat fast, like a captured bird's. "I seem to be a little dizzy, that's all."

She patted Kay's hand in a sisterly fashion. "I'm sure it's nothing to be concerned about," she said. And then she blinked and the link between them was broken. Kay felt as if a burden had been taken off her shoulders; she felt weary though, and still strangely cold. She looked away quickly from the woman's face, and stepped off the speaker's platform. "You're all right now?" Dr. Drago asked, softly.

"Yes. I am. But I've got test papers to grade back in my office. I'd better be going. It was very good to meet you, and I hope I'll see you again." She wanted to hurry out of there, hurry out of the history wing; she wasn't going to grade any more papers. She was going to get to her car and drive home and lie down. Her blood seemed to be cold, and there was some kind of strange tingling sensation at the base of her neck, as if Dr. Drago's rough fingers caressed her there. Kay began walking up the stairs, and the woman followed her.

"I hope you continue to find the village to your liking," she said when they reached the top. "Where did you and your husband move here from?"

"LaGrange," Kay told her. "It's a mill town." They walked together out into the hallway. Dr. Drago loomed over her, her face now daubed with shadows around the eyes and in the hollows of the cheeks.

"I've heard of it," she replied, and smiled again. "A smudge pot, isn't it?"

"An accurate description." Kay almost caught those eyes again, and instinctively looked away. I'm not afraid. What's wrong with you? She thought she was getting one of her headaches again, but it was just that tingling at her neck. Fading now. Fading. Thank God; I thought I was going to be sick there for a minute. "I'd better get back to work now."

"Of course," Dr. Drago said. Kay turned away and began walking back toward the math wing, but suddenly the other woman said, "Mrs. Reid? Kay? I'd like to ask something of you."

Kay turned; shadows had gathered across the woman's face, obscuring those eyes. Strange. Very strange. "Yes?"

"I was wondering . . . well, I'm having a few faculty members over on Saturday evening. If you could, I'd very much like to have you and your husband over."

"A party? I don't know. . . ."

"Not really a party. Just a little informal gathering. Conversation and coffee." She paused for a few seconds. "It would give you a chance to meet some of the others."

"It sounds nice, but I'll have to talk to Evan about it. I could let you know."

"My number's in the book. I'd love to have both of you over."

Kay hesitated. She was feeling okay now, the tingling and the chill subsiding. Her heartbeat slowing to normal. You were nervous, she rationalized to herself. Nervous as hell. "Thank you," she said finally. "I'll call you."

"Please do," Dr. Drago said. She stood without moving for a moment. Behind the veils of shadow, those strange aquamarine eyes were glittering. And without speaking again, Dr. Drago turned away and disappeared toward the other end of the corridor.

For a long time Kay didn't move. She was staring fixedly in the direction the woman had gone. I want to go to that party, she told herself. I want to meet the others. She was certain Evan would say it was okay, but even if he didn't, she would still go—alone if she had to.

Because in the last few minutes Kathryn Drago had made Kay feel that she belonged in Bethany's Sin, perhaps more than she'd belonged anywhere else. Ever.

FOURTEEN

TALES SPOKEN IN A WHISPER

"Bethany's Sin?" Jess screwed his diamond blue eyes up in thought and grunted. "No, I don't guess I've ever really sat down and done much thinking about it. Just seems like a name to me."

"Sure," Evan said, and leaned forward slightly in his chair. "But what's behind the name? What does it mean?"

Jess was silent for a moment, rolling a cigarette from a pouch of tobacco. They were sitting together in the office of the Gulf service station on Fredonia, drinking Cokes from the machine out front. In the garage Jess's son was muttering over a red Volkswagen, every once in a while circling it as if sizing up an opponent before attacking it again with his wrenches. Only a few cars had come in while Jess and Evan talked; a family had driven in for directions, and Evan had seen in the eyes of the man's wife that same expression he'd seen in Kay's the first day they'd driven through the village. Of course Evan knew why; it was a beautiful place, and its beauty would naturally appeal to women.

Evan had gotten some important mail that morning. *Fiction* magazine had accepted his short story about two former lovers, elderly now, meeting by chance on a train. And as they talked, reliving old memories, the train began to stop at stations farther and farther back in time, until at last, when they realized their love was still strong, the train stopped at Niven Crossing, their old hometown, back in the year they'd first fallen in love under summer stars on the shore of Bowman's Lake.

Evan's other mail wasn't good. A rejection from *Esquire*. That story, about a Vietnam veteran whose wife and friends had begun to take on the appearance of peo-

ple he'd killed during the war, had been terrifying for
Evan because it probed at those raw, unhealed scars
where the nerves of fear and guilt lay so close to the surface. He'd decided that he needed the distance of time to
be able to say anything articulate about Vietnam; everything he'd written so far had emerged as disorganized,
ragged screams of pain.

Perhaps he would always carry that scream within him;
it was his burden from the war, his memory of young men
ripped down like wheat beneath the dark master's scythe,
of bodies without faces or arms or legs, of shell-shocked
soldiers screaming without voices, of himself lashed to a
cot with the touch of a spider on his skin and, much later,
standing alone amid mortar fire, waiting for God's next
blow to fall. It had been very difficult readjusting to the
world after he'd come home, because it all seemed so unreal. No one leaped for cover from incoming mail; no one
screamed for medics to help hold their falling intestines in
place; no one counted the stars in the sky and wondered
if tomorrow night they'd still be there to repeat the exercise. No one seemed to really know what was going on,
or for that matter really to give a damn. And that both in-
furiated and crushed Evan, that so many had died like
little patriotic Jesuses while all the Judases at home
counted their coins. That was how he remembered Harlin, his editor at *Iron Man*: a fucking Judas of the worst
kind. From the very start of that job, Harlin, a hulking
man with a crew cut and a long lower jaw, had made it
tough for him. "You were over in Vet-Nam, huh? See
much action?" Evan had said yes. "I took on the Nazis in
World War Two. Fought in France. Got those goddamned
Nazis by the balls. Damn, but those were good times."
Evan had remained silent. "Yes sir, you can say anything
you want. But by God there's nothing better than fighting
for your country." After a long while Harlin had turned
interrogator, wanting to know how many Cong Evan had
killed, if he'd ever used napalm on any in their hutches,
if he'd ever killed any of those villagers, because by God
they all fucking look alike, anyway, don't they? Evan had
pointedly ignored him, and by degrees Harlin had grown
surly and then savage, asking him if he was certain he'd
done any fighting and why he never liked to talk about it

and why he hadn't at least brought his wife home, a fucking earlobe, for Christ's sakes?

And through this veil of savagery Evan began to see glimmers of the truth in his dreams: Harlin standing before him, his face as pale as chalk-and of the consistency of clay. Very slowly Harlin's face began to melt, as if bubbling from a vast center of volcanic hatred within the man; cheesy strings of flesh fell, sections of his face splitting away and dropping to the floor: a hooked nose, a lower lip, a jaw. Until all that was left were two hideously staring eyes set in a skull with the scalp still attached to it. And that Harlin-thing, drooling vile, dark fluids, was moving toward Kay as she slept in the bedroom of the house she and Evan had rented in LaGrange. The Harlin-thing unzipped its pants and a scaled, erect penis had risen into view, throbbing for Kay's flesh. And just as Harlin was about to throw the sheets back from Kay, Evan had awakened, gasping for breath.

It had been at a Christmas party for *Iron Man* staffers and their wives that the terror within Evan had come to a head, like a boil about to break. Harlin had begun badgering him about the war, wanting to know how many of his friends had died, and then, after Harlin had drunk a half-bottle of whiskey, wanting to know how much "little gook cunt" Evan had scored, Evan had pushed him away, and Harlin's twisted emotions had risen quickly, like a snake whipping up from a dark hole. "You're a goddamned liar," Harlin had said menacingly, as people stopped talking and drinking and turned to listen. "What d'you think you are, some kind of war hero or somethin'? I did more than you by God and you know what they give me? A pat on the back and a kick in the ass. And by God my son Jerry bless him bless my son Jerry was raised right, raised to fight for his country like a man ought to do, and he volunteered to go to Vet-Nam, didn't want to be fucking drafted, no, but volunteered because his old man said that was the right thing to do. I saw him off on the train, and we shook hands like men because when a boy's eighteen then he is a man. And you know where he is now?" Harlin's eyes had glistened for an instant, just an instant, then had burned into Evan's brain with renewed fire. "That VA hospital in Philadelphia.

Half his head gone. Just sits there, never says a word, can't feed himself, pisses his pants like a goddamned baby! And the last time I went to see him he just sat at the window and didn't look at me, like he blamed me and hated me. Hated me! And look at you, by God, standing here with a fucking eggnog in your hand and a tweed coat and a tie on and you think you're a fucking war hero, don't you?" Here the others tried to quiet him, and Evan took Kay's hand for them to go, but the man wouldn't stop. "You're not a man!" Harlin croaked. "If you were you'd be proud of killing those goddamned gooks that shot my Jerry! You're not a man, you cockless bastard! Hey!" He focused his eyes on Kay. "Hey! Maybe I'll show you what a real cock looks like someday, huh?"

And here the dream image had burst into Evan's mind, and he'd moved with relentless, terrifying speed, past Kay before she could stop him, past two other people in the way, his face contorting as the terrible things began to come up and take control of him. His arm had whipped out, faster than anyone's eyes could follow, and he'd gripped Harlin around the throat, spun him backward, and knelt to snap his spine over his knee. He'd heard and dimly remembered someone screaming and realized that madman's voice was his own. And Kay had screamed "Nooooooo!" in the instant Evan had started to apply pressure to kill Harlin in the same fashion he'd killed a young Cong who had probably been no older than nineteen. They'd wrestled Evan away from Harlin, and it was then that Kay had dissolved into soul-wracking tears. Not long after that, Evan had lost his job, been fired for "sloppiness and neglect of duty," and they'd left LaGrange.

My God, Evan thought now, in the Gulf station office, that seems like ages ago. But he knew that killer instinct he'd shown had never and would never go away; it was too deeply ingrained now, it was the black part of him that he kept hidden away, under strict lock and key.

In the past few days he'd again turned his attention to a story on the village. He'd written a letter of inquiry to *Pennsylvania Progress,* asking them if they'd be interested in something on Bethany's Sin. He'd had no answer yet, but why not try to find out what he could in the meantime? So he'd found himself guiding the conversation with Jess onto the subject of Bethany's Sin, particularly anything the man might know about the origin of that name.

Jess lit his cigarette and pulled at it. "I don't know," he said. "Do you think maybe they've got some records or something over at the library?"

"Maybe so," Evan said; he'd already decided to check the library on the walk home. "But I thought perhaps, working here, you might have heard stories, gossip, something that could help me out."

Jess grunted and smoked in silence for a while. Evan didn't think he was going to reply, and the next time Evan glanced over at him, Jess's eyes seemed to have darkened a few shades, retreated back into his head as if shrinking from the sunlight. Smoke dribbled from his nostrils, and he leaned back against a couple of crates of Valvoline oil. "There's a place up on the King's Bridge Road a few miles," he said finally. "Lot of locals hang around there. A roadhouse called the Cock's Crow. A man can hear some pretty interesting tales if he's got his ears open. Some of 'em tall tales, some of 'em . . . well, worth thinking about, if you know what I mean."

Evan didn't. "What kind of tales?"

"Man named Muncey ran this station before I came here," Jess said quietly, his eyes hooded and distant, avoiding Evan's. "I got the job because one day the man just didn't show up. He had a wife and two kids, lived in a trailer a couple of miles east of here. They didn't know where he was, either. A few weeks afterward, the troopers found the man's car, pulled out into the woods and covered over with brush." He paused, smoking his cigarette.

"What about the man?" Evan urged.

"Never found him. At first, see, they thought he'd run off with the cash receipts, just left his wife and kids and run for it." Jess shook his head. "But that wasn't so. The troopers found the cash, all bundled up in those bags the bank gives you for delivery, underneath the front seat. The window on the driver's side was broken out, and the windshield was cracked—that's what I heard from some of the locals at the Cock's Crow, and maybe they're wrong. But maybe they're not."

"That's bad," Evan said, "but I guess people disappear all the time. It's an unfortunate fact of life."

"Unfortunate. Right." Jess smiled slightly, and then the smile slithered away. "No, more than that. The sort of thing that happened to Muncey—whatever it was—has happened before around here. And more than two or three times. Enough to make a man wonder."

"Wonder? About what?"

"About what he doesn't know," Jess said, still speaking quietly and calmly, but his eyes brooding. "You hang around up at the Cock's Crow, you'll hear those stories. And you'll wonder about them the same as me. Some of the locals have seen things at night. Strange things; and they've heard strange callings in the woods, too, and heard things moving fast through the brush. Things they were scared of seeing too close."

Evan felt a chill run along his spine. He remembered the first night in his house, the fleeting image he'd seen pass the window. What had that been?

"Yes sir," Jess said. "The Cock's Crow. You hang around there a few nights and you'll know what I mean."

"Sounds like somebody has an overactive imagination," Evan said, probing for more details. Overactive imagination: how many times had Kay applied that phrase to him? More times than he could count.

"Not imagination," Jess said. "No. Me, I've never seen any of these things they tell me about. Couple of times on the drive home, my boy and me thought we'd heard peculiar cries out in the woods, but we passed it off as birds or some kind of animal. But you get close to somebody who's had a brush with the things and you look deep into their eyes and then you come back and talk about imagination. No. What you'll see there is fear, pure and simple. Now I'm not saying that Bethany's Sin isn't a nice and pretty little place. But I've been working here for a while and I've gotten a feeling about it. A feeling I don't like. That something . . . well, that something's not right around here. Like too much paint and varnish over wood that's gone rotten." Jess turned his head slightly and looked into Evan's eyes. "I stay away from this place after night falls," he said. "And I stay off the back roads."

For a long while Evan said nothing. Words weren't needed; he could see a message in this man's face. A warning, perhaps? Troubled currents churned within him, icy, gathering force. Abruptly, Jess turned away. A car was pulling into the station, and Jess left his chair to pump gas.

On the walk home, Evan stopped at the library. The librarian, a pretty young brunette with ANNE on her name tag, listened to Evan's questions about the origin of the name Bethany's Sin and jotted down his request on a piece of paper. Then she came out from behind her desk and led him over to a shelf marked REGIONAL INTEREST. She pulled down the worst of three ratty-looking books and gave it to him; it was titled *Names and Places: Pennsylvania's Village Heritage*. Bethany's Sin wasn't listed in the index, though, and turning to the date of publication, Evan found the book was published in the late thirties. He returned it to the librarian with a polite thank-you and asked her if she knew of any place he might be able to find records on the history of Bethany's Sin; she smiled and said that was a new one on her, but perhaps there might be some old papers in the basement. Why don't you give me your name and telephone number? she asked him; I'll take a look and call if anything turns up.

On the way out, Evan's attention was caught by a framed etching that hung near the front door. He paused for a moment, then approached it for a better look. It showed a woman bearing a bow with a quiver of arrows hanging at her side; at her feet what looked like wolves followed her, not menacingly but with expressions of loyalty. Forest filled the background, and above her left shoulder was the pale oval of the moon. Beneath the etching there was a brass plaque: PRESENTED TO THE WALLACE PARKINS PUBLIC LIBRARY BY DR. KATHRYN DRAGO. Evan looked into the face of the woman in the etching; it was calm and purposeful, the eyes mirroring an inner strength of will. He glanced down at the plaque again. Dr. Kathryn Drago? He wasn't familiar with the name, but the etching she'd donated strangely compelled him.

"It's from the seventeenth century," Anne the librarian

told him; she'd come up from behind while he'd been staring at the etching. "If you're interested in art, we have quite a large selection. . . ."

"Who is that supposed to be?" Evan asked her.

"The Greek goddess Artemis," Anne said. "I think. I'm not up on my mythology like I should be." She smiled apologetically.

"Mythology?" Evan paused for a moment, looking into those eyes that stared out from the etching. "I once took a course in that. A long time ago. But I can't remember anything about this one. It seems like Greek deities crawled out of the woodwork. Who's this Kathryn Drago?"

"Dr. Drago," Anne corrected. "She was voted in as mayor a few years ago, and she founded the village's historical society back in . . . oh, I guess that's got to be five or six years."

"Mayor?" Evan raised an eyebrow. "I didn't realize Bethany's Sin's mayor was a woman."

"She lives outside the village," Anne told him. "And she raises horses."

Horses? Evan thought for a moment, remembering that strange house and the horses grazing on the wide swath of pastureland. "Oh, yes," he said. "I've seen that place. That etching must have been a very expensive gift."

"I'm sure it was. Now. Can I show you our art books?"

"No, thanks," he said. "Some other time, maybe." And then he was out the door and walking in the sunlight again, his mind turning in angles like a runner trying to find his way through a darkened labyrinth. Horses? Mythology? Something working in his brain, then slipping quickly away before he could grasp it. The Greek goddess Artemis. He caught himself, almost turned back to the library to ask the librarian if they had any books on mythology, and then shrugged off the impulse, continued walking back toward McClain Terrace. Other things weighed too heavily on him right now. Like the origin of Bethany's Sin. If he couldn't find out about it by reading, he'd have to find out by listening to some of those tales Jess said circulated around the Cock's Crow. His mind began to wander, and he found himself thinking about horses again. His experience with them had been limited to riding shuffling, broken-spirited ponies at county fairs when he was a child. But another memory pricked his brain like a thorn. The shape he'd seen from his bedroom window that first night: dark, moving rapidly, almost out of view before he'd been able to register it. Could that have been a horse and rider? Possibly, he thought. Possibly.

His face began to burn. The sunlight assaulted it as if searing flesh already burned raw. He looked around, saw horses, trees, streets, but he seemed not to be able to recognize where he was. Blair? No, not yet. Walking deeper into the village as if drawn into it, one leg following the next. The sun glinting sharply through the trees, hurting his eyes. His heartbeat picking up, a heat circulating across his face with the flow of blood, burning, burning, burning. . . .

And abruptly he stopped.

The museum lay before him.

For a few minutes Evan couldn't move; his muscles wouldn't respond to the commands of his brain, and everything around him seemed ablaze with light. He remembered his dreams, and a finger of ice slipped through the curtain of heat to touch his throat very gently. Coming true? Coming true like they all did, eventually, in one way or another? The house waited for his approach in dark, grave silence. He wanted to turn away, to retrace his steps, to start again somehow from the library; but his path had been predetermined, and his steps had led him here to this waiting, beckoning house. He was afraid of it, and the fear writhed inside him, a dark, formless shape gone out of control; in the next moment he started to cross Cowlington toward the museum, and a car honked and veered away from him. Evan walked slowly and laboriously, his breath coming raggedly; he stopped for a moment at the gate and then pushed it open. As he stepped through, he felt the heat on his face even more intensely. His movements seemed heavy and dreamlike; his eyes were focused on the doorway centered beneath a columned arch, and though a voice in his soul screamed for him to turn back, he knew he must follow the directions of his dream. He must reach that door and . . . yes, open it. To see. To see what lay within.

He stood before the door, his senses vibrating, his face pinpointed with sweat. Above him loomed the museum, casting a spiderish shadow on the impeccable green lawn. Very slowly he lifted his arm, his eyes widening, widening because he knew what lay inside: a thing with gleaming, hate-filled eyes that would reach out to him with a clawlike hand. He put his hand against the door, feeling his nerves shriek. And he pushed.

But the door wouldn't open. It was locked from within.

He pushed again, harder, then took his fist and struck the wood; he could hear the sound of the blow echoing inside, echoing through long corridors filled with . . . what? Junk, Mrs. Demargeon had said. Just old junk.

Evan struck the door again. And again. No, this wasn't in the dream. Something was wrong. This wasn't the way it was supposed to be. Open and let me see you. Open. Open, damn you. Open!

"Hey!" someone called out. "What are you doing there?"

Evan turned toward the voice, blinking his eyes into focus.

There was a police car pulling up to the curb in front of the house. A man in uniform got out and began to stride hurriedly toward him. "What are you doing there?" the man asked again.

"I'm . . . Nothing," Evan said, his voice sounding strained and distant. "Nothing."

"Yeah? Well, what are you doing here, then?" The man wore a sheriff's uniform, and in his broad face, hard eyes caught Evan's and held them.

"I was just . . . going inside," Evan said.

"Inside?" Oren Wysinger's eyes narrowed. "They're closed for the day. They're not open on a regular schedule, anyway." He paused for a moment, looking into the man's eyes and seeing something there that disturbed him, as if a pool of water had begun rippling suddenly and there was no way of knowing what had moved beneath the surface. "Who are you?" Wysinger asked quietly.

"Reid. Evan Reid. I . . . live over on McClain Terrace."

"Reid? The new family just moved in?"

155

"That's right."

"Oh." Wysinger dropped his gaze away from Evan's. "Sorry I was so abrupt, Mr. Reid. But not many people come here, and when I saw you hammering at the door I didn't know what was going on."

"It's okay." Evan ran a hand over his face, feeling the heat in his flesh dying away now, degree by degree. "I understand. I was curious about this place."

Wysinger nodded. "It's closed up," he said. "Hey, are you feeling all right?"

"I'm . . . tired. That's all."

"I don't see a car. Are you walking?"

Evan nodded. "I was on my way back to McClain."

"You want a lift? I was driving that way."

"All right," Evan said. "That would be fine."

They walked back across to the police car. Evan turned and stared at the museum for a moment, then tore his gaze away and closed the car door behind him. Wysinger started the engine and drove toward McClain. "I'm Oren Wysinger," he said, offering Evan one large, rough, seamed hand. "I'm sheriff in the village; sorry I didn't recognize you back there. Guess I'm just distrustful by nature."

"You were doing your job."

"Well, yeah," Wysinger said, "but sometimes I suppose I can get carried away. You feeling any better now."

"Yes, thanks. I don't know what was wrong with me. I was very tired and I . . . anyway, I'm okay now."

"Good." Wysinger turned his head slightly, glanced at the man's profile and then back at the street. "The museum opens at nine on Mondays, Wednesdays, and Fridays. Sometimes on Tuesdays, too. It just depends on a lot of things: the weather, how many people are working on the staff that particular day, things like that. You sure seemed in a hurry to get in there."

"I didn't know it was locked," Evan said. He could feel Wysinger's eyes on him; then the man looked away again. "I'd like to see what's inside," he said.

"It's pretty interesting, if you like that kind of thing," Wysinger told him. "Statues and stuff. I find it on the dry side myself."

"What kind of statues?"

Wysiger shrugged. "To me a statue's a statue. There are other things, too. Old stuff."

"Tell me something," Evan said. "Bethany's Sin is such a small village, I find it strange that there should be such a large museum. Or a museum at all, for that matter. Who built it?"

"The house itself's been here for a long time," Wysinger said. "The historical society went in and remodeled it, tore out a lot of the smaller rooms and widened the hallways. Added another floor, too." He turned onto McClain. "It's the white house with the green, isn't it?"

"That's right. So where did the historical society get those things to display inside?"

"I don't really know, Mr. Reid. To tell you the truth, I don't turn in the same circles with those ladies in the society. I'm kind of out of touch, I guess you could say." He slowed the car and turned toward the curb.

"Are they local relics?" Evan persisted. "Indian artifacts?"

Wysinger smiled slightly. "I couldn't tell you Indian from Japanese, Mr. Reid. You'll have to go over there when they're open sometime and see for yourself." He stopped the car at the curb in front of Evan's house. "Here we are. Nice house you've got yourself there."

Evan climbed out and closed the door, and Wysinger leaned over to roll down the window. "Sorry I haven't been by to welcome you to the village. My work keeps me pretty well wrapped up, though. I'll look forward to meeting your wife and kids sometime."

"Just one," Evan said. "A little girl."

"Oh. Again"—Wysinger shrugged— "sorry I came on strong over at the museum."

"That's okay."

"Fine, then. I'd better get back. You take care of yourself, now. Be seeing you." Wysinger raised a hand and then drove away along McClain, turning back for the village and disappearing.

Evan walked along the path toward his front door, glancing over at the Demargeon house. No car in the driveway. The house silent. He wondered if Harris Demargeon was home, almost walked over there, decided not to disturb the man. He took his house key from his pocket and unlocked the front door, stepped into the entrance foyer, closed the door behind him. Kay and Laurie would be home in about a half hour. He went into the kitchen, drank a glass of water, and then sat down in a chair in the den. The manuscript returned by *Esquire* lay on a table beside him and he kept his gaze away from it. He tried to relax but found his muscles still stiff, a strange tingling in his arms and legs as if the blood had just flowed back into them from reservoirs in his heart. For a long time he sat still, his mind weaving together the pieces of a tapestry that he could not yet understand. Imagination? Were his feelings all imagination, just like Kay said? What's this fear inside me? he asked himself. And why in God's name does it seem to be growing stronger day by day, and me weaker?

His mind's eye saw the museum at the center of the village, and everything else turning around it. Then blinked. Jess's eyes, hooded and distant. Blinked again. That picture on the wall in the library, the plaque beneath it. Dr. Kathryn Drago? Another blink. A shadow across a curtained window, the figure missing its left arm. And even when he closed his eyes and leaned his head back, the eye in his mind that saw with a much more terrible clarity remained staring at the picture fragments whirling through his head like sparks thrown off a pinwheel.

For he knew what had happened this afternoon, knew why he'd been drawn to the museum, knew and dreaded the knowledge with an awful certainty. As his premonitions—imagination, Kay would say; imagination you know it's only that and nothing more I don't like to hear you cry out in the middle of the night it makes my head ache—as his premonitions were growing stronger, they were beginning to affect more than his dreams. They were beginning to seep through that curtain between two worlds. The second sight—a gift, his mother had said; a curse, his father had muttered, Eric is dead found him in the field Evan *Why didn't you help him?*—that had come down to him through generations, from his grandfather Frederick and his great-great-grandfather Ephran and God only knew how many others hidden away in the tangle of the family tree, was sharpening, intensifying, frighteningly so. That had never happened before, never, and he wasn't sure how to deal with it. Or where it would lead. As his premonitions became more immediate, would they take control of him, finally breaking entirely free of his dreams and shadowing his steps in the world of the living? Jesus, he thought: he would see everything through the eye of his mind, good or evil, beautiful or dripping with soulless horror. He didn't want to think about that because it made him afraid of what lay ahead. No. Have to control myself, have to keep those things out of myself because if I were overpowered by them what would . . . Kay's reaction be? Horror? Disgust? Pity?

And so he sat in the den, in company with those quick and fleeting visions, until he heard the door come open and Kay and Laurie were home, both smiling and happy and unaware.

FIFTEEN

KAY'S DREAM

"We were invited to a party today," Kay told Evan from the bed; he stood in the bathroom brushing his teeth. "On Saturday night," she added after a few seconds.

He rinsed out his mouth, looked at his teeth in the mirror. Straight and even. He'd never had any problems at all with his teeth, no braces and very few cavities. "Whose party?" he asked.

"The head of the history department at George Ross. Her name is Dr. Drago."

Evan stiffened suddenly, then relaxed and put his toothbrush in its proper place near the drinking cup. He grunted and said, "Did you meet her?"

"Yes, I did. A very strange meeting, too. Someone was prowling around my office this afternoon; or I thought someone was, but I'm probably wrong. Anyway, I met her in her classroom and we talked for a few minutes. Do you remember that large house just outside the village? That's hers."

Evan switched off the bathroom light and walked into the bedroom. Kay sat in bed with her knees up, supporting the July issue of *Redbook*. The soft glow of the night-table lamp at her side cast a canopy of shadows across the ceiling. "A formal party?" he asked her, crossing to the bed.

"No, nothing like that. She said it's just going to be a get-together for some of the faculty members."

He drew aside the sheets and slid into bed, sitting up against his pillow. "What does she look like?"

"Oh, she's dark-haired. Kind of a big woman, I guess." She was silent for a moment, and Evan looked at her. "Her eyes," Kay said. "They're very . . . striking and . . . it's funny. . . ."

"What's funny?"

She shrugged. "Nothing. She's a very distinctive woman. Her gaze is . . . direct, strong. And her eyes are the most beautiful greenish blue I've ever seen. Really."

Evan smiled. "You sound like someone else I talked to today."

"Oh? Who?"

"A woman named Anne, who works over at the library. I've already heard about this Kathryn Drago from her. Did you know she is also the mayor of Bethany's Sin?"

"My God," Kay said in amazement. "How does she find time to plan parties?"

"And she began the historical society that operates that museum over on Cowlington Street. I'd say she has a pretty full schedule, wouldn't you?"

"For sure. But she seems like a very composed, well-organized woman."

"I'd say she has to be. You know, I'm catching in your voice something I heard in that librarian's. A swelling admiration. Of course, I agree the woman's to be admired and respected, but you should have heard the lady at the library. It bordered on hero worship."

Kay was silent for a moment. "There's something about that woman," she said finally, "that commands respect. Yes, that's the word I was looking for, commands. When I stood before her I felt . . . small. As if she were of a huge, looming stature and I was absolutely insignificant. Does that make any sense to you?"

"Awe," Evan said. "It was sheer awe. And maybe a little nervousness about being the new kid on the block."

Kay closed her magazine and put it aside, but she didn't move to turn off the light. Instead, she sat very still for a while, and Evan took her hand and held it gently. "Sorry," she said. "I was thinking about something." Then she lapsed into silence again.

"School? Got some bad boys and girls in your classes?" He saw she was distant, her eyes unfocused and glassy. "Hey," he said softly. "What's wrong?" He waited, then nudged her. "What's wrong?" he asked when she looked at him.

"Thinking. About—and I don't know why—that woman's eyes. The way she stared at me."

Evan stroked her arm, feeling there a tension that seemed to radiate out of her as if a spring were being wound at the center of her soul. Tighter and tighter and tighter. "Her eyes?" he asked, watching her carefully. What is it I'm feeling? he asked himself. Something's wrong.

"Yes. When she stared at me I . . . couldn't move. I really couldn't. Those eyes were so incredibly beautiful and so . . . incredibly strong. I felt very strange on the drive home, as if even my bones were trembling, but by the time I picked up Laurie and got home, the feeling had gone, and instead everything seemed . . . especially right, as if everything's moving as it's supposed to."

"Everything is," Evan said, and kissed her cheek. Her flesh was tight and cool. "Do you want to go to Dr. Drago's party?"

Kay paused. "Yes," she said finally. "I do."

"Okay. We'll go. I'd like to see what this superwoman looks like, anyway. Why don't you turn off the light now?"

She nodded and reached over, switched it off. Darkness eagerly filled the room. Evan moved beneath the sheets for Kay, kissing her cheek again and then her lips, very lightly and gently at first, in the way he knew she liked. Melding his body against hers, holding her tight and soothingly, he kissed her lips and waited for her to respond.

But she didn't. She drew the sheet up around her and, without saying a word to him, moved very slightly away.

He was stung and confused. He wondered if he'd done something wrong: hurt her feelings? inadvertently forgotten something? He started to ask her what was wrong when he realized her flesh was cooling; it startled him at first, but he lay motionless beside her with a hand on her bare shoulder and thought he could actually feel the warmth being drawn from her flesh. She was silent and breathing regularly, but because he couldn't see her face, he didn't know if her eyes were open or closed. "Kay?" he said softly. No answer. "Kay?" Silence.

She didn't move. Evan lay awake beside her for a

long time. Her flesh felt strange: cool and clammy, like the wrinkled flesh of a person who has sat for hours in a tub of tepid water. Or like the cooling flesh of a corpse. Still, her breathing was normal, shallowing now as she slept. Evan leaned over, gently moved Kay's hair away from her face, and looked down at her features. She was a beautiful woman: sensitive, highly intelligent, tender and caring. He knew that he loved her, had always loved her, and he knew also how much he'd hurt her in the last few years, and despised himself for it. She sought above all permanence and security, and Evan realized he'd broken her dreams again and again because of his own insecurities and the raging inner fears that threatened sometimes to leap from his throat. He'd led both Kay and Laurie down one terrible cul-de-sac after another, and the bitter realization of how much he'd shaken both their lives cut to the marrow of his bones. They deserved better than what he'd been able to give them; sometimes he wondered if they might be in better shape without him. But he'd never voiced those thoughts; he'd only considered them.

He looked at Kay awhile longer, then lay back and closed his eyes. As he drifted toward sleep, he thought he felt Kay move suddenly beside him, as if something had disturbed her, but in another moment he decided it must have been his imagination. As the darkness took him, he suddenly envisioned that etching of Artemis in the library. Saw the staring eyes. Thought of Kay's reaction to Kathryn Drago. Drago. Drago. The name thundered hollowly within him.

And then, finally, he slept without dreaming.

But Kay did not.

She had found herself in a strange and foreign place where the sun burned red and high and vultures spun in dark circles above a death-littered plain. Bodies were strewn in bloody heaps, and the trash of battle lay scattered about her feet. But the implements were . . . different. Swords and spears, crushed helmets, battered shields, breastplates. And other things. Dead and dying horses, human arms and legs ripped from their sockets, decapitated trunks of bodies. Here a black-bearded warrior begging for mercy, the blood oozing from a gash in his belly. And Kay found herself approaching the man, and as her shadow lengthened and fell across him, he looked at her with blind terror in his eyes and held up his hands before his face. She stood over him, watching.

And knew that she wanted to destroy him. To reach inside and wrench out his dripping intestines. To grind him beneath her boot.

He spoke, in a dialect Kay didn't understand at first, but then the words seemed to take meaning inside her head: ". . . spare my life . . . in the name of the gods spare my life. . . ."

Kay knew the others were watching. She felt the hate rise within her like bitter bile. "Here is my mercy," she said, her voice sounding low and guttural and not like her own at all. And in the next instant her arm had come down, the weapon grasped in her hand cleaving the air with an eerie whistling noise. The ax blade bit into the warrior's throat, bit deeper, deeper, as a spray of blood arced into the air and the man's mouth came open in a silent scream, deeper, deeper, the blade singing in her grip, deeper.

The head toppled into the bloody sand, mouth still open, rolled a few feet, then lay still. At her feet the body began a death-dance trembling, the neck stump still pumping blood. Until slowly the heart ceased beating. Kay stepped across the corpse, picked up the head by the hair, and lifted it high above her. Blood dripped down onto her shoulder, making an old spear scar appear fresh again. She held the head up before the others and opened her mouth, and from her mouth there came a scream that both terrified and thrilled her, a long, wild, piercing scream that echoed off across the plain. The others took up the war cry until the earth shook with it and there was no other noise in the world. Then she whirled the head above her and flung it to the ground with a force that shattered the skull, making the brains ooze out like brown jelly.

Her horse, huge and lean-flanked, was waiting for her. She reached it in a few strides, swung onto it, and slipped the ax into a lion's-skin pouch that hung across her mount's shoulder. Ahead there was a pall of dust against the horizon. The three point riders were approaching from the horizon, the hooves of their horses throwing up spirals of sand and stepping nimbly, with experience, amid the clutter of war. The riders drew up their mounts, their eyes glittering with excitement and blood lust, and one of them, Demondae the Dark, pointed to the west and said the last of the enemy were crawling on their bellies in the heat now, gnawing sand between their teeth and crying for the touch of death. We can give them death in a single shadow of the sun, Demondae said, her face still splattered with gore from the ax blow that had cleaved an enemy warrior to the spine. Under her the black, gleaming horse moved excitedly, senses still keened by the clash and bellow of battle.

They began to track the enemy into the west, their approach frightening the vultures, which immediately took to the sky, wheeling about the half-eaten corpses of men and beasts.

Kay felt the singing blood and knew it was not her blood that sang. Through eyes slitted against the harsh rays of the sun she looked disdainfully down upon shattered bodies and knew it was not her eyes that saw. A long, jagged scar ran down her left thigh to the knee, the mark of earlier battle, but she knew it was not her flesh that bore the scar. No, no. The blood and eyes and flesh of another. Someone fierce and terrible and hungering for destruction as one hungers for food and drink. Someone who had hacked off a man's head and shouted a war cry ages old. Someone else within her.

Now hunting down prey in the red, streaming rays of the sun. Looking from side to side like an animal scanning the wilds for danger. Drawing a breath: sweet breath, sweet stench of decay and men's blood. Feeling the raw power of the steed between her smooth-muscled thighs. Kay could read this entity's mind, could hear its thoughts and feel its blood flowing through her veins like rivers of carnage. Perhaps I shall take one of them. I shall claim the strongest and drag him back behind my horse like baggage. And then I shall slowly strip the flesh from him as one would strip the flesh . . .

No. Kay heard her own voice as if through a distant, time-lost tunnel. No. . . . from a piece of rotted fruit. Until he screams . . .

Please. No. Please. I want to . . . I can't breathe . . . I want to wake up I want to wake up. . . .

. . . for mercy, and then I shall split his skull . . .

Please. Please. Let me go. Let me go. . . .

. . . and eat the warrior's brains from the cup of bone. I can't breathe I can't . . . I want to . . . I can't . . . please . . .

"Please . . . " Kay heard her voice echoing echoing echoing within her head, and suddenly the field of battle and the searing sun began to melt like an oil painting that had started to run together, the colors merging into a grayness unlike either life or death, and she was coming through a cold, cavernlike place. Something clicked. An orb of light. Not the sun. No more bodies. No field of carnage. Where am I? I don't know I'm lost I'm lost I don't know where I am or who I am or why . . .

"Kay?" Someone spoke softly. A man. The enemy is here, the destroyer of all things good and beautiful. Men. "Kay?"

She tried to focus on him, tried to bring the picture fragments together. For an instant she saw him with a dark beard and eyes widened in horror of her, and a cold, pure, lightninglike hatred ripped through her, but then she heard herself say I'm Kay Reid and I've been sleeping and I've awakened. The dream feeling rippled within her, leaving a tenuous heat in her blood, and then was gone.

"Oh, my God," she heard herself say, and realized she was staring fixedly at the lamp he'd switched on.

"Hey," Evan said, his eyes swollen with sleep. He nudged her lightly. "Where have you been?"

"Where have I . . . been?"

"Yes," he said. "What were you dreaming about? You started thrashing around there, and you were saying something, but it was too low for me to hear."

Kay suddenly reached out for him and held to him tightly. He could feel her heart pounding in her chest.

"Was it a nightmare?" he asked her, genuinely concerned now.

"Oh, God, yes," Kay said. "Just hold me for a minute. Don't say anything, just hold me."

They lay together quietly for a long while. The silence was broken when that dog down the street began to bark.

"Damn dog," Evan said irritably. "Whoever owns it should muzzle the thing at midnight. Are you feeling better now?"

She nodded, but was lying. She felt very cold inside, as if part of her soul had remained in the cavern that had opened for her when she'd first fallen asleep. She felt weak and drained; the same feeling, she realized, that had overtaken her when she'd met Kathryn Drago in the amphitheater. Stop it! she told herself harshly. That doesn't make any sense! It was a nightmare and that's all! But for the first time in her life a sliver of her brain refused to believe that totally, and fear flooded through her like waters that have been swelling behind a dam for years until the dam begins to crack. Just a little bit, but enough to weaken the concrete of reason.

"I thought nightmares were my department," Evan said, trying to cheer her up but realizing at once that he'd said the wrong thing. Her face clouded over with doubt. He was silent awhile longer, still holding her, still feeling the beating of her heart. Whatever it had been had frightened the hell out of her. He said, "Want to talk about it?"

"Not yet. Please."

"Okay. Whenever you're ready." He'd never seen her so disturbed about a dream, for God's sake, because she wasn't like him, and seeing her this way bothered him a great deal because she had always been so strong and logical before.

"You . . . asked me where I'd been," Kay said. "And it seemed like I was really somewhere . . . very different. Or part of me was. I don't know; it's so strange I don't know how to explain it." She paused. The dog barked. Barked. Barked. "I was on a . . . battlefield of some kind. There were bodies and swords and shields lying on the ground. The bodies were . . . mutilated. Headless." She shuddered, and he began to stroke the back of her neck to calm her. "I even . . . killed a man." She tried to smile, but the muscles wouldn't respond; her face felt frozen. "I cut his head off. God, it was so . . . real. Everything was so real."

"Just a dream," he told her. "Not real at all."

"But I could even feel the heat of the sun on me. My body was different; my voice was different. I remember . . ." She pushed back the sheets suddenly to look at her left thigh.

"What is it?" Evan asked, his eyes narrowing.

Her thigh was smooth and unmarked except for a few freckles near the knee. "I had a terrible scar on my leg in that dream. Right there." She touched the leg. "It was so real, so very real! And we were hunting down other men to kill them. . . ."

"We? Who else?"

"Some others." She shook her head. "I can't remember now. But I do know that part of me . . . wanted to find those men. Part of me wanted to destroy them because I hated them as I've never hated anyone in my life. Not just to kill but to tear them to pieces. To . . . oh, it's just too terrible to think about!"

"Okay, okay. Then don't think about it. Come on, lie back on the pillow. That's right. Now. I'm going to turn out the light, okay? And we'll go back to sleep? It was a dream, that's all."

"Funny," Kay said softly. "I remember saying that to you so many times."

Fragments of his own dreams came back to him in a flurry of hideous shapes, like things crawling out of a murk. He shoved them back, closed a mental door against them. Behind that door they roiled malevolently. "Light's going out," he said, and turned it off. Kay drew nearer to him, afraid of that vast empty space between them.

Down McClain Terrace that dog barked on, its voice rising. Then abruptly stopped.

"Thank God for small favors," Evan muttered.

"It was so real!" Kay said, unable to shake the dream images. "I could feel the weight of that ax in my hand! And I could feel the horse moving beneath me!"

Evan lay motionless. "What?"

"I was riding a horse," she said. "A large one. I could feel that strength underneath me. . . ."

"A horse?" he whispered.

She looked at him, hearing something in his voice that she didn't understand. His eyes were open; he was staring blankly at the ceiling.

"Were the others . . . riding horses as well?" Evan asked after what seemed to Kay like long minutes.

"Yes."

He was silent.

"Why does that particularly interest you?" she asked.

"It's nothing. You did know that Dr. Kathryn Drago raises horses, didn't you?"

"Yes, I did."

"There you go, then," he said. "That explains your dream. Or at least part of it. Maybe you're overanxious about attending that party or something; was Dr. Drago in your dream?"

Kay thought for a moment. "No, she wasn't."

"Well, anyway, that explains the part about the horses." He yawned and glanced over at the night-table clock. Ten minutes after four.

Overanxious? Kay wondered, her brow knitting. She had to admit she was nervous about Saturday night; nervous about meeting those people, and nervous, strangely, about being so close to Kathryn Drago again. It was the aura of power that woman radiated, she decided, that unsettled her so much. What would it be like to possess that much power? To have that much influence over other people? She wondered what Dr. Drago's husband would be like. A large man with a powerful, imposing personality? Or the opposite of her: rather small and mild? Certainly wealthy, in either case. It would be interesting to see.

The terror and revulsion of her dream had faded now, and she was sleepy again. Evan hadn't moved for a long while, and Kay assumed he'd fallen asleep. She moved as close as she could to him and let herself drift.

But in the darkness Evan's eyes were still open.

Every so often they moved, as if at the ceiling could be found the way out of a hideous and closing cage.

SIXTEEN

DR. DRAGO'S HOUSE

Long before they reached the wall between the Drago property and the highway, Kay and Evan could see the reflection of lights in the night sky. The wrought-iron gate with the scroll *D* stood open, and Evan turned into the private drive that led through the woods to the house. Ahead, rainbow-colored lanterns were strung through the lower branches of the trees, sparkling like fireflies. And then, where the drive curved slightly, the house came into full view.

The size of it stunned them. They'd seen only the roof that first day on the road, and the view had been misleading: the stone-columned house reminded Evan of some kind of sprawling Greek or Roman fortress, with four two-storyed towers at each corner. He'd never seen anything as large before; his first thought was how much money had been put into it. A million dollars? Two million? More than that? Lights blazed like fires from a myriad windows, reflected again and again from the many cars parked along the drive. Kay felt the ants in her stomach start dancing the two-step. She wondered if it was right for her to have accepted the invitation. There were going to be important people here, influential people who dressed well and spoke the language of stocks and bonds, people of intelligence and ambition with a grip on the turnings of the world. She didn't think her hair looked right, though she'd combed it until it absolutely shone; she didn't think the new beige pantsuit she'd bought the day before at the Westbury Mall did anything for her complexion, though Evan had told her again and again how stunning it looked on her; she didn't think she would fit in with these people, and she was afraid of imagined disasters: perspiration spots beneath her arms, bad breath (the Lavoris bottle in the bathroom, three days old, was already half-empty), ill-chosen remarks in the effort to be charmingly witty.

Evan had told her to relax, that these people wouldn't be any different from them, but she refused to believe it. Evan had bought a new tie to go with his navy blue blazer, gray slacks, and light blue shirt. He'd searched all over Westbury Mall until he'd found one with small gray horses on a field of dark blue.

At the last minute Kay had thought they wouldn't be able to make the party because they hadn't found a suitable sitter for Laurie. Kay had called Mrs. Demargeon to ask if she knew anyone, maybe a teenager who might like to earn ten dollars, but Mrs. Demargeon had insisted on sitting with Laurie herself, and nothing Kay could say would dissuade her. Go ahead and enjoy your party, Mrs. Demargeon had said cheerily. Laurie and I will get along just fine.

And now Evan pulled the station wagon to a halt and cut the engine. "Okay," he said, and squeezed her hand reassuringly, "here we are."

There was a long walkway between immaculate hedges to the large, imposing front door. Evan put his arm around Kay, worked the gleaming brass knocker, waited. They could hear the noise of conversation, laughter, music. A movement behind the door. On the driveway a set of approaching headlights flickered, and a slight breeze made wind chimes tinkle merrily.

The door came open, letting out the chatter and mirth. A figure filled the opening. "Ah, so there you are!" it said. "I was beginning to think you weren't coming. Please . . ." The door opened wider; the figure motioned them in . .

Kay and Evan stepped past the woman into a large, high-ceilinged foyer with a beautiful green-and-blue-tiled floor. Evan could see chandeliers glowing through a series of magnificent rooms filled with obviously expensive furniture and much greenery. There were a few guests milling about in the foyer, all with drinks in hand, but most seemed to be congregating toward the rear of the house.

"Dr. Drago," Kay was saying, "I'd like you to meet my husband, Evan."

And Evan turned toward the woman.

She wore a black floor-length gown and golden bracelets on her wrists; her hair was swept back from her face, and Evan found himself staring with frank fascination into the depths of the most beautiful eyes he'd ever seen. They were unblinking and held his gaze steadily until the woman smiled and held out a red-nailed hand. "Kathryn Drago. Very nice to meet you." He took her hand, felt his bones grind in her grip, but he kept his expression pleasant. Kay realized then how very large a woman she really was: her shoulders were square and almost as broad as Evan's, and she seemed at least an inch taller than he. Now she released Evan's hand, and Evan, still smiling, rubbed the knuckles.

"I'll show you back to the patio," Kathryn Drago said, and led them along a tiled corridor. "Kay, how were your classes this week?"

"Fine," she said. The noise of conversation was nearer.

"They haven't driven you crazy yet, I hope?"

"I think I'll make it."

"Yes," the other woman said, and smiled. "I think you will indeed."

Evan had noticed something strange about the house. There were no framed pictures on the walls; instead, the walls and most of the high ceilings were covered with brightly colored murals depicting pastoral scenes, ruins that might have been ancient Greek temples, sleek-flanked horses running in herds. He'd seen Drago's eyes flicker down briefly to his tie, narrow just a fraction, then move back to his face. And though the woman had been smiling pleasantly enough, Evan imagined he'd caught just a glimmer of something counter to her smile. Something cold and foreign. He watched her as she moved gracefully ahead of him; she was a beautiful woman, there was no doubt about that. But it was more than her beauty that Evan found attractive: from the first he'd sensed a raw sensuality underlying her cool composure. It was something he could almost reach out and touch, and he thought for a moment that he could smell a sexual musk enveloping him there in the mural-walled corridor. He realized suddenly that he was aroused, his senses sharp and alert.

"It's a beautiful house," Kay told the other woman. "Did your husband buy it or have it built?"

Drago laughed huskily. "Husband? No. I'm not married. I had this house built myself."

They came into a wide, stone-floored room with marble columns. There was a bar, behind which a professional-looking bartender in a white jacket was mixing a drink in an electric blender. A few well-dressed couples stood talking around the bar like satellites around a planet, hardly noticing Kay or Evan as they came out of the corridor. But Evan noticed all eyes flickered respectfully toward Dr. Drago. Over in a corner, near a huge fireplace with insets of carved human figures, a trio of musicians—mandolin, guitar, flute—played a foreign-sounding melody—perhaps Spanish or Greek, Evan decided. The music seemed to give life to the forest murals that adorned the walls. Glass doors opened out onto a flagstone patio, where Evan could see forty or fifty other guests; around the perimeter of the patio, torches flickered in the wake of a sudden breeze, their light adding to the ethereal glow of the tree-strung lanterns.

Drago guided them over to the bar. "A drink?" she asked. Evan shook his head no; Kay asked for a gin and tonic. The other woman gazed across the room for a few seconds, and then her eyes met Evan's. "What's your occupation, Mr. Reid?"

"I'm a writer," he told her.

"He's had quite a few stories published," Kay said, taking her gin and tonic as the bartender offered it.

"I see." Again Dr. Drago's eyes moved, very quickly, to Evan's tie. Then back to his face. She was smiling, but Evan could sense a very definite power behind her eyes; now he knew what Kay had been talking about. It seemed that this woman was trying to pick his brain with her gaze. And nearly succeeding, because Evan felt the sudden urge to tell her about his Bethany's Sin project. But he resisted. And imagined for an instant that he saw something flicker in Dr. Drago's gaze—something very brief and sharp, like the dancing of deep blue flames across a gas stove. Evan blinked in spite of himself, and then that strange illusion vanished. The noise of the music seemed louder, more irritating to his senses.

"I didn't realize until recently that you're the mayor of Bethany's Sin," Kay said. "How in the world can you handle that and your duties at George Ross, too?"

"Not without much effort, I promise you," she said, looking at Kay now. "But I suppose that, in all honesty, there's not that much difficulty in managing the affairs of a village the size of this one. And the villagers are all so willing to help, as well." She smiled. "I delegate ninety-nine percent of the work to others."

"What about the historical society?" Evan asked. "That has to take up a lot of time, too, doesn't it?"

She slowly turned her head toward him. Her eyes suddenly seemed heavy-lidded, as if she were regarding him with disdain. She was still smiling, but the smile now appeared cold and calculated. "Ah," she said quietly. "You know more about me than I thought."

Evan shrugged. "Just information I've picked up here and there."

She nodded. "Yes. That's part of your profession, isn't it? Digging, I mean? The historical society . . . takes care of itself."

"I went to the museum a few days ago," Evan continued, watching for this woman's reactions, "but it was locked. Neither Kay nor I have had a chance to tour it. I'm very interested in historical artifacts."

"Are you? That's wonderful. History's a fascinating subject. My life, as a matter of fact. After all, what would the present and the future be without the foundation of the past?"

"I agree. But exactly what kind of relics are inside there? From what period of history?"

She gazed into his eyes for no more than a few seconds. But to Evan it seemed like an eternity. Again he thought he saw that electric flame dance, and mental fingers seemed to be clawing at his skull. The scorching intensity of this woman's gaze caused a pain behind his own eyes. "Very old and valuable artifacts from an archaeological excavation I supervised in 1965, on the southern shore of the Black Sea. They're on extended loan from the Turkish government."

"Archaeology? I understood you were a professor of history."

"Quite so. But archaeology was my first love. When I left field work I drifted more into the study of history." She looked over at Kay for a moment. "Kay, wouldn't you like another drink?"

Kay paused for a few seconds, blinked, then said, "Yes. I would." She gave her glass, still half-filled, to Dr. Drago, who turned away from them to the bar.

"Mr. and Mrs. Reid!" someone said behind them. "How nice to see you!"

They turned to face Mrs. Giles, wearing a flowing gown with golden threads running through it; behind her there was a dark-haired man of medium height in a light brown suit. "This is my husband, David," Mrs. Giles said, making introductions all around. Evan reached out to shake the man's right hand, and David Giles offered his left, turning it around to clasp Evan's hand firmly. It was then that Evan realized, with an icy rush through his veins, that the sleeve of David Giles's right arm was pinned up just below the elbow. He stared at that sleeve for a few seconds dumbly, hearing his heart beat within him like a distant pagan drum of warning.

"Your gin and tonic," Dr. Drago said, giving the glass back to Kay. "Hello, Marcia, David," she said, nodding to them. "I suppose you know the Reids."

"Yes," Mrs. Giles said, "we do."

"Help yourself to whatever you want at the bar," Drago told them. "If you'll excuse me, I'd better make the rounds of my guests. Enjoy yourselves." And then she had gone out onto the patio, leaving that lingering odor of musk around Evan like an invisible, sweet-scented noose.

Kay and Marcia Giles made small talk about the village for a few minutes while Evan studied David Giles; the man seemed ill at ease, his shoulders hunched up as if he were expecting a blow across the back of his neck. He looked to be in his late forties, with dark brown eyes and cheeks that were almost gaunt. He never allowed his gaze to be held by Evan's; always he evaded Evan's eyes, as if fearful of looking at the other man. But it was that pinned right sleeve that disturbed Evan. He remembered the armless figure he'd seen silhouetted against window curtains, and he felt a cold finger, like the touch of steel, along his spine.

"What do you do for a living?" Evan asked the man.

Giles looked up at him as if he hadn't heard. "Pardon me?"

"Your work. What do you do?"

"I . . . sell insurance for Pennsylvania State Equity. We're the company with the big umbrella that covers everything."

"Right," Evan said, and smiled. "I've seen the television commercials. Do you have an office in the village?"

"No, I work out of my home." He paused for a moment, looking around the room. "Marcia's told me about you and your wife. You moved into a house on McClain Terrace?"

"That's right."

"A fine neighborhood," he said. Another pause. "I hope you've found the village to your liking."

"It's an interesting place," Evan said. "Of course, for me any place with secrets is interesting." He said it calmly and slowly, watching the man's face. It showed no reaction, though from the corner of his eye Evan saw Mrs. Giles's head turn slightly toward him.

"Secrets?" Mrs. Giles asked, smiling pleasantly. "What kinds of secrets?"

"I've been doing some research for an article on the village," Evan explained. "There seems to be a secret behind the village's name. Or let's just say it's damned difficult finding out anything about it."

Mrs. Giles laughed softly. What kind of insect does she remind me of? Evan wondered. Something cunning and aggressive. Yes. A praying mantis. "I'm sorry if you've found that to be so," she said. "I could've saved you some bother, I suppose. In the fifties there was nothing here but a few clapboard houses and a general store. But there was one important resident: his name was George Bethany, and he owned a . . . well, let's just say he was a self-made businessman with an eye for the ladies. Some of those ladies he put to profitable labor. On their backs."

Evan raised an eyebrow. "Prostitution?"

"I'm afraid so. His ladies served the farmers and woodsmen in the Johnstown area until the police ran him out of the state. Someone—I don't know who—came up with the name Bethany's Sin in dubious honor of the man. The name stuck, though we've been trying to get it changed for some time now."

Evan shrugged. "Why change it? I think it's very interesting."

"Not quite the image we'd like the rest of the state to see, though." She smiled her praying-mantis smile. "And certainly not what we'd want all Pennsylvania to read about."

"It was just an idea he was working on," Kay said defensively.

"An idea I *am* working on," he corrected her. Then looked again at Mrs. Giles. "How did you find out about all this?"

"Property is my business. I was searching for some old records of ownership in Johnstown when I came across some of the man's . . . professional records. They're stored in the basement of the Johnstown municipal building. At least they were there three—no, four years ago. Might not be there now."

"I'll have to have a look sometime."

"Well, good luck." Mrs. Giles reached over for her husband, touched the stump of his severed arm, and began to caress it. "Though I must say I hope your article remains unwritten. I'm afraid the villagers aren't as open-minded as you might think."

Meaning what? Evan wondered, looking into her flat, stony gaze. That Kay and I might be tarred and feathered and run out of the village? That we'd become social outcasts? Whatever the penalty, the veiled threat was there. Interesting in itself. Evan took Kay's hand. "I think we'll mix and mingle," he told the woman. "It was very good to see you again. And good to meet you." He nodded toward David Giles and saw in that man's eyes an unfathomable and disturbing darkness. He'd seen that empty stare before, and he searched his memory. Yes, of course. The eyes of Harris Demargeon. And the eyes of the men who'd been caged behind bamboo bars in a Vietcong POW holding camp. What could they possibly have in common?

Evan led Kay toward the patio. "What's wrong?" she

asked him as they stepped outside. "You're acting strange."

"Oh? How?"

"Preoccupied. And you were a little rude to Mrs. Giles, weren't you?"

"I wasn't aware of it," he said. "If I was rude, I'm sorry."

"And you stared at her husband's arm as though you'd never seen an amputee before."

Evan grunted. "That's the trouble," he said quietly. "I have."

She looked at him, not understanding. His gaze had darkened, and she quickly looked away so she wouldn't see those strange, haunted things surfacing from the hiding places in his soul. Not here! she told him mentally. Please, for God's sake! Not here!

He put his arm around her. "I'm okay," he said, as if he'd sensed her growing fear. "Really I am." It was a lie. The clockwork mechanisms in his brain had begun to turn around the angles of questions, vague premonitions, feelings he was unable to shake. Can't let her see it, he said to himself. Got to keep myself under control.

And suddenly, from out of the throng of people on the wide, wrought-iron railed patio, another couple stood before them. The man was shorter and stockier than Evan, and perhaps a few years older, with longish sandy brown hair and alert, intelligent-looking blue eyes. A briar pipe was clenched between his teeth, but it didn't seem to be lit. Beside him stood a pretty, petite woman with honey blond hair and attractive green eyes that reflected the lanterns' light from the trees. Somehow they seemed to fit together, though Evan could tell with one glance that they were opposites: he gregarious and outspoken, she more sensitive and thoughtful.

"Don't I know you?" the man asked, looking at Kay quizzically.

"I don't think so. . . ."

"Oh, yes, I do! You're the new math teacher at George Ross, aren't you?"

She nodded, thinking that his face looked oddly familiar. And then, seeing that patched pipe, she remembered. "Of course! You're the man who lost money in the Coke machine in the teachers' lounge one day. You're a professor of—"

"The classics," he said, and smiled, turning to Evan and thrusting out a hand. "I'm Doug Blackburn, and this is my wife, Christie." Evan shook hands with him and introduced Kay and himself. "They still haven't given me my money back yet," the man told Kay. "Cheap bastards pick your pockets over there. Have you eaten in the cafeteria yet? If you haven't, let me warn you about it. Don't go without a physician at your side. And make sure he brings a stomach pump. Better still, bring your own lunch from home!" They laughed, and the man looked around at the other people on the patio. "So many people here, but not very many we know." He put his arm around his wife. "Where do you two live?"

"Bethany's Sin," Evan said.

"We've driven through there a few times," Christie said. "It's a very beautiful village."

"Do you live near here?" Kay asked them.

"In Whittington," Blackburn said. "Boring as all hell over there. They roll the sidewalks up at five o'clock. So" —he paused for a few seconds while he lit his pipe with a match—"are your classes all right?"

"It's still touch and go," she explained. "If I can make it through August, I think everything will be fine."

"Let's hope we all make it through August. Little bastards in my eight o'clock class are driving me crazy. Never do their outside reading, never answer questions in class; they wouldn't know a Gorgon if Medusa herself gave them the eye. I'm going to flunk every damned one of them. No, I'd better not do that. At least, not for spite." He struck another match and held it above the pipe's bowl.

"Mythology?" Evan asked. "That's one of your subjects?"

"That's right. Mythology, Roman history, Latin, Greek. Are you interested in it?"

"In a manner of speaking, yes. I saw an etching over at the library in Bethany's Sin; it shows a woman with a bow and arrow in a forest setting. She's some sort of Greek deity, and I was wondering. . . ."

"Artemis," Blackburn said. "But she's recognized by other names as well: Diana, Cybele, Demeter."

"Oh. What's she the goddess of?"

Blackburn smiled and shrugged. "A little of everything. Those Greeks had a tendency to complicate things, including the powers of their deities, you know. Artemis was the goddess and protector of women, overseer of the harvest, and goddess of the moon. But she's most commonly known as the Huntress."

"The . . . Huntress?" Evan asked quietly.

Kay took his arm. "What's all this about?" she asked. "I didn't know you were so interested in mythology."

"I wasn't until just recently."

"Then you've probably been talking to Kathryn Drago," Blackburn said. "She's cornered me more than a few times, too. And since you live in Bethany's Sin, I'm not surprised you're curious about Artemis."

Evan paused for a few seconds. "I don't understand," he said finally.

"The museum in Bethany's Sin!" Blackburn said. "Artemis was the goddess of the—"

"Here you are," someone said, a figure moving alongside Evan and taking his arm. "I've been looking for you." Dr. Drago nodded toward Blackburn and his wife. She held a cut-crystal glass filled with a thick-looking red wine. "Dr. Blackburn. I see you and your wife have met the Reids?"

"Yes, and we were talking about a subject you should be interested in," he said offhandedly. "Mr. Reid was asking about the goddess Artemis. I don't suppose you've given him the grand tour of your museum yet?" He smiled thinly.

Dr. Drago was silent for a moment as she swirled the wine around in the glass. Ominously silent. Evan could feel a hostile tension building between her and the other man, and he knew Kay could feel it too, because Kay's muscles seemed to have tightened. "You're mocking me," Drago said quietly. "I'm not sure I like that."

Blackburn stood perfectly still, as if transfixed. Perhaps he felt the same thing that Evan did: the presence of something dangerous within the woman that might suddenly leap without warning.

"Your private opinions are, of course, your own," the woman said calmly. "But when you choose to make them public, in my house, you tread on dangerous ground. Dr. Blackburn, for a man of intellect you are surprisingly . . . myopic. Perhaps this autumn we'll schedule that debate we've been considering?"

"I have the feeling our debate's already begun," Blackburn said, glancing uneasily at a few of the guests who'd moved in a circle around them.

Drago smiled. Her eyes were like blazing blue bits of glass, seconds out of the kiln, still glowing with unrestrained power. But there was no heat from them; only a numbing cold. "I'll destroy you," she said. "You'll stand on your opinions, and I'll stand on my evidence."

"Evidence?" Blackburn shook his head incredulously. "What evidence? Those fragments and weapons you've put under glass in your museum? Surely not!"

A group of people had gathered, drawn by the man and woman standing like combatants beside Kay and Evan. Kay found herself staring at Blackburn's head as if she could see the skull.

"I have truth," Drago said.

"No. Only myths. And dreams."

Drago leaned toward the man. Evan thought for an instant that her hand, still clutching his arm, had begun to tighten its grip. He could feel the strength behind it, as if her fingers were flesh-covered bands of metal. "In a cavern on the shores of the Black Sea," she said very quietly, but all ears could hear her because her voice had taken on a low, threatening quality, "I found what I'd been searching for all my life. Not dreams. Not myths. But reality. I touched the cold stone walls of that tomb, Dr. Blackburn. And no man on earth can mock what I know to be true." Her eyes glinted.

It seemed to Evan that the circle of people around them had become larger and tighter. When he looked up, he saw that, oddly, they were all women.

"I'm not mocking your beliefs," Dr. Blackburn persisted, though his wife was gripping his sleeve now, "and of course your Black Sea excavation was important by anyone's standards. But I'm telling you as a professor of classics, you have no basis on which to—"

"No basis!" The woman spoke sharply and, Evan thought, bitterly. He sensed raging emotions within her, and he sensed also that she was holding herself back with tremendous willpower. "For over ten years I've been trying to prove my beliefs," she said. "I've gone back to both Greece and Turkey several times to follow whatever threads of information I could uncover—"

"Well, I'm afraid you'll follow those threads right into the ground. There's simply no hard evidence."

A chill skittered down Evan's spine. Of course he didn't understand what the man and woman were arguing about, but he now had a feeling of deep dread and sudden, inexplicable panic. The music was still playing from the house, but it sounded distant now, worlds away. The group of women who had ringed them out of mere curiosity now seemed threatening. Beside him, Kay trembled. Dr. Drago released his arm, and he was certain her grip had left bruises.

"You're an utter fool," she told the man who stood before her. "All men have closed their eyes to the truth I've uncovered, and that is a very dangerous thing."

"Dangerous?" Blackburn almost smiled. "How?"

Evan was looking around at the ring of women. Some of them he'd seen before, in the village; others he didn't know. But on all their faces there was now an eerie, shared expression: in the flickering light of the torches around the patio, Evan could see their cold hatred. Their eyes glittered darkly, and the flesh seemed to be stretched tight over their facial bones. And when he glanced to the side he realized Kay was staring at the back of Blackburn's head with the same intense, barely restrained ferocity. He turned his head, caught another man's gaze across the patio. The man seemed to be transfixed, and as Evan's eyes met his, he immediately stared down into the glass he held. Evan felt the hate rising from these women, streaming from their eyes, from the pores of their flesh, quickly, quickly, directed toward Dr. Blackburn. Suddenly he was afraid to move, as if he were standing amid a pack of savage animals.

A freezing wave had washed over Kay, numbing her brain and her reactions. She wanted to call out to Evan but found her voice paralyzed. Fear welled up in her when she realized she was no longer in control of her own body. She couldn't move, couldn't breathe, couldn't grasp Evan's arm and say let's go home something's wrong something's terribly wrong. It was if someone else, someone strange and terrible, had slid into her skin and even now clutched at her soul with ancient hands. She wanted to scream. Couldn't. Her eyes—were they her eyes now? or someone else's?—measured the size of Dr. Blackburn's skull. The width of the neck. And in the next moment she'd realized she—or the thing inside her, wearing her flesh like robes—was thinking of murder.

Her right hand came up slowly.

Reached out. Slowly.

Evan stared at her, opening his mouth to speak.

And suddenly Dr. Drago was reaching out toward Blackburn as well, and firelight flamed in the crystal glass she held. Her long-fingered hand seemed to tense, and then there was a sharp *crack!* that made Blackburn blink and jerk his head back.

"Jesus!" he said, startled.

Kay's hand was still raised just behind his neck. She had felt the hate within her rage out of control, throwing sparks like a live electric cable blown in a wind. In the image that had seeded itself in her brain and grown to bitter fruition, she was cupping her extended hand around the base of his head and squeezing until there was the brittle cracking of bone and the brains slithered out onto the ground. But now, with Drago's movement, the power that had thrashed within her seemed to be ebbing, leaving a cold emptiness behind, as if it had torn away a section of her soul in greedy, dripping claws. Suddenly she remembered where she was—Dr. Drago's party—and who she was—Kay Reid I'm Kay Reid—and that the man who stood beside her was watching her with sharp, probing eyes. She slowly brought her hand down and stared into the palm, at the crisscrossed lines dotted with pinpricks of perspiration.

Dr. Drago opened her hand and let the glass clink down onto the stones. Wine had sprayed her dress and dripped down her chest into the cleavage between her breasts like thick blood droplets. Liquid dripped from the tips of her fingers to the ground, and Evan could see several cuts in her palm, slivered with glass.

"Jesus," the man said again, staring at her. "You've . . . hurt yourself."

Her expression hadn't changed. She was half-smiling at him, though her eyes were still hard, allowing no quarter. "I'm afraid . . . discussions of this nature get the better of my temper. Forgive me."

Blackburn stood still for a minute; then he seemed to realize how close the ring of women were around him, because he turned his head from side to side like an animal seeking a way out of a trap. But Evan had seen a change come over them, just as he'd seen a change come over his wife; their expressions were placid now, no longer mirroring Drago's hatred of Blackburn. Mrs. Giles came toward Dr. Drago and took her arm. "Please," she said, "allow me to get a bandage for you."

"No," Drago said, pulling her arm free. Blood spattered the stones at her feet.

"We . . . we'd better be going, I think," Blackburn said; he held his wife's hand and she nodded quickly, her eyes still wide with shock. "I'm sorry if I . . . if I caused you to . . . do that. I didn't mean to . . ."

"It's nothing," the woman said.

"Yes. Well,"—he paused, looking from Drago to Evan and back again—"I . . . thank you for inviting us. Thanks very much."

"Marcia," Dr. Drago said, "will you show the Blackburns to the door?"

"Good-bye. Nice meeting you," Blackburn said to Kay and Evan, and then he and his wife were gone, following Marcia Giles to the front of the house.

The ring of women had melted away. Lights glinted off glasses. Across the patio someone laughed. Conversation swelled.

Drago lifted her hand and seemed to be examining the gashes. Another woman—a slender blonde Evan thought he'd seen at the village drugstore—brought her a white hand towel soaked in cold water. Drago began picking out the glass. "Foolish of me," she said. "That man goads me too easily."

"What . . . was all that about?" Evan asked her.

"His stupidity." She turned her gaze on him and then smiled. "His fears. But fortunately nothing to upset my party. I'd rather not talk about it anymore. Kay, there are some others I want you to meet. Evan, will you excuse us?"

He nodded. "Sure." Then, to Kay, "Are you all right?" She stared at him, nodded.

"We'll only be a few minutes. There are other professors from George Ross here that Kay should know." She took Kay's arm with her unbloodied hand. "Come on," she said, and they disappeared across the patio.

Evan felt like a drink. A strong one. Scotch, maybe. He went back to the bar and ordered it. He realized his pulse was pounding. What had happened out there seemed like some kind of strange dream, something beyond his control or understanding. And what had happened to Kay? What was she going to do? That look of pure hatred in her eyes still burned in his brain. I've never seen her look like that before, he thought. She looked wild and savage and . . . yes, deadly. He shook his head and sipped at his Scotch.

And looking across the room, saw what those carved figures were on the fireplace.

Warriors in armor, astride huge, rearing horses. Bearing battle-axes, some with spears and quivers of arrows about their shoulders.

He stepped toward it.

Then stopped.

The music played on. Someone behind him laughed. A female voice, light and high and free.

But he didn't hear.

Because he'd seen that those warriors were women.

SEVENTEEN

AFTER THE PARTY

On the drive back to McClain Terrace, Evan asked Kay what had been wrong.

"Wrong?" she asked. "What do you mean? Nothing was wrong."

"Oh, yes, it was. I saw the way you were staring at Dr. Blackburn. I saw you reaching for him. What were you going to do?"

She was silent for a long while; beyond the headlights the many layers of darkness swept by. She took a deep breath, let it out. How to make sense of what she'd been feeling? How to explain it to him? And to herself?

"Well?" he prompted, waiting.

"I'm tired," she said. "I didn't know there'd be so many people there."

"Kay," Evan said quietly. "You're keeping your feelings from me. I want to know because it's important."

She glanced at him quickly, then averted her eyes. "Important? How?"

"You recently told me about a nightmare, something about . . . killing a man. Do you remember? You said you were on a battlefield, and you were riding a horse, and you carried a battle-ax. . . ."

"I remember," she said dully.

"Since then I've heard you whimper in your sleep more than once. You never awakened, and I never talked to you about it. But I want to know now. Have you had any more of the same kind of nightmare?"

"I don't know," she said, realizing immediately she'd said it too quickly. Liar. Liar. Liar. There had been other nightmares, but she could recall only disjointed fragments. The last one had been particularly bad. She'd been fighting with spear and battle-ax against hordes of dark-bearded, armored warriors. There had been others of her own kind all around her, and as they struck left and right with their axes, chopping flesh, splintering bone, crushing skulls, she'd heard the war cry rising, rising, the most terrible and powerful sound she'd ever heard. The warriors had fallen back for a while, heaps of mutilated bodies everywhere, but then they'd flooded forward against swords flashing red in the harsh sun, screams and shouts and wild cries of pain echoing off into the mountains to startle the wary eagles from their clifftop nests. At that moment she'd wanted to wake up, to fight her way out of this nightmare, but she seemed trapped in it, forced to finish this frenzied, blood-soaked battle as if it were truly a part of her own memory. Fragments of faces, battle blows, ringing weapons, swept past her. She remembered lifting her gore-slick ax, and, screaming in rage and hate, she'd brought the weapon whistling down to cleave the shoulder of a warrior. Then darkness, darkness, the noise and clamor of the battle fading, darkness claiming all. And she'd known she'd gotten away from that terrible place once again, and dear God, dear God, she didn't want to have to return there when sleep overcame her once more.

"Have you?" Evan asked her. They were driving through the village, nearing Blair Street.

"Yes," she said finally. "A couple of times."

He was quiet for a while. They turned onto McClain. Lights were on in their house and in the Demargeon house. "Do you know what Dr. Drago and Blackburn were arguing about tonight?" he asked her.

"No."

"Neither do I. But I'm going to find out. I'm going to call Blackburn tomorrow."

"Why?" Kay asked. "I don't see that it's any of our business."

"Maybe not, but there's something going on around here that I can't figure out. And it has to do with—"

"Evan, please . . ." Kay began.

He turned the car into the driveway, cut the engine, and switched off the headlights. "It has to do with that damned museum," he continued, "and with Bethany's Sin itself."

"Evan . . ."

He looked at her full in the face. "Listen to me!" he said, more harshly than he'd intended. "At the party tonight, when those women began to surround Blackburn like wolves gathering around a sheep, I saw a glimmer of hatred in their eyes unlike anything I've ever seen before. As if they . . . wanted to protect Kathryn Drago. And if they could've torn that man limb from limb, I believe they would have."

"You don't know what you're saying, Evan! You're not making any sense!"

"I could feel the hate in them," Evan told her, trying to grasp the emotions that now writhed wildly within him. "And for a moment I felt the hate in you."

She looked at him, openmouthed. "Hate?" she said. "I don't . . . hate anyone."

"But you wanted to hurt him, didn't you? Because you reached out for his throat, and God knows what you were trying to do, or what you were thinking of, but I saw in your face the same thing I saw in the others!"

"Oh, Christ!" Kay said. Anger had flamed within her, and she knew she was purposely trying to cover over that seed of violence in her that Evan had seen taking root. She reached for the door handle, opened the door. "I don't want to listen to any more of these . . . dreams of yours."

He got out of the car and followed her toward the house. "My dreams are one thing. What I see is something else. And I see something happening here that . . . I can't understand."

"It's your imagination!" she said, turning toward him when they reached the door.

"It's not my goddamned imagination!" Evan's voice was raw and shaken.

"Keep your voice down! Mrs. Demargeon is—"

"I don't care!" They stared at each other apprehensively for a moment. Evan ran a hand across his face; that Drago woman's gaze haunted his brain, making it feverish and setting his senses on the knife edge of frenzy. "God," he said after he'd regained control. "God. I'm sorry. I didn't mean to shout at you. But what I'm feeling now, what I'm seeing, is not my imagination. I

know it's not!" When he looked back into her face, her eyes were glazed and distant, and he knew she'd blocked him out again. She waited for him to open the door; he fumbled with the keys.

He was about to slip the key into the lock when the door came open. Mrs. Demargeon stood there, her eyes slightly puffed, looking as though she'd just awakened. "Oh," she said. "You're home. I thought I heard someone out here." She put a hand to her mouth to stifle a yawn. "How was the party?"

"Fine," Kay said, moving past her into the house. Evan followed and closed the door. In the den there was an indentation on the sofa where Mrs. Demargeon had sat, and a stack of *Redbook*s and *House Beautiful*s on the coffee table. A half-cup of coffee, an open potato-chip bag, a few of Laurie's books and toys, lay around the room.

"Oh, me," Mrs. Demargeon said, rubbing her eyes. "I fell asleep. And when I sleep, I'm like a dead woman."

"Is Laurie upstairs?" Kay asked.

"Yes. I put her to bed around eight-thirty."

"I hope she wasn't any trouble."

"No trouble at all. She's such a sweet child. We had quite a good time just reading and watching television." She turned her head and looked at Evan. "I hope your evening went well."

"It was a crowded party," he said, running a hand through his hair. "Most of the people were teachers over at George Ross. Christ, I'm tired!"

"Can I make you a sandwich?" Kay asked Mrs. Demargeon. "Something to drink?"

"Oh, God, no! I drank enough coffee to float a battleship!" She glanced at her wristwatch. "I'd better be getting home."

While Kay talked with Mrs. Demargeon, Evan climbed the stairs wearily and took off his coat and tie in the master bedroom. He could hear the women's muffled voices from downstairs. It was going to be a bad night; he could feel it. The bed waited for him, a place where horrific dreams and twisted memories would scuttle spiderlike through his mind. And also through Kay's? he wondered. Weeks ago he'd felt certain that some terrible force in

Bethany's Sin, a presence beyond his understanding, was slowly stalking him. Now that force seemed nearer; much, much nearer. And nearer to Kay as well? he asked himself. Manifesting itself in her dreams just as it did in his own? He started to unbutton his shirt. Voices through the wall. Kay speaking. Then Mrs. Demargeon. He took his shirt off and then decided to look in on Laurie.

A sliver of light from the hallway fell upon the little girl as she lay snuggled in the covers of her bed. Evan stood looking down at her, saw her fine golden hair spread out on the pillow like a beautiful Oriental fan. He sat on the side of the bed, very carefully so as not to disturb her, and softly touched her cheek. She stirred very slightly and smiled. He felt a warm glow begin to spread through him, chasing away the fears of the night. "My princess," he whispered, and stroked her cheek with the back of his hand.

But there was something lying on the bed beside her.

It took him a moment to realize what it was, but when he did, he picked up the object and rose to his feet as slowly as a man trapped in the terrifying half-speed of a still-unfolding nightmare.

A toy. That's all. Just a toy. A little bright blue bow, strung with a white cord. Something bought at a dime store. Plastic. His heart thumped. On the night table, below a Snoopy lamp, smaller objects. Three little arrows with those harmless suction-cup tips. Lying on the floor, at his feet, a cardboard target with 100, 200, 300, 400, around the rings, and 500 at the bull's eye. He gripped the bow in his hand, tightly, turned away from the bed, and found himself walking back downstairs, toward the sound of Mrs. Demargeon's voice.

". . . just any time," Mrs. Demargeon was saying, yawning again as she stood with Kay at the front door. "Really. I enjoy being with children, and Laurie's not one bit of trouble. So the next time you—" She stopped speaking suddenly because she'd seen the shirtless man coming up behind Kay. Her eyes widened slightly, and Kay whirled around.

"Evan?" Kay said softly, her eyes moving from that terrible plain of scars to his hollowed-out, haunted gaze and back again.

Evan held out the bow. "What is this?" he asked. "Where did it come from?"

Mrs. Demargeon tried to smile, faltered, glanced quickly over at Kay. "I . . . well, we drove over to the Westbury Mall around eight. We had some ice cream, and we went into the toy store, Thurmond's Toys. She saw that little bow-and-arrow set, and she said she liked it, so—"

"So you bought it for her," he said quietly.

"Yes, I did. It's nothing, really. Only cost a couple of dollars." She dropped her eyes to his chest, to the scars that ran like a ragged tapestry across the flesh. Evan saw her eyes glisten. Her tongue darted out, licked her lower lip, then disappeared.

"I don't want it in this house," he told her, trying to keep his voice steady. "I don't want anything like it in my house."

"Evan!" Kay's voice. "It was a gift for Laurie!"

He shook his head. "I don't care. Here. Take this thing back."

"Really," Mrs. Demargeon said, backing away a step, her gaze still fixed on his scars, as if she were transfixed by them. "I meant no harm. It's just a toy. Just a toy."

"It's a toy, for God's sake!" Kay echoed.

"No. It's more than that. Please, Mrs. Demargeon. Take it back."

"I don't see what you're so upset about, Mr. Reid."

"Take it back, I said!" He thrust it out at her, and Kay grasped his wrist. Her eyes shone with anger.

Mrs. Demargeon didn't take it. She said, "I meant no harm. It's just a toy." And she began backing away, still tracing those scars with her eyes, as if physically caressing them. "Keep it for her, please," she said. Her voice lower, something harsher in it. Strained. "Keep it. I've got to go. I've got to—" And then she'd quickly turned away and was hurrying toward her own house, and they both stood where they were until they heard Mrs. Demargeon close her door in the night's stillness.

"Evan!" Kay said sharply. "What's wrong with—" She stopped, stared.

He had begun to twist the bow in his hands. The plastic whitened, cracked. The bow snapped into two pieces, and Evan flung the broken toy out into the street. Then he looked at her with a wild, hot gaze. "I don't want that thing in my house!" he told her, as if daring her to contradict him.

Abruptly, her face flushing, she turned her back on him and went up the stairs. The bedroom door closed. Hard.

He slammed his hand against the wall. Damn it to hell! he breathed, and shook his head from side to side. What's happening to me? Am I losing my mind? He could see the pieces of the plastic bow, still connected by the cord. He closed the front door and turned the lock, his nerves tingling. A child's toy, that's all it was. Just a toy. No. No. A toy. No. Because nothing was simple in Bethany's Sin; everything was complicated and secretive and connected by a darkness that seemed to be grinning just beyond the windows. Coincidence? Imagination? When he'd seen that bow, he'd immediately recalled the etching of Artemis, with her bow and arrows, and the carved frieze of warriors on Dr. Drago's fireplace, some of them bearing quivers of arrows. Coincidence? Or something strange and savage and merciless, reaching from the core of Bethany's Sin toward him, and Kay, and even Laurie?

By God I'm going to get into that museum and see for myself, he said, his hands clenched into helpless fists at his sides.

But not tonight. Tonight I've got to rest. And to think.

After a while, Evan climbed the stairs to the master bedroom.

Where Kay was dreaming fitfully of blood-dripping slaughter.

EIGHTEEN

BEHIND THE MUSEUM'S DOOR

On Sunday Laurie cried when Kay told her that her father had accidentally broken her new toy. Don't worry, Kay said. We'll get you another one.

Evan found Doug Blackburn's number through Whittington information and made his call. No answer. He spent the rest of the day in the basement, trying to work on a new story, and crumpling page after page into the wastebasket.

Kay slept badly again that night. Evan lay beside her and heard her whimper, and when he took her hand he found the flesh corpse-cold. Just past midnight he tried to wake her up because she'd cried out sharply, but he couldn't rouse her by shaking her or calling out her name or even by putting a cold facecloth against her temples. Beads of sweat had broken out on her forehead. Finally she was quiet, and Evan settled back on his pillow.

And at nine o'clock on Monday morning he stood across Cowlington Street from the museum. It was a hot, oppressive day, and sweat had already risen across his back. He stood looking at the forbidding house for a minute, and then, steeling himself, he crossed the street, moved through the gate and up the walkway. His pulse pounded, and as he reached that large oak doorway, his blood felt like liquid fire. He tried the door. Locked. He hammered on it, hearing the echoes within the house like a hoarse, bellowing voice. A trickle of sweat ran down his face, and he wiped it away with the back of his hand.

Movements behind the door. Tentative footsteps. A pause. Then the noise of a bolt sliding back.

The door slowly came open.

"Good morning!" a gray-haired woman with sharp features said cheerily. She was dressed well, in a navy blue pantsuit, and she looked fresh and alert. She opened the door wide to admit him. "Please, come in!"

He entered. There was a corridor with glass display cases, a desk with a guest book. The floor was of blue tile, and the walls were cream-colored. Similar to that corridor he'd seen in his dreams, yes, but . . . different, too. There were rooms branching off from the corridor and, at the corridor's end, a wide staircase with polished banisters leading to the second floor. Behind him the gray-haired woman closed the door. He felt air conditioning begin to loosen the shirt from his back.

"I'm Leigh Hunt," the woman said, smiling, extending a hand. A firm, cool grip. "Will you sign our book over here?"

He nodded, took an offered pen, and signed it.

"Sorry we were locked up," she said. "I'm alone here for the day, and it's rare that we have a visitor so early in the morning. It's certainly going to be a scorcher today, isn't it? The radio said in the middle nineties. And still no rain in sight. That makes for dangerous conditions, I'll tell you." She peered over at his signature. "Mr. Reid?" She looked into his face, seemed to be examining his features. "Oh, yes! Your wife is on the George Ross faculty, isn't she? Weren't you and she at Dr. Drago's home on Saturday night?"

"Yes, we were."

"I thought I'd seen you before. My husband and I were there, but we didn't have an opportunity to meet you. Are you interested in our historical society?"

"Curious," he said.

She smiled. "I see. Well, we're glad to have you. I'm surprised you and your wife haven't come to see us sooner."

"We've both been busy. Settling into the village and all that."

"Of course. Can I get you a cup of coffee?"

He shook his head.

"Well, then, let me give you a brief explanation of what these artifacts are. They were unearthed in 1965 and 1966, in an archaeological dig Dr. Drago supervised on the southeastern shore of the Black Sea, in Turkey. The fragments of statues, of pottery, coins, and the weapons you'll see in the display cases date from approximately 1192 B.C. Around the era of the Trojan War. This particular region of Turkey is now geologically unstable; there've been several killer earthquakes there in the last century, and the most recent one, in 1964, exposed a wall of earth and uniformly cut stones. Archaeologists began digging in early 1965." She began walking along the corridor, her footsteps echoing from wall to wall. Evan followed at a distance. "Dr. Drago held an archaeology post in Athens at that particular time, and for years she'd been petitioning the Turkish government to conduct a series of exploratory digs near the mouth of the Kelkit River. She'd been turned down up to that point, but Dr. Drago learned of this new discovery and petitioned the government again for permission to lead a team of Greek archaeologists in work on Ashava."

"Ashava?"

"Yes. That's the name the Turkish archaeologists gave the new site. After some professor or somebody. Anyway, Dr. Drago and her team were accepted. As a matter of fact, they made most if not all of the significant finds. The items you'll see here were all unearthed by the Greek scientists."

Evan stepped over to a display case and looked in. There were bits of pottery, all of them numbered; most were undecorated, but on several there were intricate scrollwork designs.

"Those were found on an upper stratum. In fact, the museum's laid out in order of the particular discoveries. The third floor holds those items found in the lower, and oldest, portion of the dig."

Other display cases held more pottery. Here was a fragment of what must have been a statue: it was one arm, the hand curiously curled, as if reaching for him through the glass.

"So what did Ashava turn out to be?" he asked the woman, seeing her reflection watching him in the display case.

"A city," Mrs. Hunt said. "Or, to be more accurate, a fortress. Buried by the shifting of the earth, buried from human eyes for possibly a thousand years or more. And a sheer caprice of nature uncovered its inner walls."

Evan peered into one of the rooms. A headless statue stood flanked by shadows. One hand held a spear that seemed as if it were about to be thrown at him. There were other displays: large, cracked vases, small medallions in a sealed case. "Ashava, huh?" he said, turning toward Mrs. Hunt. "I'm afraid I've never heard of it, but then I wouldn't consider myself any authority on ancient history."

"Few people are. Ashava was the name applied by the Turkish scientists. Dr. Drago identified the city by a different name. Themiscrya."

He shook his head. "Sorry. Doesn't ring a bell."

"No matter," she said. "I didn't know anything about it myself until Dr. Drago explained it to me. Themiscrya was a very ancient city, and a fabled one as well. Its origins are . . . lost in the past, but we can infer from its ruins and artifacts that it was primarily a farming community. It was a fortress, as I've said, but built as a fortress for purposes of defense against roving bands of barbarians. Of which there were quite a few. In 72 B.C. Roman legions attacked Themiscrya and destroyed it."

Evan realized there was a smell of dust in the house. Of age. Of ancient secrets, and perhaps new ones as well. "Why are these artifacts here?" he asked her as they neared the stairway. "Why not in Turkey?"

Mrs. Hunt smiled a cat-smile. "The Turkish government was in need of . . . financial aid in the late sixties. As I'm sure you're aware, Dr. Drago is quite wealthy. She . . . arranged for a loan in exchange for these relics."

"They must mean a great deal to her."

"They do. And to all of us as well."

"Oh? Why?"

"Because having this museum here makes Bethany's Sin quite a special place. An important place. There's a great deal of civic pride centered on it."

He nodded, looked up the staircase. He could see the battered torso of another statue, lights arranged around it to cast long shadows on the wall behind. "How did Dr. Drago make her money?" he asked, looking into Mrs. Hunt's face.

"She was a very lucky woman. And intelligent, too. In . . . 1967, I think it was, she married Nicholas Drago. She was his third wife."

"I'm not familiar with the name."

"The Greek financier," she explained. "The one with the shipping line and the chain of hotels. Unfortunately, Mr. Drago died in a fall barely a year after they were married. They were living in a villa on one of those volcanic Greek islands. I don't know all the details, but apparently it was a pretty grim accident." She shook her head. "Poor woman. She was supposed to have been the love of his life; he left her most of his holdings, and for a while she managed his businesses herself before she came back to America."

"Back to America?"

"Oh, yes. She was born in this country." She glanced up the stairs. "Are you going to see the rest of the museum?"

He nodded.

"Good. I'll let you go ahead, then. I've got some correspondence to answer. If you have any questions, any at all, please ask them. All right?"

"Yes, I will." He started up the staircase, and heard her footsteps retreating toward the other end of the corridor.

For more than half an hour he prowled the upper floors of the museum. There were more display cases, more fragments of statues. On the third floor there were two things of interest: bronze disks, pierced with holes, which Evan thought might have been used as currency, and a display case containing a few stone spearheads, a metallic shield shaped like a crescent moon with an angered face embossed upon it, and a battered helmet with a half-deteriorated nose guard. Evan stared at that shield and helmet for a long while, intrigued by them, and then continued through the third-floor rooms. More urns, decorated with fighting figures. A pottery fragment with a hand holding a sword. A large stone slab with part of a mural on it: he could see the outline of a man's bearded face, the eyes wide and staring and . . . yes, terrified. Those eyes seemed to be seeking his own. The expression chilled him. Strange, he thought. Mrs. Hunt had said

197

Themiscrya was a farming community. But where were the farming implements? It seemed a community more attuned to war than anything else. He continued through another room, taking his time, and then found his progress stopped.

By a large, slablike black door.

He put his hand on the gleaming brass knob. It wouldn't turn. Behind it lay probably more than half of the third floor, he guessed. Storage space? No. Wouldn't the storage area be in the basement? Possibly, possibly not. He paused for a moment and then retraced his way back downstairs.

Mrs. Hunt, pen in hand, looked up from her desk. "Everything all right?"

"Yes. Very interesting. But I was wondering about something."

"What's that?"

"On the third floor. There seems to be a locked door up there. What's behind it?"

"Everybody asks that question," she said, and smiled cheerily again. "It's a special exhibit we're in the process of setting up. A panoramic reconstruction of Themiscrya; there'll be spotlights and a slide show—that sort of thing."

"Good. When's it going to be finished?"

She thought for a moment. "Sometime in November. We hope."

He stood before her desk for a while longer, and she finally said, "I hope you've enjoyed your visit, Mr. Reid. Maybe you'll bring your wife and little girl next time?"

"Certainly," he said, and started for the front door. "Thank you. Have a good day."

"Same to you. I hope you can find some shade out there."

Evan left the museum. Reaching the street and turning toward home, he felt the harsh touch of the sun on his face. In his chest his heart beat steadily and slowly, but he felt a tension begin to radiate and spread through him from the back of his neck. He turned, looked back at the museum. So. That's all there was to it. The last vestiges of a farming community that had existed over three thousand years ago on the southeastern shore of the Black

Sea. He remembered the argument between Dr. Drago and Doug Blackburn; of course they'd been arguing about the items in the museum, but why? And what did mythology have to do with it? He made a mental note to call Blackburn's house again.

But what about the dreams? he asked himself, staring at the windows of the museum. What had they been trying to tell him? That there was danger here, something reaching for him from a swirl of dust? If so, he hadn't seen it. Hadn't felt it at all. Paranoia? Maybe. God, what if all these premonitions and feelings were only his imagination, after all? What if there were nothing whatsoever to fear in Bethany's Sin, and he'd been slowly unraveling because it was his nature to be afraid, to question, to probe.

He began walking toward McClain Terrace again. He wanted to check the mail and get started on the bones of a new story.

And then he had a curious, sudden thought: How had Leigh Hunt known he had a little girl? He'd never met the woman before, and she'd never been introduced to Kay, either. Possibly someone had told her.

Yes, that was it. There were no secrets in Bethany's Sin.

Kay had determined to put Sunday night's eerie dreams in the back of her mind and was in a better mood when she got home. Laurie seemed to have forgotten about losing her toy. Evan felt ridiculous about that incident now, and ashamed, knowing he'd embarrassed Kay in front of Mrs. Demargeon. Over dinner he told them he'd visited the museum, and Kay listened with interest while he described the artifacts inside.

He almost didn't call Doug Blackburn. Wasn't Kay right, he reasoned, in saying that it was none of his business? Wasn't it interfering where he didn't belong? But he did make the call, at ten-thirty, and Blackburn answered, sounding sleepy.

"Sure I know who this is," Blackburn said. "Mr. Reid, isn't it?"

"That's right. Sorry if I awakened you, but I wanted to

ask something. Would it be possible for us to get together and talk sometime this week?"

"What's on your mind?"

"I'd like to talk to you about Dr. Drago."

Silence. Then, "Well . . . I'm giving mid-terms this week, and I'm going to be very busy. How about—wait a minute—how about a week from Thursday? Come on over to the house and bring your wife. We'll make an evening of it."

"No, I'd better come alone."

There was a pause, and then Blackburn's voice took on a more serious note. "Hey, what's this all about?"

"It concerns Dr. Drago's museum and her archaeological dig. But I'd rather talk face-to-face."

"Okay, then. Whatever. How about making it around seven or so on Thursday?"

"That's fine."

"All right. See you then."

"Good-bye. And thanks." Returning to the den, Evan kissed Laurie goodnight before Kay put her to bed, then sat down on the sofa to watch the nightly newscast from Johnstown. The newscaster was finishing up a story on a local politician, and then he began talking about the discovery of a decomposed, unidentified corpse in the woods near Elmora.

And across the village, in Mrs. Bartlett's boardinghouse, Neely Ames heard a knock at his door over the rock music on his transistor radio. He said, "Just a minute!" turned off the radio, grabbed his blue jeans from the chair where he'd thrown them, and put them on.

It was Mrs. Bartlett, carrying a tray with a white teapot and a glass filled with ice cubes. "I brought you a surprise," she said, coming into the room and glancing around. She didn't seem to mind the clothes strewn about. "I know how tired you said you were at dinner, and sometimes a body can be so tired he can't even sleep. So I made some of my good sassafras tea for you. It'll help you relax." She put the tray on a table near his bed.

"That's very nice of you," he said; the pungent, earthy perfume of the sassafras had entered the room with Mrs. Bartlett.

"Here we are," Mrs. Bartlett said, pouring the tea. The ice cubes cracked, and the noise reminded Neely disturbingly of a night when something had smashed his truck window. "It should be cool in just a minute."

He took the glass and sat in a chair near the windows. The slightest breath of a breeze was coming through, but it was a stale, hot breath. His shoulder muscles and legs still ached from the work he'd done that day; it was almost as if that bastard Wysinger had been trying to wear him out. He'd spent the hot, muggy morning picking up litter on the outskirts of Bethany's Sin, loading plastic bags with beer cans and blown newspaper and paper cups and all manner of debris. Then, in the scorching afternoon, he'd cut down a dead tree on Fredonia Street, sawed it into small pieces, and hauled the whole thing over to the landfill. He always hated going out to that landfill; it was a filthy place, layered with garbage and inhabited by hundreds of black, biting flies.

"You look tired," Mrs. Bartlett said. "A young man needs his rest."

"Young? No, I'm not so young anymore," he told her. The glass felt deliciously cool in his hand. "I worked at the landfill today. Do you know where that is?"

She shook her head.

"It's way out in the woods, in the middle of nowhere. I hate that place. As barren as the damn moon, and hot as hell. . . ."

"I don't believe I'd like to see it," Mrs. Bartlett said.

"No, you wouldn't." He sipped at the tea. It was very sweet. "But I'm getting paid to haul myself out there, so I guess I shouldn't complain."

She smiled sympathetically.

"Must've been over a hundred out there today," he said. "And the ground's beginning to crack, like some sort of dried-up riverbed." He drank again. Almost too sweet for him. "It's good," he told her. "Thanks for bringing it."

"I hoped you'd like it. Most of my visitors do."

He nodded, drank. Sweet over bitter.

"Summers are always fierce in Bethany's Sin," the

woman said. "I can't bear to go out in the midday sun myself. They say the sun brings up all the wrinkles."

He grunted, touched the cold glass to his forehead. "Then I'd better not look in a mirror," he said. "I'd look like I was eighty years old."

"Everything'll be fine in the morning, after a good night's sleep."

"I suppose it will be. It'll have to be."

She watched him drink. "I'll let you get your rest now," she said, and moved toward the door. "We'll have pancakes for breakfast."

"That'll be great."

"Good night." She closed the door behind her, and he heard her slowly descending the staircase. In the bowels of the house another door closed. He finished the tea, touched the cool glass to both sides of his face, and then walked across the room to turn the lock in the door. When he'd switched off the ceiling light and taken off his jeans again, he lay down on the bed and tried to sleep. It was too hot, and he kicked away the sheet; the faint stirrings of breeze played across him like supple, mercurial fingers. There was a bitterish aftertaste in his mouth, and he swallowed a couple of times to get rid of it. What kind of tea had that been? Sassafras. He could still smell it in the room. His mind began to drift; sleep seemed closer, like a beautiful woman in night black robes. When he closed his eyes he had the sensation of slowly tumbling head over heels down a chill passageway. A sensation, he realized, not unlike being drunk. But different, too. Jesus, he told himself, I'm tired! Need to sleep, need to rest, just let every damned thing go. Forget about that damned hot sun, forget about the landfill, forget about Wysinger's bellyaching voice. That's right. Yes. Forget. Let sleep come. He waited for what seemed like a long time, but still he clung to that nebulous ledge between sleep and awakening. From some distant place he heard the first few lines of a song he'd been working on for several weeks: I'll fade away into the night/I'll be long gone before twilight/And I won't hear if you call my name/There's nothing but the road to blame. So much for that. Through the curtains of his eyelids Neely saw what looked like figures standing amid the darkness of his room. Standing in silence. Watching. Waiting. They had burning blue eyes like the eyes of that thing he'd seen on the highway, and he wanted his mind to sheer away from those terrible thoughts but his brain refused to obey his commands: the things with burning eyes stepped nearer his bed. Then began to fade, very slowly, until they had disappeared again into blackness. The memory of that night on the highway set in motion the churning wheels of fear in his stomach. He'd had the truck window replaced, but every morning those long rents in the metal greeted him like the nagging remnants of nightmares. If it weren't for those marks he would've shrugged off that incident as a prime example of the DTs. But he couldn't, and though he'd driven back along the King's Bridge Road to the Cock's Crow a few times since then, he'd never talked about that night, and he always took care to leave when someone else was driving toward Bethany's Sin.

Now he was falling. Falling into a corridor at the far end of which was a black abyss. Falling rapidly. Tumbling head over heels. Brackish, bitterish taste in his mouth. Sassafras tea? Or something else? Was Mrs. Bartlett—dear old Mrs. Bartlett, so much like his own mother before she'd started drinking so bad—spiking the tea? Trying to get him drunk? Preying on his weakness? Have to scold her about that. No fair.

The sudden, sharp sound of metal against metal came to him, and he knew he was still awake. It was difficult to open his eyes; he finally opened them to slits, and he could feel the light sheen of sweat covering his body from the heat that seemed to have filled the room like a living thing. What moved? he wondered. What moved? That noise again. A quiet noise. Barely audible.

The lock.

He turned his head with an effort and stared through the darkness at the door. Though he couldn't see it, he realized the lock was turning. Someone on the other side had a key.

Neely tried to lift himself up on his elbows but only half-succeeded. His head seemed heavy, his neck barely able to hold its weight. He stared at that door, his mouth slack and hanging open.

There was a quiet *click!* and he knew the lock had been turned. He tried to call out and couldn't find his voice. Drugged, he realized. Mrs. Bartlett's drugged me with something! The door began to come open; a sliver of white light from the hallway entered first, growing larger and longer and brighter, falling across the bed and blinding Neely where he lay. Until, when the door was finally open, the light stung his eyes with pure pain.

And three figures were silhouetted there, two standing in front, one behind. "He's ready," someone said; Neely heard two voices at the same time, one overlapping the other. One in English—Mrs. Bartlett's voice—and one in a hoarse, guttural language he had never heard before. That second voice, the more powerful, filled him with a dread that ate at the linings of his guts. The figures slipped through the doorway and neared him. Stood over his bed. Silent.

But now he could see their eyes in the dark blanks of their faces.

Three pairs of eyes. All unblinking. All shimering with electric blue flame that seemed to blaze out for him. He tried to crawl away, couldn't make his muscles respond; the windows were open: he could scream and someone would hear. When he tried to scream he heard himself whine instead. Those eyes moved, examining his naked body. A hand reached down; Evan saw a bracelet of animal claws on the wrist. The fingers traced the length of his penis. He tried to cringe from them, couldn't. Another hand came down, and the cool-fleshed fingers swirled in circles across his stomach. The Bartlett-thing stepped back toward the door and closed it.

Neely's heart hammered. He could hear the things breathing in the darkness, like the steady action of a bellows. Hands touched chest and arm and thigh and throat; he smelled female musk, heavy and demanding, filling the room with sexual need. Fingers at his penis, stroking the flesh. Beneath those burning, haunting eyes he knew the mouths were open, taut with fired lust. One of the forms sat on the bed beside him, bent forward, and licked at his testicles. Another one crossed to the opposite side of the bed and crawled toward him, gripped at his shoulders, bit lightly at his chest, then harder with mounting desire.

Turning his head with an effort that brought the sweat up in beads on his face, Neely saw the eyes of the Bartlett-thing, still standing beside the closed door. She was grinning.

And to his own horror he felt his body begin to respond to the caresses of the two women around the bed. It excited them even more, and they jealously shoved for position near his sexual organ. A mouth gripped him, claw-nailed hands stroked his thighs from hips to knees, leaving rising welts. Physical need shook him, setting his nerves afire. His testicles ached for release. And then he was aware that one of them, the woman-thing with the animal-claw bracelet, was standing up, slowly taking off the coarse-clothed gown she wore. Even in the darkness he could see the smoothness of her stomach, her firm, tight thighs, the triangle of dark hair between them. The fever boiled in his brain, and now he had only one need and one desire in the world. She sensed it, and moved with maddening slowness. Then the other woman-thing backed away from the bed and disrobed; he could feel the mingled heat of their bodies, and he didn't care that those hideous eyes watched him almost incuriously, didn't care that these things were nightmare visions, didn't care didn't care didn't. . . .

The one with the bracelet caressed his body like the searing touch of fire. Thick dark hair hung down over her shoulders, and he could smell a wild forest-smell in it. She mounted him, her legs pressed tight against his body. Moved forward, guiding him in with her hand. Urgently. She gasped softly and began to move, slowly at first, then with increasing passion. Her nails gouged his shoulders, and her unblinking eyes stared into his face with eerie unconcern. Neely grasped her arms, felt smooth, firm flesh; he lifted himself up and she ground down on him at the same time, mixing his pleasure with pain. In another moment he exploded inside her, with a half-human whine that he hardly recognized as his own voice. Her wetness engulfed him, throbbing against him with a strength that wouldn't let him free. She ground down on him again, locking him inside her with her legs. Orgasm ripped him like lightning, and still she moved atop him, her grasp milking him dry. As she trembled violently in the throes of her own orgasm, Neely played his fingers along her shoulders and then dropped them to her nipples.

One of them was hard and taut. The other was missing.

And Neely realized, with a new surge of confusion and fear, that this woman had only one breast. The right one was gone, and his fingers felt the hard ridges of a star-shaped scar in its place.

The woman released him and silently climbed off his body. Before she slipped back into her gown, Neely saw jewels of sweat and semen suspended in the fine down between her thighs.

At the door the Bartlett-thing hadn't moved. Her eyes, fiery blue, burned through his skull.

They waited for him to regain his strength. His body felt drained, and in his hand there was the memory of that strange and vivid scar.

And then the second woman came for him. She was lithe and blond, and her mouth and fingers played games with his body until once again he was erect and throbbing. She descended onto Neely with feverish intensity, biting at his shoulders and throat, her hips battering him. And seconds before another orgasm shivered through him, he realized this woman also lacked a right breast, because he could feel the scar pressed tight to his own chest. She lay atop him for a moment, breathing harshly, and then her weight was gone. Neely, his body aching and exhausted, saw the three women standing over his bed, staring down at him as if examining an insignificant curiosity.

"He'll sleep now." Two voices speaking. One Mrs. Bartlett's, one that guttural, foreign voice that made Neely's flesh crawl. The Bartlett-thing's hand came from the darkness, stroked his fevered forehead. And then the women slipped through the door like the rustle of cloth, into the blinding white light of the hallway. The door closed behind them; a key was turned. Footsteps on the staircase. Another door closed in the depths of the house. Then nothing but silence.

And abruptly the mountainous black wave of sleep reared up for Neely, crashing over him with the urgent touch of a lover, scorching and soothing him. Taking him down and down and down, deeper deeper deeper. . . .

NINETEEN

THINGS UNEARTHED

Behind a layer of clouds the color of corpse flesh, the sun burned, scorching the earth, browning grasses and bowing trees, searing away shade and lying like a fiery weight across Neely Ames's shoulders.

The stench of the landfill had risen up around him, enfolding him in a sickly-sweet grip. It was a wide, barren plain of dirt heaped with garbage of every description, the large mounds breeding black flies that circled hungrily around Neely's head, darting in to taste the trickles that ran down his face and arms, finding the salt taste good, circling again. Far across the landfill there were several trash fires, and from them an acrid, grayish smoke had wafted with the stagnant breeze, clinging to Neely's work clothes and making his eyes tear beneath his glasses. When he walked, his boots stirred up clouds of dust, and he stepped carefully over widening cracks in the ground, like the remnants of sudden earthquakes. God only knew how many tons of garbage lay buried beneath the ground; now it seemed to be shifting, the layers and layers of filth expanding under the fierce summer sun. At one place he could stand and peer down almost six feet at an incredible morass of rotting garbage, old bottles, baby diapers, even discarded clothes and shoes. Beneath the landfill's surface was a hideous muck emitting a stench that turned Neely's stomach inside out. Passing a mound of pasteboard boxes and glittering glass shards, he heard a high squealing from a nest of rats; he'd seen them before, usually in the early morning when it was a fraction cooler, dark shapes scurrying from garbage mound to mound in search of scraps of food. He hated this place because it was as filthy and vile as Bethany's Sin was beautiful and spotless.

And now he carried a plastic garbage bag with a half-decapitated gray cat in it. He'd shoveled it up from where it had been stuck to 219; a truck had probably barreled right over the thing during the night, and the driver in his high cab had felt only the slightest jarring of a tire. The carcass had already been bloated by the time he'd gotten to it in midafternoon, and of course the flies had gathered in sheets. As he walked on, taking the garbage bag to a trash mound deeper within the landfill, his boot crunched through weakened earth and plunged ankle-deep. Neely cursed and staggered forward a few feet before he could regain his balance. Through the thin pall of smoke he could see cracks zigzagging crazily across the plain; he envisioned holes opening at his feet and sucking him quicksandlike down into the mire of accumulated garbage, where he would die choking on the refuse of Bethany's Sin. He quickly shrugged the image off and tossed the plastic bag on the trash mound; rats squealed and ran. The stench here was infernal because here was where he dumped the carcasses of animals—dogs, cats, squirrels, once even a good-sized bobcat—struck down by cars either on 219 or in the village itself. It was a grisly job, but he'd signed on to do it and that was that. As Wysinger had reminded him several times.

He took a handkerchief from his back pocket to clean his glasses of specks of ash. Wisps of smoke swirled around him; he could taste it at the back of his throat. Bitter. Like the aftertaste of Mrs. Bartlett's tea. He suddenly shivered, though the sun was burning his face. Something began to surge in his memory—dark shapes standing over him, eyes like pools of bluish flame, hands reaching for him from the blackness—and then it slipped away before he could grasp it. All day something strange had been haunting him, shadowy images that flashed through his mind and then vanished, and though he was left with a feeling of dread, there was also a . . . yes, a feeling of strong sexual desire. He couldn't remember dreaming; in fact, it seemed that the world had gone dark after Mrs. Bartlett had left his room. He'd probably just rolled over and fallen asleep like a dead man until dawn. But when he'd awakened, his body had ached, and he'd thought for just a moment that the lingering aroma of female musk lay on his bed. No, no. Only wishful thinking.

But one thing did bother him. While he was showering he'd noticed scratches on his thighs. He'd tried to think where he could have been scratched. Possibly, when he was sawing that dead tree to pieces, the limbs had scraped across his legs without his realizing it. But funny he hadn't noticed those scratches earlier. . . .

He put his glasses back on, his eyes stinging from the smoke, and started walking across the landfill toward his pickup truck. He stopped to peer into that hole his boot had made. Jesus Christ! he thought. This whole damned place is slowly caving in. No telling how many years the locals have been using it as a dump; no telling how many tons of garbage lay underneath there. He kicked at the dirt; it was bone-dry and loose, and the hole widened.

And within it something glittered.

Neely bent down, peered in, brushed dirt and filth away. A tiny squarish object, silverish. Other things, yellow white. He picked one up and looked at it closely for a moment, trying to decide what it was.

Abruptly, he stood up, found a stick lying nearby, and probed the hole. Dirt cascaded down the sides in sheets. Flies circled him, greedy for what he might uncover. But there was nothing; only dirt and clots of filth and garbage. He threw the stick aside, wiped his hand on his trouser leg, and looked again at the object he held.

He knew what it was, and seeing it made his heart hammer in his chest. What the hell was it doing out here, in the garbage dump? Unless . . . Jesus, no! He wrapped it in his handkerchief, bent down and looked for the others. He found two more, and then he stepped back from that hole and walked quickly to his truck.

On McClain Terrace, Evan stood up from his typewriter and stretched. He'd finished about a third of the new short story he was working on, and he needed a break. Beside the typewriter there was a half-cup of tepid black coffee and a couple of chewed pencils; he took the cup, went upstairs to the kitchen, rinsed it out in the sink, and put a pot of water on the stove to boil. As the ring heated he thought about what was ahead for him: soon, he knew, he'd have to find within himself the guts to start a novel. It would be about the war, about the scarred and maimed veterans who came home and found that they'd only left one battleground for another. And here, in this broader, fiercer battleground, there was no recognizing friend from enemy until it was too late. Here the enemy wore many faces: the VA doctor explaining how in time the scars would fade; the psychiatrist with an ill-fitting toupee who said you must not blame anyone, not yourself, not those who sent you to fight, not anyone; the smiling employment agency lady who said sorry, we don't have anything for you today; people like Harlin who fell upon you and leeched your blood as a transfusion for their own tormented, decaying souls.

All that would have to come out someday.

But not now. No, now it was enough to write these smaller cries in the dark and hope that someone heard them and understood. Now it was enough to try to control the battle that waged within himself: the fight against his fears and his often unreasoning anger, the fight against those premonitions that he realized now had done so much to shake his life apart.

The pot began to whistle. He took it off the ring and then happened to glance through the window.

He could see a figure at a window toward the front of the Demargeon house. It was Harris, in his wheelchair, peering through the curtains at the street. The man's eyes looked like dark holes in his pale flesh. In another moment the curtains fell back and the figure was gone.

He could imagine what Mrs. Demargeon had told her husband about that night Evan had let his fears and suspicions grind him under. That Evan Reid's losing his mind. Took a toy I bought for his little girl and made something . . . terrible out of it, when I only meant to be kind. I tell you, I don't believe we should associate with those people anymore; that man's too unstable.

Evan switched off the eye of the stove. Unstable. Yes, that was probably right. And now, inadvertently, he'd hurt Kay again by cutting off other people. Mrs. Demargeon would probably never speak to her again. Jesus! He shook his head at his own stupidity.

No. I can make it right. I can go over there and apologize. Right now.

211

He hesitated for just a moment, and then he was going out the front and along the sidewalk to the Demargeon house. The car wasn't in the driveway, but at least he'd have a chance to talk with Harris, to try to explain that sometimes he lost control of himself, let his fears and premonitions rip parts of him away. But your wife shouldn't blame Kay, he'd tell the man. She wants friends; she wants to be a part of the village.

He stepped up onto the Demargeons' porch and rang the doorbell. Waited for a moment. There was silence within the house, and he was beginning to think the man wouldn't answer the door. He rang again, and then he could hear the quiet squeak of the wheelchair slowly approaching.

The door came open, latched by a chain. Harris Demargeon's eyes widened very slightly. "Mr. Reid," he said. "What can I do for you?"

"Well, I . . . was hoping I could come in and talk to you for a few minutes."

The other man didn't move. He said, "My wife's away."

"Yes, I know," Evan said. "But I thought . . . perhaps you and I could talk."

Demargeon looked at him, seemingly hesitant to let him in. I don't blame him, Evan thought. After all, everybody knows war vets are killers. Crazy killers, at that. Jesus! The man's really afraid of me!

But then the man reached up. There was a *click!* and the latch fell away. Demargeon wheeled backward, and the door came open. "Come in," he said.

Evan entered. The harsh glare of the sun had filled the living room with stale heat.

Demargeon wheeled across the room and then sat watching Evan. "Please," he said quietly. "Close the door behind you. And put the chain back on."

Evan did. "I saw you from my kitchen window, and I thought now would be a good time to apologize."

The other man motioned toward the sofa, and Evan sat down. "Apologize?" Demargeon asked. "What for?"

"For my bad manners toward your wife a few nights ago." He paused, watching for the man's reaction. He didn't seem to know what Evan was talking about.

212

"She bought my little girl a toy bow-and-arrow set." He shrugged. "I don't know. I was rattled, I associated that toy with . . . some things that had been bothering me, and I'm afraid, I lost my temper." As he talked, he studied Mr. Demargeon. White, short-sleeved shirt, dark trousers, black wingtips. His face a pale, pasty color. His eyes dark and darting. "So, anyway, I didn't mean to hurt your wife's feelings," Evan said. "It was very kind of her to sit with Laurie, and very kind of her to buy that toy, too. I don't know what came over me . . . I just lost control. I hope you understand."

Demargeon was silent.

"Of course you have a right to be angry," Evan said, knowing he deserved everything he was going to get. "I can see you're upset. But please, my wife likes Mrs. Demargeon very much. I wouldn't want to see their friendship—"

"Get out of here," the man whispered.

Evan wasn't sure he'd heard him. "What?"

"Get out of here," Demargeon repeated, his voice hoarse and strained. He wheeled forward and then stopped, and Evan could see his eyes were wild. "Take your wife and your child and get out. Now. Today."

"I'm sorry," Evan said. "I don't understand what you're—"

"Get out of Bethany's Sin!" the man said in a half-shout, half-sob. "Don't worry about your clothes, or your furniture, or your house! Just take them and go!"

Evan, staring into the man's frenzied eyes, felt the gnawing chill of fear rising within him. He still didn't know what Demargeon was talking about, but he thought in that instant that the man looked like a hideous, animated corpse.

"Listen to me!" Demargeon said, visibly trying to keep himself under control. He was trembling. He wheeled closer to Evan, his eyes wide and pleading. "You don't know. You don't understand. But what you're feeling is right; you don't see that yet, but it is! Now, for Christ's sake and all that's holy you've got to save your wife and child and yourself—"

"Wait a minute!" Evan said. "What the hell are you—"

Demargeon looked sharply to the door, as if he'd heard

something. His face set into a rigid mask, he swallowed, and then looked back to Evan. "They know you think something's wrong," he said. "They're watching you, and they're waiting. And when they come for you they'll come in the night, and then it'll be too late—"

"Who?" Evan said. "Who'll come?"

"Them!" Demargeon said, his hands trembling on the chair's gray armrests. "By God, haven't you seen that no man walks the streets of Bethany's Sin after nightfall? Haven't you seen?"

"No, I—"

"They killed Paul Keating in the night," Demargeon said hurriedly. "And they took his body where they take all the bodies. I heard the war cry after they killed him; I heard it and I tried to cut my throat with a kitchen knife but she wouldn't let me, she said no, no I wasn't going to get away from them like that and oh God her eyes oh Jesus God her eyes burned me. . . ."

He's crazy, Evan realized. Or been driven crazy. And what was all this about Keating? What was this man talking about . . . ?

"They'll come for you! Oh yes they'll come for you just like they came for me!" A thread of saliva had broken from the man's lip, and now it hung down over his chin onto his shirt. "In the night! They'll come in the night when the moon's strong and full and they'll take you to that place—God, that awful place!"

Evan shook his head, started to rise from the sofa to move toward the door.

"You don't believe me!" Demargeon said. "You don't understand!" Something dark and hideous flashed through his eyes. "I'll show you. I'll show you what they'll do!" And then he was rolling up one leg of his trousers, tugging at the cloth. His breathing was harsh and ragged, his muttering too jumbled for Evan to understand. His trouser leg ripped. Then his fingers fumbled, pulling at the knee. Evan could see sunlight glinting off plastic.

Demargeon's fingers worked at a strap. Then, the exertion showing on the man's face, he kicked out with one knee. The leg slithered out and lay on the floor beside the wheelchair. And then Demargeon was ripping the cloth away from his right leg, his teeth gritted, a sheen of sweat on his forehead. Another strap. He kicked out, breathing hard. The right leg fell to the other side of the chair, and the empty, tattered trouser legs dangled from Demargeon's mutilated torso.

Evan was on his feet, backing toward the door. His mouth was open but he could find no words; he stumbled, almost fell backward over the coffee table.

Sweat streaked Demargeon's face. The prosthetic legs lay akimbo, black wingtips gleaming, dark socks around plastic. Demargeon raised his haunted gaze to Evan's.

And began to laugh, hysterically, madly. And as he laughed, the tears brimmed in his eyes and dripped down over his cheeks, splattering onto his white shirt. The laugh ringed the room, strident and terrible, the laugh of someone beyond saving. "God, no . . ." Evan said, shaking his head from side to side, backing away even as Demargeon wheeled toward him. "God in Heaven, no, no, no!"

Keys in the door, jingling. The door came open, then stopped abruptly at the end of the chain. A woman's face peered through the crack. "Let me in!" Mrs. Demargeon's voice, urgent, commanding.

Evan reached for the chain.

"She'll kill me!" Demargeon said, trying to stop laughing, tears still dripping from the point of his chin. "They'll all kill me!"

Evan paused, his blood like ice, fingers inches away from the latch.

"Mr. Reid? Is that you? Let me in, please."

"She'll kill me!" Mr. Demargeon hissed.

"Mr. Reid? The door, please."

He hesitated, held by the look of pure terror in the man's eyes.

"I have to see my husband!" Mrs. Demargeon said sharply.

Evan tore his gaze away from the man and unlocked the door. Behind him, Demargeon whined like an animal caught in a trap.

The woman came through into the living room, carrying a sack of groceries; she glanced quickly at her husband, then at Evan, and set the groceries down on the table. Demargeon wheeled his chair backward, bumping over one of the discarded legs. The man's expression of terror chilled Evan, and brought back a stabbing memory: himself wired to a cot, and a silkily smiling woman holding a small cage over him in which something evil scuttled.

Mrs. Demargeon stood staring at those false legs on the floor. Very slowly she raised her eyes to her husband's face. "Harris," she said calmly, "you've been a very bad boy, haven't you?"

He stared at her, wide-eyed, shook his head.

"What the hell's going on around here?" Evan demanded, realizing his voice sounded strained.

"I'd appreciate it if you'd leave now, Mr. Reid," the woman said, her back to him.

"No! I won't leave until I know what's going on!"

Finally she turned toward him, regarded him with hooded, intense eyes. "My husband is a sick man," she said. "I don't think you're helping the situation."

"Sick?" Evan echoed incredulously. "He's . . . mutilated! His legs are . . . missing at the knees!"

"Mr. Reid!" Mrs. Demargeon said, her eyes flaming. Beyond her, Harris Demargeon was trembling, his mouth moving but making no noise. She paused a moment, put a hand to her forehead and closed her eyes. "God," she said quietly. "Mr. Reid, you don't understand the situation."

"You're damn right I don't understand it! I was told by Mrs. Giles that your husband was paralyzed, not carved up like a slab of meat!"

She looked at him with a flat, stony gaze that made his flesh crawl. "All right," she said. "All right. Come out to the porch with me." As they left the living room he heard the man begin to sob openly.

"My husband was . . . hurt very badly in a car crash on the King's Bridge Road," Mrs. Demargeon said on the front porch. "Only he wasn't paralyzed. His legs were destroyed." She frowned and shook her head. "Ever since that accident Harris has been slipping away. A gradual and terrible process, and very painful to have to watch. But what can I do?" She looked up at Evan. "I couldn't have him put in a hospital; I couldn't have him locked away."

"He acts more afraid than insane," Evan said.

"Sometimes it's worse than others. But I don't like to leave him alone, you see. When he's alone he acts like . . . what you saw in there."

Bullshit! Evan thought. Total goddamned bullshit! "Mrs. Giles told me he was paralyzed from the waist down."

"Mrs. Giles doesn't know everything!" the woman snapped. "You know how you reacted! Do you think I want everyone in the village to look at my husband as if he's some kind of damned freak? Well, do you? Jesus Christ, I've gone through enough agony!" She paused for a moment, getting herself under control again. "After the accident he was taken to a hospital in Johnstown. He stayed there for months. And when he came home I decided it was best not to talk to anyone else about his . . . injuries." She looked into Evan's eyes. "I hope you'll respect my feelings."

You're a liar, he thought. But why? He nodded. "Of course."

"Good. I'm sorry I lost my temper, but the shock of seeing that . . . I know, I should be used to Harris's moods by now, but it's still difficult." She moved toward the door. "I'd better take care of him now. Good-bye." And the door closed. He heard the chain being fastened. Heard her voice, muffled. The squeaking of the chair's wheels. He left the porch, his head pounding and dread like a sickness deep in his stomach, and walked quickly back to his house. And all the time something that frightened, half-crazed man had said echoed in his brain like an oracle's warning:

They'll come for you in the night.

TWENTY

THE COCK'S CROW

At dinner, sitting with Kay and Laurie around the kitchen table, Evan realized the hand holding his fork was trembling.

Darkness was streaming down the windows, blacking over the woodland, reducing the houses of Bethany's Sin to malevolent shapes in which lights gleamed like cunning eyes. Evan could see the white sickle of the rising moon; he thought of that half-moon-shaped metal shield on the third floor of the museum, the enraged face embossed upon it, thought of those wide, staring eyes on the fragment of pottery. And he realized now that their expression of terror was similar to what he'd seen in the eyes of Harris Demargeon.

"Are your pork chops all right?" Kay asked him, seeing he hadn't eaten very much.

"What?" He looked over at her.

"You're not eating."

"Oh." He took a bite of creamed potatoes. "I'm thinking, that's all."

"About what? Something that happened today?"

He wavered, about to tell her everything, about to tell her he thought Mrs. Demargeon had lied to him purposely, about to tell her there was a clenching fear within him now that he couldn't begin to describe. But he already knew what she'd say: you're going to have to see a doctor about these irrational fears you're wrecking our lives with these premonitions or whatever the hell they are oh God my head my head aches. . . .

"No," Evan said, averting his gaze. "I'm worried about a story I'm working on."

"I'd like to hear it."

He smiled, a thin, transparent smile. "You know I can't talk about them until I've finished."

She watched him for a moment, thinking how he looked so . . . what was it? Weary? Afraid? Burdened down? She touched his hand, could almost feel the throbbing of his pulse through the flesh.

"You know," he said, putting down his fork and looking at her, then at Laurie where she sat picking at her peas and carrots, "I've been thinking about something for a few days. It's been so hot here for the past week, and so dry, I was wondering if maybe we should all get in the car and drive over to the Jersey coast next weekend. How about that?"

Laurie's eyes brightened. "The ocean!" she said.

"Right. The ocean. Remember the summer we went to Beach Haven?"

Laurie nodded. "That was fun. But I got sunburned."

"Remember that wrecked ship that was sticking up out of the sand? We could go see that again. Remember the lighthouse that looked like a candy cane?"

Kay squeezed his hand. "That'd be nice, Evan. But I've got tests to give next week. I couldn't possibly go."

"Come on! You could go for a weekend!"

She smiled. "That's a long drive for just two days. Why don't we wait until the end of the term?"

"Awwwwwww!" Laurie said, not at all interested in her peas and carrots anymore.

"Well," Evan persisted, "maybe there's somewhere nearer we could go. Up into the mountains where it'd be cooler. Just for a weekend, then we'd be right back here on Monday morning."

"Yeah!" Laurie said.

Kay was looking at him strangely. What was all this about a vacation? she wondered. Usually it was she and Laurie who had to pull him away from his typewriter for a couple of days. Now it seemed that he was eager, even anxious, to get away from the village. "I guess I'll have to be a party-pooper," she said, watching him. "But those tests take priority right now."

"Well, when can you go?" he asked her, and now she knew that something was wrong.

"I just can't say," she told him. "When the term ends in August . . ."

He was silent, his eyes staring through her.

"August isn't that far away," Kay reminded him. "Just two weeks."

"I'm concerned about you," he said. "I think we should . . . leave this place for a while."

"Concerned about me?"

"That's right. Those dreams you've been having . . ."

"Please," she said, and put her fork down very carefully on her plate. "Let's don't talk about those."

"It's important!" he said, and realized he'd said it too strongly because he saw Laurie's eyes widen, as if she were expecting them to argue. He said more quietly, "Any recurring dream means something. Believe me, I know. . . ."

"It's not a recurring dream!" she said, "I mean, I seem to be the same person in those dreams, and I seem to be familiar with the surroundings, but . . . what happens is never the same."

"Okay. But I'm still concerned."

"Anxiety," Kay said. "You told me yourself you thought that's what it was." She narrowed her eyes as that terrible, wretched truth hit her. "So now you think this village has something to do with my dreams?"

"I think a vacation would be good for everyone."

"Let's go to Beach Haven!" Laurie said. "Please, let's go!"

"No. I can't." Kay was inwardly trembling because now she knew. She'd seen that awful, too-familiar look in Evan's face: that lost and helpless and fearful look, the look of a drowning man who can find nothing to cling to. "Evan," she said calmly, "this is the nicest place we've ever lived in. We have a chance here, a real chance to make something of ourselves. Don't you understand that?"

He sat still, then pushed his plate away like a chastised child. You've been a very bad boy, Mrs. Demargeon had said.

"This may be the last chance we have," Kay said.

He nodded, rose from the table.

"Where are you going?"

"Out," he said, his voice not angry but tense and hollow.

"Out? Out where?"

"I want to go for a drive. Where are the car keys?"

"I want to go for a drive, too!" Laurie said.

"They're . . . in my purse on the bed." She watched as he moved through the den. "Do you want us to go with you?"

"No," he said, and then he was climbing the stairs toward the bedroom.

"Eat your food," Kay told the little girl. "Those carrots are good for you." She listened, heard him coming back downstairs, heard the front door open and close. And after another minute she heard the station wagon start and pull out of the driveway. Heard it moving along McClain Terrace.

"What's wrong with Daddy?" Laurie asked. "He acted funny."

And only then did Kay feel the burning of tears in her eyes. "Your daddy . . . isn't well, Laurie. He isn't well at all." Tears broke, dripped hotly. Laurie stared.

The Cock's Crow, Evan thought as he turned the station wagon northward, driving along darkened, silent streets. A good place to drink tonight. And maybe a good place to ask some questions. He passed the black hump of the cemetery, his headlights grazing tombstones. And then he was surrounded by blackness, driving toward the King's Bridge Road, his brain filled with uncertainties that streaked like white-hot meteors behind his eyes. They'll come for you in the night, that man had said, just like they came for me. Take your wife and your little girl and get out. Now. And Kay's calm, controlled voice: August isn't that far away. This may be the last chance we have. This may be the last chance we have. He realized he was driving faster and faster, his foot steadily settling to the floorboard. Headlights gleamed off a roadside sign: SPEED LIMIT 40. His speedometer read fifty-five already. Running? he asked himself. Are you running from Bethany's Sin? The tires squealed around a curve. He passed the Westbury Mall, where comforting lights glowed, where cars were parked; it seemed part of a distant world, ages away from Bethany's Sin. In another instant, darkness took the road again.

He veered off 219 onto the King's Bridge Road, and in another few minutes he could see the glowing of a red neon sign in the sky. It was a smaller place than he'd envisioned, just an old cinder-block joint with a red slate roof and windows stickered with Falstaff and Budweiser beer decals. Above the door the neon rooster craned its head upward in a silent cry, retreated, craned again. There were only a few cars and a pickup truck in the gravel lot; Evan turned in, parked the station wagon alongside the building, and cut the engine.

Faces glanced up quickly as he came through the door into the dimly lit room, then looked away. A few dungareed farmers at tables or sitting at the bar, nursing beers. Behind the bar a hefty man with a reddish beard, wiping glasses with a white cloth. A woman with platinum blond hair drawing beer from a keg, handing it across to a gaunt-looking farmer with bushy gray sideburns. She caught Evan's gaze, nodded and smiled. "Good evenin'," she said.

He sat on a bar stool and asked for a Schlitz. "Right up," the woman said, and turned away. While she drew his beer into a frosted mug, he glanced around at the place. There were more tables in the back, and shapes sitting at them. Laughter. A white-haired man in a coat and tie with a woman who could have been his daughter. She patted his hand, and he nuzzled her ear. Other men sitting together, talking quietly. Cigarette smoke drifted to the ceiling in layers. Evan caught fragments of conversation: worries about the heat, that damn politician Meyerman and his county road program, the market price of soybeans, engine in that Ford ain't worth a damn I tell you.

The woman slid his beer across. "There you go."

"Thanks." He sipped at it, enjoying the sharp, tangy cold. When his eyes were more accustomed to the dimness he turned on the stool and looked toward the rear of the roadhouse again. The shapes were now people, mostly weathered-looking men who were probably local farmers. Evan wondered what this heat was doing to their land. Burning, cracking, drying it up so they'd have another hard year to face. His father had owned and worked land, and so he recognized these vacant, wearied faces. What the heat was doing to the earth it was also doing to these men. Cracking and withering their flesh, drawing it as tight as leather over sun-scorched bones. They drank as if trying to replace some of the fluids the sun had taken from them.

And back there Evan saw a pyramid of beer bottles stacked on a table. Light filtered goldenly through them, and he could see a form sitting behind the bottles. He thought something about the man was familiar, and he took his mug and walked back toward him. As he neared the table a voice said, "Careful. There's a loose floorboard over there. Step on it and my creation goes to hell." The voice, too, was familiar, though slightly drunk.

Evan walked around the table. The man glanced up, beer bottles reflected in his eyeglasses. "Don't I know you from somewhere?" Evan asked.

The man paused, squinting. "You're . . . the man who lives on McClain Terrace, aren't you? Mr. Rice?"

"No. Evan Reid. And you're . . ."

"Neely Ames." The man held out a hand and they shook. "Good to see you again. Grab a chair and sit down. Buy you a beer?"

"I've got one, thanks." Evan pulled a chair over from another table and sat down. "Looks like you've been doing some drinking."

"Some," Neely said. "More to do yet before this place closes. Hey, I don't smell like garbage, do I? Or smoke?"

"Not that I can notice."

"Good," he said. "Good. I thought I had that goddamned landfill in the pores of my skin. Guess I'm the only one who can still smell it." He lifted a half-full beer bottle and swigged from it. "Hell of a day," he said.

"For both of us," Evan said, and drank from his mug.

"You ever find out about your friend? The one that lives across the street?"

Demargeon's strained-to-cracking face, saying they killed Paul Keating in the night. Evan said, "No. I never did."

"Too bad. I guess he moved away. Can't say as I blame him."

"Why do you say that?"

He shook his head. "Don't mind me. Sometimes this tries to do my talking for me." He motioned toward the bottles, which seemed to tremble very slightly under Evan's gaze. "Tell me," Neely said after another moment. "What is it about that village that keeps you there?"

"Circumstances," Evan said, and the other man glanced over at him. "It's a nice little place; my wife and I got a very good deal on our house. . . ."

"Yeah, I like your house," Neely agreed. He smiled. "I haven't lived in a house for a long time. . . . Boarding-houses, of course, but nothing I could call my own. That must be a good feeling, to have a family like that."

"It is."

"You know, it wasn't that I needed money so badly that I took the job in Bethany's Sin. I was driving through, and the village seemed so clean and quiet and beautiful. It seemed that if I'd kept on driving I'd never see another place like it again. I'm a drifter, and that's all there is to me, but I thought that if ever I was going to try to find a home, then Bethany's Sin might be the place." He lifted the bottle again. "Do you understand that?"

"Yes, I think I do."

"I thought I could fit in around here," Neely said. "At first I thought it might really work out. But the way those people look at me on the street, like I'm something they could grind under if they really wanted to. And that damned sheriff is the worst of them all. That bastard would like to break me in two."

"I think he's just got a chip on his shoulder," Evan said.

"Maybe." He looked into Evan's face as if recognizing something there. "You must've run into him yourself."

"I did."

Neely nodded. "Then you probably know what I mean." He finished his beer and then was silent for a moment, staring into the amber depths of the bottle. "Now I've decided to get out of that place," he said very quietly.

"Why? I thought you said you liked it."

"I do. Are you a poker player, Mr. Reid?"

"Just occasionally."

He set the bottle down before him, as if deciding whether or not to risk the crashing avalanche of the pyramid. "There's a feeling you get sometimes in a game where the stakes are high, Mr. Reid. As if something is closing in on you from behind. Maybe you've played out your streak of luck, or you're getting a bad deal, or someone's a better player than you and he's letting you think you're winning until he snaps the trap shut on your throat. That's the feeling I've got now. Somebody's pushed the stakes up high, maybe higher than I can afford, and the final card's about to be turned. I don't know if I want to wait around to see what that card's going to be."

"I don't understand what you're getting at," Evan said.

"That's okay." Neely smiled slightly. "Nobody else would, either." When he looked at Evan again, his eyes were dark and distant, seeing shadowy forms on horseback chasing down his truck. "Something happened to me," he said quietly, not wanting anyone around them to hear, "out on the road near Bethany's Sin. I've been thinking about that for a long time, and every time I remember it I feel a little more afraid. I don't know what was going on, and I don't want to know; but I'm sure now that they would've killed me."

Evan leaned slightly forward over the table. Bottles clinked. " 'They'? Who are you talking about?"

"I don't know who they were. Or what they were. But by God they didn't look human, I'll tell you that. Listen to me!" He shook his head in disgust. "You must think you're sitting here with a real basket case!"

"No," Evan said. "Please, tell me the rest of it. What did they look like?"

"Women," Neely told him, "but not like any women I've ever seen except in my nightmares. There were maybe ten or twelve of them, and they were on horseback in the middle of the road, as if they were crossing into the forest on the other side. I left here after closing—I'd had a few beers but not enough to make me hallucinate. Anyway, I'd driven right through them before I could stop, and when I slowed down to see who they were, they . . . attacked me."

Evan was silent, his heartbeat thundering in his head.

"With axes," Neely continued, his voice still low. "One

of them broke the window out of my truck. Christ Almighty, I'd never seen anything like that before! I . . . looked into the face of one of them. I'll never forget what that thing looked like. It wanted to rip me to pieces, and if they'd forced me off the road well, I wouldn't be sitting here now." He paused for a moment, wiped a hand across his mouth. "Most of all, I remember that woman's eyes. They burned right through me; it was as if I was looking into blue flame, and by God I'll never be able to forget that."

Evan watched him, said nothing.

"I wasn't drunk," Neely said. "Those things were real."

Evan let his breath hiss through his teeth. He sat back in his chair, thoughts whirling through his brain, so many things so close to locking together and revealing a dark, terrifying picture.

"I told Wysinger," Neely said. "He almost laughed in my face. You're the only other person I've told."

Evan ran a hand over his forehead. He felt fevered and shaken, unable to piece any of it together. Get out, Demargeon had said. Get out now. Now. *Now.*

"I can see you think I'm crazy, too," Neely said. "Okay. Here's something else that's got me spooked." He reached into his back pocket and brought out a wadded handkerchief. He placed it on the table before him—the pyramid clink-clink-clinked—and began to straighten it out. There were tiny objects caught in the cloth. Neely lifted them out one by one, and Evan peered down at them. Neely held one up to the light; it glittered silverish and yellow.

"What is it?" Evan asked him.

"A tooth," Neely said, "with a filling. And these others are teeth, too, all broken to pieces."

Evan started to touch the tooth fragment Neely held, then withdrew his hand. "Where did you find those?"

"That's what's so strange: the landfill." He turned his gaze toward Evan. "Now what in God's name are human teeth doing lying around in the landfill?"

"No," Evan said, his voice hollow. "You're wrong."

"About what?"

"I don't think . . . God has anything to do with it."

Neely's eyes narrowed. "What?"

"Nothing. I'm just thinking aloud."

Neely began to wrap the tooth shards back in the handkerchief. "I was going to show these to Wysinger. Maybe have him check out the landfill or something, because I've got a hell of a bad feeling about it. Now I'm not so sure if I should even bother." He looked hard and long at Evan. "Hey, are you all right? Wait a minute, I'll buy you a beer." And then he was up on his feet, shoving the handkerchief back into his pocket, moving toward the bar. As he moved away from the table a floorboard squealed. The pyramid swayed right, swayed left, cutting swaths of amber light. Swayed right, swayed left.

And broke apart like the falling of an ancient, dark-starred city.

TWENTY-ONE

SECRETS

On Friday Kay stayed home from her classes, calling Dr. Wexler to tell him she was suffering from a migraine headache. I'll be fine by Monday, she told the man, and he said he hoped she felt better soon and wished her a good weekend.

Kay put the receiver down and lay in the bed, the curtains closed, the room darkened. She'd switched on the light a few minutes before and then hurriedly turned it off again, finding it stung her eyes. Evan and Laurie were down in the kitchen making breakfast for her; hearing them clattering around, she knew she'd have to clean up after them later. But it was nice of them, and no matter what was burned she was going to pretend to enjoy it.

She hadn't really lied to Dr. Wexler; her head was pounding. But she knew it wasn't migraine. She felt as if her nerves were trembling, felt as if an icy hand caressed her shoulders. She'd tried for weeks now to pretend that nothing was wrong, that what she was feeling inside was anxiety, that soon the anxiety would pass and she'd be the same sensible, practical Kay Reid she'd always been.

But now she couldn't do that anymore.

Something was happening to her that she couldn't explain away as anxiety or anything remotely familiar. It had begun with those strange dreams. At first she'd been an interested, if fearful, observer in them, but now, as they intensified and drew her slowly into them, she'd become a participant unable to escape. And it always seemed that she was locked within another body, one with a ragged scar on the thigh, and she viewed scenes of carnage and merciless battle through hard, slitted eyes that were not her own. She'd wanted to talk about those dreams to Evan, to tell him that fear and confusion were writhing within her, but she'd been ashamed to admit she was becoming more and more afraid of something shadowy and intangible. After all, wouldn't that be admitting that there might be something to fear in Evan's dreams as well? No. She couldn't do that. Evan seemed too preoccupied with something else to listen to her, anyway. In the past few days he'd eaten hardly any dinner at all; his eyes looked tired and hollow because he'd been staying up so late, watching television or trying to work downstairs in the basement. But Kay could have counted on both her hands the number of keys she'd heard strike paper. Those were familiar symptoms, and they were setting her nerves on edge as badly as were her nightmares.

The one the night before had been the worst yet. She'd awakened in the gray hours with a cry of pain caught in her throat. Through the whorls of smoke and dust, the hordes of swarthy, black-bearded invaders had advanced, swinging blood-edged swords; archers on horseback wheeled across fallen walls and around roaring fires where corpses crackled and split. She and three comrades had fought back to back, swinging their gore-splattered axes from side to side like a ferocious, maddened fighting machine. She'd cleaved one of the enemy with a blow that had burst his skull into fragments, and then she'd heard a name—Oliviadre—which she'd recognized as her own, called in warning. Whirling to the side, she'd met the strike of the sword with her battle-ax and slashed the invader's hand off at the wrist. The stump had gouted blood, and it had been a simple blow to end his life. Behind her, Coliae had fallen with an arrow in her throat; Demusa shrieked her war cry even as a blade struck her shoulder and a second blade pierced her chest; Antibre was struck in the face by a flashing sword, and even as she fell to her knees, she cleaved the head from the warrior who'd struck her down. Through the smoke the warriors came forward, shoulder to shoulder, their chests heaving. Oliviadre backed over a heap of fallen comrades, hand clenched around the handle of her weapon. All around burned fires of defeat: the great city, the great nation, finally trodden down beneath the boot of the destroyer. Torn bodies littered the stone pathways, and blood splattered murals of glorious, breathtaking color.

And now Oliviadre, her gaze sliding from side to side like a cunning animal's, saw the fear in their eyes, but knew the time of her own death was fast approaching. One of the warriors, a large man both courageous and foolhardy, rushed forward, his arm coming back to fling a spear. Oliviadre shrieked in rage, felt the hot graze of the spear as she stepped quickly to the side; at once she was upon the man, striking, striking, striking. The mutilated body fell, head hanging from strings. She spat upon it and readied herself for the others. They hesitated, sensing in her the fury that had almost brought Athens to its knees over a hundred years before. A bow hissed, and an arrow flashed over the heads of the men. It struck Oliviadre in the shoulder, forcing her back a few paces. The warriors, seeing the stream of blood, pushed forward.

Until Oliviadre's wary retreat was stopped by a firescorched, broken ruin of a wall. The warriors paused, looking for an opening.

But Oliviadre gave them no chance. At once she screamed the chilling war cry of the eagle, and then she was leaping over the mounds of corpses onto the terrified men. She struck one down with a single blow, slashed out and saw an arm fall, still gripping a sword; a searing, burning pain at her spine; slashing, slashing, spraying red droplets across crumbling faces, slashing; volcanic pain at the back of her head; still slashing, the ax heavier now, the warriors crowding in closer as she fell to her knees; one of them lifting his sword high, and then . . .

Darkness.

Gray light.

Morning on McClain Terrace. God, my head! Got to call Dr. Wexler. . . .

"Breakfast!" Laurie said, coming into the room with Evan close behind her, carrying a plate with bacon and eggs and a glass of orange juice on a tray. She put the tray carefully across her mother's lap. "We burned the toast up, though," Laurie said cheerily.

"Oh, that's all right. It looks very good."

"Don't you want a light on in here?" Evan asked her.

"No. Please. My head's still aching." She reached to the night table for a bottle of Tylenol. Two tablets remained; she swallowed them with the orange juice.

"You're not feeling any better at all?"

She shook her head. The final image in her dream remained fixed behind her eyes: a warrior lifting his sword, muscles rippling in his arms, to strike across her skull. No. That wasn't me. That was . . . Oliviadre. Oliviadre was struck by that sword, not me. So why do I feel this terrible, throbbing pain? She winced and touched her forehead.

"Does it hurt bad, Mommy?" Laurie asked.

"Yes, it does."

Evan picked up the empty Tylenol bottle. "I'd better drive down to the drugstore and get you another bottle of these, then." He looked at her for a moment, seeing her obvious pain in the lines around her eyes. "Do you want to see a doctor?"

"Oh, it's not that bad," Kay said quickly. She took a tentative bite of an egg, reached for the salt shaker on the tray. "I'll be just fine."

"You've been working too hard," Evan said. "Probably reading too much."

"That's probably it. It'll be good for me to rest today because I've got those tests to give next week."

"Am I going to school today?" Laurie asked.

"No," Kay said. "Why don't you stay home and keep me company?"

"But Daddy can do that!" Laurie protested. "Mrs. Omarian was going to finish her story today!"

Kay grasped her little girl's hand. "I thought you'd want to stay home, honey. You can watch television, and go outside to play, and—"

"The queen!" Laurie said. "I'm going to miss the part about the queen!"

Evan's eyes flickered quickly over to Kay, then back to Laurie's face again. "What queen?"

"The real queen!" Laurie said. "The one right here in this place!"

"In this place? What place do you mean?"

The little girl shook her head, irritated that her father didn't understand. "Right here!" she said emphatically. "She lives in a big castle!"

Kay began to stroke the child's hair. "Stay home with me, honey. We'll have a good time together."

Laurie paused for a moment. "Awwwwww, I miss out on everything!"

"Tell you what, princess," Evan said. "Why don't you drive with me over to the drugtore? Okay?"

Another pause, and then she finally nodded. "I guess so."

As they crossed the lawn to the driveway, Evan found himself staring at the Demargeon house. Nothing moved over there; the Demargeons' car was gone. Evan, with Laurie on the seat beside him, backed the station wagon into the street and turned toward the Circle.

"You must like Mrs. Omarian a lot," Evan said while he drove.

"I do. She's nice."

"Are there many others who go to the Sunshine School?"

She nodded. "It's hot. Can I roll my window down?"

"Sure. Go ahead." Evan came to a stop sign, slowed and stopped, looked both ways, and then drove on, past silent houses. "Mrs. Omarian must tell you some good stories," he said in another moment.

"Oh, she tells very good stories. Just to us and not to the boys, either, because she says we're special."

"Of course you're special," Evan said. "How many little boys go to the Sunshine School?"

"Oh . . . four or five. It's mostly girls like me."

He nodded, glanced in his rearview mirror, got a quick glimpse of the museum's roof before he looked away. "I'd like to hear some of Mrs. Omarian's stories," he said. "Especially about this queen who lives in a castle."

"Can't," Laurie said. "Mrs. Omarian said they're just for us because we're special. She said daddies aren't supposed to know."

"Oh," Evan said easily. "Secrets, huh?"

"It's fun to have secrets."

Evan's vision clouded over. He was only dimly aware that he was still driving through the streets of Bethany's Sin, because some other part of him stood in a corridor, surrounded by swirling dust and heat, watching a dark shape with burning eyes slowly come closer and closer to stand just before him now. A hand pierced the veil of dust, reaching out for him. Took his arm in a cold, hard grip, pulled him forward. *Daddy,* someone said. His heart pounded, but there was nothing he could do to resist; the thing pulled him onward, along the corridor to a huge room where others waited. *Daddy!* A voice, very close. The floor of rough stones, the ceiling of glass and the moon burning white in a black sky. Things with flaming, hideous eyes ringing the room. A slab of black rock in the center, and someone standing there. *Daddy, please!* Laurie's voice. Kay. Kay standing there, but a . . . different Kay. A Kay with two faces: one half snarling, the single eye blazing blue and filled with hate; the other half screaming, eye widened in fear. Behind her, other figures, waiting. *Daddy, you're* . . . Kay lifting one arm, the hand holding a battle-ax that glowed with the same spectral power; her other hand clenched for him, the fingers trembling in a frenzy. . . .

". . . *going too fast!*" Laurie screamed, close to his ear.

And then he jerked himself back away from the hideous place and saw the stop sign coming up fast and knew that even as he jammed on the brakes the car's momentum would carry them across and he prayed to God there would be no other cars coming into that intersection. The tires squealed, squealed, squealed. The car shuddered violently. Ahead a looming black figure, twisting aside. "Christ!" Evan said, gritting his teeth and easing the station wagon to a halt in the middle of the intersection. He looked to Laurie, who was shaking and biting her lip, her eyes wide. "I'm sorry, princess," he said. "Christ, I'm sorry! Are you all right?"

She nodded, her eyes darting.

"Christ, I'm sorry," he said again. "I didn't mean to do that. I don't know what I was thinking." And suddenly he was aware of another presence, and eyes drilling through him. He smelled an animal smell and looked sharply to the side.

Beside the station wagon there was a gleaming, massive-flanked black horse, nostrils wide, still nervously tossing its huge triangular head. Red fire seemed to burn in that horse's eyes. And astride the animal, riding bareback, was Kathryn Drago, her hand clenched in the horse's mane. "Steady, Joker," she was saying softly. "Steady. Steady." The horse jerked its head and then

233

stood quiet while the woman stroked its neck. And then she gazed across at Evan. "That was very careless of you, Mr. Reid," she said coldly. "You could've killed my horse while we were crossing the road."

"I'm sorry," he told her. "I didn't see you there."

"We were in full view," the woman said. "Do you make it a point to break traffic laws?"

"My wife's not feeling well," Evan said, for lack of a better excuse. "I'm on my way to the drugstore."

The woman continued stroking the horse's neck. The animal rumbled with pleasure and seemed calm now. "Kay's ill?" she said, her visage softening a fraction. "Is it serious?"

"Headache," he said. "But she's staying home from school today."

"I see." She peered through the window, beyond Evan. "That's your little girl?"

"Yes, it is."

"She's very beautiful. Hello, there."

" 'Lo," Laurie said.

Drago's eyes moved back to Evan's. "You should be more careful. Someone could have been hurt."

"Is that your horse?" Laurie asked her, leaning forward to peer up at her.

"His name's Joker," Drago said. The horse's ears twitched. "I've been exercising him this morning. He's a fine horse, isn't he?"

"He's so pretty!" Laurie said, the near-accident now fading into the past. "I like horses!"

"That's good. I have twenty horses at my stables. Perhaps your mother and father will bring you to go riding someday soon."

"Could I, Daddy?" Laurie looked to him.

"We'll see," he said, smoothing her hair. When he looked into Drago's eyes he saw something flash there, something quick and dark and dangerous.

"I hope you'll bring her out," Drago said. "Every woman should know how to master a horse."

"She's got time for that."

"Indeed she does," the woman said, and smiled very slightly.

A car's horn blew for Evan to clear the intersection.

He said, "I'm sorry this happened, Dr. Drago. I'll take more care in the future."

"Yes," she said. "You should." And then she expertly wheeled the horse around with one hand and her heels, and rode off in the opposite direction. Evan waved to the driver of the other car and then drove on toward the Circle.

"She's so nice," Laurie said. "I'd like to go see her horses."

Evan was silent. The Circle was ahead, with its neat little shops. In the center he noticed that most of the flowers had died under the extreme heat.

And on the outskirts of Bethany's Sin, near the large welcoming sign, Neely Ames paused behind the red lawn mower to mop his face with his arm. The sun was searing him, and there was a lot more ground to cover before he'd be finished. He felt as if his eyelids were puffed from the heat, and around him trees drooped toward the earth. He was beginning to look forward to that special sassafras tea Mrs. Bartlett had ready for him almost every night now.

It was always so cold, and made him sleep so well.

TWENTY-TWO

WYSINGER, AFRAID, AND EVAN SEEKING

The patrol car with BETHANY'S SIN POLICE on the driver's door rolled to a halt before the massive black gate with the large *D* in it. Wysinger left the car and walked over to a speaker imbedded in the wall beside the gate; he pressed a button and waited.

A metallic voice, female: "Yes?"

He cleared his throat nervously. "It's Sheriff Wysinger. I'd like to see Dr. Drago."

"On what business?"

"It's personal."

There was a long pause, and Wysinger shifted his stance several times. Then, "Very well. Return to your car and drive through." The speaker clicked off, and the gate came open, slowly, with the hum of concealed machinery.

Wysinger did as he was told, then drove toward the house. Unease always crept into his bones like a disease when he came here; he avoided the place as much as possible, though sometimes he found it necessary to speak to Dr. Drago in person. He disliked her, even hated her, because she had money and land, because she was well-educated and had traveled so much, because she was intelligent and powerful.

But far beyond the boundaries of his hate was a fear that now gnawed at him, slowly eating away whatever semblance of courage remained inside him, until when he reached the door to the house he would be so much walking, breathing, blood-filled jelly. He always wished he'd had a drink before he saw her; he wished he carried a pint of Beam in the glove compartment. But no. She'd smell it. Shit, she could smell the odor of a man a quarter of a mile away, couldn't she? She could smell his fear, too; he knew it, knew the way she—and all of those others who were like she was—could sharpen her senses by releasing that strange and terrible power lying deep within her soul.

His fears were heightened now by the fact that evening was fast falling into limitless night. Through the trees he could see the shadowy hulk of that huge house waiting ahead. His skin crawled beneath the sweat stains on his shirt. He craned his neck, scanning the sky. No moon tonight; it had waned away to blackness. God in Heaven, he thought, I dread going inside that woman's house! Stepping across her threshold was like stepping into a different, terrifying world where her word was law, over and above the laws of men. The house was dark and seemed deserted, but as Wysinger parked his car before it and walked slowly toward the door, a light came on in a front window. The door came open, and a slender young blond woman in violet robes awaited him. Wordlessly, he followed her inside, along the dim corridors with their earth-hued murals, toward the rear of the house.

"Wait here," the woman told him when they reached a pair of gleaming oak doors. She went inside; Wysinger took off his hat, his heart already beating fast, and glanced up and down the corridor. A herd of horses, muscles straining, raced along one wall.

The blond woman reappeared and held the door open for him. He moved past her into the room, and the door swung closed behind him. Instantly he felt trapped.

He stood in Dr. Drago's study, a room of rough stone walls with a huge fireplace and ghost-eyed, life-size statues standing in the four corners. Beside a large picture window that looked out across the pasture was a highly polished walnut desk adorned with intricately carved human figures; Dr. Drago, in black robes, sat there, writing on a sheet of pale blue stationery. A single lamp burned beside her shoulder. "What do you want?" she asked coldly, without looking up.

Wysinger approached her desk. When he got within six feet of it the woman's head came up and her eyes froze him where he was.

"I want to . . . to talk to you about . . . the others," he said quietly. And carefully.

"What about them?"

"I hadn't said anything . . . before, but the hunting time's coming soon, and I . . ."

Her eyes narrowed. "What have you to do with the hunting time?"

He paused a moment, gathering himself. His legs seemed about to give way. "It's not safe," he said. "That workman, Ames, saw them on the King's Bridge Road. He's the only one who ever saw them and lived. They attacked him too close to the village. I don't like that."

She was silent. She put down her pen and folded her hands before her. "I'm not concerned with what you do or don't like, Wysinger. It's of no importance."

"Yes, it is, by God!" he said, his voice whipping out of control. "I've had to deal before with state police nosin' around here looking for people! Somebody finds another truck or another body out in the woods near the village, they're going to start putting it together!"

"As you did?"

"Like I did!" Wysinger said. "I took a real personal interest in it because I found the first ones, the Fletchers; but somebody else, some smart son of a bitchin' trooper, is going to put it together sometime, too!"

"That's part of your job," Drago said quietly. "To keep them away."

"Sure, I know that's my job, but if there's too many questions, I won't be able to handle the situation."

"What are you suggesting?"

He took a deep breath. "Keep them off the King's Bridge Road. Keep them off all the county roads. Let them do their hunting in the woods, or on the back roads, far away from the village."

"I was unaware that the workman was involved," Drago said. "He was chosen for a purpose, not for the pleasure of the others."

"I don't care what happens to that little bastard, but he saw them and he can describe them. And he's been spending time up at the Cock's Crow, probably shooting his mouth off to anybody who'll listen."

"No one will believe him."

"I wouldn't be so certain about that," Wysinger said. "From what I hear, someone else has been asking a hell of a lot of questions about the museum and—"

"Yes," Drago said. "I know. Mr. Reid."

"He may know something," Wysinger said. "If he does, what's going to happen?"

Drago's eyes glittered. "Patience," she said. "Mr. Reid is a curious man, but he's groping in the dark."

"I think you ought to get rid of him," Wysinger said.

"I'll decide that!" Drago said sharply. "When the time is right. Mrs. Reid is undergoing the transformation now. Soon she'll be ready for the rite, but until that time she'll be unstable, slipping back and forth from what she is to what she will be. Killing her husband now would be . . . unwise."

Wysinger ran a hand over his face. "He's dangerous. He's asking too many questions."

"Mr. Reid is being taken care of. Mrs. Hunt satisfied his curiosity about the museum, and Mrs. Giles gave him a perfect story about"—she smiled slightly—"Bethany's Sin. Did you know that Mr. Reid was a military man? He served in the Marines. That makes him a much more interesting opponent."

"That man's trouble," Wysinger persisted. "I found him hammering at the museum door one day, like he was in . . . a damned trance or something."

"Strange," the woman said, darkness lying in the hollows of her eyes. "Several days ago he ran a stop sign and almost struck my horse. I caught a glimpse of his eyes through the windshield. They were . . . distant, unfocused. A trance? Interesting. Very interesting." She picked up her pen and tapped it several times on the blotter before her. "Perhaps there's more to Mr. Reid than I've suspected." She raised her eyes to the man before her. "I'll take your suggestion into consideration. Now leave."

He nodded and turned toward the door, his heart still beating fast; no matter what the damned bitch decided, he thought, he'd be glad to get behind the safety of his own walls tonight.

"Wysinger," Drago said. The man shivered involuntarily and looked back. "We have two new arrivals in the village. Mrs. Jensen and Mrs. Berryman had baby girls last week at the clinic. Mrs. Gresham had a baby boy on Wednesday night; I want you to look in on Mr. Gresham from time to time to make certain . . . everything remains in control. Now you may go." She returned to her correspondence.

In the police car, with his hat back on his head and his heartbeat slowly returning to normal, Wysinger drove along the road to the gate, waited for it to swing slowly open, then turned toward Bethany's Sin. In his rearview mirror he saw that gate begin to close again, like a barrier between worlds. He breathed an almost audible sigh of relief at getting away from that damned place. Of course Dr. Drago paid him well, and had given him the house on Deer Cross Lane, but he knew all too well that she could easily have him killed. And God, what a horrible way to die that would be! Like Paul Keating, or like any of the dozens of others. Like the Fletchers, mutilated in the gray dawn hours just before they were going to sit down for breakfast. They voted him in as sheriff term after term, but he knew that in their hearts they despised him; he knew that in their hearts they wished they could get their hands on him and tear him into grisly, dripping pieces. That scrapbook of murders had become a good insurance policy. Now, if he sensed any threat, he could seal it up and hide it somewhere safe, maybe in a Johnstown bus locker, even; or he could send it to his cousin Hal in Wisconsin, with strict orders not to open it unless something happened to him. That way he'd have an edge over them. He wondered what they'd do if that scrapbook were found. Kill him? No, probably not. They needed him for the sake of appearances. All's well in Bethany's Sin; no dark deeds in this village. Bullshit.

Night had fallen over the village. Stars glittered in the sky. No moon tonight. No moon. Thank God. He was approaching the Gresham house; it was dark, but he knew Mr. Gresham sat inside, staring at a wall or the ceiling. There would be an empty bottle on the floor beside him, and the television or the radio would be on, filling those rooms with phantom figures, phantom voices. Mr. Gresham would be drunkenly mourning the death of his infant son. Perhaps contemplating suicide? No. Gresham didn't have the courage. Wysinger left the

Gresham house behind. Suddenly a pair of headlights rounded a curve and passed him, fast but within the posted speed limit. He watched the red taillights recede in his rearview mirror, then disappear. A station wagon? Whose? Except for that car the streets of Bethany's Sin were deserted; in the forest the insects began to whine, louder and louder, and the heat had already settled to ground level, like a steaming fog. Wysinger turned onto Deer Cross Lane, then into the driveway of his house. For him the day was over.

But for Evan the most important part of it lay ahead. He was on his way out of Bethany's Sin, past the Drago property, and along Highway 219 toward Whittington where Dr. Blackburn was expecting him. He'd almost called the man to postpone their conversation because Kay wasn't feeling very well, but he'd decided that talking to Blackburn was vital. Kay had missed two more days of school; that disturbed him deeply because it wasn't like her to take time off from work. She certainly wasn't a hypochondriac, nor was she especially prone to illnesses barring an occasional bout with the flue. But now she was staying in bed most of the time, eating very little and practically living on those damned Tylenols. Evan wanted her to go to the Mabry Clinic for a checkup, but she said she didn't have time right now, she'd do it as soon as the term ended. It seemed to Evan that in just the last couple of days her face had begun to change; she'd paled, and purplish shadows had crept beneath her eyes and into the hollows of her cheeks. At night she cried out in her sleep but refused to talk about what was haunting her. Evan had brought her some vitamins from the drug store, thinking that perhaps she wasn't eating well enough, but those bottles sat unopened in the bathroom medicine cabinet. He felt ineffectual, helplessly watching his wife . . . yes, waste away before his eyes. She'd been sleeping when he'd left home for Whittington.

Evan found 114 Morgan Lane in the quiet little community of Whittington; Blackburn's house was smaller than his own, of weathered red brick with a white picket fence. When Evan rang the doorbell a dog began to bark inside. Blackburn's voice, nearing the door, said, "Be quiet, Hercules!" and the dog stopped. The door opened and Blackburn, in jeans and a casual pullover shirt, smiled and said, "Come on in!"

The house was decorated well, if inexpensively; in the living room were a brown plaid sofa and a couple of chairs, a dark gold carpet, a glass-topped table with *National Geographic*s and *Smithsonian* magazines arranged on it. Christie, also in casual clothes, looked up from the sofa and smiled; at Evan's feet a small brown bulldog sniffed, sniffed, sniffed.

"Good to see you again," Blackburn said, shaking Evan's hand. "Here you go. Have a seat. Can I get you something to drink? A beer, maybe?"

He sat in one of the chairs. "No, thank you."

"We've got wine," Christie said. "Boone's Farm."

"That sounds good."

"Fine. Doug, do you want a glass?" She rose from the sofa.

"A small one." Christie left the room, and Blackburn took her place on the sofa; the bulldog jumped up beside him, still eyeing the stranger. "Well," he said, "how are things in Bethany's Sin?"

"It's still there," Evan said. "Other than that . . ." He shrugged.

Blackburn stroked the bulldog's back, and it stretched out lazily. "You can see what goes on in Whittington. Seven o'clock and lights out, by municipal decree. No, really, it's a nice little place. Christie and I prefer peace and quiet. And Hercules does, too." He scratched the dog's head.

Christie came with a strawberry wine; Evan took a glass from her, and she settled herself on the other side of her husband. "I'm sorry your wife couldn't come with you, Mr. Reid. I'd like to see her again."

"She's not feeling too well these days."

"Oh, that's too bad," Christie said. "What is it? A virus or something?"

He sipped at the wine. "To tell you the truth, I don't know what it is. I think perhaps she's overworking." That lie stung him.

"Probably so," Blackburn said. "This is her first term; I suppose she's breaking her back to do a good job."

"Yes," Evan said, "I guess that's it."

Blackburn drank from his glass and then put it down on the table before him. He reached into his shirt pocket for that briar pipe and began to fill it from a tobacco pouch. "Now," he said after he'd gotten it lit, "what exactly's on your mind? I'll tell you, you sounded very anxious over the phone. And concerned. I hope I can help you with whatever your problem is."

"I hope you can, too." Evan leaned forward slightly. "At Dr. Drago's party you and she . . . well, you got into an argument over her museum exhibit. I didn't quite understand what was going on, but I saw clearly how disturbed Dr. Drago was. Since then, I've been through the museum myself; I've seen the artifacts from Themiscrya and now I have a question."

"Shoot," Blackburn said.

"Why all the disagreement between you and her over a three-thousand-year-old farming community?"

Blackburn stared at him, blinked, smiled slightly. Then the smile broadened. "Oh, come on! Who told you Themiscrya was a farming community? Not Dr. Drago herself, surely!"

"No. A woman at the museum, a member of the historical society."

"I don't understand that," Blackburn said, his brow knitting. "Maybe some of those ladies in that so-called society have got some common sense after all."

Evan shook his head. "I'm afraid I don't understand what you mean."

"Since 1965," Blackburn said, a wreath of pipe smoke above his head, "Kathryn Drago has maintained that the city of Themiscrya was the capital of the Amazon nation. A center of warfare, not a damned settlement of farmers!"

"Amazons?" Evan smiled slightly. "Like Wonder Woman?"

"No." Surprisingly, Blackburn's voice was grave. "That's pure fiction, and ludicrous at that. The Amazons were glorified in Greek mythology; if they ever existed—and that's a huge *if*—they were bloodthirsty female killers who looked upon battle as recreation. Men were their sworn enemies; those they didn't slaughter on the battle-fields, they mutilated and kept as sexual slaves—"

"Wait a minute!" Evan said. That word had thudded into him with the force of a blow, ripping the smile off his face and exposing the raw nerves beneath. "What do you mean, 'mutilated'?"

"Crippled them in some way. They held the barbaric belief that cutting off an arm or a leg would strengthen the male's sexual organs. Of course, they didn't particularly crave the attentions of men, but they needed female babies to keep their tribe strong. Usually the Amazons slaughtered the men after they weren't needed any longer." He paused for a moment, seeing something odd in Evan's eyes. "Is something wrong?" he asked.

"No," Evan said. "Nothing's wrong." Silhouette behind a curtain. Reaching for a hand that wasn't there. Legs falling away from a torso. Nothing's wrong nothing's wrong. . . .

"Mythologically," Blackburn was saying, "Dr. Drago's correct. Throughout the fables that have come down from the Greeks, the city of Themiscrya was a massive Amazon fortress, from which the female warriors planned their marches on the Greek state. Realistically, it just simply wasn't the case, much as it would thrill me and countless other mythologists if it were. Oh, Themiscrya existed, all right; that's a historical fact. The Romans attacked and destroyed the city in 72 B.C., but no Amazons were found in the ruins. Only men. So . . ."

"What about the earlier inhabitants of Themiscrya?" Evan asked. "The ones those artifacts in the museum belonged to?"

"Ah!" Blackburn said, the pipe clenched in his teeth now. "That's where it gets a little tricky. Historians don't really know that much about the beginnings of Themiscrya; that's why Dr. Drago's finds were so important. Since 1965 a picture of the early Themiscryan civilization has been slowly emerging: they were a warlike culture who raised horses and some staple crops, and who worshiped the deities Ares and Artemis. There's evidence in some remaining wall paintings that it was at one time a very beautiful, well-planned city. But somewhere through the ages it gradually began to decay, as most cities did and still do; when the Romans attacked, there probably wasn't much left of it."

"And there's no evidence at all to support Dr. Drago's belief?"

Blackburn smiled. "Inconclusive evidence. And that's not good enough."

"Such as?"

"Pottery adorned with Amazonlike figures. Fragments of wall paintings showing figures that might be female warriors standing over their fallen foes. That sort of thing. But at that time, you see, the Amazon legend was very popular; a great many sculptors and painters of the period used them as subjects. Amazons popped up on drinking cups, vases, pots and pans, even the Parthenon. So why shouldn't they be depicted at Themiscrya as well? But Dr. Drago found something that's made the historians wonder a little bit. She crawled through a tunnel of fallen rock into a cavern, and there she found a primitive statue of Artemis over an altar of black stone. This Artemis was covered with what were clearly female breasts. Dozens of them."

Evan raised an eyebrow.

"There's speculation among mythologists, mostly unfounded, that the Amazons may have seared off their right breasts with either a heated sword or some kind of branding-iron-like thing. It was done as a test of courage and as a sacrifice to the goddess. Also, some say, the right breast might have interfered with the drawing back of the bowstring." He traced a star on the right side of his chest. "Scar's supposed to have looked like that. That statue's over at the museum in Bethany's Sin. Didn't you see it?"

Evan shook his head, remembering a black door that cut off his progress. Remembering a black altar stone in a vision, and women waiting.

"One interesting thing," Blackburn said as he struck another match to his pipe. "Themiscrya was rumored to be haunted."

Evan locked eyes with the other man. "Haunted?"

"Right." The tobacco fired; he exhaled smoke. "There was a village called Caraminya near the dig site; from what I've gathered, the villagers thought the area's earthquakes were caused by the wrath of the slain Amazons.

Soon after the excavations began, some of the Caraminya women . . . went off the deep end, I guess you'd say."

"How?"

"Tried to kill their husbands, ranted and raved in a language nobody could understand. Anyway, Caraminya isn't there anymore. After the quake of 'sixty-five, and after Themiscrya began to reappear out of the earth, those villagers packed up their belongings and left."

"This cavern that Dr. Drago found," Evan said quietly. "What else was in it?"

"Scorched statues. Evidence that a huge fire had burned there at one time. A lot of ashes; mounds and mounds of ashes that everyone at first thought were only dust. That cavern had been closed up for God knows how long; the quake broke it open again."

Evan sipped thoughtfully at his wine. "Ashes? Of what?"

"Bones," Blackburn replied, watching Evan's eyes. "The cavern had been used as a huge funeral pyre, ages ago. The historians are still working on that one."

Evan ran a hand across his forehead, finished his wine, set the glass aside.

"Would you like more, Mr. Reid?" Christie asked. Evan shook his head.

"Now, how about explaining to me what this is all about?" Blackburn asked.

Careful, Evan cautioned himself. Careful. "Do you believe the Amazons ever existed?" he asked the man. "Anywhere?"

Blackburn smiled again, but the smile wasn't reflected in his eyes. "If you want to believe, then yes, they did exist. Homer says they did. Arrian says they did. Herodotus does, too. Historical records say Amazons attacked and almost overcame the city of Athens around 1256 B.C. The last great Amazon queen, Penthesilea, is supposed to have been killed by Achilles at Troy. And Troy did exist. Who knows? The only thing that endures is the legend—of wild, cunning female fighters who came out of the mists and returned to the mists. But imagine if you can, Mr. Reid, hearing across the plain of battle the long and fierce war cry that would freeze the marrow in your bones; in the distance you could see the dust boiling as their horses approached, and long before they reached your ranks, the skies would sizzle with arrows. Then it would be hand-to-hand combat, sword and spear against the bipennis, the Amazonian double-bladed battle-ax; their horses would twist aside from spear thrusts, or a bipennis would shatter the arm that gripped a blade. And during the terrible din of bloodletting, their eyes would be wild and shining; their senses would sing with the stimulation and tumult of war, as necessary for them as breathing. There would be no end to the fighting until the last man had been beheaded or dragged back to camp to be mutilated. That would be a horrifying way to die, Mr. Reid; and I thank God that, if the Amazons did live, our destinies never met." He raised his wineglass, drank, returned it to the table.

Evan rose from his chair. There seemed to be an abyss inside him, somewhere between the soul and the physical body; within that cold darkness, terror churned, about to break free and flood like bile from his lips. He moved toward the door.

Blackburn stood up. "You're not leaving, are you? I imagine there's most of a bottle of Boone's Farm left."

"I've got to go," Evan said; he placed his hand on the doorknob.

"You know, I still don't understand what's going on," Blackburn said. "I assume you're not going to tell me?"

"What happened to the male babies?" Evan asked him. "Surely some of the Amazons did have baby boys?"

"Of course." Blackburn took the pipe from between his teeth and examined Evan's face, not certain precisely what he was seeing. "That couldn't be helped. The Amazons kept some of the males, to be used as breeding stock later on. Most of the male infants they killed. Why are you so interested in the Amazon civilization? I want to know."

"Sometime I'll tell you. For now, let's just chalk it up to curiosity." Evan opened the door; stale heat waited to embrace him. Hercules yipped once, twice, and Christie put a hand on him to quiet him. "Thanks for having me over," Evan said. "And thanks for the wine."

"Bring Mrs. Reid next time," Christie said.

"Yes, I will. Good night."

"Good night," Blackburn said.

Evan drove toward Bethany's Sin, his mind working furiously, sheering away from the terrible truth, but always, always coming back because there was no other way out of the labyrinth.

And at the Reid house on McClain Terrace the thing moved in the dark, down the stairs, through the den, toward the kitchen. Where the knives were. It could smell the fetid stench of man in these rooms; the man this pitifully weak woman named Kay lived with, slept with, allowed to touch this mansion of flesh. The girl-child, sleeping upstairs. A sheet wadded under the door to jam it shut and muffle noise. The thing moved into the kitchen, senses tingling. Almost able to see in the dark. Almost. Glasses, dishes stacked on the counter next to the sink. An arm swept through them, scattering most of them to the floor. Opening drawers, wrenching them out, spilling their contents. And then it found what it sought. A large-bladed butcher knife, hardly used. The blade was so keen it drew a thread of blood from a testing finger.

In the darkness the thing waited for the man to come home, as the cheery yellow kitchen clock showed three minutes into August.

IV

AUGUST

TWENTY-THREE

HOME

From the blackness shadow-shapes slowly materialized. Headlights gleamed briefly off windows, awakening the squat, heavy-lidded, unnamable, malignant creatures lying indolent on their jealousy guarded square plots of lawn. As Evan swept past those houses he wasn't altogether certain the eyes of the beasts didn't shift in their wooden and brick frames to follow him; when he glanced quickly into his rearview mirror, he saw that the blackness had swelled again, midnight currents engulfing Bethany's Sin.

He switched on the radio, searched for stations. Rock music, Mick Jagger's snarl rising and then fading away into static; soft piano playing "Moon River"; a woman breathily talking about the action at Jimmy K's in Johnstown; crackles and shrill static from the real world beyond the boundaries of the village. Dear God, Evan said suddenly, afraid that something inside him was about to give way as if he stood on flooring that could hardly bear the strain of more weight. He ran a hand across his face. Dear God. Oh Christ oh God in Heaven. Fear and disbelief ran through him, almost splitting him apart. Dark Bethany's Sin streets. Dark Bethany's Sin houses. Dark Bethany's Sin forest. Blending, merging into one greater darkness, lapping at the windows of the station wagon, trying to get in at him.

By the time he reached silent McClain Terrace, the full weight of the terror had clamped itself to his back like some huge, venom-dripping spider. That he and Kay and Laurie had stumbled into the nest of some unholy, murderous Amazonlike cult. He turned into his driveway, stopped the car, switched off the radio and the headlights, then sat still for a few minutes, gathering his thoughts together as best he could while the heat slithered in around him. Was this what his premonitions had been warning him of, he wondered, ever since the first day they'd arrived here? That the evil in Bethany's Sin was centured around the museum with its remnants of long-dead Themiscrya? Or was there something even more incredibly terrible yet to come? He shivered suddenly, felt his mind slip out of control for an instant. Am I going crazy? he asked himself. No. I'm all right. I'm all right. But I've got to get Kay and Laurie out of here. And I've got to be very careful. He took the keys out of the ignition, left the car.

He unlocked the front door and, stepping inside, switched on the light in the entrance foyer. Shadows scuttled. Was there anything to drink in the house? Yes. Beer in the refrigerator. He turned on the living-room light on his way to the kitchen, stopped in the kitchen doorway, stepped forward, stopped, stepped forward, like a marionette pulled on by strings held by claw-nailed hands. His shoes crunched on fragments of broken glass and dishes. He reached for the light switch, then paused and dropped his hand; his heart had begun to beat faster, and the cold noose of uncertainty had dropped around his throat. Had Kay been up since he'd left, and had there been an accident here in the kitchen? He stood looking around at the breakage, his back to the pantry door.

Could these dishes have slid off the counter by themselves? he wondered. The house was so quiet; unnervingly so. It was a quiet not of peace but of events hanging in time by a slowly unraveling thread. Evan pushed some of the glass fragments out of the center of the floor with his shoe. Then, the beer forgotten, he retraced his way back through the living room, turned off the light, and climbed the stairs; one of them squealed beneath his weight.

Both bedroom doors were closed. Moving in the dark, Evan opened the door to the master bedroom and slipped in.

Table shape. Lamp shape. Bed shape. And in the bed the hills and valleys of Kay's body in the sheets; she was lying on her left side, facing away from him. He could see the darkness of her hair fanned across the pillow. Wake her, he told himself. Wake her and tell her everything you suspect and take her and Laurie out of this godforsaken place. Wake her now. Now. Now. His hand moved toward the hill of her shoulder. No. Wait. She'll think you've lost your mind; she'll think you're drunk or you're raving or that finally the threads of your fragile sanity have snapped. *Goddamn it wake her now this may be your last chance!* He hesitated. No. Not tonight. In the morning. In the morning I'll tell her, and maybe, just maybe, I can make her understand we've got to get out of here.

Evan undressed in silence, put on his pajamas, slid into bed beside his wife; through her back he could feel her heartbeat, strong and steady. For a while he stared at the ceiling, seeing the eyes of Harris Demargeon hanging faceless above him, and to escape that vision he closed his own eyes and sought sleep.

The slow shifting of weight on the bed. An inch at a time.

Something leaped behind Evan's eyelids, trembling with fire. Like the sudden reflection of light on the blade of a knife.

Evan's eyes came open.

And he could see the faint outline of his wife standing over him. He lifted his head, started to ask her what was wrong. But found no voice.

For in Kay's face tendrils of blue flame burned in a terrible, unblinking gaze. In that searing instant Evan knew that the woman-thing before him was no longer truly Kay.

She shrieked—a cry that rattled the window glass and ripped at Evan's soul—and drove down with a knife she'd raised high above her head. As Evan leaped to one side, the nerves in his shoulder and back cringed; the knife plunged into the pillow where his head had been, the tearing of cloth electric, filling the room. Evan had rolled to the floor, was now rising to a crouch, moving backward. The Kay-thing turned her head, eyes piercing him; she ripped the knife through the pillow, lifted it again, and came for him, her breathing harsh now, and rapid.

"*Kay!*" Evan screamed. "*What in God's name are you . . . ?*"

And then she leaped forward, was almost upon him before he could even think to grasp for the doorknob. The knife glinted, swung for his face in a vicious, hissing arc. As Evan jerked his head back, he felt a hot, grazing pain just above his left eyebrow. She came forward, snarling like an animal, quickly adjusting her grip so she could stab with the blade. He realized she was backing him away from the door, and blind panic surged through him. *"Kay!"* he shouted at her, but those eyes, those eyes, those terrible, unblinking, flaming eyes scorching him with utter hatred. Not Kay, no. Something else. Not even human. Something beyond the black door of nightmares. A wetness, collecting in his eyebrow. Streaming down. He wiped it out of his eye. When he did, she leaped forward again, her hand darting in with the speed of a cobra, the fang of the knife yearning for his blood. He twisted aside, felt the metal rake his ribs. The Kay-thing's free hand whipped out, clutched him around the throat, and began to squeeze with a power he'd never imagined could be harbored within that body; he gripped her wrist, tried to struggle free. The knife rose, a cold glimmer of stainless steel in the darkness. Fingers dug into Evan's throat, and now he found breathing difficult. He balled up his fist to strike her in the face; the knife rose, rose; his knuckles whitened; knife blade gleamed. *Strike her!* No. *Strike her!* No. *Strike her . . . !*

The knife reached its zenith. Arm trembled slightly, gathering strength for a blow that would drive the blade through his heart.

Something pounding. Pounding. Pounding. "Mommy?" Laurie's voice from behind her bedroom door. "Mommy? Daddy?" The tremor of panic, of tears about to break.

The knife hesitated. *Strike her this is not Kay this is something within her body but not her dear God not her dear God not her. . . .*

His fist came forward almost involuntarily. He struck her on the cheekbone and her head rocked back, but still the eyes did not blink; her fingers loosened a fraction, and then Evan struck again, hammering into the crook of her arm, fighting his way out of the grip that had almost crushed his windpipe. The knife whistled down for him, missing by inches; she shrieked again, a bloodcurdling, savage shriek, and before the next blow came, Evan had picked up a chair, holding the legs out to ward her off.

"Mommy!" Laurie screamed. *"Daddy open the door!"*

As the Kay-thing reared back to strike again, a guttural growl rumbling from her throat, Evan thrust forward with the chair. It caught her off-balance, staggered her; something ripped, and the knife blade tore through the cushion of the chair toward Evan's face. He pushed against her with all his strength, shoulder muscles cracking. She slipped, the folds of her nightgown flying around her, and went down in a corner, her head slamming hard against the wall. Evan threw the chair aside, the knife still piercing it, and spun toward the light switch.

Clicked it on. Blinding light. *"Daddy!"* Laurie was almost hoarse now. *"Daddy please let me out let me out!"*

In the corner, Kay lay with her eyes closed, her face as pale and drawn as that of a corpse. She seemed to be laboring to breathe; her chest was heaving, and beads of perspiration clung to her face. He bent over her carefully and felt for her pulse. It was racing. A drop of blood splattered down onto her chest. Followed by another. Evan put a hand to the cut above his eye to stop the bleeding; the blood trickled in a thin line between Kay's breasts. Her head lolled to one side, and Evan could see the eyes moving quickly back and forth behind the lids. He shook her for a moment, trying to wake her, but she was unresponsive. He stepped across the chair toward the telephone on the night table, paged quickly through the phone book. What's that doctor's name? Myers? No. Mabry. Hurry. Hurry. Laurie sobbed across the hall. He found the listing: Mabry, Eleanor, physician. Two numbers: home and office. Blood drops on the page. He chose the home number, misdialed, tried it again. Kay moaned softly from the corner.

The doctor was alert when she answered. Evan, trying to keep his voice calm, told her who he was and where he was calling from, and that his wife had had an accident. Dr. Mabry asked for no other details. She said she'd be there in fifteen minutes.

Evan mopped at his forehead with his pajama shirt tail, pulled the knife out of the chair, and laid it on the bed, out of Kay's reach; he put the chair back where it had been, and then he crossed the hall, finding Laurie's door jammed. When he wrenched that wadded-up sheet out, the child leaped into his arms. "I couldn't get out," she sobbed. "I heard something awful I heard you shouting Mommy's name and I couldn't get out 'cause the door was stuck!"

"Shhhhhh," he whispered, holding her close, feeling the tiny heart beating in her chest. "Everything's all right."

She drew back, looked at him, saw the blood. New tears welled, and her lower lip trembled.

"Daddy hit his head," Evan told her quietly. "I had another one of those old nightmares. You know, the kind I always have? And I bumped my head on the night table. It's just a little scrape."

"Where's Mommy?" She tried to look over his shoulder.

"She's in the bathroom getting a Band-Aid for my hurt. A doctor's going to be coming here in a few minutes to look at me." He peered into his daughter's eyes, tried to keep his own gaze steady. "Now. Will you do something for me?"

"Is Mommy all right?"

"Sure she is. But you know how she gets mad at me for having those dreams. I want you to go downstairs in the den and stay there until the doctor leaves. Will you do that for me?"

She paused, wiped away tears, finally nodded.

"Good. I think there are some cookies down in the kitchen, and some Kool-Aid. I don't think your mom would mind if you had some. Go on, now." He waited until she went reluctantly down the stairs; the lights came on in the den. Evan turned away; in the master bedroom Kay was still lying where she'd been, moaning very softly.

Dr. Mabry was a slender, fiftyish woman with slightly disarrayed gray hair and a high, heavily lined forehead. As Evan led her quickly up the stairs, her hazel eyes moved behind thick-lensed eyeglasses like fish in watery bowls. "In here," Evan said, leading her into the bedroom.

She looked down at Kay and saw the knife on the bed; she put her medical bag on the night table and popped it open. "What happened here?" she asked in a cool, evenly modulated voice.

"My wife's been having some strange dreams lately," Evan said, his hand still pressed to his wound. It had stopped bleeding, and blood was crusted in his eyebrow.

"I think I must've disturbed her during one of them, and she . . . attacked me. I don't think she knew what she was doing."

"Does your wife always sleep with a knife in her bed?"

Evan was silent. Dr. Mabry took a stethoscope from her bag and listened to different places on Kay's chest for a moment; she carefully moved Kay's hand to the side and felt through her hair. "Nasty bump there," she said softly. "And what's this?" She placed a finger alongside the purpling bruise on her cheekbone.

"I had to defend myself."

"I see. How has your wife been feeling lately, generally speaking?"

"Tired. She's hardly been eating at all; I can tell she's losing weight, and she doesn't sleep very well anymore."

Kay trembled, moaned.

Dr. Mabry reached quickly into her bag, brought out an ampul and snapped it open under Kay's nose; Evan smelled the aroma of ammonia. Kay's eyelids fluttered, and she shook her head from side to side. "She'll come around now," Dr. Mabry said.

"I know this looks bad," Evan said, "but I'd prefer that you not tell Sheriff Wysinger."

"I have no intention of telling him anything," the woman said, lifting first Kay's right eyelid, then her left. White rolling to blue.

Kay moaned again, louder now, and gradually her eyes opened, squeezing tears from the corners. She struggled up, winced, and felt at the back of her head. "Oh, God, I'm hurt," she said. "I'm going to be sick. I'm going to—"

"Mr. Reid," Dr. Mabry said, "I want you to go downstairs to your kitchen and boil some water. Pour the hot water into a cup and bring it back up for us, will you?"

He left them and did as the woman asked, telling Laurie downstairs that everything was just fine, but he saw all too clearly that she didn't believe him.

When he returned to the bedroom he smelled the reek of vomit; Kay had thrown up into the toilet, and Dr. Mabry was saying softly, like a mother to a child, "There, there. Now you'll be fine. Are you feeling better now?"

"My head," Kay muttered, wiping her face with a wet washcloth. "My head is hurting."

"Here's your hot water," Evan said.

"Fine. Put it down out there, will you?"

Dr. Mabry led Kay, looking paler and more feeble than ever, back to the bed. Kay lay her head gingerly on the pillow. She was still trembling, and Evan wasn't certain yet that she really knew where she was or what had happened. Dr. Mabry reached into the bottom of her medical bag and brought out an amber-colored, unlabeled bottle. She unscrewed the cap and poured into the hot water what looked like a mixture of honey and herbs; it had a sweetish smell to it, and bits of herbs floated on the top. "I want you to drink this," Dr. Mabry said, offering the cup to Kay.

"What's in that?" Evan asked her.

"It's a home remedy," Dr. Mabry replied without looking at him. "Something to calm her nerves. That's right, dear. Drink it all down. Finish the last of it."

Kay did. The doctor took the cup back and laid it aside. "How do you feel now?"

"Funny. Still a little sick. Where's my husband?" Kay gazed into Dr. Mabry's eyes as if she didn't realize Evan was in the room.

"Here, Kay. I'm right here." He sat beside her and took her hand. Cold. Pulse still fast, but gradually slowing.

"What happened to your head?" she asked him, lifting a finger to touch his eyebrow. "That's blood!"

"Mr. Reid." Dr. Mabry rose to her feet, snapped her medical bag closed. "I'd like to talk with you in the hall, please."

"What's wrong with my wife?" Evan asked the doctor quietly when the bedroom door was shut behind them. "She doesn't seem to remember anything of what happened."

"I believe she's in a mild state of shock; there's disorientation due to that blow to her head. But to be perfectly honest with you, I'm not certain what her overall condition is. She seems to be relatively healthy, and yet you say her appetite's fallen off, she's tired and doesn't sleep well. I'd like to do some tests on your wife at my clinic. Starting tomorrow morning."

"What kinds of tests?"

"Blood, urine, cardiogram. And electroencephalogram."

"Her brain? Do you think something's wrong with her—"

"I'd like to find out," Dr. Mabry said. "As quickly as possible. Can you bring her to the clinic in the morning? Around nine?"

No, Evan thought. I want to take my wife and child and get out of this place in the morning.

"Her condition may be serious," Dr. Mabry said, her voice cool but emphatic. "There's a possibility she might have to stay at the clinic for several days."

"I don't know . . ." Evan said.

"If it's a question of payment . . ."

"It's not!" he said sharply. No. Hold on. Hold on. Kay's sick; she's really sick after all. He paused for a moment; Dr. Mabry watched him. A thought sizzled in his brain: They'll come for you in the night. He tore it out of himself, as if it were diseased tissue. Nodded. "I'll bring her in the morning."

For the first time the hint of a smile flickered across her face. "That's the wise thing to do. Your wife will be sleeping soon. I'll find my own way out. Oh"—she paused, popped open her bag again, and brought out an adhesive bandage—"this is for your forehead; I can tell just by looking that it's a graze. No stitches necessary. You might clean it with alcohol and then put this bandage on, though." And then she'd turned from him and was making her way down the stairs. The front door opened, closed.

In the bedroom Evan sat down beside Kay; she was on the verge of slumber now, her eyelids heavy. Evan grasped her hand and held it. "Kay?" he said softly. "Can you hear me?"

She stirred; her eyes were half-open. "Sleepy . . ." she whispered.

"When I came in, when I climbed into bed with you, I think you were dreaming again. Do you remember if you were? And what it was about?"

"Can't," she whispered.

"Try. Please. It's important."

"No." She winced, shook her head. "Terrible."

"Just relax. Think, now, and try to remember."

"My head hurts." She tried to lift her hand toward her

face, but the hand fell to her side before she could. Her eyelids squeezed closed very tightly, as if dark things were surfacing inside her that were tearing her to pieces. "I couldn't get out," she whispered. "She wouldn't let me out."

"Out? Who wouldn't let you out?" He leaned forward to hear.

"Her. Oliviadre. Her. Because I was her, and she was me. And she had me and wouldn't let me out."

"Oliviadre? Kay, what are you talking about?"

"My dreams. That's who I am in my dreams." She was quiet for a long time, and Evan thought she'd fallen asleep. But then her lips moved again. "Oliviadre is me, and I am her. And this time she wouldn't let me come back." Her eyelids squeezed. Wetness at the corners. "I was alone in the dark, and I couldn't . . . get back to here because . . . she's too strong now." Wetness thickening.

"Were you dreaming again?" he asked her; out of the corner of his eye he saw Laurie standing at the door.

"Yes. Oliviadre was . . . dead, and those men . . . those men dragged her body by the hair where they dragged the bodies of the others. Sleep. I want to sleep." Tears broke.

"What men?"

"The ones with swords. The awful ones. They dragged Oliviadre and . . . left her on the heap of corpses. And then they . . . set fire to us and we burned and I felt us all burning." The tears trickled slowly down her cheeks. "But after we were burned to bones, and after our bones were . . . burned, too, we lived . . . we lived still. . . ."

"Kay?" Evan whispered.

"But we were in darkness." Her voice had dwindled to a sigh. "All of us like wisps of smoke, still there, waiting. Waiting. Terrible darkness. Cold and terrible."

"Where were you?" Evan asked her. "Can you tell me that?"

"All dead, all dead but not gone. Still waiting. A long time waiting." A tear dripped from her chin. "Until the light. And the . . . woman."

"What woman? Kay, what woman?"

"Don't know. Sleepy. They were all around her, like dust, and they . . . went into her."

Evan's mouth was dry. "Went . . . into her?"

"Oliviadre wouldn't let me come back," Kay whispered; a breath escaped her like a slow, tortured gasp, and as another tear slipped down her cheek she was silent and motionless.

"Daddy?" Laurie said softly.

He stood up, his face touched by shadows. "Mommy's sleeping," he said. "Let's tuck you into bed now. Okay?"

TWENTY-FOUR

IN ROOM 36

The wide halls of the Mabry Clinic were spotless. How does the saying go? Evan thought as he walked, Laurie's hand in his. So clean a baby could eat off the floor. Yes. that was it. Tiles gleamed beneath the circular ceiling lights; the walls were two-toned, flat pale green and beige. On many of the walls hung framed original oil paintings or watercolors: sailboats running before a breeze, bright yellow daisies in a sun-dappled field, two puppies with wide, innocent eyes, a wistful clown playing a flute. Antiseptic odors wafted through the hallways: soap smells, detergent smells, Lysol smells.

It was Saturday afternoon, and beyond the air-conditioned halls of the clinic the sun scorched Bethany's Sin, softening pitch on the roofs of the buildings in the Circle, glancing off windows in rays of solid heat, shimmering above the ground like burning tides. Evan could feel sweat drying on his face, and his shirt slowly separating from the skin on his back.

Dr. Mabry had told him the day before, Kay's first day, that there were five full-time nurses at the clinic and five ladies who worked part-time in the afternoons, but now the place seemed deserted. Many of the rooms on either side of the hall were open; there were empty beds, blankets folded at the bottom. Yesterday Evan had seen two patients: a man lying on his back in bed, staring at the ceiling, in Room 36, and a pregnant woman in Room 27. She'd been watching "The Price Is Right" on her television, and had stared quietly at Evan as he'd walked past her open door. But there were closed doors as well, with INTENSIVE CARE and POST-OP and SURGERY in burnished metallic letters.

Kay was in Room 30, a nice room at the front of the

clinic with a wide window and beige curtains. The afternoon before, she'd wanted to come home and had started to climb out of bed, asking Evan and Laurie to help her get dressed, saying that nothing in the world was wrong with her and she was missing too many of her classes. But a slim young black nurse had come in to take her blood pressure, and Kay had been told rather severely to get back into bed. Immediately.

In her book-lined office on Friday afternoon, Dr. Mabry's gaze had been cool and direct across the black-blotter-topped desk. Possibly by Monday or Tuesday, she'd replied when Evan had asked what day his wife could come home. We're not finished with our tests by any means, she'd said, and it takes time to evaluate them. And if we do find something, we'll recheck ourselves to make certain, of course.

Do you suspect anything in particular? Evan had asked her.

Please, she'd said. Let's wait until the results are in, shall we?

"Here we are," Evan told Laurie, and rapped on the door marked 30.

"Come in." Kay sounded tired.

Inside, Evan's first impression was that, yes, Kay was looking worse. Her eyes seemed to be retreating into her head, and they'd taken on a sharp, shiny look, as if they were bits of polished glass. Her cheekbones protruded now, as if the flesh were tightening around her skull.

"Hi there," Kay said, and smiled at both of them.

"Hi," Laurie said softly. Uneasily.

"Come here and give me a kiss." Kay sat up against the pillows, held her daughter to her; Laurie kissed her on the cheek. "Are you being a good girl?"

Laurie nodded.

"How are you feeling?" Evan said, sitting beside her on the bed and taking her hand.

"Fine, just fine. Nothing's wrong with me. Have you talked with Dr. Mabry?"

"Yesterday afternoon, after I left you."

"What did she say?" Evan told her, and she shook her head. "Those tests are pointless; they're not going to show anything. All they're doing is sticking me with a few needles and taking my blood pressure at all hours of the night. At two o'clock this morning that nurse gave me the most horrible thing I ever drank in my life. It looked like orange juice, but it was just awful."

"Do the shots hurt?" Laurie asked.

"Like bee stings," Kay said. "Not too bad."

"How's the food?" Evan asked her. She looked as though she hadn't eaten a bite in a week.

"Okay. A little chalky-tasting. But my nurse, Mrs. Becker, went over to the delicatessen for me last night and brought back a pastrami sandwich. She said if Dr. Mabry found out she'd be in real trouble because I'm supposed to be on a special diet. For the tests, you know."

"Laurie and I both miss you," he said, squeezing her hand. "A lot."

"It's nice to know you're missed," Kay said, and smiled.

Evan caressed the back of her hand, where he could see blue veins snaking underneath statue white skin. "I have to ask you something," he said quietly. "Do you remember anything of what happened Thursday night?"

A shade passed briefly across her eyes. She lay her head back. "I remember putting Laurie to bed around nine. I went to bed a little before eleven. And then the lights were on and Dr. Mabry was standing over me."

"Nothing else? Please, think hard."

She shook her head. "No, nothing else."

Evan leaned forward, held her gaze with his own. "That's not what you told me before. You were drugged and sleepy, and you were telling me that you'd been dreaming. . . ."

"Dreams!" Kay said, so harshly that Laurie blinked, stepped away from the bed. "No one in the world puts so much faith in dreams as you do, Evan! For God's sake!"

"You spoke a name;" he continued, still holding her hand. "Oliviadre. Do you know who that is?"

"Of course I don't."

"I do," he said calmly. "It's the woman you see in those dreams. And more. It's who you are in them."

She looked at him incredulously, but he could see in her face the fear and the realization that he'd nicked the dark, shapeless thing that passed for truth in Bethany's

Sin, drawing yellowish ichor. For a long while she was silent, her eyes flickering nervously over toward where Laurie stood. "Yes," she said finally. "In my dreams I'm a woman called Oliviadre. But what difference can that possibly make?"

"What kind of woman is she?"

"A . . . warrior of some kind," Kay said. "Proud. Merciless. For God's sake, listen to me! I'm talking like she really exists!"

"You said something else, Kay. That Oliviadre wouldn't let you free; that she's too strong now. . . ."

"I never said anything like that!" Kay said sharply.

He paused for a moment, watching her. "Yes. You did."

"She's not real, damn it!" the woman said, not caring now what Laurie heard or saw. "She's a shadow, not flesh and blood! What's wrong with you, Evan? Are you losing your—" She stopped abruptly, her mouth already curled around the word.

"My mind?" he prompted. "Losing my mind? No. Now listen to me. Don't turn your face away! Listen!" She looked at him with the eyes that had flamed in the darkness of their bedroom. "Something terrible is happening in this village. Don't say anything, just listen! There are forces in this place, Kay, forces I don't understand and never will, but by God I'm afraid for all of us. When this terrible thing gathers itself, it won't come only for me but for you and Laurie as well." He gripped her shoulders and peered into her face. "Believe me this time, Kay. Please believe me."

Her eyes were hooded. She said very quietly, "You're frightening Laurie."

"I want to make you believe!" he said, and she recoiled slightly because his eyes had been wild for the briefest instant and his voice lay on the cracking edge. "I'm afraid that they've already done something to you, and we've got to leave here before it's too late!"

"Evan," Kay said softly. "Evan, let me go. Let me go, please."

"No!" Evan hissed. "I won't let you go! They're killers, they're all killers, and somehow they're making you into what they are! You attacked me with a knife, Kay! And

265

you never knew what you were doing because you weren't in control! Don't you see? It wasn't you!"

"Daddy!" Laurie said, grasping at his arm. "Mommy doesn't like this!"

"They're all like the woman in your dreams!" Evan said. "All of them!"

"Daddy!" Laurie whined. "Please let go!"

"Yes," Kay said quietly, her tone hollow and weary. "Let go of me."

He stood over her a moment longer, seeing that she thought the fear inside him had finally and irreversibly brought him to the edge of the abyss. He released her, put his hand to his forehead; the bandaged wound on his head was throbbing. "This isn't like the other times," he told her. "I've talked to Doug Blackburn, and I know now what they are. . . ."

Kay drew the sheet around her, stared at him vacantly as if finally the remnants of love she'd felt for him had been scattered by the winds of reason. She was wondering what to do about him: he'd never gotten really violent before, or anything like that, but still it worried her that Laurie would be in the house alone with him. No! No! she told herself. This is my husband standing here; this isn't some damned stranger! He's kind and good and wants only the best for us, but . . . dear God, Evan needs help. He needs help so badly.

"Don't turn away from me," he said, window-blind-striped sunlight across his face. "I need you now more than I ever have. Just let me in a little bit. Just admit to me that this . . . this thing in your dreams is—"

"No!" Kay said, and winced at the vulnerability in her own voice. Her mother hadn't raised her to be weak; her mother had taught her the virtues of reason and common sense to shut out the demons that came in the night bearing doubts and fears and superstitions. And that's how she'd always planned to raise Laurie. "No," she told the man who stood before her. "You're wrong."

There was nothing more he could say. Kay turned her head, held her hand out for her little girl. "We're going to have to get you registered for real school in a couple of weeks," Kay said.."Won't that be fun?"

Laurie nodded, her eyes still wide.

Evan left the room abruptly, his head throbbing dully. His shoes clattered in the spotless hallway. There was a water fountain up ahead somewhere, and he needed to clear out the ashen taste in his mouth. He found it, drank, and then stood over it with his head bowed, like a man awaiting the executioner. Or executioness? As he walked back along the empty corridor with its mindlessly cheerful pictures, he saw that one of the doors was cracked slightly open. Room 36, where he'd seen that man the day before. He paused, almost walked on, paused again; looked up and down the hallway and then approached the room. And standing before the door he felt a sharp, tingling in his veins, his vision was beginning to mist, quickly, quickly, as it had that day he'd almost run Kathryn Drago down. He tried to step away, found instead that he was stepping forward purposefully, his hand coming up.

And then he was in the room—into a wall of light that streamed thick and hot through a window. As he stared, stared, stared, the light faded quickly until the heat had cooled and the room lay in the grip of darkness.

There was a wheelchair, empty, in a corner of the room. Three figures. Two women standing, a man lying naked on the bed, arms and legs spread-eagled, wrists and ankles strapped. One of the women was taping the man's mouth shut so he couldn't scream, and above that white slash of adhesive tape, his eyes were bulging from his face in stark horror. A grinning oil-painted figure hung framed above the bed, dangling a spider from red-nailed hands. The second woman held an ax. Double-edged and gleaming, catching the blue light that night cast on the walls like dripping paintings done by a darker hand. The man thrashed, veins standing out on his neck. His eyes rolled back, whitened. The woman reached out and touched his penis, fondled it lovingly, touched the testicles, and then lifted the ax.

The man's body arced.

The ax fell.

Droplets of blood were flung across Evan's face. Flesh blued and withered, and one leg rolled off the bed, severed at the knee.

The ax rose. Fell again.

The other leg jerked; gouts of blood flowed across the sheets. Evan opened his mouth to scream, and droplets of blood dripped down, thickly and slowly, to his chin.

And when he blinked and tried to step backward, the light increased, flooding in until he realized it was not blood on his face, no no not blood not blood, but rather drops of sweat. Through the window the fierce August sun clawed at his flesh. August is our killer month, Mrs. Demargeon had told him a long time ago. In the room the bed was neatly made, covered with a white spread. No wheelchair. He stepped out quickly, closed the door behind him, and stood leaning against the wall, for a moment, one hand pressed to his face.

God. God in Heaven.

He'd recognized the man on the bed.

Himself.

They're not wrong, he told himself. My premonitions are never wrong, and now they've taken me over, growing more and more insistent. Warning me. Warning me that this is what could happen. No! Yes. This is what could happen to you if you don't take Laurie and get her away from this village. *What about Kay? What if you're wrong and she's really ill?* They'll come for you in the night. Burning blue eyes: the merciless gaze of the Amazon. *No no no no!* His mind reeled, and he thought for an instant that his knees would buckle there in the clinic corridor. Losing my mind losing my goddamned mind! Hold on. *No no no!* Hold on. *I cannot leave Bethany's Sin while Kay is sick!* The image of Harris Demargeon casting off those legs slashed his brain like a jagged-edged razor. Of course. This is where they did it, in the clinic. And this is where they'd bring him when they were ready to cripple him to keep him from ever escaping Bethany's Sin. Yes. Dr. Mabry had brought Kay here for two purposes: to prevent him from seeing the terrible woman-thing that was crawling out to wear her body like a robe of flesh, and to prevent him from leaving the village before they were ready. And when the thing called Oliviadre had taken over Kay, they'd come for him in the night. And Laurie? What would they do with Laurie?

A hand reached for him. Clasped his shoulder. "Mr. Reid?"

He spun around.

Dr. Mabry's eyes searched his face. "Aren't you feeling well?"

"I'm fine," he said quickly.

"You look a little pale," she said.

"I felt dizzy for a minute. I'm okay now."

She paused, her hand still gripping his shoulder. "I hope so. I was just on my way to tell you that your wife has some more tests scheduled for this afternoon. It might be best if you and your daughter went home." She smiled, dropped her hand. "I'm sorry because I know how much you enjoy visiting with her."

"Will she be able to come home on Monday?"

"I think we can safely say that by Monday she'll be at home on McClain Terrace," the woman said.

Evan looked into her eyes. Haunted. Themiscrya was haunted.

The smile stayed in place. "We'll be running our last tests in the morning. Mrs. Reid may be under some medication, so it may be best if you . . ."

Haunted. Themiscrya. Bethany's Sin?

". . . just plan on calling Monday morning. If anything comes up, I'll let you know then. All right?"

He nodded. Haunted. Both haunted. Themiscrya, then. Bethany's Sin, now.

"Good," Dr. Mabry said.

Evan ran a trembling hand across his face.

"You look tired, Mr. Reid. I have something you could take that would help you . . ."

The queen, Laurie was saying inside his skull; the real queen. She lives in a big castle. . . .

". . . sleep," Dr. Mabry said.

Dr. Drago.

"Can I prescribe some of those pills for you?" she asked him.

He finally was able to focus on her. "No," he said. "I'm fine. I'd better go get Laurie now, and take her home."

"Yes." Shifting shadows across her face. "That might be best."

Evan thanked her, turned away, walked back to Kay's room. "We're leaving now," he told the little girl, and took her hand.

"Where did you go?" Kay asked him.

"Just down the hall." He stood framed in the doorway, Laurie beside him. "Don't worry about me," he said, managing a tight smile. "I'm not going off my rocker."

"I never said you were," she replied nervously.

"You didn't have to. But I want you to know one thing, whatever happens. I love you. I always have, and I always will. You're a strong, special person; God knows, you're a stronger person than I've ever been. Just remember that I love you, alright?"

"Evan . . ." Kay began, but it was too late. Her husband and child were gone.

In the car on the drive home, Laurie sat very still on the seat next to her father. "I hope Mommy gets all better," she said. "She's so sick."

"She'll be better," Evan said hollowly. Home by Monday, Dr. Mabry had said. Yes. But would it truly be the Kay Reid he'd just left in that clinic room?

"Mommy acts funny," Laurie said softly. "Will she be okay when she gets home?"

He reached over and pressed his daughter close to him. Tiny objects had begun to glitter behind his eyes. Silverish and yellow. Stained with bits of dirt, like Eric's dead grin when he turns his face from the fire. Evan accelerated slightly; they'd turned onto McClain Terrace, and now he drove past their house without even glancing at it.

"Daddy!" Laurie said. "You're passing home!"

"Well," he said easily, "I thought we'd drive out to the Westbury Mall, princess. I thought maybe you could use an ice-cream cone."

"Oh, yes. I could. I wish Mommy could be with us."

"I want to get something from the hardward store, too," he said. And then he was quiet as they turned away from Bethany's Sin. Because he'd already decided what had to be done. For the sake of his sanity. For the sake of knowing whether the Hand of Evil had scuttled spider-like through Bethany's Sin or if it had grasped his mind in a death grip and there would never, never be any escaping it again. For the sake of knowing whether either the things inhabiting Bethany's Sin or he should die beneath God's stern, wrathful eye.

What the hell are human teeth doing lying around in the landfill? Neely Ames had asked him at the Cock's Crow.

Thank God the moon would be out tonight, Evan thought. There would be enough light to dig by.

TWENTY-FIVE

MRS. BARTLETT'S KITCHEN

"Mrs. Bartlett?" Evan asked the matronly, gray-haired woman who answered the door.

"That's right." She stood half-in, half-out of the door, as if she suspected he were some kind of brush or appliance salesman.

"I'm Evan Reid," he said. "I'm sure you don't know me, but I live over on McClain Terrace. Doesn't a man named Neely Ames have a room here?"

"Mr. Ames? Yes, he does."

"Is he in right now?"

She glanced down at her wristwatch. "No, I don't believe he is. You didn't see his truck parked around back, did you?"

Evan shook his head.

"Neely doesn't get back from work until after six o'clock; he works for the village, you know. Sometimes it's way after seven when I hear his truck drive up. Can I give him a message for you?"

Now it was Evan's turn to look at his watch. Five-fifteen. "I'd like to wait, if I could. It's really very important."

"The sheriff might be able to tell you where Neely is." Her eyes examined him from head to toe.

"I'd probably have better luck catching him here," Evan said. "May I come in?"

Mrs. Bartlett smiled, stepped back, and opened the door wider for him. "Surely. Oh, that sun's still ferocious out there, isn't it?"

"Yes, it is," he said, stepping across the threshold into the boardinghouse. Instantly he was met by a musty odor, the combination of life smells and heat bound up behind the walls of this house. There was a large sitting room with a brown-and-green Oriental carpet thrown across a hardwood floor, chairs and a sofa arranged around a scorched brick fireplace, lamps on low tables, a few Sears prints hanging on the walls. Sunlight streamed whitely through curtains drawn across a high bay window. "Please sit down," Mrs. Bartlett said, motioning toward a chair. "I was just mixing some lemonade in the kitchen. Let me get you a glass."

"No, thanks. I'm fine as I am."

She sat down across from him; her legs were varicose-veined and puffing beneath grayish-looking hose. "Are you a friend of Neely's?"

"In a way."

"Oh?" She raised an eyebrow. "I don't recall Neely saying he'd made any friends here in the village."

"We met one day over on McClain Terrace," he explained. "And then we ran into each other at the Cock's Crow."

Mrs. Bartlett frowned. "Oh, that's a nasty place, that Cock's Crow. Shame on you two decent men to be going up there. It's got a bad reputation, I'll tell you."

Evan shrugged. "It's not all that bad."

"I can't understand those places where adult men go to act like children. Seems to me like a waste of time." She fanned her face with a *Good Housekeeping* magazine she'd picked up from the sofa beside her. "Goodness, it's been hot these last few days. Unmerciful hot. Going to get hotter, too. Always does around here at the last of the summer. Gives us one more good bite and then it's gone into autumn. Sure I can't get you anything to drink?"

He smiled, shook his head.

"No telling when Neely might get home," Mrs. Bartlett said after a few minutes. "Maybe he's going out to the Cock's Crow again; maybe he won't be home until after midnight. Why don't you just leave a message for him, or I could have him call you?"

"I need to talk to him in person."

She grunted. "Must be something serious, then." She gave him a little sly smile. "Man-talk, is it? Things us women don't have any business knowing?"

"No," he said politely, "that's not quite it."

"Oh, I know all about menfolk's secrets." She laughed and shook her head. "Just like little boys."

"How long have you been running this boarding-house?" Evan asked her.

"The better part of six years now. Of course, I don't do a whopping big business. But you'd be surprised how many traveling salesmen and insurance men come through Bethany's Sin. There's a Holiday Inn about ten miles north of here, on past the Cock's Crow, but I'll tell you they charge a lot for a room, and here I throw in meals with the rent. So I do all right."

"I'm sure you do. Does your husband work in the village?"

"My husband? No, I'm afraid my husband passed away soon after we moved here."

"I'm sorry." He was watching her carefully now.

"He had a bad heart," Mrs. Bartlett said. "Dr. Mabry told him he needed one of those pacemaker things, but he just waited too long. Thank God he died peacefully, in his bed one night."

Evan stood up from his chair, walked over to the window, and moved the curtain aside. Sunlight stung him. The street was deserted. Houses on the other side: neat boxes of wood and brick, neat lawns, smooth, clean carports. Evan turned away from the window, his cheeks tingling from the touch of the sun, and saw on the fireplace mantel a group of photographs. The first one was a wedding photo, snapped in front of a church, showing an attractive dark-haired woman kissing a stocky man in an ill-fitting powder blue tuxedo. Everyone was smiling. In the second photograph the woman was lying in bed, holding in the folds of a blanket a newborn baby; a shadow—the man's?—had fallen across a wall. The same woman stood holding a baby—the same one or a different one?—on the neatly trimmed lawn of a white house in the third photograph. Something about this picture disturbed Evan; he stepped forward, picked it up. The woman's eyes were harder, sunken deeper into her head; her mouth was smiling, but those eyes mirrored a soul in which all smiles had faded. There was something else in this photograph, too: an object just on the edge of it, beside the woman. And staring at it Evan realized it was a hand clutching an armrest. There was a slice of wheel rim. A few spokes. A shadow.

"That's my daughter, Emily," Mrs. Bartlett said. "Em for short. She's a fine young woman."

"This is your grandchild, then?" he asked, holding up the photograph.

"My granddaughter, Jenny. She'll be eight months old in October. Jenny's my second grandchild. See that other picture, the first one on the mantel?" Evan reached for it, and Mrs. Bartlett nodded. "That's it. Her name's Karen, and she'll be two years old in April. Do you have any children of your own?"

"A little girl named Laurie," Evan said; he replaced the photographs as they'd been. "Where does your daughter live?"

"Just a few streets over from here. She and her husband, Ray, have a beautiful little house on Warwick Lane." She fanned herself with the magazine. "Oh, that sun's made it so hot in this house! I'll thank God when it's autumn, I'll tell you! This year I won't mind the blizzards. Are you sure I can't get you a good glass of lemonade with plenty of ice?"

He checked his wristwatch again. "All right," he said. "I'd like that."

"Good." She smiled, rose from the sofa, disappeared toward the back of the house. He heard a cupboard opening, then another.

Evan turned toward the mantel, stared for a few minutes at the photographs. How simple and normal they looked. But dear God what a terrible story they told. He could look into the eyes of the woman in that third picture and see the change that had come over her. The same change now enfolding Kay. Evan left the mantel, peered back through the corridor that connected the front of the house with the back; there was a narrow stairway leading up to a series of closed doors. The boarders' rooms. At the end of the corridor a door stood open, and Evan could see Mrs. Bartlett moving around back there. He could see shelves, a stove, potted plants in a window, wallpaper with apples and oranges and cherries on it. Glass clinked. He moved quietly along the corridor toward the kitchen.

An instant before Mrs. Bartlett realized he was there, Evan saw bottles and vials in an open cabinet. All unmarked, they held bluish green, brown, grayish liquids, viscous-looking. There were solid substances in a few of the vials: white powder, something that looked like wet ashes, something else that looked like shards of charcoal. Beside the glass of lemonade that Mrs. Bartlett was laboriously stirring was a vial of slightly yellowish liquid. The cap was off. Mrs. Bartlett spun around; her eyes widened. But in the next second she composed herself. Her mouth smiling tightly, she reached up ever so casually and closed the cupboard. "I hope you don't mind artificial sweetner," she said, standing with the vial behind her.

"Not, not at all," Evan said.

"You must be thirstier than you thought. I was going to bring it out to you." She stirred again, dropped in a couple of cubes from an ice tray, held the glass out to him. "Here we are." When he took it she walked past him back toward the sitting room; he followed her, wondering what sort of hellish substance she'd mixed into it. He could trust none of them now, none of them. Perhaps this old, unassuming woman was the true druggist of Bethany's Sin, mixing strange and ancient elixirs here in this house, in that kitchen with the tacky wallpaper. What would she concoct in there? Potions for strength? Sleep potions? Aphrodisiacs? Remedies passed down from the Amazonian culture, liquids distilled from nightblack roots and the marrow of men's bones? And if he drank this brew, what would it do to him? Make him physically ill? Make him sleep? Or simply pierce his brain, drawing from it the desire to defend himself against them when they finally came for him?

In the other room she sat down on the sofa again, smiled, fanned herself, waited for him to drink. Her eyes gave no indication that she realized he'd seen. "Hot," she said. "That's all it is, just plain hot."

Evan heard the squealing of aged brakes from outside. Looking through the window again, he saw Neely Ames's battered truck pulling up at the curb. "Well," he said, setting the full glass of lemonade aside. "I think Mr. Ames is home."

"He'll be using the rear entrance," the woman said quietly. "There are stairs up to his room." Her eyes glittered; she glanced from him to the glass and back again.

"Thank you, Mrs. Bartlett," Evan said at the front door. "I appreciate your hospitality."

"Surely, Mr. Reid." The woman rose, winced at pain in her legs, and approached him. "Please come back and sit some other time, will you?"

"I will," he said, and then he was out the door and walking toward the pickup truck. Ames, his T-shirt soaked with sweat and his face burned raw by the sun, swung out of the cab and onto the ground. He looked up, saw Evan, and continued rubbing lawn-mower oil out of his hands with a stained rag.

" 'Evening," Neely said; there were dark hollows under his eyes, and his cheeks were gaunt. He massaged a kinked muscle in his right shoulder. "What are you doing over here?"

"Waiting for you," Evan said. He turned his head toward the house. The curtain at the window moved very slightly. "I have to ask your help in something."

"My help?" He took off his glasses, cleaned the lenses with a dry spot on his shirt. "Doing what?"

"Why don't we go up to your room? It might be better." Evan motioned toward the rear of the house.

"Excuse the mess," Neely said when they were upstairs. "Just throw those damned clothes out of that chair and sit down. You want a beer? Sorry, but they'll be warm."

"No, thanks." Evan sat down.

Neely shrugged, pulled the last remaining Schlitz from a carton on his night table, and popped it open. Drank, closed his eyes, sat down in a chair, and threw his legs up on the bed. "Christ. Jesus Holy Christ I burned my ass off out there today. God Almighty!" He drank again from the can.

Evan glanced around the room. There was a guitar case propped against a wall; what looked like songs on sheets of paper lying on a desk; an open, empty suitcase on the floor.

"So," Neely said after another moment. "What can I do for you?"

"Is that door locked?" Evan motioned toward it.

"Yes." He looked at Evan quizzically. "Why?"

Evan leaned forward, watching the man's face. "Do you still have those teeth you showed me? The ones you found in the landfill?"

"No. I threw them away."

"Did you ever tell the sheriff about them?"

"Was going to. Decided he'd only blow hot air my way. Besides, I started figuring that maybe there's a reasonable explanation for them. Maybe they came out of some dentist's garbage can; hell, maybe somebody got his jaw busted and spit his teeth out. I don't really care anymore."

"That's bullshit," Evan said. "You don't believe that any more than I do." He glanced over at the suitcase. "Are you planning on leaving?"

Neely drank from the can, crushed it, tossed it into the wastebasket. "Tomorrow morning," he said. "I'm settling with Mrs. Bartlett tonight."

"Does she know yet?"

He shook his head.

"How about Wysinger?"

"Fuck that bastard," Neely snarled. "That son of a bitch has given me nothing but grief since I've been here. Today was payday." He patted his back pocket. "This will take me a long way from Bethany's Sin."

"Where are you going?"

"North. Into New England. Who knows? I'm going to try to find myself a nice, dark little club to play my music in. If I can still pick a guitar with these damned blisters on my hands. No. I'm through here. I'll be heading out at daylight."

"Finding those teeth in the landfill didn't have anything to do with this decision, did it?"

"Hell, no. People throw away every kind of thing. More junk than you can imagine." He paused, looked into Evan's face. "Maybe it did. Maybe. Like I told you before, at the Cock's Crow, I've got a bad feeling about this village. I want to get out of here. You probably can't understand what I'm talking about, but I feel like . . . like something's coming closer to me. And I don't mind telling you that it scares the shit out of me." He reached for a pack of cigarettes from the night table, lit one, and inhaled. "I'm not going to stay and wait for it."

"I need your help," Evan said, keeping his gaze steady. "Tonight."

"How?"

"I want you to take me to the landfill. I want you to show me where you found those teeth."

"Huh?" Neely narrowed his eyes over the burning cigarette. "What for?"

"Because I'm going to be looking for someone. Paul Keating."

"Keating? The guy that lives across the street from you . . . ?" His voice trailed off.

"Lived across the street. Lived. I believe he's dead, and I believe his body's buried in the landfill."

Smoke streamed from Neely's nostrils. He took the cigarette out of his mouth and stared across the room. "What the hell are you talking about?"

"You heard me right. Now listen to me. I believed your story about those women who attacked you on the road; I think they've attacked and killed a great many others. Now, I ask you to believe what I'm saying, and I ask you to help me. I can't search across the landfill without you."

"I'm getting my ass out of here in the morning," Neely said.

"Okay. Fine. Do what you want. But *I* have to stay here, and by God I've got to know the truth about this place. Just lead me out there, that's all I ask. And help me dig."

"Jesus," Neely whispered; he drew from the cigarette, exhaled smoke, crushed the butt out in an ashtray beside him. "You're going hunting for a body?"

"Or bodies," Evan said. And from the corner of his eye he caught the swift sliding of a shadow, moving across the strip of light at the bottom of the door. He rose quietly to his feet, was across the room in a few strides as Neely watched him from the other chair; Evan unlocked the door, turned the knob, and opened it.

There was no one in the stairway leading downstairs. The other doors along the corridor were closed. He wondered behind which of them the cunning old bitch was hiding. He shut the door again, locked it, stood with his ear pressed to the door for a moment. Heard silence.

Neely had lit another cigarette. He drew on it as if the smoke would chase away the nagging fears that now were chewing steadily at his stomach. When Evan looked at him again, Neely saw that his eyes were slitted and steady.

"Are you going to help me?" Evan asked, still standing against the door.

The cigarette burned toward Neely's fingers. He shivered suddenly because he'd felt that a figure with flaming blue eyes was standing just behind him, and it was slowly lifting an ax.

Evan waited.

Neely muttered, "I don't know who's crazier, you or me. What time?"

"Two o'clock."

"What? Christ Almighty!"

"I don't want anyone to know."

"Okay, okay," Neely said, and stood up from his chair. "Then you'd better let me get some sleep. Do you have a couple of shovels?"

"A shovel and a pickax. I bought them this afternoon."

"Good. That should do it."

Evan opened the rear door and then turned back to him. "Something else. If I were you, I wouldn't eat or drink anything Mrs. Bartlett tries to give you tonight. I'll meet you out front at two o'clock sharp." And then he'd turned away and was going down the back stairs.

Neely watched him go. Not eat or drink anything Mrs. Bartlett offered? What the hell was that all about? A voice within him screamed *no don't do this!* but he brushed it aside, refused to listen. It faded away. He closed the door and stood looking down at the suitcase. The man needed his help. What would one more day mean? But by God when he'd finished at that vile, stinking place he was going to fill that suitcase with his meager belongings, take his guitar and his songs, and get out of this village. Fast.

He pulled his T-shirt over his head, rolled it up, and tossed it into the suitcase. He was hungry, but he decided not to ask Mrs. Bartlett to make him anything for dinner. Maybe that man wasn't as crazy as he appeared to be. He touched his shoulder gingerly, the fingers running across the scabbed line of a scratch that he'd first noticed in the bathroom mirror a few days before.

TWENTY-SIX

TO THE LANDFILL

Wearing dark clothes and the thick-soled combat boots he'd found in a dust-covered trunk in the basement, Evan quietly climbed the stairs. He eased Laurie's door open; a shaft of light fell across the child in her bed. Evan stepped in and stood looking at her. She was sleeping peacefully, her face untroubled; beside her lay the rag doll, grinning up at him as if they shared a secret.

Evan reached out and gently touched her cheek. She stirred very slightly, and he drew his hand back. My princess, he thought. My beautiful princess. I pray to God you always sleep the sleep of the innocent. He leaned over, kissed her forehead softly, then backed away from her and closed the door to her bedroom.

It was time to go.

Through the den windows he could see the moon, not completely oval yet, but as white as ice and casting a clear light. A sluggish night wind was blowing large, silver-edged clouds across the sky, and when they crossed the moon's cunning face, the light became murky, twisted with shadows that looked like figures on horses of gargantuan scale. And now Evan felt as he had so often during the war: leaving the safety of camp for a recon mission under cover of night, trusting his instincts to keep him alive, knowing that all eyes were enemy eyes and morning was ages away. Perhaps it was best, he thought now, that he'd been captured those many years ago, and forced to lie on a cot beneath the contemptuous gaze of that female officer; now he knew that he couldn't underestimate these women of Bethany's Sin because if he did he could expect no mercy. With them it was either kill or be killed. He took his keys, left and locked the house. McClain Terrace lay cloaked in darkness. He slid into the station wagon and started the engine, switching on the parking lights instead of the full headlights. As he backed out of the driveway, slowly, slowly, the new shovel and pickax clinked together behind him.

As Evan drove away from the house on McClain Terrace he never saw curtains move from a window at the front of the Demargeon house. Never saw the flaming eyes that peered through.

On the drive to the boardinghouse, following the yellow glow of the parking lights, Evan wondered what he would do if he found the bones of Paul Keating. Go to Sheriff Wysinger? To the state police? He realized there was danger in going to Wysinger; he didn't know on which side the man stood. Was it possible these terrible events were swirling around Wysinger without his even knowing it? Perhaps, but Evan had decided he couldn't take that chance. There was too much to lose. But how in God's name could he ever explain to anyone what he thought to be true of Bethany's Sin, that it was as haunted as ancient Themiscrya had been, that the deathless essence of the Amazon nation had taken root here, in this village, and one by one the women had been taken over by a fierce, nameless evil that reveled and rejoiced in the slaughter and mutilation of men? The secrets of Bethany's Sin were layered, and dripping with black filth; a beautiful village on the outside, all-perfect, designed to lure its victims closer, and closer, and closer, until they were inescapably entangled. Those things-beyond-death, those bloodthirsty warrior-shadows had clutched leechlike to the soul of Kathryn Drago, and she had brought them out of that ancient cavern and now released them like sparks from a huge blaze to burn within other souls. The queen, Laurie had said. The real queen. Dr. Drago. Was it possible that the bones of an Amazon queen had lain in that cavern and been burned to ashes with the rest? And now that fierce lioness of a woman had claimed Kathryn Drago's body for her own, as a fitting receptacle for a hate and power that had spanned the ages?

Silent streets unwound before him. Mrs. Bartlett's boardinghouse ahead. He slowed, pulled to the curb, and stopped. A figure coming across the lawn.

Neely, beads of sweat already shining on his face, slid in and quietly closed the door. Evan accelerated, turned in a circle, and drove away from the village.

"It's west—" Neely began.

"I can find it," Evan said. At the limits of the village he reached over and switched on the headlights. The road leaped up at him.

Neely could almost grasp the tension radiating from the other man. His own heart was thundering dully within his rib cage. He fumbled at his shirt pocket. "Mind if I smoke?"

Evan shook his head.

Neely took a cigarette out, stared for a few seconds at the climbing match flame, then blew it out. The green lights on the dashboard dials glowed in the ovals of his glasses. "One cigarette is all it would take," he said, mostly to himself.

But Evan had heard. "What?"

"One cigarette. Toss it out the window, and *poof!* Sun's burned and dried out everything around here for miles. The woods are so dry they're crackling. No rain for weeks. Yes sir. Just one cigarette." He regarded the red-glowing tip.

There was a fork in the road ahead.

"Take the right one," Neely said, and put the cigarette back in his mouth. In another moment he shifted on the seat and said, "What makes you so sure you're going to find anything out here? And why all this damned secrecy?"

"You didn't say anything about this to Mrs. Bartlett, did you?" Evan twisted his head to the side to look at him.

"No. Nothing."

"Good." Evan was silent, watching the road. A deer burst out of the brush ahead, leaped into thicket, and was gone. "I'm not certain I'll find what I'm looking for in the landfill. As a matter of fact, I'm hoping I don't. I'm hoping I'm stark raving mad; I'm hoping that I'm so crazy I'm not seeing or thinking straight." He paused. "But that's not how it is."

"You're not making any sense."

"This has to do with those women you saw on the

King's Bridge Road," Evan told him. "I believe they broke into Paul Keating's house and killed him. And I believe they brought his body to the landfill. As for the secrecy"—his eyes flickered over toward Neely—"we don't want to end up like Keating, now, do we?"

"Turn to the left here," Neely said quietly. He had begun to smell the sweet-and-sour-and-a-thousand-vile-odors smell of the landfill, and he dreaded what was to come. Digging through that mess? Actually lifting out layer after layer? Jesus Christ what have I gotten myself into!

Tendrils of smoke lay across the road, shifting like gray-scaled serpents. "Slow down," Neely said, his nostrils full of the putrid stench of baking garbage. "We're here."

Evan put his foot to the brake and pulled the station wagon off onto the side of the road. He cut the engine, switched off the lights. To the right he could see a flat, unbroken blackness and, in the distance, the red gleamings of minute fires. They got out of the car, went around to the back; Evan hefted the shovel, handed Neely the pickax and a bull's-eye lantern he'd bought at Western Auto. "Now show me," he said.

"Okay. Watch your step." Neely clicked on the lantern, shouldered the moon-gleaming pickax, and made his way carefully across the black plain. Evan followed in his footprints, his boots cracking earth and awakening thick swirls of dust. Acrid smoke wafted around them, clutching at their hair and clothes like something alive; garbage mounds took vague shapes; rats squealed on all sides. The stench assailed Evan; he ground his teeth and forced back a wave of nausea, thinking only of what he had to do. Great cracks had split the earth, and by the moon's light Evan could see in those cracks a steaming morass of garbage, layer after layer of it, shifting by degrees as the sun had mercilessly burned, burned, burned. Now it seemed to him that even the moon was brutal, searing his face with a cold fire that made his nerves shriek. Ahead, Neely moved the lantern's beam back and forth across the ground, his shoes crunching dead earth in a no-man's-land; the heat had fallen upon them, cloaking them, and sweat beaded their flesh.

And like whirling, buzzing clouds of darker dust, the flies came. A dozen of them struck Neely in the face, tangled in his hair, spun around his head. "Christ!" he said in disgust, and waved at the things with his lantern. They parted, buzzed, came at him again. Flies attached themselves to the drops of sweat on Evan's face and arms, drinking greedily of human fluids.

"Wait a minute," Neely said; he stopped, waved at flies, waved again. His eyes followed the track of the lantern on the ground. A huge mound of decaying garbage stood just to the left, topped with bald tires and automobile fenders. A battered, rusted refrigerator lay on its side like an open coffin. Neely moved forward a few yards, looking around to get his bearings; he shone the beam from side to side, searching for that wide crack in which he'd found the teeth. But Christ in heaven the earth was jigsawed with cracks out here, but there was no way to be sure where it had been. I should be packing my suitcase right now, he told himself, not out here in this miserable place. God, the stench of it! And these fucking flies!

"What's wrong?" Evan said behind him.

Neely walked a few steps to where the dry ground had split; glass gleamed in the crack: beer bottles. Why not let this guy do his digging right here, he thought. Get this over with so I can get my ass out of this place? "This is it," he said without looking at the other man.

"You're certain?"

"Yes, I'm certain!" he said, placing the lantern on the upturned side of the refrigerator so the beam would shine down into the split. Might as well get this over with! He waved flies away that had been dancing before his eyes. "Stand back," he told Evan, and, bracing himself, he lifted the pickax, brought it down into the earth with a smooth, strong swing. Glass cracked; Evan heard the noise of metal scraping metal. Neely pulled the pickax out and struck again, and again, and again. Then he wiped a drop of sweat from the point of his chin and stepped away. "It's all yours."

Evan dug in with the shovel, uncovering bits of glass, empty tin cans, flattened milk cartons, fragments of magazines and newspapers. He dug deeper, putting his shoulders against the shovel; uncovered more glass, cans, Bethany's Sin trash.

"What's that?" Neely said suddenly.

Evan thought the man was talking about a clump of rusted steel wool. He turned and said, "Nothing. Just junk."

But Neely wasn't staring into the deepening hole; instead he was staring off to the right, into the darkness. "No," Neely said quietly. "I heard something." The moon glistened across his glasses. "A long way off."

"What did it sound like?" Evan rested on his shovel.

"I don't know. Like a whine or something."

A train whistle? Evan thought. He glanced off in the direction the other man was looking, then turned back to the hole. Thrust in with the shovel again. Met harder earth. "Need the pickax again."

Neely swung into the hole, broke earth; a boil of dust engulfed them, then the flies. Death's here, Evan thought, his blood chilling. Death's here somewhere. He stepped forward after Neely was through and began to dig again. In a few minutes more, he uncovered what at first appeared to be a whole shirt, but holding it up he realized it had been torn into rags for some household chore; he threw it aside, shoveled dirt.

The moon's light lay heavily on Neely's face; he stared into the distance, listening. What had that noise reminded him of? he wondered. Yes. Something he'd heard before.

"Pickax," Evan said.

When he'd finished, Neely said, "This is pretty pointless, don't you think? I mean, if you're looking for bones, there's a hell of a lot of territory to cover."

Evan said nothing; he thrust downward, lifted dirt and held it up to the light, cast it aside. Thrust, lifted. Thrust, lifted. Flies gathered around his sweating face, and he shook his head to get rid of them. Death. Death. Death somewhere. And then, abruptly, he froze. He'd heard a high, screeching noise in the distance; he looked up, scanned the dark, forest-studded horizon.

"You heard that, didn't you?" Neely said. "What the hell was it?" His eyes were wide and shining behind his glasses.

287

"Some kind of animal off in the woods," Evan replied evenly. His gaze shifted, searched, saw nothing but moonlight and garbage mounds and shadow. "Pickax."

"Animal, my ass!" Neely said sharply. "That didn't sound like any damned animal I've ever heard before!"

"I need some more earth broken," Evan told him, stepping up out of the deepening trench.

Neely, muttering, stepped down. The pickax rose, fell, rose, fell, rose, fell. In the distance something screeched. Pickax flashed with moonlight. "There's nothing here, by God!" Neely said. "Christ, I don't know if this is the right place or not! How can I tell?" He pulled himself out from a morass of dirt and trash.

Evan, his shirt soaked, sifted dirt. Coke bottles, crushed beer cans, Tide detergent boxes, clumps of tissue paper, Lysol cans. A strengthening, sickening stench. The flies swarmed, waiting.

Screeeeeech. Nearer. Off from the left now. An eerie whine that made Neely's stomach tighten.

Evan dug in, lifted. A dark, solid object came free from the dirt. He bent and picked it up, held it to the light. A dirt-and-filth-clumped loafer, creased from wear. While he held it, flies dropped down to examine it, then whirled away. He tossed it out of the trench, now hip-deep, and continued digging.

"You're not going to find anything," Neely said, his voice tense. "Let's get out of here!"

"In a minute," Evan said. Digging. Digging. Digging. The sides of the trench were beginning to crumble. Dirt rolled around his boots. The flies hovered above him, all of them heralds of Death and scavengers of flesh. His shoulders were aching fiercely, and he hardly heard the next half-human shriek when it came from the right, closer than any of the others had been.

Neely whirled toward the sound, his heart pounding. He'd heard that noise before, on the King's Bridge Road, when a woman with scorching blue eyes had peered at him through the window of his truck an instant before an ax had flashed. The heat had surrounded him, and now he found it difficult to breathe.

"Pickax," Evan said. Neely didn't move. *"Pickax, damn it!"* He reached up, took the pickax from the fear-frozen man, and began to strike at the earth in a sweat-flinging frenzy.

"They're coming," Neely whispered, staring into blackness, afraid of what he might see. "Dear God, they're coming. . . ."

The trench had deepened to Evan's waist; he closed his ears to the approaching war cries, closed his mind to the horror that was now racing on horseback toward them, axes glittering blue with moonlight. *"Goddamn it I know they're here!"* Evan shrieked, his voice shredding, and struck with all his strength into one of the walls of the trench. The wall cracked, crumbled, split, and began to fall to pieces around him.

And the bones began to spill out like an obscene flood breaking the walls of an earthen dam.

Full skeletons in rotted clothes, broken skulls, pelvises, arms and legs with remnants of gray flesh still clinging, spines that looked like hideous staircases, tumbled out around Evan's legs; he spun, a scream gagging his throat, and struck deeper into the trench with every ounce of strength he could summon. More household trash: boxes, cans, bottles. Struck again. Bones. Grinning, toothless skulls. Again. Dirt cascaded. Shattered femurs, broken fingers, jawbones, here a skull with a scalp of black hair still clinging, here a rib cage, clotted with dirt, wearing a blue-checked shirt. Struck again, the scream ripping him. The tiny bones of skulls and spines of infants poured out of the dirt. Yes. Yes. Terror gripped his heart and tore at it. The little boys. This is where the little boys come to rest and sleep forever. His mind, reeling with pure shock, groped: a line from a Beatles' song came insanely to him. All good children go to Heaven. All good children go to Heaven. He swallowed dust; the flies encircled him, feasting on the Death smells, feasting on dried flesh still dangling from human bones. This was the unholy place of Death in Bethany's Sin; not the cemetery, no, because that was a holy place and probably only women lay there. No, this was where the murdered men and the male infants were brought, thrown in with the rest of the garbage, covered over with filth, forgotten. This was the slaughter ground of the Amazons, the corpses heaped here like bodies on blood-drenched, smoke-drifting ancient battlefields.

". . . *they're coming!*" Neely screamed at him, had been screaming because he'd seen the first of the rapidly moving shadows approaching, but Evan hadn't heard.

Evan felt his mind slip. He couldn't find the strength to climb out of this godforsaken slaughter pit. My wife and child; got to get my wife and child. . . .

"*Come on, damn it!*" Neely shouted, and held out his hand for Evan to grasp. "*Come on! Hurry!*" He glanced back over his shoulder. Shadows taking shape. The rumbling of horse's hooves, a trembling of the earth; burning blue orbs hunting him down. He looked back to Evan, saw that the man had been overcome by shock. Neely reached down, his nerves screaming, and grasped Evan's wrist, pulled at him.

And in the next instant there came an earsplitting *screeeeeeech* just behind Neely Ames; he twisted around, his mouth coming open to scream. The night black horse loomed over him like a storm cloud, and an ax blade that glittered with a power like live electric cables whistled down for him. He heard the shriek of air as the metal parted it.

Neely's head, throwing spirals of blood, was flung over Evan's shoulder by the blow; blood spattered his face. The decapitated body, still gripping Evan's wrist, crumpled to its knees and slid down into the trench. The hot droplets of blood brought Evan back to where he was, and to the reality of the nightmare things that were closing in. Evan jerked his hand free of the death grip and reached for the pickax. The Amazon on the black horse was rearing back for a blow that would split his skull; Evan, his shoulders hunched, swung the pickax into the horse's front legs. The horse shrilled, staggered, lost its balance, and fell heavily, crushing the woman-thing underneath it; there was the sharp, brittle sound of bone breaking and an inhuman, guttural cry of pain.

And then Evan had heaved himself out of the trench and was running across the landfill for his station wagon. The others wheeled their horses toward him, eyes flaming with hatred, axes swinging high; they dug in their heels, and dirt spun from the hooves of their mounts. He glanced over his shoulder as he ran. The one in the lead, on a dappled horse, would catch him before he made the car. He ran on, his legs pumping against the earth; he could feel the ground trembling as the horse gained. He spun around as the ax blade shrieked for him. It whistled past his cheek, and he fell on his stomach to the ground, dug his fist into the earth, ran again; the horse wheeled alongside him, and the Amazon's arm came up for a second blow. Evan stood his ground and flung the handful of dirt into her face; when the ax fell it shaved past his left arm, peeling back the cloth of his shirt. The horse spun in a wild circle as its rider tried to clear her eyes, and the others were fast approaching.

But Evan had reached the station wagon. He flung himself behind the wheel, locked all the doors, rammed the keys into the ignition. His tires threw chunks of earth as he slammed down on the accelerator. Behind him he heard the shrill, bloodcurdling war cry, and he knew they were after him. Bethany's Sin, he thought, his brain throbbing with his heartbeat. Got to get back there. Got to get Laurie and get away. And Kay? What about Kay? No, I'll come back. Get the state police first. Then bring them back. First get Laurie. *Laurie.*

He wrenched the wheel to the left, and the station wagon spun, tires shredding, in a circle that almost threw the car into a ditch on the far side of the road. Then he was accelerating again, his teeth gritted, the headlights showing deserted highway ahead. He heard the next Amazon shriek almost directly in his ear, and then there was a figure on the road before him: a large-flanked chestnut horse bearing a rider whose burning gaze pierced him to the bone. The Amazon's teeth were bared, and he had an instant to realize that this woman was the librarian who'd inquired if he wanted to see any art books. But now she wore a different, masklike face, and hatred screamed from her open mouth. Evan slammed on the brakes, but the horse was too close; the station wagon smashed hard into the animal, staggering it backward and to the side. He heard the grille shatter, and one of the headlights flickered out; but then the Amazon's body, thrown from the horse by the impact, came flying across the car's hood, struck the windshield, and sprayed jagged glass that whined around Evan's face, nicking his cheeks and forehead and neck. The body, face slashed, throat pumping thick blood from a sliced jugular vein, dangled down over the dashboard; the sightless eyes mirrored for another moment the tremendous power of the entity within that form of flesh, and then the blue darkened. The eyes looked like black, empty holes, and the flesh seemed to have withered around the face, giving it the look of a long-dead skull.

Evan pressed his foot to the floor, wound his way back toward Bethany's Sin, back into the vile, evil nest of . . . *them*. This time he made no attempt at silence; his tires squealed as he took corners, and the station wagon's engine screamed at the limits of its power.

Dark streets. Dark houses. A terrible, gathering darkness. The moon, grinning in window and window and window.

McClain Terrace. His own house, pitch-black and silent. He drove the car up onto the lawn, leaving tread marks on the grass, and leaped out, running for the front door. They would be after him, of course, and in minutes they'd find him. He fumbled with his keys in the lock. Hurry. Have to hurry. Have to. They're coming. They're coming. His key slid home. A dog barked, barked, barked.

And in the next instant the door was ripped from his grasp. A hand with manicured nails grasped his wrist, wrenched him into the darkened entrance foyer with a strength that threw him to the floor. From the darkness a figure reaching, reaching, eyes aflame and terrible, and he heard himself whine like a trapped animal. He was hauled up, pushed through parting darkness, and thrown onto the floor in the moon-dappled den.

Evan, crouched on the floor awaiting the fiery blow of an ax, looked wildly around.

Four figures touched by moon-shadows. Four women. Four sets of merciless, murder-hungry eyes.

One of them sat in a chair on the other side of the coffee table, watching him without speaking.

Dear God, he thought, his mouth as dry as landfill dirt and the image of a crumpling headless body flashing through his head. They were waiting for me all the time. They were waiting.

From the chair the Drago-thing spoke, with two voices: one her own, in her Greek-accented English, the other a guttural harsh language that was the strange tongue of the Amazon, both voices meshing perfectly from the same throat. "Now," she said softly, the Amazon tongue sounding hollow and eerie within the confines of the den. "We shall talk."

TWENTY-SEVEN

THE WOMEN

"You're a much more intelligent man than I'd at first believed," the Drago-thing said from her chair. "I admire intelligence. I admire strength of purpose as well."

Evan's eyes moved slightly. Mrs. Giles—or what had once been Mrs. Giles—standing in a corner of the den; No-longer-Mrs. Demargeon standing at the foot of the stairs; a young blond woman wearing a mask of callous hatred standing to the left of Drago's chair. He measured inches against seconds.

"Don't be a fool," the woman in the chair said.

He glanced up at her. The woman-thing's eyes burned bright and fierce. Laurie. The fear slashed at him like a gleaming ax blade. "Where's my child?"

"Sleeping."

His gaze moved toward the stairs.

"Not here," the woman said, the rumble of-the Amazon language echoing from wall to wall, as if the words had been spoken within a time-lost cavern and not within the den of a wood-framed house. "Somewhere else."

"Where is she?" He forced himself to keep his gaze steady, but even so, he felt the power within this woman as surely as if he stood before a white-hot blaze.

"Safe, I promise you. Interesting. The end of your own existence may be seconds away. Why do you concern yourself with the child?"

"Because I'm a human being," Evan said, choosing his words carefully. "I doubt if you know much about the feelings of real humans anymore."

The Drago-thing paused, regarded him for a moment without speaking. "Oh, yes," she said finally. "You're referring to the maternal instinct. Unnecessary. The strong will always see to themselves. The weak must be weeded out as a threat to the perpetuation of the race."

Evan's eyes narrowed. "I saw an example tonight of what you've 'weeded out.' "

"Yes," the woman said. "So you did. You went into the Field of Bones, where our enemies lie fallen by the will of Artemis. . . ."

"Enemies?" Evan said incredulously. "Men and infants?"

"Men and men-to-be," Drago said softly, her voice velvet and iron, the Amazon voice lower and harsh. "Two of you went into the Field of Bones. Only you returned; where is the workman?"

"He's dead. Killed by one of those . . . things on horseback."

"Warriors. A pity Mr. Ames was struck down; he'll never see his children now."

"Children?"

She responded with a tilt of the head. "Two women are pregnant by his seed. We hope one of them will bear us a daughter. Of course, Mr. Ames never knew; Antigatha's potions strengthened his sexual potency and blanked his memory."

"Antigatha?" Evan's heart pounded. "Mrs. Bartlett?"

"The one you call Bartlett, yes. You underestimated our superior senses of sight, of smell, and of hearing. Antigatha easily overheard your conversation behind that locked door. But unfortunate about the man; the younger warriors have yet to learn restraint, even against the enemy. I had hoped that the man would be a successful breeder."

"Then they weren't sent out there to kill us?"

"No. Only to"—she paused, searching for the proper word—"herd both of you back to the village. I assure you, if I had ordered you dead, you would now in fact be dead. And buried by now, along with the others." She shook her head, eyes blazing eerily. "I don't want you dead. Not yet."

Evan looked quickly around the room; the other women hadn't moved. They watched him like animals eager for the kill. A shudder rippled up his spine; he could see the spiderish shadows cast across the walls by the moonlight. Creeping nearer and nearer. "What in the name of God are you?" he asked her, his voice trembling. "What are all of you?"

"We are . . . survivors," the Drago-thing said, two voices echoing, intertwining. "Survivors by the sheer force of our individual wills, gathered together in a place of cold darkness for . . . a long time of waiting. We are the chosen of Artemis, the vanguard of Her might, and our hatred sustained us when we were broken to our knees and cast into the maw of Hades." She closed her eyes for a moment, opened them and stared down at the man on the floor before her. "We are warriors first and always, and one can fight in Hades as fiercely as on the steppes of Athens. One can fight Master Death in a clash of wills, and with the divine help of Artemis, win. Yes! Win!" Her eyes flamed; the power seared Evan's face, and he drew back. "You know nothing of the desire to survive," she said, her lips curling as if she were snarling at him. "You know nothing of the will to live, to walk the earth and the forests, to smell the sea again, to stand beneath a burning sun and scream toward the sky! We know all that, and we know bitter, limitless cold and dark, and we know wanting to shriek but having no voices, and wanting to see but having no eyes!" Her voice rose, rose, hammering at the walls. "We know the grip of Thanatos, with his scaled hands and his red burning eyes, and we know what it is to fight that grip as one raging power fights another! And we know what it is to wait and to *wait and to wait!*" Her arm flashed out, golden bracelet gleaming around the forearm; the fist crashed down on the coffee table, and there was a piercing *craaaaaack!* as the table split from one end to the other. She blinked, as if for an instant the power within that flesh sought to burst free, out of control. She brought her hand back and sat staring at him over the broken table.

His mind slipped, slipped; he gritted his teeth, tried to quiet the scream that had begun in his soul. "You're not Kathryn Drago any longer," he said after another moment. "Who are you?"

The woman-thing lifted her fist up, clenched tightly. It trembled with repressed rage. "The last of the royal blood," she whispered. "After Troy"—she spat the word out—"after the murder of Penthesilea, the Chair of Power fell to me. But that was in the last days, and we were weak from the wars that had depleted our ranks." Her eyes were half-closed now, hooded with memories. "And so the cowards came, horde after horde of them; black-bearded destroyers lapping at our shores, at the gates of our city. We fought them back again and again; Artemis lifted up corpses and gave them life to fight still, and we battled day and night without rest. Until the end. Until the end." Her voice had dropped to a whisper.

"The end came in that cavern, didn't it?" he asked her.

She looked at him sharply.

"The corpses were heaped together and burned. The cavern was sealed, and the invaders took over Themiscrya. . . ."

"Enough!" the Drago-thing shrieked, the word a hoarse bark in the Amazon tongue. Not-Mrs. Giles stepped forward a few paces, as did not-Mrs. Demargeon.

"Why gather within Kathryn Drago's body?" he asked her, watching her carefully, ready to leap backward if she attacked him. Knives. There were knives in the kitchen. Could he get to them in time?

But she didn't move. Instead, she smiled—a thin, haunting smile that drew the flesh tight across her cheekbones, giving her a look of a flaming-eyed death's-head. "Because this one had been brought to us by the will of Artemis. Because this one was fulfilling her own destiny, drawn to where we waited in darkness. And this one had already delivered justice to the destroyer."

Evan didn't move; his mind was racing. Knives. Knives in the kitchen.

"Perhaps you would understand if I told you her maiden name. Bethany Katrina Nikos. Her father and mother emigrated to America from Greece in 1924; the father purchased a plot of farming land and built a wood-frame house, and in 1932 his daughter was born. But he was a rough, uneducated man, and he knew only how to work with his hands; his wife was frail and intelligent, but she bent to his wrath because she knew no better. When his crops began to fail, he spent his rages by drinking and beating her bloody; very often the little girl was awakened in the night by the sound of blows and piercing, terrible screams." She blinked suddenly, and Evan knew that the small portion of Kathryn Drago that served as a disguise for the fiercer power was remembering. "Terrible screams," she hissed. "By this time a village was beginning to spring up. Everyone knew that the man beat his wife, but what could they do? It was his business. And at night I remember . . . I remember my mother, her face puffed by bruises, sitting on the edge of my bed, telling me stories of a land where men did not dare inflict these pains on women, of a land where women were the masters, and men in their rightful place. She told me the legends of the Amazons when we were alone, when he was drunk and sleeping, and those stories seemed to take fire in my soul. . . ." She blinked again; the face contorted, grinning. "He killed her on a night when the winds howled around the house and snow had frozen the earth. He hit her, and hit her, and she fell down a stairway and her neck snapped. The little girl heard the bones breaking." She gritted her teeth, stared into his face. "Of course the police came, but the little girl was afraid to speak. He told them they'd had a fight over his drinking and she'd slipped and fallen. Those men all . . . grinned at each other, as if they shared a secret with"—she blinked again, and a shade passed over the eyes—"my mother at the center. Oh, yes. A fine, fine secret. And so I lived in the house with him, as he drank more and more and began to seek someone else's flesh to strike his hand against. But I knew what I must do, and I . . . waited . . . .

"Until he was drunk with wine again, and he lay in a bathtub filled with tepid water." The power had returned to her eyes again; her lips were curled savagely. "The little girl waited until he'd fallen asleep, and she took his straight razor and stood over him in the bathtub." The tongue flashed out like a lizard's, licked across the lips. "Slashed. Slashed. Slashed while the bitter tears streamed down her face. The water ran red with his blood, and the walls were streaked with it. And then she went to the police to tell them what she'd done, and why she'd done it. Justice. She'd wanted justice. She was sent to live with relatives in Athens. And from there she began her search."

"Bethany's sin was murder," Evan said tonelessly. "The villagers named this place after what she'd done."

"Not murder!" the Drago-thing hissed, leaning forward. *"Justice! The true justice of the Amazons!"* She paused for a moment, gaze glittering, pockets of moonlight caught beneath her cheekbones. "When we returned with her, she purchased that land and built the temple of Artemis on the foundations of her father's house. And to give thanks to Artemis we directed her to begin the hunting time. We found other suitable vessels, and some unsuitable, which we destroyed. Now the youngest of us gather at the estate and ride in Artemis's honor when the moon is at its height."

The heat seemed to be slowly strangling Evan; he shook his head, dazed, unable to think what it was he should do. Run for the kitchen? Fight here? What? His brain shrieked, and above that noise he could hear the other things breathing.

"This world is strange," the Drago-thing whispered. "So very strange. Filled with mysteries we did not even dare to imagine. But still the same; you and your kind are our enemies, and we will have no rest until we destroy you."

"What are you going to do with me?" he heard himself ask.

"We need your intelligence and stamina in our daughters," she said quietly. "We wish to use you for breeding purposes."

Images of mutilation streaked through his mind: slashed and severed arms and legs, screaming faces. He shook his head. "No! No, I won't!"

"It can be good for you, if you don't try to resist. We'll honor you as a special captive. . . ."

"No!" Evan shrieked. *"No by God no!"*

The woman stared at him, fury churning in her face. Stared at him until he thought he would either scream or go mad. "You have a second choice," she whispered, and reached down to the floor beside her chair; the golden bracelet caught moonlight, reflected it briefly into Evan's face.

She lifted up Harris Demargeon's severed head by the hair and placed it before her on the cracked coffee table. The dead eyes were rolled back to white, like the unseeing orbs of a statue; the mouth hung limply open.

"Now decide," the Amazon said.

TWENTY EIGHT

THE DECISION

Even as the woman's menacing words were echoing from the den walls, Evan threw himself forward, knowing that if he didn't move with lightning speed the others would be upon him like avenging lionesses. He gripped the edge of the coffee table and jerked upward on it, sending it flying backward onto Drago; Harris Demargeon's head spun into shadows, thumped against a wall, the Giles-thing screamed a scream of dripping hatred and flashed toward him; Drago slammed out with one hand, her teeth bared, knocking the table aside. But by then Evan had crossed the room, bent, picked up a chair, and used it to shatter the picture window; glass exploded from the casement. When Evan looked back over his shoulder, he saw them reaching, reaching, reaching as if in a slow-motion nightmare, and the Drago-thing had risen to her feet and was pointing toward him in a command to the others. Evan flung the chair into their midst, saw the Giles-thing brush it away as if it were made of papier-mâché. And then he spun around and leaped into space through the broken window.

He ran through the down-sloping backyard, not daring to look back. He reached the chain-link fence, climbed it, and leaped over into the concrete-bottomed drainage ditch. Then he glanced back, expecting to see them coming across the yard for him, but saw only the form of Kathryn Drago, standing in the broken window frame, watching him. He stared at her for a few seconds; their eyes met, burned. And then Evan was running into the forest.

His legs pumped. Brush stung his face, and shadows loomed heavily on all sides. His only thought now was to get away, to thread a path out of these woods somehow and get to Spangler or Barnesboro—anyplace with lights, telephones, real people. Anyplace where he could get help. He ran on, the moonlight flashing whitely through the dense overhang of trees like a searchlight stabbing for him. And then he felt his boot catch in a clump of low brush, and he was pitching forward to the ground. He slammed down hard, the breath whooshing from his lungs, and he lay with his face pressed against ashen-smelling earth. He was panting like an animal, his chest burning with the stale heat that pressed at him from all sides like a searing vise. His head throbbing with pain and confusion, he drew himself up against the trunk of a tree and clung to it.

And then, abruptly, he realized what he was doing.

Running. Running again, like all the other times he'd turned his back on the evil that crawled through this world; like the time he'd turned his back on his own brother, lying broken in a golden field while the specter of Death crept closer; like the time he'd turned his back on ragged men behind bamboo cages, leaving them to the mercy of their captors. Evan's mind staggered, like a man trying to run with weights strapped to his shoulders. Yes. The Hand of Evil was real; it was real, and it had been waiting for him all this time in Bethany's Sin. And all these years, when he thought he'd been escaping its grip, he'd only been running nearer and nearer to it. Until now, finally, it was reaching for him again.

And, clinging to the tree, Evan felt his sanity begin to unravel. Oh God, he breathed. Oh God help me help me help me! Like red slashes of a razor blade, the visions streaked through his mind, one after the other: an Amazon with scorching eyes, reaching for him with one hand while the other raised a blood-dripping ax; a place where hollow-eyed statues stood, casting spiderish shadows on stone walls, where the moon burned fiercely down through a ceiling of glass, where Amazons crowded around and came nearer, nearer, nearer; Kay standing with her eyes closed and her breasts bared, and smoke swirling around her; the Drago-thing's face, grinning; and himself burning in what must have been the leaping fires of Hades.

He jerked himself back to reality, sweat dripping from his chin to the ground. God help me. God help me. His sanity ripped, ripped. *No!* he screamed at himself. *No! Hold on! For God's sake hold on!*

Because through the veil of those horrible visions he had seen what he must do. He must go back among them, and get his wife and child away from them. For if he turned away, if he ran on to Barnesboro or Spangler or Marsteller or wherever, they would be forever lost to him. He clung to the tree as if it were the last solid, real thing in his life, and a thought of cold crystal clarity came to him: Why had they let him get away at all? Why had they let him run?

In the next instant he knew.

He heard the high shriek of the Amazon riders off to the right, and he knew they were less than a mile away. They would be able to see in the dark in these woods, and their horses would know the shadowed paths by instinct. So even here, in the silence and darkness, there would be no hiding. His heart pounded; he rose to his feet, looked around. Another shriek, to the left and nearer than the first. They were closing in on him, hunting him down. Barnesboro and Spangler were cut off to him now, and behind him lay Bethany's Sin, an evil-pregnant spider in the center of her web.

Now enfolding his wife and child.

He peered into the darkness a moment longer, listening. Cries from the left and right, as they moved relentlessly toward a vertex where he stood, utterly defenseless. And then his decision was made. He turned and began to run back for the village, his head turning from side to side to pierce the darkness; he stayed close to the trees, avoiding the white slashes of moonlight, and in a few minutes he had crawled down into the drainage ditch behind his own house. Another war cry, rippling through the night, perhaps a half-mile away and closing in. The sound hammered at his eardrums. He crawled on his belly up against the chain-link fence and stared across his backyard. His house was full of the night, as if it, too, had been consumed by utter evil. Moonlight sparkled on glass edges in the broken window. He thought he heard the snapping of a branch just behind him, and he whirled around, ready to leap to the side. But nothing was there. Then he lay perfectly still, a shadow among a thousand others. His brain burned; of course they were waiting for him, and of course they would expect that he might try to return to his own house when he realized the riders had cut off his escape route, either to seek a weapon or to try to use the telephone to call for help. His eyes, narrowed into slits, slid to the left.

The Demargeon house, dark. He could see the door leading into their basement: four panes of glass, just like his own basement door. Behind him another war cry rolled across the forest. Near. Very near. He couldn't stay out in the open any longer. Would they expect him to break into the Demargeon house? Would they expect him to try to hide there until daylight cleansed these streets?

He crawled along the fence, steeled himself and quickly climbed over, dropped down into the yard. Crouched there, listening. All still, all quiet. Then he was running from shadow to shadow, staying low to the ground; he moved through Mrs. Demargeon's vegetable garden, now withered and dry from the heat. When he reached the basement door Evan balled his fist and struck the bottom glass pane; it starred and cracked. He picked out the pieces, let them fall to the grass, groped for the doorknob. Pressed the button that unlocked the door, twisted the knob, and then he was inside.

Evan closed and locked the door behind him and, breathing raggedly, let himself sink down along one of the basement walls. For a long time he listened and heard nothing but the occasional shrieking of the wariors in the woods; eventually those cries faded and died like half-remembered echoes. The basement was about the same as his own, with a wooden stairway leading up to a closed door into the house. There were stacks of boxes with junk in them: old clothes, musty-smelling magazines, a broken lamp, a heap of cracked flower pots. A chair missing its left leg sagged in a corner, and beside it there was a barbecue grill on rollers and a couple of cans of lighter fluid for charcoal. Near the basement door there was a rack with garden implements dangling from it: a Weed-Eater, a hand trowel, a rolled-up green hose. In the corner beside Evan was a sack of chalky-smelling fertilizer.

Now there was nothing to do but wait for dawn, still

hours away. He put his face in his hands and tried to sleep, but every few minutes he'd imagine a nightmare shape had slithered down into the basement and was slowly stalking across the floor toward him, and he'd open his eyes with a cry about to burst from his lips.

When he did sleep, Evan dreamed of fire. A great roaring red-and-orange conflagration, a sky filled with churning ashes and shards of wood. And then embers flaming amid ruins, houses black-charred, bricks toppling from walls as a stain of purplish smoke slowly obscured the horizon. And after that, a place of ghosts, where ashes stirred in sluggish spirals and no grass or flowers grew among the cracked, scorched walls and blackened fields. Even as he dreamed, Evan realized that was the fate of Spangler, or Marsteller, or Saint Benedict, or any of the dozens of small towns ringing Bethany's Sin, when the warriors began to ride in full strength. When the Amazons taught their daughters how to wield the fire-edged ax of wrath, and those daughters taught their own, and the legacy of evil and murder and rage passed on from generation to generation, their lust for violence would turn against whole communities. They would strike in the night, swift and without warning, and this would be a place of ghost towns where dogs howled in darkness and the cry of eagles shrilled among the broken ruins. Whispered tales of night terror would make this a desolate, haunted land, but still there would be those who by accident or curiosity drove along the stretch of Pennsylvania Highway 219 that swept past the village of Bethany's Sin. And for those people there would be no turning back.

The dreams faded.

Hot white sunlight striped Evan's face; he came awake as he had during the war—senses sharp and questing, vision clear, his brain already working out the steps needed to stay alive. He pulled himself out of the light, into shadow where he'd be hidden. Birds sang in the trees, and Evan heard the distant sound of a car's horn, probably at the Circle. He glanced through the four-paned door—no, three-paned door—and looked for the sun. It was probably a little before eight o'clock. Something sparkled silver against the blue sky: an airplane, coming in for the airport in Johnstown. He wondered what the things thought of planes, of skyscrapers, of cars and ocean liners, of televisions and electric can openers and lawn mowers and all the thousands of items he took for granted. What could the things understand of the modern world, and how could they cope with it? But it seemed to Evan that in possessing the body they must possess also the memory, the intelligence, and to some degree the personality as well; he'd seen the woman sitting before him in the den slip back and forth between two worlds, from Kathryn Drago to the power that had lodged itself within her. Possibly the Amazon entity lay hidden away, using Drago's personality as a disguise, until there was the need for its savagery to surface from that pool of flesh in full force. Perhaps that was true of all the rest of them, too. Even the language lay between two worlds, the English-speaking voice and that guttural, chilling growl.

And now he thought of Kay, lying in a bed in the clinic while the Amazon known as Oliviadre slowly claimed her soul. He ran his hands over his face. When the transformation was complete, would the Kay he knew and loved still be locked within that form, or would Oliviadre crush out her life-spark entirely? *I've got to go to her!* a voice screamed inside him. *I've got to go now and get her out of there!* No. No, not yet. They'll kill you before you can get away from McClain Terrace. But how, then? How in God's name am I going to get my wife free of them? And what's happened to Laurie? He was confident they hadn't harmed her, but the idea of what they might be planning for her made his flesh crawl.

He jumped suddenly. He'd heard a phone ringing upstairs. Ringing. Ringing. Ringing. Then a door-muffled voice.

Evan quietly rose and moved toward the stairway. Then stopped, realizing he needed some kind of weapon; he reached over to the rack of garden tools and took the trowel. He slipped up the stairs carefully and put his ear against the door.

". . . I've heard nothing from any of them." Not-Mrs. Demargeon was speaking in her Mrs. Demargeon voice now, and Evan pictured her in a robe and slippers; the Amazon entity within her lay submerged now, waiting. A long pause. "Yes, that's right." Another pause. "He could not have gotten very far from the village. This we know. They've been searching the forest between his house and the highway all night. If he's there, they'll find him." Pause. She cleared her throat. Evan started to crack the door open and decided against it. "No. Cybella says we're in no danger; I stayed with her until early this morning, waiting for reports. The man has not reached the highway."

Come here and open this door, bitch, Evan breathed. Come here.

The woman listened, said, "No." Listened again. "No," emphatically. Then, in a more soothing tone of voice, "We shall wait and see. The man poses no problem. In the meantime, we shall proceed with the Rite of Fire and Iron. Tonight; Oliviadre grows restless."

Evan's throat tightened. What was that about a rite? And Oliviadre? He leaned forward, pressed his ear tightly against the door. The wood made a slight creaking noise, and Evan winced.

". . . met a young couple at the Westbury Mall yesterday," the woman was saying. "The Daniels. He's an insurance executive with Hartford in Barnesboro; she's a housewife, five months' pregnant. Very nice people, I understand. Bremusa believes they would fit into the village very well; she's going to show them that empty house on Deer Cross Lane next week." A pause. "Yes. Yes, I will." Then, "I have to go now. Good-bye." The sound of the receiver being placed on its cradle, footsteps moving away.

Evan stood pressed against the door for another moment. Bethany's Sin was going to beckon and ensnare a couple called the Daniels; Bremusa—Mrs. Giles?— had plans for them. Oh, yes; just as she'd had plans for Kay and Evan. Show them a beautiful house on a beautiful street in a beautiful village, offer it to them at an unbelievable price, and then—

The door came open so quickly Evan had no time to react, and there stood the woman, her face still lined with sleep, wearing a bright canary yellow robe. Her eyes were dark and staring, but in a split second the power began to flood into them, fierce and blue and wild with the unleashed strength of the Amazon; in another instant they were orbs of flaming hatred, and with a guttural snarl of pure rage the woman lifted the ax she held and brought it whistling down toward Evan's shoulder.

But he hunched over and drove himself into her with all his strength; the ax crashed down and split the railing at the top of the stairway. They clawed at each other, falling to the floor and rolling, upsetting table and lamp and telephone. As she retrieved the ax he grasped at her wrist, caught it before she could strike at him again; she twisted, snarling like an animal, gripped the wrist of his hand that held the trowel, and began to squeeze. He dropped the trowel as he felt his bones grind together, and he cried out in pain. They rolled back and forth, slammed into a wall. She spat into his face and tried to jerk her arm free, but he held onto it for dear life. Then she twisted again and got one slippered foot between them; she kicked out, throwing Evan off her and halfway into the living room. He fell over a chair, regained his footing and picked up the trowel just as she leaped at him, the ax flashing for his head.

When he jerked his head back, he saw the reflection of his own face in the ax blade, and he was certain it had cleaved away the hair that hung over his forehead. He gritted his teeth, feeling rage and anguish screaming within him, feeling the killer instinct rising within him now, rising, rising. Evan stepped in, drove upward with the trowel. But the woman was faster; she gripped that wrist again, twisted his arm to the side. Pain flooded through him, and his fingers involuntarily opened, dropping the trowel again. The woman-thing struck a backhanded blow at him that caught him alongside the jaw and almost broke his neck. Evan staggered. She rushed in, gripped at his shoulder with flesh-clawing nails, and tore half his shirt away, exposing the plain of ragged scars. He fell backward, his head still ringing from her blow, and dropped down to his knees. The thing that had been Janet Demargeon loomed over him, lifting the ax for a death blow. When he was able to look up into her face, he saw the blood hunger in her eyes, saw the way she stared at the scars crisscrossing his chest; it was the way she'd looked at them that night in the entrance foyer, and he realized now those scars must've brought back memories of gore-splattered battle to the entity within her, and she'd gotten away quickly that night before she'd been compelled to attack him. Now the ax rose, rose; its shadow fell across him, and he felt too weak and beaten to move.

The killer instinct took over. It bared his teeth in a snarl, made his right hand whip out to grasp the trowel that lay only a few feet away. Made him dig his heels into the carpet and plunge toward her even as the ax reached its gleaming zenith and hesitated there for a fraction of a second. Made him thrust out and upward with that garden trowel with all the strength of his shoulders and back behind it. Canary yellow cloth stopped his hand.

The woman threw her head back and screamed, a scream not entirely of pain but of anger as well. The canary yellow reddened. Reddened quickly.

She tried to stagger back to deliver her blow, but Evan chopped at her ankles with his free hand, and she fell, still gripping the ax in waxen white hands. At once he withdrew the trowel and, snarling, drove it in again. She screamed, struggled, screamed, clawed at his face and missed; Evan threw his weight against the makeshift weapon and felt it sink deeper. The body beneath him thrashed wildly, seemingly stronger now; her arm came up with the ax and slashed wickedly past his left shoulder. Then her other hand flashed out, caught his cheek, nails digging rents in the flesh. He shook away from her; struck again and again and again.

Until finally he realized he was stabbing a dead woman.

He fell back away from her, his hands sticky with blood; the trowel was buried in her midsection up to the handle, and a pool of red had collected around it. Evan crawled away, shaken and sick, and threw up in a corner of the living room. For a long time he lay on his back, unable to move, thin red rivulets trickling down his cheek from three deep scratches. He realized the woman must have heard that door creak, and sensed him hiding there; perhaps she'd smelled his sweat or fear. When he could look at the corpse again, he saw that her eyes were dark and lifeless, the face shrunken and skull-like, all the terrible power gone now. But still he was afraid to turn his back on her. He stared down at his bloody hands; the fingers twitched and trembled. After a while he staggered into the bathroom to clean himself, and saw in the medicine-cabinet mirror a face that shocked him: hollow-eyed, pale, a blackening bruise at his jawline, another on his right cheek, the three bloody scratches. Red gouges in both shoulders, a long, jagged scratch across his chest. His torn shirt flagged around him. He washed his face in cold water, almost threw up again, and then explored the rest of the Demargeon house.

The rooms were small, neatly decorated, as if from a Sears furniture catalogue. In a room at the very back of the house he found Harris Demargeon's headless body, still sitting in that wheelchair. There were no windows in the room, and no furniture but a bed with a dark brown spread.

Evan closed the door quickly.

In the living room he sat down on the sofa and found himself staring with curiosity at the woman's corpse. So, he told himself. When the body dies, they die. Or do they? He couldn't be certain. But he knew one thing for sure: there must be a physical hand to hold the ax, and this woman's hand would never hold another one. He rose up from the sofa, bent beside the body, and loosened the robe.

The left breast sagged, the nipple flattened and gray-looking; where the right breast had been there was a brown, starlike scar that indicated a severe burn.

The Rite of Fire and Iron, this woman had said. To-night; Oliviadre grows restless. Evan closed the robe because he didn't want to look at that scar anymore. The woman's dead eyes, half-closed, stared at the ceiling.

And now Evan, sitting on the floor in the presence of Death, put his head in his hands and saw clearly what it was he must do to save his wife and child.

TWENTY-NINE

EVAN, WAITING FOR THE NIGHT

Evan's search of the Demargeon house turned up six empty Coke bottles beneath the kitchen sink. He withdrew two of them, carried them downstairs to the basement, and began to sift through the assortment of boxes for suitable rags—not too dirty, thin enough to be jammed into the necks of the bottles. When he found two rags he could use, he filled the bottles about three-fourths of the way to the top with lighter fluid. He twisted the rags and fit them into the Coke bottles as fuses for his makeshift firebombs.

Then he went back upstairs to wait. At the top of the stairs, he recradled the telephone, afraid a prolonged busy signal would attract suspicion.

He was going to have to create a diversion, something that would allow him time to get to the Mabry Clinic and find Kay; he'd already decided he was going to set fire to the Demargeon house, and with those two firebombs he could pick a couple of other targets and unleash enough confusion to shield him. But there was another problem: where was Laurie? The Drago house? The Sunshine School? Yes. Possibly there, under the watchful eye of whatever hideous entity lay within Mrs. Omarian's form. And now, as the hours moved sluggishly through the afternoon, Evan kept a surreptitious watch from the living room, moving the window curtains aside perhaps half an inch, one eye peering through at McClain Terrace.

At first it seemed deserted, but as Evan looked he caught the shadowy outline of a figure sitting before a window in a house diagonally across the street. And another figure in the house next door to where Keating had been murdered. They were both sentries, watching the street. Probably Mrs. Demargeon was supposed to be watching for him as well. Damn them all to hell, he breathed.

The light began to fade. As evening crept across Bethany's Sin, Evan saw several cars drive slowly along McClain Terrace, heading toward the Circle. Across the street no lights showed in houses, but he knew they were still there, watching and waiting. There was a plastic-based table lighter on the floor, thrown from the overturned coffee table during the fight; Evan bent and picked it up, sat on the sofa, and clicked the flame on and off a couple of times. Fire reflected dully from the eyes of the corpse at his feet.

Night fell.

Bethany's Sin lay silent; but somewhere in the depths of the Demargeon house a clock ticked, ticked, ticked. Evan wiped his face with the back of his hand, wincing as droplets of sweat touched the raw scratches. Now he was alone, totally alone, and whatever happened in this place tonight depended solely on his own instincts, on his ability to slip quietly from shadow to shadow, on his will to survive. Tonight he must face the Hand of Evil, and there would never be any running again. His heartbeat echoed the ticks of the clock.

At twenty minutes after eight the phone rang. He tensed, stared at it as it rang again. Again. Again.

Let them know. Yes. Let them know I'm ready to fight them.

The phone rang on.

Evan stood up, crossed to the phone, and ripped it from the wall.

And now it was time to go.

He took the lighter down into the basement, used the remainder of a can of fluid to soak magazines and newspapers and cast-off clothing in boxes, then dragged the boxes to a spot beneath the stairs. He broke the crippled chair into pieces and threw them onto the fluid-gleaming pile; there was enough fluid remaining in the second can to douse the stairs themselves. Then he clicked the flame on, touched it to the edge of a scrapped dress; the cloth smoked, sputtered, burst into fire. The newspapers and magazines caught quickly, pages curling and blackening;

tendrils of fire snaked upward toward the stairs, and bluish flame rippled across the wood. Evan waited until the pile of boxes had caught completely, the fire hot enough to make him step back a few paces, and he watched the steps begin to blacken; then the lowest step caught, and the dangling railing. Grayish, sour-smelling smoke swirled thickly around the basement. Evan put the lighter in his back pocket, picked up the two firebombs, and slipped through the basement door into the backyard. Ran for the fence and climbed over, cradling the two sloshing bottles in the crook of one arm. He glanced back, could see red light streaming through the door-panes, and then he was running along the ditch in the darkness, planning to circle the perimeter of the village until he reached the clinic. Overhead, the near-perfect orb of the moon bathed him in hot, lunatic light. He ran on, keeping his body low, looking from side to side for any trace of movement; to his right lay the backs of houses, to his left the solid darkness of the forest.

And in another moment there came a terrible, high-pitched shriek, and three Amazons on horseback burst toward him from that darkness, axes swinging. This time he knew they would kill him, for he recognized the death-look in their eyes.

Evan reached for the lighter, flicked it on, touched that yellow flame to one of the fluid-sopped fuses. He took no time to aim, but threw the bottle into their midst. When the bottle hit, there was a brief, white-startling ball of fire and the horses screamed, rearing. Two of them collided and went down, and the third spun in a fearful circle as the fire leaped along bone-dry brush and tangles of thicket. And then Evan was past them and gone, his legs churning. He looked back for an instant, saw a patch of woodland trembling with flame and the dark horse-shapes caught in it. Then he didn't look back anymore. He ran on, knowing he was still on the perimeter of Bethany's Sin but not exactly certain how far away the clinic was. From the abyss of the forest he thought he heard more shrieks, closing in, and he kept one hand firm around the remaining bomb. Shadows leaped at him; the night was a mad-house of moonlight and darkness, fighting each other and the man who struggled through them. He tripped, almost fell, kept running; if that bottle should break, his last weapon would be gone.

And then, his chest heaving and his lungs burning for oxygen, Evan abruptly stopped. Peered into the blackness ahead. Listened. What was that sound? What was that terrible, hellish sound?

Hoofbeats. Four or five horses. Coming along the ditch toward him.

And before Evan could leap for the fence, they were upon him: four Amazons with hate-twisted faces, axes shimmering with moonlight and the eerie, pulsating power of the things that gripped them. The red-eyed horses rumbled like world-splitting earthquakes. Shrieks from five raging throats tore at him, and even as he was stepping back he was touching the flame to his last fuse; it sputtered, leaped. He reared back and threw the bottle among them; it glanced off an elbow, off a shoulder, leaving ripples of flames, finally exploded like a hand-grenade blast. Fire and glass shards pierced the air, into the hair and eyes of the woman-things. One of them screamed wildly, began chopping the air while her eyes caught fire; another ripped at her flaming gown; a third clutched to a rearing horse with a burning mane. Evan turned away, leaped for the fence and caught his fingers in it, pulled himself up. An ax slammed the mesh beside him. Evan pushed against the top of the fence, landed in grass, ran through a backyard toward the street, his nerves screaming.

When he reached the street he saw it was Fredonia; he'd completely circled Bethany's Sin, gone past the clinic. In the distance he could hear the pain-screams of the horses, and toward McClain Terrace the sky was beginning to redden very slightly. He knew they'd have found the fire, and would be trying to put it out. He stood where he was for a moment, trying to get his bearings; he'd have to go through the village to get to the clinic, and they would be waiting there for him. Evan looked around: there was the Gulf station, a few silent houses, the road leading out of Bethany's Sin toward safety, and . . .

. . . something lying across that road.

Lights came on. Evan was caught between them, like a

moth frozen by double flames. He squinted, tried to see beyond those lights. Realized they were headlights. A car had blocked the road.

"Mr. Reid," someone said. A man's voice. "Mr. Reid, I think you'd best step on over here now. Come on. And be real careful how you move." A figure stepped out of the car, walked forward so it was framed against the headlights. Sheriff Wysinger, holding a gun loosely at his side. "Come on, now," he said, as if coaxing a little boy out from his hiding place. "There's no use in running. You ought to know that by now, Mr. Reid."

Evan didn't move. "I'm going to find my wife and child," he said, his mouth bitter-dry.

"Oh, no, you're not. That's not what they want. Your wife's one of them now, Mr. Reid, or she soon will be. You can't fight them. Nobody can."

"I can fight them!" Evan shouted, trembling; his voice echoed along the street. *"For God's sake help me!"*

"God's no good in this place," Wysinger said quietly. "At least, not the God you and I pray to." He smiled like a lizard. "Used to pray to. No. Even God stays out of Bethany's Sin."

"You and I can fight them together!" Evan said desperately.

Wysinger shook his head, brought the gun up, and pointed it at Evan. "I'm too old, and I'm too weak. You're just a fool. And mister, my little niche in Hell is all carved out for me and waiting, and I'm in no hurry to get there."

"What's wrong with you?" Evan raged. "You're the sheriff here, and you're sitting in a nest of murderesses!"

"I'm alive because they need me," Wysinger said, his eyes glittering over the gun barrel. "If they didn't need me, I'd be out in that place by now, my bones rotting with all the rest: It's a matter of survival, Mr. Reid; either you do or you don't. Now step on over here, and hurry up about it." He motioned with the gun.

Evan, his mind racing, walked slowly toward the man.

Wysinger suddenly cocked his head to the side; Evan had caught the smell of fire in a stale, sluggish breeze, and he knew the other man had smelled it too. Wysinger's eyes widened; he'd seen the faint red smear in the distance, over on McClain, and the brighter burst of light where the forest had caught fire. "You . . . set a . . . fire . . . " Wysinger whispered incredulously. His face reddened with fury. *"You son of a bitch! You crazy son of a bitch!"* He reached out, gripped the remnants of Evan's shirt and wrenched him foreward, holding the gun up under his throat. *"I ought to blast your fucking head off right here and now! That forest'll burn like dry tinder!"* He shook Evan mindlessly. *"Do you know what you've done? Do you know . . . ?"*

"Yes," Evan said. "I know." He locked eyes with the man. "You don't have the equipment to battle a blaze like that. Neely Ames told me so. When they can see the fire from Spangler or Barnesboro, they'll send their trucks to help you. And then they'll find you, and me, and . . . those women."

"Goddamn you!" Wysinger breathed, his teeth gritting. His eyes slid over toward the forest. Sparks were spinning toward the sky, flaring out across the sunbaked woods and setting new fires. He shoved Evan toward the police car. *"Get in there!"* he roared, fear cracking his voice. *"Hurry!"*

Evan slid across the seat. Wysinger, his face drawn and sweat-beaded, climbed beneath the wheel, keeping the gun aimed into Evan's side; he started the engine. "I'll kill you if you move," he said fiercely. "I swear I'll kill you."

"Where are you taking me?"

"To them. To that . . . temple." He put the car into gear with his free hand. "They'll know what to do about that goddamned fire." He gritted his teeth. "And they'll know what to do about you!" He put his foot to the floor, and the car leaped forward.

Evan spun, gripped the man's bearish wrist, jerked it upward; the gun cracked and cracked again; glass shattered; Wysinger lost his grip on the wheel, reached for Evan's throat, and Evan, clinging to the gun hand, threw his weight against the slipping wheel. The tires screamed into the night, banshee wails, and the car rocketed across the street toward the gas station. Too late, Wysinger realized what was about to happen; he cursed, tried to get control of the car again, but in a fraction of a second Evan had slammed his own foot down atop Wysinger's, forcing the accelerator to the floorboard.

The police car struck the gasoline pumps with a rending shriek of metal against metal; the pump housings shattered, were thrown to each side by the passage of the car, and then the car was going forward, forward, smashing through the glass front of the main office, where Evan had sat talking with Jess the manager. Evan was jerked forward and then backward, forward again, striking his forehead on the dashboard, striking his shoulder against the door; he caught a glimpse of Wysinger's sweating face, open mouthed, screaming. The car ground over a sea of glass and slammed heavily into a wooden counter, splitting it into two sections; the cash register spun away, crashed into a wall, and exploded. And then the car stopped, engine grinding grinding grinding.

Through a red haze of pain Evan saw the first tongues of fire licking around the hood. He couldn't make himself move: pretty fire, he thought. Pretty red fire burn everything down. His shoulder throbbed, and he thought it must certainly be broken, but when he tried he could move all the fingers of that hand except his thumb. Pretty red fire, he thought, staring as it grew. Burn. Burn. Burn. After another moment he could turn his head.

A livid blue bruise, blackening, covered one side of Wysinger's face; half of the steering wheel had been broken off and lay in the man's lap. He moaned softly but didn't move.

The fire had bubbled paint on the hood. Evan watched the bubbles burst. And then he was moving again, slowly, painfully, trying to get out of the car. He pushed against the door and it ground open, and then he was falling out, onto his injured shoulder, and then crawling, crawling through glass and oil and flattened cans. He crawled out through the broken window, blood streaming from his shattered nose; crawled out across the gas station pavement; crawled, trailing blood, into the streeet, and lay there, unable to crawl anymore.

There was a quiet *whump!* and then an explosion of glass and metal. A ragged scream that went on and on and on. Evan turned his head to look. Wysinger's gas tank had blown, and flames covered the car; as Evan watched he saw the swirling fires churn within the station office and then snake in long red tendrils toward the remnants of the shattered pumps, following the path of the rising fumes from the open tanks, disappearing into the ground.

The explosion that followed cracked Evan's eardrums. Metal and glass and slabs of pavement burst high, and sheets of flaming gasoline sprayed out in a deadly mist. The station office and the police car disappeared in a column of white fire, and Evan saw what looked like a burning human body explode into minute pieces. He curled himself into a ball as the debris came down, striking all around him. The flaming gasoline spattered trees and rooftops and lawns, and the air was filled with the reeking stink of it, like a thick perfume or a wine that has turned to vinegar in the bottle.

Just as Evan remembered where he was, he realized his shirt had almost been burned off him, and his hair and eyebrows were singed. He wiped his face, and the hand came away bloody. He lay against hot concrete, hearing the growing roar of Hades lapping at the shore of Themiscrya.

The Rite of Fire and Iron. Oliviadre. The temple, Wysinger had said; that's where they are. The temple. All there for the rite.

We're having a party. And everyone's invited. Even you, Mr. Reid. Oh, yes. Especially you. Come on, now. We're waiting for you. Come on. You don't want to be late, now, do you?

"No," Evan said between cracked lips. "No." He heaved himself up, stood on unsteady legs, staggered. We're waiting. All of us. Your wife, too. Your wife, Oliviadre, she of the burning eyes and wicked grin. Standing amid the heat and the smoke and the far-scattered flames, Evan could see the museum through distant treetops. It was blazing, too, but blazing with light—the only house in Bethany's Sin that looked alive tonight. Alive and waiting for him; he thought for a fleeting instant that those windows did indeed look like blank, cold eyes, the eyes of a statue, perhaps, or of an all-sleeping spiderish monstrosity that sat in the center of Bethany's Sin waiting for its next offering of flesh.

Evan summoned his last reserves of strength. I'm okay, he told himself. I can make it. *I can.* I can make it because if I don't they will have won. *I can.* Yes. They will have won and the Hand of Evil will have my wife and child. I'm okay. *I can. I can.*

Something within him laughed long and loud, the laugh becoming hysterical and twisted. We're waiting. Come on. Come on to the paaaaaarrrrrrttttttyyyyyyy.

The eyes of that house sought him, beckoning him on.

And Evan staggered forward, through the streets of fire.

THIRTY

FIRE AND IRON

By the time Evan reached the museum his muscles were twisted into aching knots of pure adrenaline. He could look back over his shoulder and see the trees burning near the circle, their leaves spinning from black branches, leaving flaming scrawls of red against the sky. Glass shattered in the distance; a huge gout of fire shot toward the stars, followed by what might have been a rise of bats with flame-edged wings. Roofing tiles, Evan realized; one of the buildings across the Circle had caved in. He thought of those beautiful flowers arranged in the Circle's center; now they would be wispy ashes, and around them the fires would be crawling up and down the trees, across the grass, licking at windows and front porches, sitting rooms and kitchens.

Evan turned his head, looked to the right. A hideous red rent in the darkness: the forest was burning, and it wouldn't be very much longer before the firemen from Barnesboro and Spangler came. He looked toward McClain Terrace, could see more trees outlined in livid orange flame. And carried on the waves of smoke and heat coming from the direction of McClain, screams and shouts were audible now; they were trying to fight the fire themselves, and they were most certainly losing. A dark green Buick, tires shrieking, turned onto Cowlington and roared past Evan, almost striking him down; he heard the scream of brakes as the driver skidded before the fire that burned at the other side of Bethany's Sin. Another car swept past, turned off Cowlington, and disappeared into the night. Followed by another.

Evan wiped his face, breathing through his open mouth rather than his broken nose, and neared the museum's gate. Six cars had been parked along Cowlington before the looming building, and Evan recognized a gleaming black Buick as Mrs. Giles's. As he went through the gate and up onto the lawn, red embers and ashes wafted around him, and he was engulfed by a pall of smoke. In the distance he heard a car screech and crash with a sound of rending metal. Good. Good. Let them all die.

And then he realized that his vision of charred ruins had not been the fate of any other village, but instead what lay ahead for Bethany's Sin. Even on the first day, when he'd stared at the museum through the trees, he'd felt the raging heat of the conflagration that would consume this place of utter evil. Now it was coming true: fires burning at each side of Bethany's Sin, slowly coming together like advancing armies. The pawn of Hades, he thought suddenly, gripping the gate and looking up at the looming house. I was the pawn of Hades all along.

A figure appeared at a window on the upper floor, stared out for a few seconds, and then disappeared. Perhaps, he thought, that hellish rite was already in progress and, once begun, wouldn't be interrupted until the end; or perhaps they're simply waiting for me. Another car roared past and vanished into a tunnel of flame and smoke.

Evan went through the gate, his heart pounding, and reached the door. It was locked from within, and though he slammed against it with his uninjured shoulder, it wouldn't budge. He heard a sudden *whooomph!* and twisted around, seeing that one of the trees across Cowlington had burst into flames; droplets of fire rained down onto a rooftop, snaked across the tiles. Beside that house shrubbery was flaming, and lawns were blacktopped with ash. Evan stepped back, away from the door, and looked up at the museum, no footholds or handholds on the walls, nothing to help him climb to the top floor, where Kay now lay at their mercy. Could he climb along a gutter? he wondered frantically, feeling the heat at his back now. No, no; it wouldn't hold his weight. Ashes spun into his face and hair. *I've got to get up there!* the voice screamed within him. *I've got to find some way to get in!* He ran alongside the house, eyes scanning the walls; his boots crunched on browning grass. And then he stopped, staring up at the huge oak tree that stood directly behind the museum; those branches, scorching now, touched the roof.

A bellowing breath of fire reached for his back; the trees on Cowlington and beyond were traced with orange white flame. A burning branch cracked, split, fell onto a roof, followed by another. Houses were enveloped in fiery webs, and now Evan could see an occasional figure running through the streets.

We're waiting. Come on to the party. We're waiting just for you, and we have your lovely wife here with us. . . .

Evan turned away from the flames, ran for that oak tree, and pulled himself up through the lowest branches. Climbed, his muscles shrieking; climbed, climbed, climbed toward the roof. Burning ashes stung him, and around him the foliage was smoking, bursting into flame even as he struggled through it. And as he made his way along the uppermost branches, not caring about the pain or the fire anymore, he tore off the last of his scorched shirt and let it drop. He leaped for the roof and landed on it just as the oak, filled with burning debris, burst into a searing ball of fire.

And he found himself staring down through a skylight into the section of the museum that had been closed off by the black door.

It was a wide, hardwood-floored room. At the center was a dark slab of stone, and on it lay Kay, naked, her flesh pale and translucent against the stone. She seemed to be asleep, or drugged, because she wan't moving. Beside the stone altar stood a red-glowing brazier with iron instruments heating within it. Around the room stood fully intact statues, all frozen in positions of combat, gripping sharp-pointed swords or axes or bows; another statue, its back to Evan, stood poised on a pedestal directly at Kay's feet.

And the Amazons, draped in black robes, ringed the naked woman; they were chanting something in that unintelligible language, and as Evan watched they knelt before the poised statue and extended their hands out to it. And it was only then that he saw their hands were dripping with blood. Blood stained their mouths like an obscene lipstick; Evan, his heart hammering, craned his neck. At Kay's head there was a copper pot brimming with blood and six copper cups. And just above that pot there was a macabre iron post on which had been placed the severed triangular head of a black horse, still dripping blood.

The chanting continued, a drone of voices. Evan could see their flaming, cruel eyes. Ashes and sparks swirled around him, touching the museum's roof. A shard of wood stung his shoulder. The Amazons seemed to have no fear of the conflagration, nor did they seem to care that soon the fire brigades would most certainly be coming; in that instant Evan felt a grudging respect for their courage, however evil and twisted they were, for these women feared nothing, not even Death in its gaudy robe of fire.

The Drago-thing, her black robe dragging the floor, came into his field of vision. Around her the things that had gnawed away the souls of Mrs. Giles, Mrs. Bartlett, Dr. Mabry, and others he'd seen before but didn't know bowed their heads slightly in deference to their queen. Drago stood before the higher statue, spoke a few sentences in a singsong dialect, and then stepped toward the glowing brazier; her right hand, clad in a metal glove, reached out and withdrew one of the iron instruments. A scissorslike pincer pulsated a deep, terrible red. Then she turned again toward Kay.

The other Amazons rose, their eyes gleaming. Dr. Mabry stepped beside Drago to assist her.

The pincer opened, dropped down toward the swell of Kay's right breast. Kay, her eyes still closed, opened her mouth and writhed silently as the glowing pincer came down.

Her breast, Evan realized. They were going to take her breast!

And then he struck out with one boot, smashing through the skylight. Shards of glass rained down; the Amazons looked upward, faces contorting. Evan kicked out again and then leaped through the shattered opening. Landing beside the stone altar, he went to his knees and struggled upward. They closed in, breathing hatred, their hands clawing for him. Evan threw his weight against the brazier, and coals tumbled out as it hit the floor, driving them backward for an instant. The coals began to smolder and spark; Evan turned his head, gazed upon the statue on its pedestal. It was of a woman, arms outstretched, one hand broken away. Around the neck and shoulders were draped row upon row of marbled, taut-nippled female breasts; in the solemn face of the statue blank eyes burned a fiery, unholy blue, that fire leaping now, leaping, leaping. . . .

And Evan realized he gazed upon the terrible visage of Artemis, goddess of the Amazons, bearing her symbolic sacrificial gifts from the women who had devoted their lives and beings to the destruction of men.

Those eyes flamed his skull, made him almost reel back and drop to his knees. *No!* the voice within him screamed raggedly. And then he threw himself at that statue, upsetting the pedestal; the statue wavered, wavered, crashed to the floor. The head and left arm cracked away, but in that severed head the eyes still flamed.

A hissing sound behind him; the shriek of air parting. He ducked down, stepped back as the red-hot pincers swung past his face. The Drago-thing, her face a mask of cold and absolute hatred, rushed him, forcing him backward and into the arms of the two Amazons who stood on the other side of him; they gripped him across the chest and throat, arms like steel bands.

Drago held the hissing pincers before his face. "Now your time has come," she whispered, two voices whispering, intertwining, echoing. On the altar Kay stirred slightly. "Hold him while I finish," she commanded the women; they tightened their arms around him until he could barely breathe. And then she turned again toward his wife.

"Leave her alone, goddamn you!" Evan shouted. He struggled, found he couldn't move. *"Get away from her!"* Tears of rage and terror sprang to his eyes.

The pincers, gripped by that metal glove, were lowered toward Kay's white body.

"Stop it! Stop it!" he shrieked, his throat shredding. *"If you want a sacrifice, take me!"*

Drago blinked, held the pincers just above Kay's breast. She slowly turned her head toward him; her evilly grinning visage froze the marrow in his bones.

"Leave her alone!" Evan said, daring to stare back into

her face. "Take me as your sacrifice, unless you're afraid . . ."

Drago didn't move.

In the distance a siren began to wail. Then another. Smoke had swirled into the room, and Evan heard the flames gnawing at the museum's roof. The sirens grew louder.

"You and me," Evan taunted. "Alone. Come on, you gutless bitch!"

Drago's lips parted in a snarl, but still she didn't move.

"You haven't got much time," he said. "They're coming soon. Themiscrya is burning, bitch, and I set the first flame." A hand tightened at his throat. *"Come on, damn you! Decide!"* Smoke swirled between them; somewhere within the house, glass shattered.

"Take Oliviadre and leave," Drago whispered to the others, her eyes not leaving Evan's face. "All of you leave, and quickly. Make certain the children are gotten out and away from the village." The other women paused. *"Go on now!"* Drago said, her voice vibrating with power.

The Amazons released Evan, backed away. The Giles-thing and another blond woman began to try to rouse Kay; she stirred, mumbled, sat up on the altar. The Giles-thing helped her to her feet, and it was then that Evan saw his wife's face. One eye burned with the terrible, spectral power, and one side of the face was twisted with hatred as she turned her gaze upon him; the other eye was clear and terrified. And he realized that without the rite the transformation wasn't complete; without the blessing of the bitch-goddess Artemis she was still partly Kay after all. But partly Oliviadre as well—caught between two worlds.

"Take her out!" Drago commanded.

"Kay," Evan said.

She stared at him, one eye flaming blue. Her mouth began to work, but no words came out.

"Don't let them have you, Kay," he whispered. "Please, for the sake of all that's holy, don't let them have you. I love you. Please remember I love you. . . ."

Drago stepped toward him with the pincers. "Get her out of here now," she told the Amazons. *"Hurry!"* The last word was a bark in the Amazon language.

Kay's face contorted, rage fighting love. A tear streamed from the unclouded eye, broke over her cheek. "Ev—an—?" she whispered hoarsely. "Evan? Ev—?" And then the women spun her around, one of them giving her a black robe to hide her nakedness; they took her out through the door into the museum, and Dr. Mabry paused for an instant to stare back at the man.

Then the black door closed.

Sealing Evan in with this blood-eyed warrior.

Evan backed away from her; she gripped the pincers and followed, like a lioness stalking her victim, one step at a time, slowly, slowly. . . .

"No man can stop us," she hissed. "No man."

And then she struck, faster than Evan's eye could follow; the pincers whistled down, struck across his chest, drawing a line of bubbling blood. He threw back his head and screamed a scream of piercing pain; Drago lifted the pincers again, stepped in quickly for another blow. But Evan, fever about to blow his brain apart, met her attack. They crashed together with a fury that shook the floor, Evan reaching for and grabbing the wrist that held the weapon; Drago's free hand shot out, the fingers groping for his eyes, finding one of them. She wrenched at his face, tore him in two with pain, and then Evan was screaming with blood-mad rage and backing her toward the altar, one hand gripping that wrist, the other clamped about her throat. She spun him around as if he were a toy, leering into his face, and he was picked up bodily and slammed against the far wall.

He fought for breath. Through his unbloodied eye he saw fire leaking down through cracks in the roof, saw pools of fire gathering on the floor. The rest of the skylight exploded into rubby red slivers, and through the opening he saw the face of the oval moon. Then Drago was upon him again, swinging those pincers for his head; he jerked backward, and the burning iron seared a line across his cheekbone. He struck out at her with his fist, caught her full in the face but didn't stagger her; then he struck again, and again before she could bring that weapon back. Her head finally went to the side, and Evan struck with all his strength at the point of her chin. Her teeth clicked together, and blood drooled from one corner of her mouth; she spat out flesh, and Evan realized she'd bitten her tongue in two. But still the eyes burned, more fiercely now, and she grinned at him the crazed grin of a warrior who has seen Death and dares it to strike. Evan clamped both hands around her throat and squeezed; they fell to the floor, rolled through fire and glass, the woman's free hand striking at his forehead and temples, her other hand, white-knuckled, gripping the pincers. Above them the roof cracked, and streamers of fire, like party confetti, fell through.

Drago twisted, flung him against one of the combat-frozen statues. A stone spear grazed his side. The pincers sang for him, whistled past his head again. This time he reached up and put his hands against the scorching iron, ripping the weapon from her grasp and throwing it aside. She shrieked with rage and struck him with that metal glove, knocking him to his knees. He lay there, pain arcing along his rib cage, head battered and throbbing. Fire chewed at the floor all around, and in its glow he saw the woman's shadow on a wall: a huge, distorted thing that dripped with the venom of nightmarish evil.

The Amazon stood over him, panting for breath, blood streaking a face that seemed as fierce and inhuman as those of the warrior-women statues. She wiped thick blood from her mouth, looked down with disdain upon the man, and spat at him, bloodily. Then she turned, groping for the fallen pincers to sever her enemy's head from his body. She reached down for it, gripped it, started to turn for Evan again.

But he had already leaped from the floor and launched himself at her like a human projectile. Drago grunted as the air was forced from her lungs, and screamed out as he gripped her throat and drove her backward, backward, backward, off balance. . . .

Toward that statue in the far corner. The one with the drawn, sharply tipped sword.

Drago's eyes writhed with blue fire; Evan drove her back with every shredding fiber in his body.

And then Drago's shriek of bloodcurdling fury was intermingled with a cry of pure pain. The stone sword pierced her back and then her stomach; the gleaming point of it emerged from her body, red against black robes, and the woman-thing thrashed against it, still trying to strike him with the pincers; she got a hand on his shoulder and wrenched him forward, and before he could jerk away, he felt a white-hot pain lance his own stomach. And then he realized, with sharp and sudden clarity, that she had driven him onto that part of the sword that protruded from her own body.

Drago gripped him, wouldn't let him free. The flame in her eyes wavered. "Die," she breathed, the word as mangled as her tongue. Red-flecked spittle clung to her lips. "Die. Die. Die. Die. . . ."

Evan sagged, the pain brighter and hotter than a thousand August suns. But even as he sagged he pushed forward, driving her back father upon the merciless Amazon blade. Her mouth opened, opened, and remained open even as that terrible flame of spectral power flickered, flickered, and died from her eyes. Then he was looking into the black eyes of a corpse, and a red mist of pain and fire swept between him and the dead woman, obscuring his vision.

Replacing it with the soft and silent sheen of a golden field where a dead tree stood, naked branches reaching toward the sky. A body lay in that field, near a branch that had broken and toppled to the earth. A young body, a boy's body, lying motionless. And Evan standing over it, grown-up Evan now, but still the Evan he always was. I'll run get help, he thinks. I'll hurry and get Dad and then he'll say that Eric's okay, he's okay, he's not dead after all. But the grown-up Evan knows now that one cannot run from Death, not really, and that one must fight the Hand of Evil wherever it is, even on its own pestilent ground.

Evan steps forward, puts a hand to the young boy's shoulder.

And Eric looks up, grinning widely. "Fooled you, didn't I?" he says impishly. "Whooey, I took a fall! 'Bout knocked the stuffing out of me!"

"You're . . . all right?" the grown-up Evan asks softly.

"Me? Sure!" Eric stands up, little-boy Eric who has never changed at all, and rubs the dirt from his knees. "But that sure scared me, I'll tell you!"

"That was . . . dangerous," Evan says, squinting in the warm sunlight. "You shouldn't do that anymore."

"Oh, I won't. Just once is enough, I'll tell you! Whooey!" Eric suddenly looks past his brother, into the distance. "Hear that?"

"No. Hear what?"

Eric grins. "Aw, come on! Mom and Dad! They're calling for us to come home! It's time, y'know."

"Yes," Evan nods. "I guess it is."

"Let's go, then!"

But Evan still stands staring, as if he's trying to remember something just beyond the reach of his memory.

"Come on, slowpoke!" Eric shouts, laughing. "They'll be along in a while, you'll see! Come on! I'll race you!"

And grown-up Evan turns toward his still-small brother, and he smiles and says, "I always could beat you in a race," and together they run laughing toward the edge of a golden field that seems to stretch on forever.

From fire-ravaged Cowlington Street Kay saw the museum roof collapse, sending up a geyser of sparks and flame. There was a great, earthshaking rumble as if the museum itself were about to fall into a fast-opening bottomless fissure. She blinked, the flame scorching her face; two women stood on either side of her, pulling; their hands were ice-cold. Like corpse hands. My hus—band, she thought. *No no not your husband anymore!* another, more terrible voice within her shrieked. Yes. My husband. Evan. *No no not your husband!* Evan's . . . in there. He's inside that place! *Let him die let him die let him. . . .* My husband! *Oh dear God where's my husband!* She tried to jerk free of those women, but she couldn't move her arms, and they were pulling her along, faster and faster, and everywhere there was fire and smoke and a high, wailing noise. *Where's Evan I've got to find Evan!* The heat puffed her face, and within her that more terrible voice seemed distant now, and fearful: *Go with the others hurry go with the others!*

She shook her head from side to side, both eyes leaking hot tears. Tried to pull away, was wrenched on. "Evan!" she called out, trying to fight them. "I've got to find him!" Windows in the museum exploded, a hideous cacophony that split her head with pain. The voice within her, dying, dying: *Get away! Hurry! Get away!* "Where's my husband?" Kay shouted, struggling from something that lay upon her like the cold, clammy grip of an unseen hand. A voice, fading to nothingness, screaming within her soul. "I want to find my husband!" The voice gone.

And through the wall of smoke and fire that lay across Cowlington emerged a monster with blazing white eyes, its voice an eerie, rising wail. White light froze Kay where she stood, and suddenly the two women who had been beside her—who had they been?—were gone, running in opposite directions through the smoke, vanishing from sight. There was a long, heart-stopping squeal of brakes, and the firemen were leaping from their truck toward the dazed woman who staggered in black robes.

"You okay?" one of them, a burly man with thick black sidburns, yelled above the noise. "What's your name?"

"Kay," she said, trying to think. "I'm Kay Reid."

"Jesus Holy Christ!" another fireman shouted beside her. "This whole damned village is burnin' to the ground! Where'd this damned fire start?"

Kay shook her head, tried to focus on the men.

"She's out of it, Jimmy," the black-sideburned fireman said to the other. "Come on, ma'am, let's get you to the truck!"

"Jesus Holy Christ!" Jimmy said again; his double-chinned face was streaked with ashes. "Where are all the people? Where are all the damned people?"

They led her quickly to the truck. Behind them a tree crashed flaming across Cowlington.

"My husband," Kay said, fighting to breathe through the smoke. "I have to find him." She turned, stared back at the house as it began to melt and run. *"My husband was in there!"*

"It's okay, it's okay," Black Sideburns said soothingly. "We'll find your husband. Right now we've got to get you out of here. Come on, just lean on us and you'll be—"

"Laurie!" Kay shouted, gripping at the man's shoulders, new panic welling within her. "Where's my *little girl?*"

"Hold on, now," Jimmy said. "She's probably fine and waiting for you." A roof exploded into a million cinders. He ducked his shoulders slightly, hurried her toward the truck. "The emergency unit found a bunch of little girls over at a house a couple of streets over. The nursery school."

"Oh, God," Kay sobbed, feeling her legs give way beneath her. The firemen caught her, guiding her forward. "Oh my God oh my God oh my God . . ."

"You're gonna be just fine," Jimmy said. "Here you go, get up into there. Holy Christ, how'd this damned fire start?" He blinked a couple of times, glanced over at the other firemen, said in a low voice, "Christ, Steve! This lady doesn't have a stitch on underneath that robe!" He took off his coat, gave it to her as he sat beside her in the truck's cab; she bundled up in it, hardly realizing that it smelled of sweat and acrid smoke.

And then she began to cry. Couldn't stop.

"There, there," Jimmy said. "There, there."

V

AFTERWARD

THIRTY-ONE

RUINS AND BEGINNINGS

Two figures standing on a plain of charred ruins. A woman and a little girl, holding hands. The September breeze, cooling into autumn, whispering through cracks in freestanding walls, sighing eerily around jutting black chimneys and the ashen stumps of trees long hauled away.

What little remained of Bethany's Sin had been cordoned off for weeks by the police and fire departments as they sifted through the sea of ashes looking for clues that might explain the sudden and terrible holocaust. Kay had been questioned repeatedly, first by the police and then by reporters. To all of them she said the same thing: I don't know. In the last week or so, the reporters had started calling the small, one-bedroom apartment Kay was renting in Johnstown—God only knew how they'd managed to get the telephone number—badgering her day and night, treating her like some sort of macabre celebrity. Recently they'd even begun hanging around the private school Laurie was attending, hoping to ask questions of her; but Mrs. Abercrombie, bless her soul, was a smart lady, and she could spot those reporters a mile away. On several occasions she'd called Kay at George Ross and told her that Laurie would be waiting at the back door today, because you-know-who's outside again this afternoon.

Kay's last session had been with a Lieutenant Knowles, a fiftyish man with curly gray hair and blue-as-flint eyes. He'd offered her coffee, a cigarette. No thank you, no thank you. Let's just get this over with, shall we?

"Right," the man had said; he'd smiled apologetically

and then eased himself down into a black-vinyl swivel chair. "I know how painful this is for you. . . ."

"Then why do you keep asking me to come back? Of course it's painful!"

"Well, I'm really sorry," Knowles said. "Really I am." His eyes meant it. "But it seems that you're just about the only person who came out of that fire. Well, you and the children, of course. But the children don't know anything. . . ."

"And neither do I."

"Mind if I smoke?"

Kay shook her head.

Knowles reached for a pack of Trues and a lighter. "This whole thing is so . . . crazy. So really crazy." He lit the cigarette, pushed the pack away across his desk. Pictures of a smiling wife and two children were placed to his right, Kay's left. "The sheriff's car crashed into the gas station, nothing left of him to speak of; that crazy place with all the statues and old junk; a few skeletons lying around. . . ."

She shifted uneasily.

"Sorry," Knowles said over his cigarette. "But that's the truth. One skeleton even missing its head! Another one with a spade or something stuck in its gut. And you know how the firemen found your husband and that Dr.—" He paused, flipped through a few pages of notes he had before him.

"Drago," Kay said. Something about that name made her skin crawl now.

"Right. Well, I'll tell you, nothing makes sense." He looked at her, narrowed his eyes. "And you still can't remember? I mean, nothing's come back to you at all?"

"I've already told you people what I remember. I've told you again and again. I remember seeing my husband inside that museum. Then I don't remember anything else until I was out in the street."

"How about up to that point? Anything?"

She took a deep breath. Oh, God, this was where it got confusing. It seemed that she recalled lying in a bed in the clinic, staring at the shadows on the ceiling; the nurse had just brought her some of that awful, chalky-tasting orange juice, and she remembered thinking that orange juice isn't for nighttime, it's supposed to be for breakfast. She remembered worrying about Evan, about what he might do in his present state of mind—she'd told no one that—and then she'd felt suddenly and strangely cold, unable to reach for the buzzer beside her bed when she wanted to call for another blanket. Nothing after that, at all. Just empty darkness. "No," she said, and Knowles looked disappointed.

The man drew on his cigarette, tapped it into an ashtray; his brow was furrowed, had been furrowed ever since this nasty business had begun. There were so many damned unanswered questions! The gas station explosion; the skeletons of the man and woman, melded together by the heat, found in the ruins of that museum; a few female skeletons in the ashen forest, along with the charred remains of horses, of all things; other fire-ravaged corpses in several of the houses, where they'd been trapped by fallen debris; the fact that Bethany's Sin had been deserted but for the children, this woman who sat before him, and assorted bits and pieces of burned-beyond-recognition bodies. The coroner was still counting; he'd already passed fifty. The other people who'd lived in that village had just vanished. Strange. Maybe the strangest thing he'd ever heard of.

Other things bothered him, too, made him sit awake nights now trying to figure them out, but he realized that he'd probably never grasp the whole picture, no matter how long he and his team investigated. Fragments of some kind of scrapbook had been found in the sheriff's office; clippings of murders and disappearances dating years back. In another half-charred notebook, calculations of when the moon would be full, the lunar sequence painstakingly worked out through December. Who the hell could explain that? What had Wysinger been, some sort of astronomy nut or something? And from the reports he'd seen, Kay Reid had lain in a hospital bed for three days after the fire, alternately feverish and shivering, hysterical and silent. Complaints of recurrent nightmare, of seeing figures standing over her bed, some doctor had written on one of her medical forms. Nightmares vague, but indicative of severe trauma.

And now this woman, possibly the key to whatever had happened that August night in Bethany's Sin, sat here in his office and insisted she could remember nothing. He could look into her face and see the new lines around her eyes, and he knew she'd come a long, hard way back from Bethany's Sin, but was she lying to him? Trying to pretend she knew less than she really did?

So he decided to take a gamble. "Are you still having those nightmares, Mrs. Reid?" Knowles asked her, watching for her reaction as he stabbed his cigarette out.

She winced, quickly regained her composure. "What do you mean?"

"The nightmares you were having in the hospital. Do they still bother you?"

Kay paused for a moment. "No," she said finally. "No, they don't."

"That's good to hear. What were they about?"

"Have you decided to trade your badge in for a psychiatrist's couch?"

Knowles smiled, shook his head. "No. Just curious."

For a long while she pretended to examine her nails, still uncertain whether to tell him or not. And then she seemed to relax visibly, as if ridding herself of a haunting, terrible weight. She looked up at him. "Yes," she said softly, "the nightmares. I was afraid to sleep at first because they came every night. They were . . . especially bad when I was in the hospital because being there reminded me of somewhere else. The clinic in Bethany's Sin. I was . . . sick, and the doctor put me in a room there."

"What was wrong with you?" the man asked.

She shook her head. "I don't know. When I try to remember what happened to me from then on, my mind just . . . well, it's like my memory's blanked out or something. I know it sounds strange, but it's as if I . . . ceased to exist entirely. I was cold, terribly, terribly cold, and in a place of utter darkness." Kay looked into the man's face, her own gaze intense and fearful. Knowles clicked his lighter, lit another cigarette. "I couldn't find my way back," she said, "until I heard Evan call my name, as if he were off in the distance somewhere and trying to help me. And then I began to fight toward where the light was; I began to repeat my own name over and over again, and I tried to remember everything in my life that had made me who I am." She saw that Knowles's eyes were vacant above his cigarette, and she knew he couldn't possibly understand or believe. "It was like drowning in a bright blue pool, and trying to struggle toward the surface where the sun was shining." She saw him blink suddenly, and she lapsed into silence.

Knowles cleared his throat uneasily, shifted in his chair. "All that was part of your nightmares?"

Kay smiled thinly. "Yes, that's right." She wouldn't tell him what she'd really seen in those night visitations: herself in black robes, drifting along a wide, stone-floored corridor, flanked on both sides by grinning statues with volcanic, half-human eyes; and at the far end of that corridor stood a black rectangle. A mirror, Kay realized as she neared it, but reflecting nothing but its own dark, evil-glowing self. And as Kay leaned forward to peer into that mirror, she saw a shape within it, something ancient and scabrous, wafting like dust, turning in on itself, churning like a maelstrom of agonized hatred. As she stared, unable to tear herself away, the shape coagulated, became something mimicking human form, with blue-burning, un-blinking eyes that touched her to the soul.

And from the mirror the hand of a skeleton reached out, gripping her around the wrist and pulling. It was then that she realized, in numb-beyond-thinking terror, that this was not a mirror, no, not a mirror, but instead a doorway to that region of entities drifting in the bodiless void between Life and Death. The skeleton had tight-ened, tightened, pulling her slowly toward the doorway. But always she found her voice and screamed, wrenched away from the nameless horror, turned and ran back along the corridor even as the statues began to shamble toward her, raising their swords and axes and spears to strike her down.

She always escaped.

And in time those nightmares had faded. Thank God.

"What are your plans now?" Knowles asked her.

"I have an apartment," Kay said. "I've been given the opportunity to stay on at George Ross. Laurie . . . still cries, but I think she'll be all right." Kay smiled; or tried to, because her lips trembled. "I never realized how very much I loved and needed Evan until he was gone. Sometimes in the night I still reach over to the other side of the bed for him." Her eyes glistened. "I want him so much to be there. Love's funny, isn't it? What's the old saying? You never know how much you've got until it's gone. But he's not really gone, not really. No one's ever really gone unless you forget."

Knowles sat still for a moment, examining her face. No, he decided. This woman wasn't lying. He felt more certain now than ever that whatever had happened in Bethany's Sin was locked away from him. Perhaps forever. No, no, he thought, scratch that. I'm a police officer, and maybe someday I'll dig up something. He rose to his feet. "I suppose that about wraps it up, Mrs. Reid. Thank you very much for coming in."

Two figures standing on a plain of charred ruins. A woman and a little girl, holding hands.

"I don't like this, Mommy," Laurie said. "Let's go home."

"We will, sweetheart," Kay told her softly. "In just a little while, we will." They stood on what remained of McClain Terrace: blackened facades of houses with collapsed roofs. Nothing but timbers left of the Demargeon house, as if it had been struck by God Himself. The house where the Reid family had lived was a charred shell: roof sagging; windows empty, gaping holes. Kay had wanted to come to this place one last time; after today she would not return here again, and their lives would start fresh from this place and point in time. It was such a beautiful house, she thought, looking at the ruins. Such a beautiful village. She moved closer, shoes crunching ashes and shards of glass. Something fluttered on the ground, and Kay bent to pick it up.

It was a page from one of Evan's short stories. She could see the typewritten characters only faintly, and before she could read it the breeze had crisped it into ashes that spun out of her grasp, floating, floating, floating away. That same breeze made ghost-voices moan from empty doorways.

Kay wiped her face—quickly so Laurie wouldn't see and become disturbed—and then said, "Come on. We'd better be getting home now." They crossed the lawn of ashes toward Kay's second-hand Vega, climbed in with ashes still clinging to their shoes. Kay hugged Laurie to her for a moment, then started the car and left McClain Terrace behind.

Yellow lights blinked on Blair Street. A detour: a maze of trash and fallen trees still awaited the cleanup crews. Kay had to turn onto Cowlington.

And as they passed the burned-out hulk of the museum, Kay slowed, staring up at it. She pulled the Vega to the curb and sat for a few minutes, her heart slowly beating, beating, beating. Evan's tomb, she thought. But why? What had happened in those last days? What kept hammering at the door of her mind, even now the memories trying to force their way in? Something that Evan had been trying to warn her of, all along? Something she'd dismissed with a wave of her hand and an accusation? The breeze whispered around the corners of the house. Spirals of ash spun up, twisted, dancing back and forth; one of the spirals, caught in the teeth of the breeze, whirled down toward the Vega. Kay smelled a hot, scorched smell.

"I don't like it here, Mommy," Laurie said.

"We're going," Kay said. She put the car in gear and pulled away from the curb, accelerating. "We won't come back to this place anymore." Someday I'll know, Kay told herself. Someday I'll be strong enough to let those memories in, and I'll see what it was that Evan saw. She stroked Laurie's hair. "Home in just a few minutes," she said, and glanced down at her child.

Laurie smiled. For the briefest instant Kay thought she saw something strange in the little girl's eyes, but then Laurie blinked and that half-seen, half-recognized glimmer was gone. Laurie slid across the seat against her mother, thinking of how much she was going to miss Mrs. Omarian. Mrs. Omarian with those funny stories about

341

those funny women, those stories that were too funny for daddies to know.

But, somehow, Laurie didn't feel like laughing anymore.

They left Bethany's Sin.

And turned toward the city.

Time shall come when the female shall conquer the male, and shall chase him far away. . . .

—ANCIENT ORACLE

*It passed
from the dead
to the living,
a beautiful gift
with a frightening power—*

THE AMULET

A sweltering southern town . . . a mysterious
necklace . . . a family's burning house . . . a
doomed policeman . . . a jealous woman turned
killer . . . a babysitter enraged at a crying child.
Where did it come from? Who would it strike next?
And why? The horror was unspeakable, the terror
unstoppable, and the chain was unbroken . . .

A Novel of Pure Terror
by MICHAEL McDOWELL

 Avon / 40584 / $2.25

THE BIG BESTSELLERS
ARE AVON BOOKS

☐ **The Second Son** Charles Sailor   45567 $2.75
☐ **People of the Lake** Richard E. Leakey &
     Roger Lewin   45575 $2.75
☐ **"The Life": Memoirs of a French Hooker**
     Jeanne Cordelier   45609 $2.75
☐ **Adjacent Lives** Ellen Schwamm   45211 $2.50
☐ **A Woman of Independent Means**
     Elizabeth Forsythe Hailey   42390 $2.50
☐ **The Human Factor** Graham Greene   41491 $2.50
☐ **The Train Robbers** Piers Paul Read   42945 $2.75
☐ **The Brendan Voyage** Tim Severin   43711 $2.75
☐ **The Insiders** Rosemary Rogers   40576 $2.50
☐ **The Prince of Eden** Marilyn Harris   41905 $2.50
☐ **The Thorn Birds** Colleen McCullough   35741 $2.50
☐ **Chinaman's Chance** Ross Thomas   41517 $2.25
☐ **The Trail of the Fox** David Irving   40022 $2.50
☐ **The Bermuda Triangle** Charles Berlitz   38315 $2.25
☐ **The Real Jesus** Garner Ted Armstrong   40055 $2.25
☐ **Lancelot** Walker Percy   36582 $2.25
☐ **Snowblind** Robert Sabbag   44008 $2.50
☐ **Fletch's Fortune** Gregory Mcdonald   37978 $1.95
☐ **Voyage** Sterling Hayden   37200 $2.50
☐ **Humboldt's Gift** Saul Bellow   38810 $2.25
☐ **Mindbridge** Joe Haldeman   33605 $1.95
☐ **The Monkey Wrench Gang**
     Edward Abbey   46755 $2.50
☐ **Jonathan Livingston Seagull**
     Richard Bach   44099 $1.95
☐ **Working** Studs Terkel   34660 $2.50
☐ **Shardik** Richard Adams   43752 $2.75
☐ **Watership Down** Richard Adams   39586 $2.50

Available at better bookstores everywhere, or order direct from the publisher.

WILLIAM H.
HALLAHAN

KEEPER
OF THE
CHILDREN

▲ 45203 $2.50
AVON

Novels have been written about children possessed. Novels
have been written about unnatural evil—in most of its dis-
guises. But nothing can prepare you for the unspeakable frenzy
of this . . .

Dolls move. Scarcrows animate and kill. Toys wield axes
against parents. Cats band together and attack humans in a
fury of fur, claws, and teeth. And in a terrifying dimension beyond anything ever before explored in fiction, a lone father
battles a demonic force—a new kind of evil—for his daughter's
life . . . and his own.